MELTING THE ICE QUEEN'S HEART

BY
AMY RUTTAN

MILLS
BOON

Published in Great Britain 2014
by Mills & Boon, an imprint of Harlequin (UK) Limited,
Eton House, 18-24 Paradise Road, Richmond, Surrey, TW9 1SR

© 2014 Amy Ruttan

ISBN: 978 0 263 90749 0

Harlequin (UK) policy is to use papers that are natural, renewable and recyclable products and made from wood grown in sustainable forests. The logging and manufacturing process conform to the legal environmental regulations of the country of origin.

Printed and bound in Spain
by Blackprint CPI, Barcelona

Dear Reader

Thank you for picking up a copy of MELTING THE ICE QUEEN'S HEART. I don't think authors can ever truly express how much it means to us that readers like you enjoy our stories.

MELTING THE ICE QUEEN'S HEART is set in one of my most favourite cities of the world: San Francisco. My grandmother had a painting in her dining room of the Golden Gate Bridge. I used to stare at it for hours on end. It's now in my home.

I always wanted to go to San Francisco, and in 2008 at a Romance Writers of America conference I had that chance. It was amazing, and I knew I had to set a romance in that city some day.

This story is about two stubborn surgeons who have never wanted a family of their own because they've both lost someone they cared about deeply and it has made them afraid to love.

Yet somehow love always finds a way, and even the most stubborn man can melt a heart of ice.

I hope you enjoy MELTING THE ICE QUEEN'S HEART. I love hearing from readers, so please drop by my website www.amyruttan.com or give me a shout on Twitter @ruttanamy.

With warmest wishes

Amy Ruttan

Dedication

This book is dedicated to one of my best friends, Diane. You are so strong and my awe and admiration of you is so much I can't even begin to explain it. Love you.

And to a great friend, Chris. There are friends you make who you feel like you've known your whole life in just a few short moments upon meeting. You were one of them. My family and I miss you every day, Mr. Baxter.

Recent title by the same author:

SAFE IN HIS HANDS

CHAPTER ONE

"WE HAVE A state-of-the art facility here at Bayview Grace and we're staffed with some of the top surgeons in the country." Dr. Virginia Potter gritted her teeth, but then flashed the board of directors and investors the best smile she could muster.

She hated this aspect of her job, but as Chief of Surgery it was par for the course. She'd rather have her hands dirty, working the trauma floor with the rest of the emergency doctors, but she was used to schmoozing. Earning scholarships and being on countless deans' lists had helped her perfect the fine art of rubbing elbows. It's how she'd got through school. Her childhood certainly hadn't prepared her for that.

Still, Virginia missed her time on the floor, saving lives. She still got surgery time, but it wasn't nearly as much as she used to get.

This is what you wanted, she reminded herself. It was career or family. There was no grey area. Her father had proved that to her. He had spent more time with his family instead of rising up in his job and because of that and then an injury he had been the first to be let go when the factory had moved its operations down south. Virginia had learned from that. To be successful, you couldn't have both.

It was the values her father had instilled in her. To always strive for the best, go for the top. Again, that was a sacrifice one had to make. It was a position she wanted.

To not make the same mistakes in life he had. Keep a roof over your head and food on the table. That was what she had been taught was a mark of success.

Others have both. She shook that thought away. No. She didn't want a family. She couldn't lose anyone else. She wouldn't risk feeling that pain again.

"I'd really like to see the hospital's emergency department," Mrs. Greenly said, breaking through Virginia's thoughts.

Anywhere but there, her inner voice screamed, but instead Virginia nodded. "Of course. If you'll follow me?"

Why? Her stomach felt like it was about to bottom out to the soles of her feet. Virginia had planned to steer clear of the emergency room. There were so many more "tame" departments at Bayview Grace.

Departments with Attendings who were more polished and less dangerous to her senses.

Bayview Grace's ER Attending was the quintessential bad boy of the hospital.

She led the investors and the board of directors towards the emergency department and tried to think back to the posted schedule and whether Dr. Gavin Brice was scheduled for the day shift, because even though Dr. Brice was a brilliant surgeon he and the board of directors didn't see eye to eye.

Maybe he's not working?

Oh, who was she kidding? He was always working and she admired him for that, except this one time she wished he wasn't so efficient.

Virginia had been the one to push for them to hire Brice. They hadn't been impressed with his extensive CV. The board had wanted a more glamorous, "citified" surgeon. Not one who'd gotten his hands dirty and lived rough.

"It's all on your head, Dr. Potter. If Dr. Brice fails, you fail."

The threat had been clear.

At first Virginia had been nervous, because hiring Dr. Brice had put her job on the line, but then she'd realized she was being silly. His work with Border Free Physicians, practicing surgery in developing countries around the world, was an experience in itself. His survival rates were the highest she'd ever seen.

There was no way Dr. Brice would not succeed at Bayview Grace.

She'd see to it, but the board still wasn't impressed with him.

His survival rates were still high. Topnotch, in fact, but Gavin was unorthodox and a wild mustang on the surgical floor.

He had no patience for surgical interns. No patience for anyone really.

Gavin followed his own rules when it came to practicing medicine. He was the perpetual thorn in Virginia's side.

Please, don't be on duty. Please, don't be on duty.

The board of directors and their investors headed into the emergency department.

"Get out of the way!"

Virginia just had time to grab Mrs. Greenly out of the line of fire as a gurney came rushing by from one of the trauma pods.

Speak of the devil.

Gavin Brice was on top of a man, pumping an Ambu bag and shouting orders to a group of flustered interns.

"There's no time, he has a pneumothorax. We have to insert a chest tube." He climbed down and handed the operation of the manual respirator over to a resident.

Oh. My. God. Did he just say what I thought he said?

"Dr. Brice," Virginia called out in warning.

Gavin glanced over his shoulder and didn't respond, effectively dismissing her presence. "Get me a 20 French chest tube kit." One of the interns ran off.

"Dr. Brice," Virginia said again. "Think about what you're doing."

The intern returned with the chest tube kit, handing it to Dr. Brice as he finished wiping the patient's side with antiseptic. "Ten blade."

Virginia gritted her teeth, angered she was being ignored. She spun around and gauged the expressions of the board members. Most had nasty pallors. Mrs. Greenly looked like she was about to pass out.

"Dr. Brice!"

"I said ten blade! Have you actually studied medicine?" he barked at an intern, ignoring Virginia.

She stepped towards the gurney. "You can't place that chest tube here, Dr. Brice. Take him to a trauma bay or an OR, stat!"

"Dr. Potter, there are no rooms free and I don't have time to mince words. As you can see, this man has sustained crush injuries and has pneumothorax from a motor vehicle accident. He could die unless I do this right here, right now."

"I really think—"

Gavin didn't even look at her as he cut an incision in the man's chest and inserted the chest tube. "Come on, damn you!"

Virginia watched the patient's vitals on the monitor. It didn't take long before the man's blood pressure and systolic regulated and for the fluid to start to drain through the silicone tube.

"Great. Now we need to clear an OR, *stat*." Gavin shot her a look. One of annoyance. He shook his head in disgust as the trauma team began to wheel the man off towards the operating rooms, his hand still in the patient's chest.

All that was left in his wake was a spattering of blood on the floor from where he'd made the incision to insert the tube.

Virginia rubbed her temples and turned to the board and the investors. "Well, that's our ER. How about we end this tour here and head back to the boardroom?"

It was probably the dumbest thing she'd ever said, but she didn't know how to recover from this situation. In her two years as Chief of Surgery this had never happened to her before. She'd never had an emergency play out in front of the board in the middle of a tour.

Investors had never had to watch a chest tube be inserted in front of them before.

The stunned members nodded and headed out of the department, except for Mr. Edwin Schultz—the tight-lipped head of the board. Another thorn in her side. It was no secret that he thought the hospital was bad from a business perspective. He was the one holding Bayview Grace back, because as far as Virginia was concerned, Edwin Schultz wanted to drop the axe on her hospital.

"Dr. Potter, I'd like to speak with you about Dr. Brice in private."

"Of course," Virginia said, rolling her eyes when his back was turned. She opened a door to a dark exam room, flicked on the lights and ushered Mr. Schultz inside. When she had closed the door, she crossed her arms and braced for a verbal onslaught of tsunami proportions.

"What was that?" Mr. Schultz asked.

"A pneumothorax. The chest tube insertion probably saved the man's life."

"Can you be certain?"

"If Dr. Brice hadn't have performed that procedure, the patient would've certainly died."

Mr. Schultz frowned. "But in the middle of the ER? In front of the investors and other patients?"

"It wasn't planned, if that's what you're implying." Virginia counted to ten in her head. Her whole body clenched as she fought back the urge to knock some common sense into Edwin Schultz's addled brains.

"I didn't say it was, Dr. Potter." He snorted, pulling out a handkerchief to dab at his sweaty bald head. He folded it up again and placed it in his breast pocket. "I'm suggesting that maybe you should have a talk with him about the proper place to perform a medical procedure."

She wanted to tell Schultz that sometimes there was no time to find a proper room or an OR in trauma surgery when a life was at stake, only that wasn't the diplomatic way and she'd worked so hard to become one of the youngest chiefs at Bayview Grace, heck, one of the youngest in San Francisco at the age of thirty. She wasn't about to give that up. Job stability was all that mattered.

Her career was all that mattered.

"I'll have a talk with Dr. Brice when he's out of surgery."

Mr. Schultz nodded. "Please do. Now, let's go take care of the investors because if they don't invest the money we need, the emergency department will have to be cut."

"Cut?" Virginia's world spun around, her body clenching again. "What do you mean, cut?"

"I was going to speak to you later about this, but the hospital is losing money. Many members of the board feel that Bayview Grace could make a lot more money as a private clinic. The emergency department is the biggest detriment to the hospital's budget."

"We're a level-one trauma center." And they had just got that distinction because of two years of her blood, sweat and tears.

Mr. Schultz sighed. "I know, but unless we get the investors we need, we have no choice."

Virginia cursed under her breath. "And how do you feel, Mr. Schultz?"

"I think we should close the emergency department." The head of the board said no more and pushed past her.

Virginia scrubbed her hand over her face.

What am I doing?

As a surgeon, she wanted to tell Mr. Schultz what she thought about shutting down Bayview Grace's ER, but she didn't. She held her tongue, like she always did, and her father's words echoed in her ear.

"Don't tick off the boss man, darling. Job security is financial security."

And financial security meant food, home and all the necessities.

Virginia wanted to hold onto her job, like anyone did. She wouldn't wish a life of poverty like she'd endured as a child on her worst enemy.

So she was going to hold her head up high and make sure those investors didn't walk away. She was going to make sure Bayview's ER didn't close its doors so the people who worked in trauma didn't lose their jobs.

Though she respected Dr. Brice and his abilities, she knew she had to rein him in to keep control of her hospital.

She just didn't know how she was going to do that, or that she really wanted to.

"Where's the family?" Gavin asked the nearest nurse he could wrangle.

"Whose family?" the nurse asked, without looking up from the computer monitor.

Gavin bit back his frustration. He knew he had to be nicer to the nurses. At least here he had them.

"Mr. Jones, the man with the crush injuries who had the pneumothorax."

The nurse's eyes widened. "In the waiting room. Mrs. Jones and her three teenage sons. They're hard to miss."

"Uh, thank you…"

The nurse rolled her eyes. "Sadie."

"Right. Thanks." Gavin cursed inwardly as he ripped off his scrub cap and jammed it into a nearby receptacle. He should really know her name since he'd been working with her for six weeks, but Gavin couldn't keep anyone's name straight.

Except Virginia's.

It wasn't hard to keep her name straight in his head. The moment he'd met her, his breath had been taken away with those dark brown eyes to match the dark hair in a tidy chignon. She was so put together, feminine, like something out of a magazine, and then she spoke about all the rules and regulations, about everything he was doing wrong, and it shattered his illusion.

No wonder the staff called her Ice Queen. She was so cold and aloof. There was no warmth about her. It was all business.

The woman was a brilliant surgeon, he'd noticed the few times they'd worked together, but she was always slapping his wrists for foolish things.

"It's not sanitary. Legal is going to talk to you. The hospital could get sued," Virginia had stated.

In fact, when he had a moment, he planned to discuss the functionality and the layout out of this emergency department with her and the board.

It was horrendous.

When he'd been working in the field, in developing countries, everything he'd needed had been within arm's reach, and if it hadn't been then he'd made do with what he'd had and no one had complained. No one had talked about reprimanding him.

He'd been free to do what he wanted to save lives. It's why he'd become a trauma surgeon, for God's sake.

If he wasn't needed in San Francisco, if he had any other choice, he'd march into Virginia's office and hand in his resignation.

Only Lily and Rose stopped him.

He was working in this job, this suffocating, regimented environment, because of them. He didn't blame them; it wasn't their fault their mother had died. It's just that Gavin wished with all his heart he was anywhere but here.

Although he liked being at home with them. He wanted to do right by them. Give them the love and security he'd never had.

Gavin stopped at the charge desk and set Mr. Jones's chart on the desk to fill out some more information before he approached the family with news.

"You know that was the board of directors you traumatized today," Sadie said from behind the desk.

Gavin grunted in response.

What else was new?

Board of directors. He pinched the bridge of his nose. "I suppose Dr. Potter wants to have a little word with me?"

"Bingo." Sadie got up and left.

Gavin cursed under his breath again. "When?" he called after her.

"Ten minutes ago," she called out over her shoulder.

Damn.

Well, Virginia would have to wait.

He had to tell Mrs. Jones her husband, who'd sustained severe crush injuries in a car accident, was going to be okay.

All thanks to his minor indiscretion over the chest tube insertion in front of the board.

Only he wouldn't get any thanks. From Mrs. Jones, yes, but from the people who ran this place, no.

It would be another slap on the wrist. Potter would tell him again how he was skating on thin ice with the board of directors.

It would take all his strength not to quit. Only he couldn't.

No other hospital in San Francisco was hiring or had been interested in him. He didn't have a flashy CV after working as a field surgeon for Border Free Physicians.

He didn't make the covers of medical journals or have some great research to tempt another hospital with.

All he had were his two hands and his surgical abilities.

Those two hands had saved a man today, but that wasn't good enough for the board. The bottom line was the only thing that mattered and it made him furious.

If it wasn't for the girls, he'd quit.

He couldn't uproot them. He wouldn't do that to them, he wouldn't have them suffer the same life he and Casey had endured as army brats, moving from pillar to post, never making friends and having absentee parents who had both been in the service.

Although he understood his parents now. He respected them for serving their country and doing their duty. He lived by the same code, only he wasn't going to raise a family living out of a backpack, and because he loved his life and his work he'd never planned on settling down.

He planned to die doing what he loved. Like his father had done.

Working until he'd dropped.

Of course, that had all changed seven months ago when Casey had called him.

Casey wanted stability for her girls and that's exactly what Gavin was going to give them.

Stability.

He picked up Mr. Jones's chart and headed towards the waiting room.

Virginia could wait a few moments more and he'd smooth things over with the board. Mrs. Jones, however, wouldn't wait a second more.

CHAPTER TWO

HE'S GOOD PR for the hospital.

Virginia felt like she was running out of ways to praise Dr. Gavin Brice to the board of directors. None of them were physicians.

None of them understood medicine.

And because none of the board understood medicine she constantly had to explain to them the actions of Dr. Brice; just like she'd done for the past hour.

Virginia rubbed her temples, trying to will away the nagging headache that gnawed her just behind her eyes.

It'd been grueling, but she'd managed to smooth things over. By again reminding them of Dr. Brice's phenomenal survival rate. It was probably that way because of the unorthodox techniques he used.

Of course, what was the point when the head of the board seemed so keen to shut down the hospital's emergency department and make Bayview Grace a private hospital? Private meant only for the wealthy.

And catering only to the wealthy made her sick.

When she'd first decided to become a doctor she hadn't just want to help those who could afford it. It was one of the reasons she'd chosen Bayview to do her intern and residency years. Bayview, back then, had had a fantastic pro bono fund and a free clinic.

The free clinic had been closed two years ago when

she'd done her boards. When she'd become chief she'd tried to get it back, but that would have meant dipping into the pro bono money and that money had been needed.

Mr. Schultz had feigned regret, but Virginia had seen those dollar signs flashing in his eyes. It made her feel a bit sick.

Her stomach knotted as she thought about the countless people from all walks of life who came to her hospital. The pro bono budget was dwindling and she wished she could help more, because at one time in her life she'd been in the poorest of the poor's shoes, getting by on only sub-par medical care.

It was why her sister Shyanne had died.

Shyanne had hidden her pregnancy from her parents, knowing they couldn't afford to help her with medical bills, but the pregnancy had turned out to be ectopic. Virginia had happened to be home on a school break in her first year of medical school and had kicked herself for not seeing the signs early enough.

By the time the ambulance had come to take Shyanne to the hospital, she was gone. Ruptured fallopian tube. She'd bled out too fast.

It was one reason why Virginia donated so much time to the pro bono cases, why she didn't want Bayview's ER closed, like the free clinic had been closed.

There was a knock on her office door, but before she could answer the man in question swaggered into the room and she had to remember herself. She had to control the flush that was threatening to creep up her neck and erupt in crimson blooms in her cheeks.

It was a damn pain in the rump that she was basically his boss and that he was so devilishly sexy. Reddish-gold hair, green eyes like emeralds. Even the scar on his cheek, which just grazed that deep, deep dimple, made the young woman she'd buried under her businesslike façade squeal just a little bit. He was the quintessential bad boy and she'd always had a soft spot for bad boys. Even though her mother had warned her not to give them the time of day.

Virginia and Shyanne had listened. Shyanne had got involved with a good boy. One who had been a golden son of De Smet, South Dakota. A golden son who had knocked Shyanne up and taken off on a football scholarship, leaving Shyanne in the lurch.

"You wanted to see me, Dr. Potter?"

"Yes. Please, take a seat." Pulling at the collar of her blouse, she motioned to the seat in front of her desk. When he moved closer she caught a whiff of his scent. A clean scent of something spicy but rugged and the smell made her insides flutter. With a calming breath she folded her hands neatly in front of her on her blotter. "The board has asked me to speak with you."

A brief smile quirked on his lips as he sat down. "Again?"

"Yes. Are you surprised?"

"Not really. I did happen to catch the expression of some of those investors today."

"You think it's funny?"

Gavin cocked his head to one side. "A bit."

Virginia bit her lip and silently counted to ten. "I managed to smooth things over."

He rolled his eyes. "Look, can I lay something out for you, Dr. Potter?"

She was stunned. "Of course, by all means."

"I don't care what the board approves or disapproves of. I don't care if they think the way I practice medicine is barbaric."

"I don't think they actually said barbaric, Dr. Brice."

He grinned. "Please, call me Gavin."

Virginia swallowed the lump in her throat. It was the first time since they'd met that he'd asked her to use his first name. Not that they'd had much social interaction, besides work-related conversations, and these seemingly frequent discussions about the board and his disregard for following hospital policies.

"Gavin, if you're unhappy, perhaps there's something we can do, or I can do, to make your practice here better?"

"There's nothing you can do. Frankly, I wouldn't be happy anywhere outside Border Free Physicians."

Intriguing. "Then can I ask you a personal question?"

"Of course, but I may not answer."

Touché. "Why did you leave Border Free Physicians and apply here?"

Gavin's easy smile faded and his mouth pressed into a thin line, his brow furrowing. Virginia couldn't help but wonder if this was something he wasn't going to answer. In his few weeks here she'd ascertained he was a private man. He didn't socialize with many people, ate his lunch alone and did his job efficiently, as far as Virginia was concerned. Maybe not to the board's approval, but as long as the patients lived and there were no lawsuits she was happy.

"I'm needed here," he said finally. Only that's all he said. No explanation about why he'd applied for the job or why he'd told her he wasn't happy here and wouldn't be happy anywhere but with Border Free Physicians.

So why had he left?

"You look confused," Gavin said, the teasing tone returning to his voice.

"Not confused." *Oh, who am I kidding?* "Okay, a bit confused."

"I'm sorry. I didn't really want to put you in this position."

"You haven't put me in a position, Dr. Brice."

"Gavin."

Heat bloomed in her cheeks. "Gavin. I only want to help you, even if this position is not the one you want."

Gavin nodded his head. "I thank you for that."

"For what?"

"For trying to help, but I really don't think I need it."

"I know it's difficult, you came from a job where you worked in rough conditions and had to think on your feet and quickly, but the board of directors has to protect the hospital's best interests."

"Isn't that basically what all trauma surgeons do?"

Virginia smiled. "Yes, but there are certain rules and regulations that have to take place in a hospital setting. They feel what happened today was inappropriate."

He snorted. "Inappropriate to save a man's life?"

"There are rules and the board is protecting the interests of the hospital."

"So you keep reiterating."

"It seems I have to." She crossed her arms. "Do you understand what I'm saying?"

"The bottom line." That look of disdain returned and he shook his head slightly.

Virginia knew and understood what he was feeling, but what choice did they have?

"Unfortunately."

Gavin stood. "I have to protect my patient's best interests, Dr. Potter. I won't change the way I practice medicine."

"I'm trying to help you." Now she was getting irritated. How could she help someone who didn't want her help? Easy. She couldn't. She was losing an uphill battle when it came to Dr. Brice.

He pulled out his pager and glanced at it. Not looking at her, thus silently ending their conversation. "I appreciate that, but I'm needed back in the ER."

Stunned, Virginia stood as he left and then watched

through the glass as he jogged down the hall towards the ER.

What just happened?

She slowly sank back down into her chair, feeling a bit like a deer caught in headlights, like someone had just pulled a fast one on her.

The board wouldn't be happy with her for not reining him in, but then again she didn't really want to. Dr. Brice was someone who moved to the beat of his own drum. He annoyed the nurses because he couldn't remember their names, didn't have much time for interns and, yes, performed a medical procedure in front of a bunch of rich investors, but the point was he saved lives.

His curriculum vitae was impressive. As far she was concerned.

His image, his work in Africa, doing surgery on refugees, brought in good press for the hospital. People had a soft spot for good Samaritans.

Even if the board thought he was a bit of a rogue surgeon.

Virginia rubbed her temples. Her tension headache was becoming stronger. Couldn't he see how she was trying to make his transition to a metropolitan hospital setting just a bit easier? There was one thing Virginia took away from this meeting today and that was that Dr. Gavin Brice was a bit of a pompous ass.

Dammit.

Gavin glanced at his wristwatch and noticed the time. He was late and Lily was going to kill him. Rose wouldn't, though, she was so sweet, but Lily was a force to be reckoned with. This was the third time he'd missed taking her to ballet lessons and he'd pinky-sworn that he'd be the one to take her this time instead of Rosalie, the sitter.

He had no idea what he was doing and he was a terrible father figure, but that was the crux of the matter—he wasn't Lily's and Rose's father. He was their uncle, but as he was their only caregiver since their mother, his sister, had died of cancer, he was no longer cool Uncle Gavin who sent them postcards from new and exciting locations as he traveled to different developing countries with Border Free Physicians.

Now he was Mr. Mom and not very good at it. Lily, who was eight, had reminded him of it every day for the last couple of months.

"That's not how Mom did it."

Rose was four, all smiles, but she didn't say a single word.

It's why he was here, in San Francisco, instead of continuing with Border Free Physicians. He hated not being where he wanted to be, but he'd do anything to take care of those girls. To give them the home life and stability he and his late sister, Casey, had never had.

After all his nieces had been through, there was no way he could drag them from pillar to post, living rough while he worked. He'd had to give up his life as a field trauma physician and get something stable, reliable and in the girls' hometown.

He needed to give them structure and not rip them away from all they knew. Especially not when their world had been shattered after their mother's recent death and their father's when Rose had been only an infant.

He had to be reliable or he could lose the girls to their paternal grandparents. He'd promised Casey he wouldn't let that happen. It had been only three months since Casey had died and though he'd always said he didn't want to be tied down, he wouldn't give the girls up for anything.

Even though he was a hopeless failure.

A cool breeze rolled in off the bay and Gavin shivered. He pulled his coat tighter. Even though it was August, there was a nip in the air and he still wasn't acclimatized to anything that wasn't subtropical.

He stuffed his hands in his pockets and headed for the grey minivan he'd inherited from Casey. His motorbike was sitting alone and forgotten under a tarp in the garage, because you couldn't ferry kids to and from various dance rehearsals, art classes and Girl Scouts' meetings on the back of a motorcycle.

As he made his way across the parking lot he caught sight of Virginia walking toward her dark, sleek-looking sedan. Gavin paused a moment to watch her move. She was so put together and she moved with fluid grace. Even if she seemed tight, like a taut bowstring most days.

Her dark hair was piled up on her head, not a strand of hair loose. There was a natural look to her and she didn't need to wear garish makeup to accentuate those dark, chocolate eyes or those ruby lips. Her clothing was stylish and professional but sexy. Today it was the pencil skirt, paired with a crisp shirt and black high heels that showed off her slim but curvy figure in all the right places.

She climbed into her car, and just as she was sitting down her skirt hiked up a bit, giving him a nice view of her stocking-clad thigh.

Gavin's pulse began to race. If any woman could emulate the princess Snow White it was Dr. Virginia Potter.

He let out a hiss of disgust; he'd been reading Rose far too many fairy tales if he was comparing the chief of surgery to Snow White.

Did that make him a dwarf? Though the way some of those surgeons and nurses moved through the hospital, it was like they were on their way to the mines for the day.

Virginia drove away and Gavin scrubbed his hand over his face. He needed a beer and to veg out in front of the television for a while.

One of the perks of being in the city.

He drove through the streets in a trance, letting the day's surgeries just roll off his back. When he pulled up into his sister's pink-colored marina-style home in the outer Richmond district, a twenty-minute commute from the hospital, he finally let out a sigh of relief mixed with frustration.

It had to be pink.

His whole life seemed to be wrapped up in various shades of pink from coral to bubble gum. At least his scrubs weren't pink.

The lights were all on in the living room above the garage, which meant the girls were home from dance rehearsal. Rosalie's car was on the street outside. The garage door opened and he pulled the van inside, next to his tarp-covered Harley.

I know, baby. I miss you too.

He sighed with longing, pulling the garage door down and locking it. Rosalie, having seen him pull up, was leaving as he opened the locked gate onto the street that led to the front door.

"Dr. Brice, how was your day?" Rosalie asked, brightly.

"You don't really want to know. How's Lily?"

Rosalie gave him a broad, toothy grin as she heaved her bag over her shoulder. "You don't really want to know."

"That bad?"

"It's been a rough day for her." Rosalie moved past him to the car. "When is your next shift?"

"Tomorrow, but then I'm not on call this weekend. I don't go back until Wednesday afternoon."

"Ah, a four-day weekend. *Que bueno.* I'll see you tomorrow, Dr. Brice. Have a good night." Gavin waited until Rosalie was safely in her car and had driven away before he locked the gate and headed inside.

The stairs from the entranceway to the main level were scattered with various dance paraphernalia and pink things. As he took a step something squished and squeaked under his feet, causing Rose to materialize at the top of the stairs, scowling with her chubby little arms crossed.

Gavin peeled the rubber giraffe from under his foot. "Sorry, I didn't mean to step on Georgiana."

Rose grinned and held out her hand. Gavin placed Georgiana in Rose's hand. "How's Lily?"

Rose rolled her eyes and then skipped off. Gavin groaned inwardly and dragged himself up the last few steps.

He found Lily sitting at the kitchen table, her chin resting on the table with a dejected look on her face. The same face Casey had made when he'd been taking care of her when their dad and mom had left them while they did their duty to their country.

It made his heart hurt just to think about how much he missed his sister.

"Lily."

Lily glanced at him sideways, her blue eyes so like Casey's. "I know. There was an emergency. I get it."

Gavin took a seat opposite to her. She talked so much like a little adult. "There was an emergency, in fact, a car accident. I had to perform surgery."

"Did you save the person's life?"

"I did."

Lily sat up straight. "Then I guess that's worth it."

At least someone thinks so.

"Very mature of you, Lily. Look, after tomorrow's shift I have the next four days off. I'm not on call and I can spend it with you and Rose."

Lily chirked up. "Really?"

"Really. We can go down to the piers, watch the sea lions." Rose skipped into the room then and crawled up on his lap.

"Can we get some clams?" Lily asked brightly.

Clams? I was willing to offer ice cream...

"You girls like seafood?"

"Yeah, Mom used to take us down to the fish market all the time. We'd get some seafood and she'd make her famous chowder."

Gavin nodded. "Sure. I'll try to make you guys some chowder. How about you two get ready for bed?"

"Sure." Lily got up and took Rose by the hand, leading her towards the front of the house. When Gavin had made sure they were out of earshot he laid his head down on the table. He had never thought he would be a father because he had always been afraid he would be terrible, like his own father was. Oh, his father was a hero all right, but he'd never hugged them, never complimented them and had never been there. It was the same with their mother and it terrified Gavin to his very core. He didn't want to become like them.

Only Casey had had the same fears about becoming a mother and she had been one of the best.

God, I miss her.

He just hoped he was doing right by his nieces.

He owed Casey that much.

CHAPTER THREE

Virginia picked up Mr. Jones's chart and read Gavin's notes quickly. When she glanced up she could see Gavin through the glass partition in Mr. Jones's room. Mr. Jones was still unconscious, so he needed to be in the ICU, but Gavin was speaking to Mrs. Jones.

At least Virginia assumed it was Mrs. Jones, as the woman had been by Mr. Jones's bedside all night. Which was what the night charge nurse had told her when she had started her shift at five that morning.

"Is everything okay, chief?" the charge nurse at the desk asked.

"Yes, Kimber, everything's fine." Virginia smiled and handed the binder back to her. "Just checking on the ER's newest celebrity before I head into surgery."

"Who?"

"Dr. Brice."

Kimber grinned. "Oh, yes, I heard about the excitement in the ER yesterday. I always miss the drama when I'm off."

Virginia cocked an eyebrow. "Is that so? What did you hear?"

"That Dr. Brice inserted a chest tube in front of the investors." Kimber shook her head and chuckled to herself. "I bet they were impressed."

Virginia didn't say anything else as Kimber walked

the file back to where it belonged. Before Virginia had been the Chief of Surgery, she'd had friends and comrades she'd been able to talk to about anything. Now, because of her position, she had to be careful of everything she said.

There was no one she could blow off steam with. No one to vent to.

Except the cactus in her apartment.

Even then it wasn't the most animated of conversations.

She missed the days when she could go down to the cafeteria and sit down with fellow attendings and residents and shoot the breeze.

Heck, she could even talk to the nurses back then.

Now they all looked at her for what she was. Their boss.

Their careers were in her hands.

Kimber returned back. "Chief, really, is there anything I can do?"

Deal with the board for me? "No, why?"

"You were staring off into space."

"Thinking."

"About?"

Virginia cocked her eyebrow. "What do you think of Dr. Brice?"

"Dishy." Kimber waggled her eyebrows, but then she instantly sobered. "Sorry, chief."

"Professionally, what do you think?"

"Oh, well…" Kimber hesitated.

"Go on," Virginia urged.

"He's pretty brusque with nurses, doesn't remember our names. Refers to most of us as 'hey you'. Rarely says thank-you. But he's good with the patients and he's a great surgeon."

"Thank you, Kimber."

"Is Dr. Brice in trouble, chief?"

Virginia shook her head. "No, I just wanted to see how well he was getting on with the other members of the staff."

"The answer to that is not well." Kimber walked away from the charge desk, just as Dr. Brice left Mr. Jones's room.

He was staring at his pager, headed right for her. Finally he glanced up and saw her there and his eyes widened momentarily. "Dr. Potter, what brings you to the ICU today? I thought you'd be in more investor meetings."

Virginia gritted her teeth. "No. No meetings today, Dr. Brice."

"Gavin." He flashed her a smug smile, which she wanted to wipe off his face. Instead she ignored him.

"I'm headed for the OR, actually."

"Amazing, I didn't think chiefs of surgery were able to operate."

"I'm a surgeon first and foremost. Now, if you don't mind, I'll be off." She turned from him and headed for the OR suites, but Gavin followed her, keeping pace.

"What surgery are you preforming?"

"A routine cholecystectomy."

"I thought you were a trauma surgeon."

"I'm a general surgeon, but I did work in trauma during my fellowship years. Besides, our ER is staffed with several capable surgeons."

Gavin chuckled. "Not me, though."

Virginia cocked an eyebrow, but continued toward the ORs. "What do you mean?"

"We had this talk yesterday, Virginia. I'm not an asset to Bayview Grace."

"Dr. Brice—"

"Gavin," he interrupted.

She took a calming breath. "Gavin, who said you weren't?"

"You did."

"When?"

"Yesterday, after I saved Mr. Jones's life in front of the

board, or have you mentally blocked that catastrophe of public relations proportions from your brain?"

Virginia chuckled. "I never said you weren't an asset. You're a fine surgeon, Gavin, you just have to work on your interpersonal skills." The doors to the scrub room slid open and she stepped inside. Gavin followed her.

Lord. Just let me be.

All she wanted to do was this surgery. Here she could clear her head and think.

"Interpersonal skills?" A smile quirked his lips. "In what ways?"

"I don't have time to talk the semantics over with you. I have a choly to attend to, that is, unless you want to scrub in?"

Please, don't scrub in, one half of her screamed, while the other half of her wanted to see him in action. To work side by side with him.

"I haven't done a routine choly in…well, probably not since my residency, and it wasn't done laparoscopically. The attendings and indeed the hospital where I obtained my residency weren't up to par with Dr. Mühe's ground-breaking procedure."

"I would love to have you assist, Gavin." Virginia stepped on the bar under the sink and began to scrub.

Gavin grinned, his eyes twinkling in the dim light of the scrub room. "Liar."

"Pardon?"

"You don't want me in your OR. I think you've had enough of me."

"That's true. You've been a thorn in my side since I hired you."

He laughed. "I know."

Virginia shook her hands and then grabbed some paper towel. "I would like to see you work, though. I haven't had the chance to observe you, and the nurses tell me you're a brilliant surgeon."

He raised his eyebrows. "I didn't think the nurses cared much for me."

"They don't." She smirked. "You really need to work on remembering their names."

"Not at the top of my priority."

Virginia shook her head and moved towards the sliding door that separated the suite from the scrub room. "Make it a priority, Gavin. You'll find things run a lot smoother if you do. Are you joining me?"

"I think I'll pass, Dr. Potter. I may be needed in Trauma."

"Virginia." She shot him a smug smile and headed into surgery, both relieved and disappointed that he wasn't joining her.

I should've gone into surgery with her.

Gavin was beating himself up over not taking the opportunity to sit in on a surgery with Virginia, the ice queen, even if it had been a routine one.

Emergency had been quiet. Eerily so. He'd resorted to charting, though secretly he was trying to learn the nurses' names but couldn't.

He could remember the most complicated procedure, but when it came to mundane, everyday things like dry-cleaning or remembering a name he couldn't.

What was wrong with him?

Something was definitely wrong with him, because he'd turned down the chance to get to know Virginia by operating with her. She'd been so uptight every time they'd spoken, but this time there had been something different about her.

She was more relaxed, more receptive to gentle teasing. He'd enjoyed his verbal repartee with her, even if it'd only been for a moment. Gavin had seen the twinkle in her eyes before she'd entered the operating room, that glint of humor, and he'd liked it.

And it had scared him.

He had no time to be thinking about women. The girls were his top priority.

"I won't say what you're thinking, because if I say it we'll be bombarded with a bunch of trauma."

Gavin looked up from his chart to see Dr. Rogerson leaning over the desk, grinning at him. Moira Rogerson was another trauma surgeon, but only a fellow as she'd just passed her boards.

"Pardon?" Gavin asked.

"You know, like how actors don't say 'Macbeth' in the theater."

"Oh, I get what you mean."

ER physicians never remarked on a slow day. If they did it was bad juju and they'd have an influx of patients. Gavin returned to his charting, dismissing Moira.

At least he hoped it gave her the hint. The woman had been pursuing him like a lioness hunting a wounded wildebeest since he'd first set foot in the hospital.

"I was wondering if you'd like to grab a bite to eat with me after work?"

The lioness obviously couldn't take a hint. It wasn't that there was anything wrong with her, she was pretty, intelligent and a brilliant surgeon, but he wasn't interested in her.

He didn't like to be pursued and he wasn't interested in starting a relationship with anyone at the moment.

"I can't."

"Why?"

Gavin sighed in frustration. "I just can't."

"I know you're new to this city. What can you possibly have to do?"

Gavin slammed the binder shut and stood up, perhaps a

bit abruptly. "Things." He set the chart down and headed towards the cafeteria. Maybe grabbing some lunch would clear his head.

Moira, thankfully, didn't follow.

Sure, he'd been harsh with her and, yeah, he had an itch that needed to be scratched, but since the girls had come into his life he had to be more responsible.

A year ago he would've taken Moira up on her offer and then some. As long as she hadn't wanted anything serious.

She was attractive.

Now that he had his nieces, he just couldn't be that playboy any more. His dating life could be summed up in two words. Cold. Showers.

In the cafeteria he grabbed a ready-made sandwich and a bottle of water. He was planning to take them outside and get some fresh air when he spotted Virginia on the far side of the cafeteria. It surprised him, as he never saw her in here.

She was sitting in the corner of the cafeteria at a table for two, but she sat alone. She was reading some kind of medical journal as she picked at a salad.

The cafeteria was full of other doctors, nurses, interns, but Virginia sat by herself.

She's the chief of surgery. The boss.

The ice queen.

No one would want to sit with their boss at lunch. They wouldn't feel comfortable, and he felt sorry for her. She was so young and she didn't have it easy.

Just like me.

He crossed the cafeteria and stopped in front of her. "May I join you, Virginia?"

She looked startled and glanced up at him. "Of—of course, Dr. Potter. I mean Gavin."

Gavin took the seat across from her. "How was your choly?"

"Routine." She smiled and his pulse quickened. He liked the way she smiled and especially when it was directed at him, which wasn't often. "How was the ER?"

"I think you can guess."

"I know. I won't say it."

"I'm trying to work on interpersonal skills, but I'm having a hard time putting faces to names."

She cocked an eyebrow. "You don't seem to have that problem with patients."

He nodded. "This is true."

"You're agreeing with me? Amazing." The twinkle of humor appeared again.

"You're mocking me now, aren't you?"

Virginia stabbed a cherry tomato. "So what's the difference between the nurses and the patients?"

"The patients aren't all wearing the same kitten-patterned scrubs."

Virginia chuckled. "Not all the nurses wear kitten scrubs."

"Well pink, then." Gavin snorted. "Always pink."

"What do you mean by that?"

"Nothing." Gavin didn't want to talk about his nieces. His private life was just that. It was his and private.

"What did you do in Africa? How did you remember names there?"

"It was easy. There were only ten of us at the most at any given time."

"It's a number thing, then."

Gavin swallowed the water he had taken a swig of. "There are so many nurses. I think they're multiplying and replicating in the back somewhere."

Virginia laughed. It was a nice one, which made him smile. "Please, don't tell them you think they're cloning themselves. You're a good surgeon, Gavin, and I'd hate to lose you to a pyre they'd light under the spit they'd tie you to."

Gavin winked. "I'm trying."

"Good." She leaned forward and he caught the scent of vanilla, warm and homey like a bakery. He loved that smell. Gavin fought the sudden urge to bury his face in her neck and drink the scent in. "I have a secret."

"Do tell."

"They wear nametags."

Gavin rolled his eyes. "Ha-ha. Very funny."

Virginia just laughed to herself as she ate her salad. "So, do you have any plans for the weekend?"

He cringed inwardly and then picked at the label on his bottle of water. "Nothing in particular. Are you off this weekend?"

"Yes, surprisingly."

"And do you have plans?"

"I do."

Gavin waited. "Not going to tell me?"

"Why should I? You don't divulge aspects of your personal life."

"Touché." He downed the rest of his water and stood. "I'd better get back to the ER. It was nice chatting with you, Virginia."

"And with you, Gavin. I hope the ER remains quiet for you for the rest of the day."

A distant wail of an ambulance could be heard through an open window of the cafeteria. Several people raised their heads and listened.

Gavin groaned. "You had to jinx it, didn't you?"

And all that minx did was grin.

CHAPTER FOUR

VIRGINIA WAS TIRED of sitting in her apartment alone. Not even the cactus could get her mind to stop racing.

The two things on her mind were the board's threat to close the ER and Gavin.

After lunch yesterday she had felt the eyes of the other staff members boring into the back of her skull. They had obviously been shocked that the lone wolf, Dr. Brice, had sat with the ice queen of Bayview Grace, and the kicker had been that they'd both seemed to enjoy each other's company.

Well, ice queens could get lonely too.

Virginia couldn't let a slip up like that happen again. She couldn't afford to have rumors flying around about them.

She'd eat in her office from now on.

At least, that's what she'd decided on during her drive down to the pier in the calm serenity of her car.

Virginia had forgotten how crowded and noisy the pier was. It was a Saturday and it was August.

Tourist season.

The height of it.

All she wanted to do was get some fresh produce and maybe some shrimp down at the pier for dinner later, but she'd forgotten how jam-packed Fisherman's Wharf could be. If she had a nickel for every middle-aged guy in an

Alcatraz T-shirt wearing sandals with dark socks hiked to their knees who had bumped into her today, she'd have twenty bucks. At least.

Virginia moved through the crowd towards the pier. Her favorite vendor had a stall right near the edge of the market. Nikos knew her by name, knew what she liked and had her order ready every third Saturday of the month.

She liked the conversation and the familiarity, but it also reminded her of how utterly alone she was. How much it sucked that she'd be returning to her apartment in Nob Hill with only the echo of her own voice, her mute cactus and cable television to keep her company.

You can't have it all, Virginia.

At least, that's what she kept telling herself. She needed to keep her job so she could keep a roof over her head and send checks to her parents in De Smet. She'd make sure her younger siblings had a better childhood than she and Shyanne had had. Money was what her family needed. Not her presence, even though her mother begged her to visit all the time. A pang of pain hit her. She missed her twin sister and her family with every fiber of her being.

Only she couldn't earn the money her family needed and take time off to visit them.

A shriek across the market shook her out of her dull reverie and she glanced to the source of the sound. A flurry of pink could be seen in the midst of the crush of locals and tourists.

The cloud of pink, in the form of a very puffy and frilly tutu, was attached to a golden-haired cherub on the shoulders of someone one could only assume was her father.

A pang of longing hit her and hit her hard.

Kids weren't part of the plan. It was why she was single,

but in that moment Virginia couldn't remember for the life of her why.

Right, because I don't want to have to worry about anyone else. I don't want to lose any one else.

Another girl was pulling on the man's arm and he turned around.

Virginia let out a gasp of shock to see a very familiar face peeking out from under the tutu. None other than the lone wolf Dr. Gavin Brice.

She hadn't known he was married and with his vehement stance on where he'd rather be practicing medicine, Virginia would never have pegged him for a family man.

The pained expression on his face also confirmed her assumptions. Why hadn't he mentioned his children before? Or the fact that he was married?

Virginia knew she shouldn't get involved, that she should just turn the other way, but, dammit, Nikos would have her shrimp ready. She wasn't going to change her plans just because it might avoid an awkward conversation.

No. She was going to stay on her present course.

Besides, curiosity was getting the better of her.

"Curiosity killed the cat!" Her mother's voice nagged in her ear.

Shut up, Mom.

"Lily, I think we have everything we need." Gavin's voice was pleading.

"No way. You're missing the key ingredient. Besides, you said we could go watch the sea lions after this."

"Dr. Brice, what a surprise to find you here," Virginia said, interrupting them.

Gavin's eyes widened as he looked at her. His eldest

daughter inched closer to him, her keen blue eyes probing her, picking out her weaknesses.

Virginia recognized the look because she'd done the same many a time when she'd been younger. Only Gavin's daughter was giving the stare dressed in a ballet leotard and tutu. Virginia envied her, because ballet was something she'd always wanted to do as a little girl but her parents couldn't afford it.

"Dr. Potter, what a surprise to see you here."

"I always come to the market when I have a Saturday off." Virginia grinned at the little cherub who was peeking out from the top of Gavin's hair. The cherub had a very messy blonde bun on the top of her head, like whoever did her hair had no idea what they were doing. Virginia could feel her heart turning into a great big pile of goo, which was starting to coat the insides of her chest cavity like warm chocolate. "Are you going to introduce me to your daughters, Dr. Brice?"

The eldest snorted. "He's our uncle, *not* our dad."

Gavin nodded. "Yes, these are my nieces. This is Lily. Lily, this is Chief of Surgery at my hospital, Dr. Potter."

Lily's eyes widened, obviously impressed. She stuck out her hand; the nails were a garish color of red, sloppily painted on. Virginia took her hand and it was a bit sticky. In fact, both girls looked a bit of a mess. Just as Gavin appeared to be, which was so different from his put-together appearance at the hospital.

"Nice to meet you, Dr. Potter."

"Likewise."

"And this little one who's latched herself to my brain, apparently, is Rose." Gavin poked at the chubby cherub, but she wouldn't release her death grip on her uncle.

Virginia smiled. "Nice to meet you, Rose."

Rose didn't utter a word, just continued to stare.

"Sorry, Rose doesn't talk," Gavin explained, and then sighed in exasperation.

"Shy?" Virginia asked.

"No," Lily said, piping up. "She hasn't talked since our mom died."

Gavin wished Virginia hadn't run into them. Mainly because he didn't want any of his work colleagues to know about his private life. On the other hand, he was glad he had run into her and she didn't even bat an eyelash after what Lily had blurted out. Not that he would've even recognized her from the polished businesswoman who graced the halls of Bayview Grace Hospital.

Her dark hair, usually pinned up and back away from her face, hung loose over her shoulders, framing her oval face perfectly.

Instead of a tight pencil skirt, crisp blouse and heels, she wore a bulky cardigan, jeans and ballet flats, but the rest, well, it suited her. He liked the relaxed, affable Virginia.

The cardigan he could do without. It hid too much of her curvy figure, which Gavin liked to admire on occasion, like when she wore those tight pencil skirts and high heels. Just thinking about that made his blood heat.

Get a hold of yourself, Gavin.

"I'm so sorry to hear that," Virginia said, and he could tell by the sincerity in her voice she really meant it. It wasn't one of those polite obligatory outpourings of grief. Virginia meant it.

Lily was growing bored with the conversation and was gazing around the teeming market. Rose had released her death grip on Gavin's head and was wiggling to get down off her perch to join her sister.

"Thanks," Gavin said, depositing Rose down on the ground beside Lily. He breathed a sigh of relief and stretched his neck.

"Well, I'd better go. I'm going to pick up some shrimp and head back to my apartment."

"That's what we need, Uncle Gavin. Shrimp," Lily piped up.

"Shrimp? I thought it was clams?" he asked.

Lily rolled her eyes impatiently. "Mom *always* added shrimp to her clam chowder."

Virginia chuckled. "Sounds like quite an undertaking."

Gavin lifted the cooler he was holding with his one arm. "This clam chowder is becoming more and more complicated."

"So it seems." Virginia smiled and warmth spread through his chest. He liked the way she smiled. "Well, I'd better go," she repeated.

"Can I come with you, Dr. Potter? I'll get the shrimp we need, Uncle Gavin."

Gavin watched as Virginia's eyes widened, but only for a moment. She appeared nervous.

"Uh, it's Lily, right?"

"Yep! So, can I come with you?"

"Okay," Virginia said, her voice shaking and her expression one of utter shock. Like a deer in headlights.

"That sounds great!" Lily took Virginia's hand and Gavin took a step back, surprised by his niece's familiarity with a perfect stranger. Gavin handed Lily some money and watched as Virginia guided her to a booth on the outskirts of the market. Virginia, though still looking stunned, handled it well.

They were in view the whole time, so there was nothing for Gavin to be worried about. He shook his head over Lily's behavior. She wasn't that open or friendly with strangers usually. Lily didn't like change. She was a creature of habit, but here she was seemingly at ease with his boss and buying shrimp with her.

A tug on his shirt alerted him to the fact Rose needed his attention. "Yes?"

Rose nodded in the direction Lily had gone with Virginia and shrugged. Gavin chuckled and rumpled her hair. "Got me, kiddo."

Gavin wandered closer to the stall. He watched in awe as the old Greek fishmonger doted on Lily. Virginia was so affable, laughing and totally at ease with his niece. There was a natural connection between Lily and Virginia. It made him a bit nervous. He didn't want or need a relationship. He wasn't looking for a mother for his nieces.

Aren't you? a little voice niggled in the back of his mind. It made his stomach knot.

This was not the life he'd planned, but it was what he'd been dealt.

A bag of shrimp was passed over, Lily handed the old man his money and they turned and headed back. Gavin looked away quickly, not wanting to be caught staring at them. Like he was studying them or something.

"Got the shrimp!" Lily announced triumphantly. Gavin set the cooler down and she placed the plastic bag in beside the clams and the container of scallops.

Virginia knelt down. "That's quite a catch."

"I don't think it'll be clam chowder any more," Gavin said under his breath.

Virginia chuckled again and stood up. The scent of vanilla lingered and as she brushed her hair over her shoulder, he was hit with it again.

He loved the scent of vanilla. It reminded him of something homey. Something he'd always longed for as a child.

"I think you're past the realms of a simple clam chowder and headed toward a seafood chowder or a bisque." Virginia grinned.

"What's the difference?" Lily asked.

"Bisque is puréed and chowder is chunky," Virginia replied.

"Definitely chunky," Lily said.

Gavin just shook his head and shut the cooler. "I guess we're making seafood chowder."

Virginia crossed her arms. "Have you ever made chowder before?"

"Does making it from a can count?"

Virginia cocked a finely arched brow. "No, it doesn't."

"Dang." He grinned and was shocked by the next words that were suddenly spewing from his mouth. "Would you like to come over for dinner?"

Virginia was stunned.

Did he just ask me to dinner?

How was she going to respond? Well, she knew what she had to say. She had to say no, she was his boss.

"Please, come, Dr. Potter! Hey, maybe you could walk down to pier thirty-nine with us and watch the sea lions?" Lily was tugging on her hand, her blue eyes wide with excitement.

How can I say no to that?

She couldn't, but she should.

"I'm not sure, Lily. How about I just walk down to the pier with you? Then I should go home and get these shrimp into the fridge."

"Want to place them in my cooler?" Gavin asked, popping the lid.

Now she had no excuse to bolt. "Sure. Thanks." Virginia set her bag in the cooler. They made their way through the crowd and onto the boardwalk, heading away from Fisherman's Wharf and toward the loud barking sounds of San Francisco's famous occupants.

Lily and Rose rushed forward and climbed up on the

guard rail to watch the sea lions lounge on the docks, sur-rounded by sailboats lining the pier.

"I've been here six months and I haven't come to see these guys yet. They're pretty loud."

"They are." Virginia winced as the sea lions broke into another course of barking. Lily laughed outright, but Rose didn't make a sound. She just beamed from ear to ear. Rose was such a little angel, or at least appeared to be. "How did your sister die?"

"Cancer," Gavin answered.

"I'm so sorry for your loss." And she was. If anyone understood, it was her, but she didn't share her own pain. She couldn't.

"Thank you." He gazed at her and butterflies erupted in her stomach. He looked so different today. The navy-blue fisherman's sweater accented the color of his hair and brought out the deep emerald of his eyes. His hair was a bit of a mess from Rose's handling, but the tousled look suited him.

It made her swoon just a bit.

Get a hold on yourself.

"Well, I'd better head back to my place." She bent down, opened his cooler and pulled out her bag of shrimp, drop-ping it in her canvas carryall. "Good luck with the chow-der."

Virginia turned to leave, but Gavin reached out and grabbed her arm to stop her from leaving. "I'd really like it if you came to dinner tonight."

"Gavin…" She trailed off, trying to articulate one of the many excuses running through her brain.

I'm your boss.

Do you think it's wise?

People are already talking.

Of course, all those excuses were lame. What did she have to lose? Yeah, she was technically Gavin's boss, but it wasn't like he was an intern or even a resident. He was an attending, the head of trauma surgery, so why couldn't they be friends?

Who cares what other people think?

"Okay. Sure, I'd love to come to your place for dinner." She pulled out an old business card and a pen. "Write down your address."

Gavin did just that and handed it back to her. "I know Lily and Rose will be excited to have you join us tonight. We haven't had a real house guest since the funeral."

"What time should I be there?"

"Five o'clock. The girls are on a schedule for sleeping and since it takes me ten hours to get them to fall asleep once they're in bed…"

Virginia laughed with him. "Five o'clock it is. I'm looking forward to it."

Gavin nodded. "So am I. I'll see you then." He picked up his cooler and walked to where the girls had moved down the boardwalk for a better view of the sea lions.

Virginia glanced down at the card. Gavin didn't live very far from her apartment. The shrimp linguine she had been planning to make for herself tonight could wait until tomorrow.

Tonight she'd actually have company to talk to instead of four walls and a cactus.

The first thing Virginia noticed about Gavin's house was it was pink. Very pink. She parked her car and set her emergency brake. She'd been passing time for the last couple of hours, waiting for five o'clock to come.

The thing that struck her was that she was very nervous, like she was a teenager again, going on her first date.

She'd even done her hair and her makeup. So different from her usual Saturday attire of yoga pants, no bra and a tank top.

With one last check in the rearview mirror she got out of the car and opened the back door. Before she'd left the market she'd managed to pick up four small sourdough loaves. She was going to hollow them out so they could serve the soup up in them.

She hoped Gavin was a good cook, but she didn't have much faith in that. The thought made her laugh as she headed towards the gated front door. She pushed the buzzer and waited. As she was waiting she noticed a flicker of the drapes in the bay window above her and she spied quiet little Rose peering at her through the lace.

Poor little soul.

The door was unlocked and opened and Gavin opened the gate. "Welcome."

Virginia stepped over the threshold as Gavin locked the gate and then the front door again. He was dressed the same as he had been earlier, but at least his hair wasn't as messy. Still, he looked handsome and it made her heart beat just a bit faster.

"Are you afraid I might escape?" she teased, hoping he didn't hear the nervous edge to her voice.

"No, just force of habit. I'm not used to living in a big city."

"You live in a pretty nice neighborhood but, yeah, I can understand your apprehension." She regretted suggesting he might be nervous when he furrowed his brow.

"You live in a very pink house, Gavin," she teased, changing the subject.

"Yes, well, that's my sister's taste. She always loved the color pink." He began to walk up the steps. "You can leave your shoes on—actually, I'd advise it as I'm not the niftiest cleaner. My maid has the weekend off."

Virginia chuckled and followed him up the stairs to the main floor. Rose dashed out from the living room at the front of the house and wrapped herself around Gavin's leg.

"You remember my boss, Rose?"

Rose nodded and then gave Virginia a smile. It wasn't a verbal greeting, but at least it was a start. It was then Virginia noticed that there was no lingering scent of dinner cooking.

"Did you have some problem starting the chowder?"

"Yeah, as in I have no idea what I'm doing."

"I guess it's a good thing I decided to come tonight. Show me to the kitchen."

Gavin grinned and led her to the back of the house where the kitchen was. Lily was in the kitchen with a battered old recipe book in front of her and looked a bit frantic.

"I can't find it," Lily said, a hint of panic in her voice.

"What?" Virginia asked, setting down the bag of bread.

"The recipe my Mom used. I can't find it." Lily was shaking and Virginia wanted to wrap her arms around the little girl and reassure her that everything would be okay. Only she couldn't. She had never been very good at hugging.

"It's okay. Look, why don't we try out my recipe for tonight? What do you think?"

Lily nodded her eyes wide. "Okay."

"Virginia, you don't have to do that. You're our guest."

"It's okay, Gavin. I don't mind." Virginia hung her cardigan on the back of the chair and pushed up the sleeves on her top. "Lily, you want to help me?"

"Of course!" Lily jumped down from the chair where she was sitting and whipped open the fridge, pulling out various items.

"I didn't know you could cook." Gavin watched as Lily plopped the bags of clams, shrimp and the container of scallops on the kitchen table.

"I have hidden depths." Virginia winked. "Do you have any cream, Lily?"

"Yep!" She ran back to the fridge and pulled out a carton.

"Where are your pots?"

Gavin pulled out a stainless-steel saucepan. "Is this good?"

"Not in the least. Do you have a stockpot?"

"A what?"

Virginia rolled her eyes and began to open random cupboards, finally locating a stockpot in a bottom cupboard. She held it up. "This is a stockpot!"

"Impressive." Gavin pulled out a chair and sat down. Rose was there in a flash and climbing in his lap. "Mind if I watch?"

"Why?" Virginia asked skeptically.

"It's how we surgeons learn, by observation, is it not?"

"Perhaps I'll employ the Socratic method on you while I'm dicing the potatoes." Virginia reached down and began to peel one of the potatoes Lily produced.

"I don't think that's fair. I know nothing about cooking."

"He really doesn't," Lily said. "All he can make is grilled cheese. Rosalie does most of the cooking."

Virginia cocked an eyebrow. "Who's Rosalie?"

"My housekeeper slash nanny slash cook." Gavin poked at the bread. "What's in the bag?"

"Ah, that's a surprise that will have to wait until the chowder is ready." Virginia finished peeling the potatoes and began to dice them. Then she went to work on the onions and carrots. When the vegetables were diced she placed them in the stockpot with some salted water and set them to boil.

"Why would I put potatoes on to boil, Gavin?" Virginia asked as Lily grabbed Rose's hand and led her out of the kitchen. They'd obviously lost interest in making dinner.

Gavin shook his head. "I told you, I'm an observer. I don't adhere to the Socratic method."

"And how do you teach your interns?"

"Shut up." There was a twinkle of humor in his eyes.

"Did you just tell me to shut up?" She picked up the knife and pointed it at him. "Very dangerous, my friend." Virginia went to work on the clams, scrubbing them and shucking them. "I'm afraid your strict bedtime rule will be kyboshed tonight. This is going to take some time to cook."

Gavin sighed. "Well, at least it's Saturday and the summer break, so no school. Would you like some wine?"

"I would love some. I actually brought a bottle."

"We'll save yours for dinner." She took a seat at the table as he set a wineglass down in front of her and poured some red into the glass.

He sat back down and poured some into his own. "I'm glad you came tonight. The girls were so excited."

"Thank you for inviting me." Virginia took a sip of wine. It was good, from a local winery in Napa. "So, where is the girls' father?"

Gavin sighed and fingered the stem of his wineglass. "Dead. He was a soldier, he died in Afghanistan just after Rose was born."

Well, that explained why he'd left Border Free Physicians and taken a job in the city as a trauma surgeon. It hadn't been his choice, he was just doing his duty to his sister and his nieces. It was quite admirable of him to give up his career for two little girls.

"How terrible."

Gavin nodded. "I was on a leave from my work in Africa at the time. I spent a couple months helping Casey out. She was a rock, though, and of course my brother-in-law's parents helped too."

"Do they see the girls often?"

"They do. Their grandfather is a marine and they're stationed in Japan, but they come to San Francisco as often as they can to see them. Last time they were here I just worked double shifts at the hospital and allowed them free rein of the house."

She'd sensed a bit of bitterness when he'd mentioned the grandparents and she thought it best to change the subject.

"What about your parents?"

Gavin's lips pressed together in a firm line and Virginia wondered if she crossed some sort of line. "My parents are dead."

"I'm sorry," she said, trying to offer some sort of apology for prying.

"Don't be."

Virginia was stunned by the way he shrugged it off and cleared her throat nervously.

"I'm sorry. I know I sound heartless but they weren't the most loving of parents."

"No, I'm sorry, Gavin. I shouldn't be prying. It's none of my business."

"You're right. It's not."

CHAPTER FIVE

His gaze was intense and riveting, making her feel very uncomfortable, but not in a bad way. In a way that was dangerous. If she hadn't been his boss and if he hadn't been working under her she could almost swear he was going to kiss her, or strangle her maybe.

If she hadn't been his boss she might even have kissed him back, but she was and she wasn't looking for a relationship.

Not now. Not ever.

Why not?

The question surprised her because she'd never entertained the notion before. The fact Gavin made her question the life path she'd chosen for herself was scary.

Virginia had had passing flings, not many, but the moment the man wanted to take it to the next level and become serious she'd break it off, put up her walls and plug the plug.

All her relationships had a DNR lifeline attached to them.

It was so easy, but looking at Gavin now, feeling the blood rush through her like liquid fire, her stomach bottoming out like she was on a roller coaster, she knew once she'd had a taste of him she'd want more.

Much more, and it frightened her to her core.

A hiss from the pot broke the connection and she got

up to stir the potatoes and turn down the heat, hoping he didn't notice the blush rising in her cheeks.

"I hope I didn't offend you, Virginia."

"Why would that offend me? I have a tendency to pry to get to the truth." She looked over her shoulder at him. "It's a bad habit of my job unfortunately."

"I bet it's a pain in the rump to have to deal with all that bureaucratic nonsense that goes on behind closed doors at the hospital."

Virginia snorted and checked on the potatoes bubbling in the pot, before draining half the water away. *You don't know the half of it,* she was tempted to say. Only she had to keep those thoughts private. She couldn't be blabbing about hospital politics to another physician. Not when she was the head honcho. Instead she said, "I'm sure you had to deal with red tape with Border Free Physicians."

"To an extent. Of course, I wasn't getting my fingers slapped for inserting a chest tube in the ER in an emergency situation. Life over limb was the motto."

"Touché." Virginia started stirring the soup. The old first-aider motto was how all doctors should practice in a hospital setting. Lawyers, board members and insurance companies thought differently. Though they wouldn't come right out and say it. She changed the subject. The last thing she wanted to do was talk about work. "Too bad you didn't have any crab. This would be great with some fresh bay crab."

Gavin set down his wineglass, headed to the fridge and pulled out a container. "Left over from dinner last night."

"Awesome." Virginia dumped the crab into the pot. "You're quite a seafood connoisseur."

"Yes, lately I am. It's what the girls like and I try to make them happy."

"You're a good uncle."

"I try to be."

Virginia got lost in his riveting gaze again. This had to stop or she was going to forget her rules completely.

"So, are you going to tell me what's in the bag you brought?" he asked, breaking the silence, much to her relief.

"Sourdough bread. It's the secret ingredient to any good seafood chowder, especially in San Francisco."

"I'm not originally from San Francisco. I'm from Billings, Montana."

"That's…"

"Not exciting in the least." Gavin grinned, that dimple she liked so much puckering his cheek. Heat flushed in hers. She cleared her throat and went back to stirring the soup. "Well, I'd better make sure Rose is still conscious and hasn't passed out from hunger."

When he left the kitchen, Virginia let out a breath she hadn't even realized she'd been holding. What was she doing? This wasn't her. If only her mother could see her now, cooking for a man and two young girls. Her mother would be pleased, because her mother felt she worked too much.

"You never come home."

Though there was nothing much to go home for and her parents' double wide trailer in rural South Dakota was quite cramped when everyone was home.

If her mother could see her, she'd be pleased. Especially if she knew how much she was actually enjoying the company.

Gavin watched Virginia from across the table. This was not the cool, aloof and businesslike professional he'd been dealing with yesterday. This woman was not the ice queen.

This Virginia was warm and kind. She had an easy rapport with them. At the hospital there was a tangible barrier between Virginia and the other surgeons. A mix of fear and respect. The woman currently sitting in his dining room was not Dr. Virginia Potter, Chief of Surgery.

Only she was.

He was amazed at how well she got on with his nieces. Lily had been so closed off and cold with strangers since Casey had got sick and died. Even with him it had taken some time for Lily to warm up and trust him.

And you couldn't blame Lily for that reaction. Death had hit her hard, twice, in her young life.

With Virginia, Lily was chatting happily and engaging her in conversation. A smile touched his lips as he watched the two of them talk. Virginia was asking Lily about dancing and school. Was this what it was like to have a real family dinner?

He wouldn't know.

His parents had never been around. Casey and he had lived off of cereal and peanut-butter and jelly sandwiches. Sometimes, when Mom hadn't gone shopping, there would only be enough bread or cereal for one. Those were the nights he'd gone to bed hungry, because he had been taking care of Casey.

Now he was taking care of Casey's girls, making sure they wanted for nothing and that they were happy. It was why he was in the city instead of some far-flung country.

"I think your sister is out for the night. What do you think, Gavin?"

"What?" Gavin asked, shaking those painful childhood memories from his head. "What's up?"

"Uncle Gavin, Rose is passed out in her chair." Lily gazed at her little sister lovingly.

Lily and Virginia were right. Rose was sound asleep, curled up on her chair with her arms tucked under her chubby cheek and her bottom up in the air.

"Lots of excitement today." Gavin pushed out of his chair and scooped his younger niece into his arms. She let out a small huff of air but didn't wake up. "I'll be back momentarily."

"At least she ate her soup, but she didn't get a chance to finish off her bowl," he heard Lily say with an excited giggle as he walked down the hall toward Lily's and Rose's shared bedroom. He smiled again as he remembered the look of pure excitement on the girls' faces when their chowder had been served up in their own individual bread bowls.

"Bowls we can eat? No dishes!" Lily had chirped excitedly.

Rose hadn't said a word, but the twinkle in her eyes and the smile on her face had spoken volumes. She had been excited too. He'd salvage what he could of the bread bowl so she could have some tomorrow. Rose would be so disappointed in the morning to find out she'd missed out on her dinner bowl.

Gavin tucked her into the bottom bunk. Lily would climb in beside her sister later. The bunk beds were fashioned for a single on top and a double underneath. Though Lily's bed was technically the top bunk, that's not how they slept.

If they weren't waking up in the night, as far as Gavin was concerned, that sleeping arrangement was fine with him.

He tiptoed out of the girls' bedroom, stepping on the darned rubber giraffe again, but Georgiana's pitiful squeak didn't even cause Rose to stir. Gavin just cursed silently under his breath and made his way back to the kitchen.

When he got there, he could see that Lily wasn't far behind her sister. Her eyelids were beginning to droop and she was leaning pretty heavily on her elbow.

"Hey, kiddo, why don't you get ready for bed?" Gavin suggested.

"Aw, do I have to?"

"I think you should. You were an awesome help to me today, Lily. Thank you," Virginia said, standing and starting to clear the table.

"Okay." Lily got up and dragged herself down the hall to the bathroom.

"Brush your teeth!" Gavin called, and Lily's response was a groan of derision.

Gavin picked up the remainder of Lily's and Rose's dinners and took them into the kitchen. Virginia was filling the sink with water.

"You don't have to do that," he said. "You were our dinner guest and I made you cook."

"I don't mind."

"No, seriously. Come and have another glass of wine while I put the leftovers away."

"One more glass. I do have to drive home."

Gavin chuckled and poured her another glass. "The girls really enjoyed the dinner tonight."

Virginia smiled and warmth spread through his chest. She had a beautiful smile, with her full red lips. If it was any other woman, he'd be putting the moves on her.

She's my boss.

"I enjoyed tonight too." She took a sip. "I think there's one thing you need to learn about managing a house full of girls."

"Are you critiquing my parenting skills?" he teased.

"Just a bit."

"What can I approve on, then?"

"Don't take this the wrong way, but you seriously have no idea when it comes to a little girl's hair."

Gavin laughed and she joined in. It was the first time he'd really heard her laugh, a deep, throaty, jovial laugh, which not only surprised him but delighted him too.

"And you do?"

"Yes," she stated confidently. "First, because I was

a little girl at one point in my life and also I have two younger sisters."

It was the first time she'd opened up to him. It was the first nugget of information he'd got from her.

"Sisters, eh?"

"Yes." She smiled. "And even though you may have grown up with a sister, you really don't know anything about hair."

"Little girls' hair baffles me. Actually, it drives me squirrely," he said, and he meant it. No matter how many scrunchies or ties or pins he used, he couldn't put their hair up in a bun or braid to save his life, but it was a necessity for dance class. "Anything else?"

"Also the nails. That red color is not flattering on Lily and it's pretty messy."

"Yes, I admit I need some boning up on those finer aspects, but she wanted to paint her nails and I got home from the hospital tired and some nights I don't have any fight in me. I just give in."

Virginia nodded. "I understand about giving in."

Tension settled between them. He wanted to ask her what was stressing her out, but he knew it had something to do with him and what the board deemed his crazy, unorthodox methods. The last thing Gavin wanted to do was talk about work with *this* Virginia.

The laid-back, affable, warm and caring Virginia who had just spent part of the day and the evening with him and the girls.

The Virginia who made him forget about his worries. How he feared he was a terrible father figure to his nieces. That he'd lose them to their paternal grandparents. The girls were all he had left. Only he felt like he was failing them.

Not once since his sister had died had he and the girls enjoyed an evening like this together. It had been nice and he found himself wanting it all the time, even though a long time ago he'd sworn he'd never have a family or a wife, because of the lifestyle he wanted. Living rough and always traveling.

"I should go," Virginia said, breaking the silence that had settled between them. She got up and picked up her purse from the kitchen counter. "Are you sure you don't need a hand with those dishes?"

"Positive. I'll walk you out."

Gavin escorted her to the front of the house and down the stairs. He unlocked the outside gate and stood with her for a few moments. The night was clear and the moon full. The water on the bay was still, like a mirror.

You could see the lights from across the bay, twinkling in the darkness; the two bridges dominating the San Francisco skyline.

"What a beautiful night." Virginia let out a little sigh, which sounded like one of regret. "I should go. Thank you for a lovely evening."

"Thank you for coming." He wanted to say that he'd really enjoyed getting to know her somewhat better, but instead said, "The girls really enjoyed it."

"I enjoyed meeting them." Virginia hesitated and then ducked her head. "Well, I'd better be going. I'll see you on Wednesday afternoon, Dr. Brice."

And just like that it was no longer Gavin and Virginia. It was Dr. Brice and Dr. Potter and he didn't like that connection at all.

She turned and walked away from him, heading towards her car. "Wait!" he called out, surprising even himself.

Virginia paused and turned. "Yes, Dr. Brice?"

"What are you doing tomorrow?"

CHAPTER SIX

WHAT AM I doing? What am I doing?

Virginia was standing in the middle of Union Square in the evening, waiting for Gavin and the girls. She'd been so flabbergasted that he'd invited her out, but it wasn't like a date. It was just another outing with Gavin and his nieces. Just an innocent outing between friends.

At least, that's what she kept telling herself.

The plan was to walk up from Union Square to China town and have some dim sum. She had nothing better to do and it was a nice August evening.

Virginia nervously glanced at her watch. They were late, only five minutes but she'd been waiting for twenty, because when she was nervous she was always early, or, as she liked to call it, overly punctual.

Relax. They'll be here.

What if they didn't show? She'd appear like a real dork. Virginia shook that thought away. No one knew where she was. No one at the hospital knew she was meeting Gavin and his nieces here.

She needed to get a grip.

"Sorry I'm late."

She turned and saw Gavin, without the girls, behind her. He was dressed in jeans, a sport jacket and a nice button-down shirt. His hair wasn't a complete mess but still stuck up here and there from a troublesome cowlick.

He had a nice five-o'clock shadow, but she liked scruffi-
ness on a man. She could smell the spicy scent of his soap,
which made her feel a bit weak in the knees. Gavin presented a neat and tidy appearance but there was a hidden
depth of ruggedness to him that appealed to her.

She'd always had a penchant for bad boys, wild boys,
but she tended to date respectable, clean-cut men.

For some reason, when she saw Gavin, she pictured him
on a big motorcycle clothed in leather and denim as he rode
down the California coast. That brief little thought caused
a zing of anticipation to race through her, but it was just a
fantasy. She knew Gavin drove his late sister's minivan.

"Where are the girls?" she asked, her voice cracking.
She winced, worried that she was probably sounding as
dumb as she felt at the moment.

"Ah." He rubbed the back of his neck. "Their grandparents flew in unexpectedly from Japan. They have a lay-
over for a couple of days, so the girls are spending time
with them."

Virginia just nodded, suddenly feeling really nervous,
like a shy teenage girl standing at the edge of a dance floor,
waiting for someone, anyone to ask her to dance.

Why isn't he saying something?

"Maybe we should schedule this for another night, when
the girls are able to join us?"

"Why?" he asked.

Virginia's cheeks flushed. "Do you think it's appropriate for the chief of surgery to go out with an attending?"

"We're going to have dinner, as friends. Just think of
it that way, if you're nervous. I think a boss can have a
friendly dinner with an employee." He grinned. "We'll
save Chinatown and the dim sum for the girls. How about
we catch the streetcar and head down to a diner on the
Embarcadero?"

Virginia hesitated. "I don't know."

"Come on, Virginia, help me out. I want to give the girls space with their grandparents. Don't make me be a fifth wheel to their time together and I rarely have a moment free without them."

Go on. Live a little.

"What the heck. You're right. Lead the way."

Gavin took her hand, her heart beating just a bit faster at the intimacy. His hand was warm and strong as it squeezed hers gently. "Come on, then." He pulled her through the square as they jogged down to catch the F Market streetcar and she was glad she'd decided to wear flats instead of wedges or boots. Flats helped her keep up with Gavin's long strides.

When they crammed onto the streetcar, Virginia finally caught her breath. "Where are we going?"

"Fog City Diner."

"I hope you made reservations. That place is a San Francisco institution."

Then he grinned deviously, like a Cheshire cat. "We'll just have to play it by ear, won't we?"

She was going to say more, but more people got onto the streetcar and they were separated in the crowd.

When their stop came she got off and met him at the back exit. "It was a bit of crush in there, wasn't it? Seeing how you're not from around here, I thought you might miss your stop."

"I'm a pro at public transportation and large crowds. I rode a train across India and stood for six hours. Not fun."

"No, I bet."

They walked toward the diner and from the look of the crush of people going in and out of the doors Virginia knew it would be busy, and there weren't many other options around. The other couple of restaurants nearby would be overflowing with rejects from Fog City.

"Why don't we catch the next streetcar and head down to the wharf?" Virginia suggested.

"You have so little faith." He took her hand again, making her pulse race and her palms sweat.

Great. Sweaty palms are so alluring.

"It looks busy," she said nervously.

"Appearances can be deceiving." He pulled her inside and walked up to the seating hostess. "Reservations for two, Gavin Brice."

The hostess checked her list, smiled and grabbed two menus. "Ah, right this way."

Gavin grinned at Virginia with smug satisfaction. "After you."

Virginia shot him a dirty look as she followed the hostess to their booth overlooking the Embarcadero. He slid in across from her, the polished black tabletop reflecting his smug pleasure.

"You had reservations."

"I did. As you said, Fog City is a San Francisco institution."

"It's almost as if you planned this."

"Well, when the girls' grandparents flew in early this morning I made the reservation. I would've told you but I don't have your home number."

"You have my pager," Virginia teased. "Everyone in the hospital has my pager."

"You carry your pager around when you're off duty?"

She pulled it out of her purse and flashed it at him, like the big nerd she was. "I'm Chief of Surgery. What if there was some kind of freak accident and the press swarmed the hospital?"

"High-profile cases don't go to Bayview Grace."

Virginia bit back the feeling of annoyance that was threatening to rise. It was always a bit of a sore spot for her. She'd raised Bayview Grace to a level-one trauma center, but other hospitals still got all the press.

"That's part of my five-year plan for the regeneration of Bayview Grace Hospital. I plan to make it the top hospital in San Francisco. It's well under way."

Gavin leaned back against the cushioned seat. "Does it matter? We're a level-one trauma center and we practice good medicine. Who cares if we're not the top?"

"I care," Virginia snapped. When she'd become Chief of Surgery at Bayview Grace the hospital had been in a sorry state and it had ranked low on the list of hospitals nationwide and statewide. It had been her mission to change that, to bring back its glory days.

It was what she'd lived and breathed for the first two years in her position. She would fight to the bitter end to keep Bayview open.

Two lonely, busy years and now Gavin was suggesting it didn't matter?

That her life didn't matter?

Gavin regretted the words when he saw the change of expression on Virginia's face. When they'd first got to the diner she'd been smiling so brightly and had been so at ease, just like she'd been the night before.

As soon as he'd brought up the hospital, that amiable woman had been replaced by the workaholic, tight-lipped and controlling chief of surgery that most staff at Bayview Grace avoided.

Virginia was not the most popular surgeon in the hospital, but it was hard to be popular when you were responsible for budget cuts, staffing and all the other mundane administrative stuff that Gavin wouldn't wish upon his own worst enemy.

Tonight wasn't supposed to be about work.

Then what's it supposed to be about? You're out with your boss.

It was supposed to be about fun. A night away from the girls and the responsibility of fatherhood.

"Are you saying the hospital's standing isn't important?" she asked, her voice rising an octave.

"That's exactly what I'm saying." No, he didn't care about the hospital's standing. He'd spent years in dirty holes of medical facilities, trying to bring medicine to those people who had no access. He'd worked in sweltering temperatures, monsoons, festering cesspools to treat people.

That's all that mattered when it came to medicine, as far as he was concerned. A hospital rating meant nothing, as long as people were being cured.

"I think I should go." She slid to the edge of the seat, but he reached out and grabbed her.

"Don't go. Look, I know it's important to you, but it's not important to me. I come from a different world."

She eyed him with misgiving but slid back to where she had been sitting.

"I don't want to talk hospital politics."

"Isn't that what coworkers do?" she asked.

"How about, just for tonight, we don't. Let's just forget about it all and enjoy ourselves."

Her expression softened. "You're right. I'm sorry too, for what it's worth."

"Why are you apologizing? You have nothing to apologize for."

"I do. You see, I don't go out. I live and breathe that hospital. I've forgotten what it's like to talk to another adult human being."

Gavin chuckled. "I understand. How about we take it slowly? Hi, my name is Gavin Brice and I'm a fishmonger."

Virginia laughed. "You're a what?"

"You know, one of those guys down at the wharves that monger fish."

"Do you know what monger means?" she asked, cocking a thinly arched brow.

"Doesn't it mean clubbing the fish to death or something?" He made a gesture of beating a fish against the table. "Like bashing in their brains?"

She laughed again. "That's not what a fishmonger does and that's not how you use that word properly in a sentence. It means to peddle, to sell or stir up something that's highly discreditable."

"Well, thank you, Merriam-Webster." He winked.

"What would you like to order?" the waitress asked, interrupting their conversation. Gavin quickly glanced at the menu and ordered the catch of the day and Virginia did the same.

When the waitress was out of earshot he continued.

"So, as I said. I'm a fishmonger. I like screwball comedies and aspire to own a macadamia farm in Hawaii one day and populate it with llamas."

"That's the most absurd thing I've ever heard anyone say."

Gavin grinned. "Come on, play along. Tell me who you are."

"Dr. Virginia Potter."

"No."

"No?" she asked in shock.

"No, you're…" He paused, trying to think of some crazy name.

"Fifi La BonBon?" she offered.

"I like it. It's very French and naughty."

A pink blush colored her cheeks and she cleared her throat. He didn't mean to get so personal with her, but he couldn't help himself. Virginia intrigued him and he wanted to get below the surface of her prim and proper exterior.

Beneath that cool professionalism he knew someone warm existed, a passionate woman, he hoped. By the way her cheeks flushed he was positive one did and his blood fired as he thought about exploring that woman.

Gavin fought the urge to run his fingers through her silky brown hair, to crush those rose-colored lips under his, bruising them in passion as he peeled those crisp, pastel-colored clothes from her body. He cleared his throat and fidgeted in his seat.

She's your boss.

It'd been some time for him; yes, that was a fitting explanation for his sudden infatuation with Virginia. A woman who had been a thorn in his side since he'd arrived at Bayview Grace. Always calling him into her office to tell him what he was doing wrong.

It's not her choice. It's the board.

But he knew the reason. She didn't chase him like other women did.

"Okay," Virginia said, breaking the silence between them. "I'm Fifi La BonBon and I'm a tank cleaner at the Monterey Bay Aquarium. I spend my day avoiding sharks and tickling starfish."

Now it was his turned to look stunned. "Really? A fish-monger and a tank cleaner, what an interesting pair we make."

The waitress brought them their drinks and caught the tail end of his sentence, shooting them both a quizzical look before disappearing again.

"The waitress is going to think we're nuts." Virginia swirled the wine in her glass. "I've never lived on the edge like this."

"What, wine in a diner?" Gavin teased, taking a sip of his Scotch. "You rebel, you."

Virginia leaned forward across the table and he caught a whiff of her perfume, vanilla. So different from when they were at the hospital, where scents were banned due to allergy reasons. Everything was so antiseptic and sterile.

So not like his work with Border Free Physicians, where every scent known to man seemed to trudge in and out of his clinics. Some intriguing, some not so much.

"No, this fantasy talk. I guess I'm not used to lying."

"Oh, come on, Virginia. You must have to bend the truth to some of your employees sometimes. Don't we bend the truth to our patients one time or another to make the blow sting just a little bit less?"

Her smile disappeared, but only for a brief moment, and he was worried he'd crossed some invisible line again. "Whatever do you mean? I clean tanks."

Gavin laughed out loud, surprised by the way she broke the tension and eased into the icebreaker conversation he'd started. It surprised him and pleased him. The waitress brought their meals and they chatted about their fake personalities, coming up with the weirdest stuff they could imagine, until it was time to leave the diner.

There was a chilly breeze coming off the bay when they headed outside and walked along the Embarcadero towards the next pier, where they could pick up the streetcar and head back to Union Square. It was where he'd parked his motorcycle.

"Did you drive down to Union Square?" he asked, because he didn't know exactly where she lived.

"No. I walked. I only live in Nob Hill, not far from Union Square."

Damn. He was disappointed. He'd wanted to offer her a ride on his bike, take her to her door, like a proper gentleman would.

This is not a date, he reminded himself for the umpteenth time, but who was he kidding? It was. He knew it and he was pretty sure she knew it too. Only it didn't have to be anything more than just this.

They wandered along the Embarcadero in silence. The only sounds were traffic, the waves and the wind, and they finally stopped when they could see the Coit Tower clearly.

"We've wandered quite a piece away from Market Street," she said, and she turned to look out over the water. The sun was setting, just behind the Golden Gate Bridge, in a fiery ball of liquid gold.

"It's been a while since I was able to enjoy a sunset." She let out a sigh. "I've been so busy, so damn busy."

Gavin wondered if he was supposed to hear that last admission, but if he wasn't supposed to be privy to that thought, he was glad he was.

He liked this Virginia. Very much.

"It's a nice sunset," he said. "But it's not my favorite."

"Where was your favorite sunset, then?"

Gavin leaned against the railing of the boardwalk. "Egypt. The sun setting behind the pyramids as the full moon rose above them. It was...magical."

Virginia sighed. "You've been so many places. I envy you."

"You haven't traveled much, I take it?"

She shook her head. "I went to Harvard and then came here. Like I said, I was too busy trying to fix Bayview Grace."

"What about summers off from school?" he asked.

"I worked. Scholarships and what I could save myself paid my way through. My parents couldn't afford to send me." A blush crept up her neck, as if she was embarrassed by that admission.

"That's a shame."

"You're going to bring up this again?" she asked, annoyance in her tone.

"No, it's just that you haven't traveled or cut loose. I

can't imagine not. It's hard for me to stay put and take care of my sister's kids. My wandering foot is itchy."

"You're doing the right thing, giving them the stability they deserve."

Gavin nodded, even if it was a bitter pill to swallow. He knew all about wanting that stability and craving it in his childhood, but it was hard to do when you spent most of your adult life living out of a rucksack. The whole world was your home.

"I can't tear them away from their home. I won't."

Virginia nodded. "I do envy your travels, though."

"You should try it, at least once or twice."

She smiled and ducked her head, tucking a strand of hair behind her ear. "Perhaps one day."

There was a sparkle in her eyes. Maybe it was the way the fading light from the sun reflected on the water but Virginia seemed to glow and Gavin couldn't help himself. He wrapped his arms around her, tipped her chin and kissed her.

He cupped her face in his hands; her skin felt like silk. Virginia softened a bit. The taste of the wine she'd drunk still tainted her lips. It was sweet, like her. He wanted to press her body against his, feel her naked under him. When he tried to deepen the kiss, Virginia pushed him away.

Her cheeks were flushed and she wouldn't look him in the eye. "I think...I think I'd better go."

"Virginia, I'm sorry."

"No, it's okay. There's no need to apologize and there's no need to mention it again." She hailed a cab and it pulled over. She turned, but still wouldn't look him in the eye, obviously mortified by what had happened between them. "I'll see you Wednesday, Dr. Brice. Thank you for the lovely evening."

And with that she climbed into the cab and was gone.

CHAPTER SEVEN

VIRGINIA LOOKED DOWN and realized she'd been holding the same file for a while. Janice would be furious, because all the "sign here" stickies were still void of her signature. Since Sunday when Gavin had kissed her she'd been walking around in a bit of a haze.

More like a stupor. His kiss had been like nothing she'd ever experienced. It had made her melt and if it had been anyone but Gavin she would've taken it a little bit further.

Since their stolen kiss and her panicked reaction to it, she'd tried to get her mind off it. Only she couldn't. All she thought about was the feel of his lips against hers, his stubble tickling her chin, his tongue in her mouth, his fingers in her hair.

Her knees knocked and she felt herself swooning like some lovelorn heroine in a romance novel.

She'd been berating herself for walking away, and she couldn't face being alone in her apartment, reliving that kiss over and over again. So she went back to work on Monday instead of taking the rest of her time off. Janice didn't even question her early return to work. Virginia often came in on her days off.

Truthfully, Virginia didn't want to admit to her or anyone else that she just couldn't stand the oppressive loneliness of her apartment and Gavin invading her dreams, her thoughts, her every waking moment.

One kiss had made her realize how lonely she was.

Dinner had been so wonderful, as had the company. The walk along the waterfront had been the same. She'd gone on other casual dates with men, but nothing compared to the time with Gavin. Usually she couldn't stop thinking about work.

For one stolen moment she'd forgotten she was Chief of Surgery. She'd forgotten about all her duties, all the problems, everything that made up the core of her existence.

Gavin made her forget everything, made her think of traveling, something she'd always dreamed of, though she'd never entertained the idea of doing it for real. Travel was expensive and a luxury. That was just it, Gavin made her feel frivolous, like doing something more than being a surgeon and working her fingers to the bone.

She couldn't remember the last time she'd enjoyed herself so much,

I shouldn't have left him. I should've taken a chance.

Only she knew why she had walked away. It'd been a one-off. When she'd got home and thought about it, she'd realized she shouldn't have done it.

She shouldn't have let him kiss her.

She was Gavin's boss. Nothing could happen between them. They couldn't date.

It was better to put an end to it now, before the girls became attached to her or something, and there was no way she could hurt those girls.

They'd already been put through the wringer enough.

Only a part deep down inside her wanted to risk it all to get to know them better. Gavin was handsome, but it wasn't his looks that attracted her to him and it definitely wasn't that pompous air he had when he marched through the halls of Bayview Grace. Far from it. That Gavin was a jackass.

It was the Gavin she'd briefly got a glimpse of on

Saturday at his house. The Gavin who'd kissed her down by the water.

The man who had been thrust into fatherhood appealed to her greatly and that thought scared her. Kids weren't in the plan, she reminded herself for the umpteenth time.

Why can't they be?

She was a doctor, she wasn't going to end up poor, like her parents. Even though she could give a child what they needed, she didn't want to risk it.

What if something changed and she couldn't support a child any more? What if something happened to that child? She'd witnessed the pain and suffering her mother had gone through when Shyanne had died. It had almost killed their mother and she never wanted to experience that kind of loss.

It was far too risky.

Her pager went off in her pocket and she pulled it out. She was wanted in the trauma department. For one moment her courage faltered, because it was Wednesday and Gavin would be back on duty and, like the shy wallflower she'd been in high school, she cringed inwardly over the thought of facing him.

Get a grip.

Virginia pocketed her pager. She was Chief of Surgery. This was her hospital and she was first and foremost a surgeon.

Just because she was chief and did a lot of paperwork, it didn't mean she didn't belong in the trauma bay, getting her hands dirty.

And she had nothing to be ashamed about.

Nothing to be embarrassed about, because nothing had happened between her and Dr. Brice and that's the way it had to remain.

She had to forget about the kiss. It'd been a mistake and thankfully no one knew about it.

When she entered the trauma bay her gaze naturally gravitated towards Gavin, but she took a step back when she realized he wasn't in his scrubs but in his street clothes. Of course, it was only ten in the morning. He wasn't due to start until two. He also wasn't leading the paramedics, he was traveling with them and on the gurney was a little figure.

Virginia's heart skipped a beat and she ran towards them.

"What happened?" she asked as she followed the gurney into the trauma pod.

"Female age eight, fell off the monkey bars at the playground. No obvious head trauma, but there appears to be a fracture of her right ulna," the paramedic stated.

Lily was on the gurney, her face grey with pain. Virginia looked at Gavin and his pained expression said it all. Suddenly she saw her twin sister Shyanne on the gurney in agony, bleeding out. Lily had a fracture. She was not hemorrhaging because of a ruptured fallopian tube.

Get a grip, Virginia.

"Glad you could come, Dr. Potter," Gavin said.

"Of course. I'm the trauma surgeon on duty."

Gavin nodded, but didn't look at her.

Lily's gaze met hers. "Dr. Potter?"

"Hi, Lily."

"Wow, the chief of surgery." Then she sat up and retched into a basin.

I feel the same way some days.

"Let me just do an examination of your arm." She turned to the nurse and fired off instructions for an X-ray and pain medication.

Lily winced as Virginia gently palpated the site.

"It hurts." A sob caught in Lily's throat, but she kept up her stiff upper lip.

"Yeah, I'm sure it does." She leaned down and whispered, "You can cry if you want. Breaking a bone is a huge deal."

Lily shook her head and glanced at her uncle. "I told him I'd be brave."

Virginia glanced over her shoulder at Gavin and then back at Lily. "We're going to do an X-ray and check out what kind of fracture it is, and Nurse Jo here is going to give you some pain medicine in a moment."

Lily nodded and Virginia walked over to Gavin. "Is she allergic to anything?"

"No. Nothing."

"Good. Where's Rose?"

"With her grandparents. They were supposed to fly out, but then Rosalie called as I was getting ready for work." Gavin scrubbed a hand over his face. "I appreciate you coming down, but couldn't one of your ortho attendings handle this?"

"No, Lily knows me. I'll make this as painless as I can for her."

Gavin's eyes narrowed. "You don't have to."

"I want to. She's frightened, though she doesn't want you to know it."

Gavin sighed and mumbled thanks before pushing past and sitting next to Lily. A pang of longing hit her, and hard, watching him sitting next to Lily, stroking her hair as Nurse Jo administered pain medication.

Her parents and other siblings were so far away. If she got hurt or sick no one would be here for her. Her parents couldn't afford to come see her.

There was no one.

No boyfriend, no kids and no family.

I want that.

The thought frightened her and she looked away, stepping out of the trauma room. She was just being emotional. It was not part of the plan.

She wanted to bring Bayview Grace to its former glory. That's what she wanted. That was the plan she'd crafted for herself the moment she'd taken her Hippocratic oath.

"Can you page me when Lily Johnson's X-rays come in?" she asked the nurse at the desk.

"Do you want someone from Ortho to handle it, Chief?"

Instead of snapping, Virginia just shook her head and smiled. "No, I'll see to the patient personally. Thanks, Deborah, and this is pro bono. Don't charge them for my services."

The nurse looked stunned, but only for a moment. "Of course, Dr. Potter."

It wasn't often Virginia dealt with minor fractures, let alone wrote off her time, but Lily was a staff member's ward and Gavin had enough to worry about without having to deal with billing. He'd have to fill out the forms, but at least he wouldn't have to deal with his insurance.

"Thank you." Virginia headed back towards her office. She had to put a safe distance between herself and Dr. Brice.

Gavin was fighting hard not to take over the situation. He was after all a trauma surgeon, his life in this hospital was running from room to room and assessing the most serious cases. He wanted to help Lily and it was killing him but he couldn't. He was family and there was a strict rule about physicians and family members.

He'd been shocked to see Virginia come into the room.

It had made his pulse race when she'd walked into the trauma pod, but the woman he'd kissed on the waterfront was gone, replaced by the austere chief of surgery.

And for a moment, when she'd been talking to Lily, she hadn't been that cold professional he'd first met when he'd come to Bayview Grace. For one brief moment he'd seen the woman from this last weekend.

The one he'd kissed.

Stop thinking about her.

He had to get her out of his mind. Virginia had made it quite clear what she thought about his kiss when she'd climbed into that cab and left him standing alone on the Embarcadero.

Of course, she'd made it clear to him that she was uncomfortable with the thought of it being a date and he'd promised her it was nothing more than coworkers going out for a quick bite.

And, honestly, that's what he'd thought when he'd shown up at Union Square.

They had just been going out as friends, but as the evening had worn on, he'd been unable to help himself. He was setting himself up to fall for a girl like Virginia.

She was his boss, she was taboo and he was like a moth to her flame. He always liked a challenge, the woman who was hard to get.

He was so rusty, though, when it came to dating women like Virginia. When he'd been traipsing around the world with Border Free Physicians there had been little time for romantic notions. There'd been the odd fling, but that had been all.

Just enough to relieve the itch, and even those had been few and far between.

This is not part of the plan, he reminded himself again for the ten thousandth time. He couldn't settle down and bring a strange woman home to the girls. The girls were his life now.

The girls like Virginia.

Gavin watched her walk out of the emergency department. Her chestnut hair was in a tight twist again, instead of falling loose over her shoulders. Her white lab coat was crisp, without a crease, the colors she wore were dark, professional, and her black pumps were flawless, without a single scuff.

Even the scent of vanilla was gone from her. Only the antiseptic scent of the hospital burned his nose.

This weekend the Virginia who made his heart race had been soft, both in the colors she'd worn and the scent of her hair.

"I feel funny," Lily said, her eyes wide and a bit dazed.

Nurse Jo chuckled and looked at Gavin. "It's the pain medication."

Gavin smiled and smoothed back the hair from Lily's forehead.

"I can feel my eyeballs, Uncle Gavin. They're round and b-i-g." Lily dragged out the word "big."

Gavin laughed. "It's right about now I should start filming, something to blackmail her with later when she hits those teen years."

"That's about right, Dr. Brice." Jo smiled. The woman had never smiled at him once since he'd started working here. Then again, he'd never really conversed with her before.

"We're ready for her in X-Ray," the orderly said, stepping into the room. "Hey, Dr. Brice."

Gavin nodded to Chet the orderly. "Should I go with her?"

Jo shook her head. "Nope, you know the rules. No family in Radiology. You get to take a seat in the waiting room."

"I'm a doctor here. In fact, I'm head of this department."

Jo crossed her arms. "Are you really going to try and challenge your head nurse, Dr. Brice?"

Gavin held up his hands. "Nope, you're right. I'll just head to the cafeteria. Page me when she gets out of Radiology."

"Will do, Dr. Brice."

Gavin leaned over and pressed a kiss against Lily's forehead. "I'm going to call your grandparents and check on Rose. She was pretty upset when you went to the hospital."

Lily nodded, still wide-eyed.

Gavin had left the room so they could prep Lily for Radiology. He was veering off towards the cafeteria when the charge nurse called after him.

"Paperwork, Dr. Brice. Lots of nice forms for you to fill out."

Gavin groaned. "I'll give you fifty dollars to fill them out for me."

The charge nurse gave him a look that would have made hell freeze over and handed him a clipboard.

"Well, it was worth a shot."

"It was, but no dice, Dr. Brice, and make sure it's legible. I'm *very* familiar with your handwriting."

Gavin rolled his eyes and headed towards the cafeteria, clipboard in hand. He too busy flipping pages and wasn't watching where he was going until he ran smack into a warm, soft body and was spattered with lukewarm coffee.

"Dammit!"

When he glanced up he was standing in front of Virginia, whose crisp white lab coat and blouse were now stained and drenched with coffee.

"Why don't you…?" She trailed off when she realized who it was and her cheeks flushed crimson. "Of course, it had to be you."

CHAPTER EIGHT

Virginia stepped into a boardroom as a janitor came to clean up the mess of the two coffees that had just been dumped down her front. Gavin followed her with a roll of paper towels. She could feel the eyes of most of the staff and the patients in the trauma bay boring into the back of her skull. She was absolutely humiliated.

This was the last thing she needed. She peeled off her lab coat and tossed it on the table.

Gavin set down the clipboard beside it and then ripped off a sheet of paper towel, about to mop up the front of her chest.

"I'll take care of that, thanks." She tried not to snap at him, but she was more than annoyed. She had a board meeting later.

"I thought you were heading back to your office."

"I was, until I thought I'd bring you a coffee. You looked like you need a pick-me-up." She dabbed at her shirt, but there was no saving it at the moment. She'd have to change into her scrubs and attend the board meeting like that.

She was sure she'd get comments from some of the snootier members of the board about it.

Forget about them.

"It was nice of you to go to the trouble," Gavin said.

"It was no trouble. I was at the coffee cart and thought of you."

Gavin picked up the clipboard and grinned. "So I was an afterthought?"

Virginia sighed impatiently and tossed the soiled paper towel in the garbage. "I told you, you looked a bit pale."

"Well, thanks for the thought."

"You're welcome."

"By the way, I'm not going to be in to work later today." The twinkle in his eyes returned, that mischievous look that she liked so much.

"I assumed that. Your niece happens to be my patient." She eyed the clipboard. "Patient forms?"

Gavin *tsked*. "Yeah, and I've been given dire warnings from the charge nurse about curbing my terrible handwriting."

"Ah, Sara can be a bit of a bull about that. Why don't you fill out the forms here?"

"Only if you keep me company."

"I have a hospital to run," Virginia said. "I have a VIP patient who needs my help."

"She's in Radiology." Gavin pulled out a seat and sat down at the table, beginning to fill in the forms.

"I thought you'd be down in Radiology with her."

"They wouldn't let me. Jo, I think that's her name, can be a bit of a bull when it comes to that."

"Good to know you're learning names."

"Well, someone gave me a hint about name tags."

Virginia chuckled. "Do you want me to talk to them, get them to bend the rules?"

Gavin shook his head. "Nah, I don't want to ruffle any feathers." He cursed under his breath and slammed down his pen.

"What's wrong?" she asked as she pulled another sheet off the roll of paper towels.

"I know none of this information." He dragged his fingers through his hair, making it stand on end. "Dammit."

Gavin stood and stalked toward the far end of the room, muttering and cursing under his breath. She felt sorry for him. Of course he wouldn't have all this information memorized. A mother would, but an uncle who had been thrust into a fatherhood role wouldn't.

"Dammit, what good am I if I can't even remember something simple like her date of birth? Terrible. I shouldn't be doing this."

Virginia closed the boardroom door. "Gavin, what're you talking about?"

"I don't know Lily's birthday!" he snapped, and his hands fisted at his sides. "I know nothing. Everything is at home, in a file, and I've been so damn crazy at work and just trying to get the girls on schedule."

"It's not your fault."

"It is my fault, Virginia, I should know this by now." He cursed again and kicked the wastepaper basket.

Virginia wanted to reach out and hug him, to reassure him that it was okay he didn't know, only she didn't know how. Instead, she picked up the clipboard and began to fill in what she could.

"What're you doing?" he asked.

"Filling out what we can. The rest can come later, we know where you live." Virginia winked at him.

"You don't have to do this."

"It's okay, Gavin. I don't mind."

"Well, maybe I mind."

Virginia set the pen down. She was overstepping her bounds. What right did she have to help him? None. She'd made that clear on Sunday when she'd pushed him away and climbed into that cab.

"I'm sorry," Gavin said, as he scrubbed a hand over his face. "I didn't mean to snap. You were just trying to help."

"It's okay, Gavin." She stood and picked up her soiled

lab coat. "Fill in what you can, bring the forms to me and you can phone me with the rest of Lily's information later."

"Don't go. Please stay."

"I have to." Her pager went off and she pulled it out of her coat pocket. "Besides, they're back from Radiology and I have a fracture to assess. Bring the paperwork. Come on."

Gavin nodded and followed her out of the boardroom.

She stopped and realized she needed to change. There was no way she was going to apply a cast to Lily's arm with a coffee-soaked shirt.

"Lily's in room 2121A. I'm going to change and I'll meet you there."

"Sure. See you there." Gavin turned and walked in the other direction towards the ortho wing. Virginia took a deep breath, trying to calm the emotions threatening to overtake her.

And for the first time since meeting Gavin and learning about his situation, she realized that the life he'd fashioned for himself, his plan, had been torn asunder.

Her plan was still sound. She was where she wanted to be.

Am I?

She shook those thoughts away as she changed in her office bathroom. She put on her green scrubs, replaced everything in the new lab coat and tossed her soiled lab coat in the hospital laundry bag. As for her clothes, she left them in the sink. She'd take them to her dry cleaner's after work.

Janice cocked an eyebrow as she came out of her office in her scrubs.

"What happened to you?" Janice asked.

"Don't ask."

"Did it involve Dr. Brice?"

What? Virginia panicked inwardly. "No, why would it?" she asked cautiously.

"The man is a brilliant surgeon, but he's a bit of a klutz. He walks around these halls with his head in the clouds. If you see him barreling towards you, you'd best get out of his way because he won't see you."

"He has a lot on his mind."

Janice's eyebrows arched again in surprise. "You're defending him. Well, this is a first."

Virginia pinched the bridge of her nose. "I have to go put a cast on a little girl. Hold my calls."

"Can't someone from Ortho do that?"

"I can too."

Janice grinned. "I know, but usually minor cases like this you don't bother with. Especially ones involving a child."

Virginia rolled her eyes. "Why are you grinning like that?"

"Because I like this side of you. Could the ice queen be melting?"

Virginia groaned. "Just hold my calls, will you?"

"Of course, Dr. Potter."

Virginia headed off toward the ortho wing, cursing Janice and her uncanny ability to talk about the last thing Virginia wanted to discuss, and that was Dr. Brice. She was sure Janice would interrogate her later about her change of heart when it came to Gavin, because Janice had been listening to Virginia moan and gripe about Gavin since his arrival.

Now she understood him. Gavin wasn't just a faceless jackass, trying to make her life as Chief of Surgery impossible.

She understood where he was coming from, from a certain point of view.

Her life plan was still on track. Gavin's had been derailed.

The first thing Virginia noticed when she entered the room was that Lily wasn't as pale as she'd been before.

"How are we feeling, Lily?" Virginia asked, as the nurse handed her the films.

"Great!" Lily chirped.

Virginia hid her smile as she slid the films onto the light box to study the fracture. "It's just a greenstick fracture. Easy-peasy to fix."

Lily craned her neck to take a look. "Cool, but what do you mean by greenstick?"

"It means your bones are soft and you need to drink more milk," Gavin teased.

Lily rolled her eyes at her uncle. "Do I get a cast?"

"Yes, it's closer to your elbow, so you'll get a fancy cast you'll have to wear for a month."

"Awesome." Lily's eyelids fluttered.

"The pain meds are making her a bit loopy." Gavin rubbed his eyes. "Damn, I need to call her grandparents. I forgot before. They'll be worried sick."

"Go," Virginia said. "I've got it here."

"Thanks." Gavin left the room and Virginia readied the supplies to make the cast. Lily opened her eyes again.

"Rose is upset."

"I bet she is," Virginia said. "You broke your arm. Was she there when it happened?"

Lily nodded. "She hates hospitals."

"Why?"

"Mom died in one. This one, actually."

Virginia's chest tightened. "I'm sorry to hear that."

"She was worried I was going to die."

"Did she tell you that?" Virginia asked, hopeful Rose only had selective mutism.

"No, but I know what she was thinking when the ambulance came. I was worried too."

Virginia bit back the tears that were threatening to spill. Even though she'd only known these girls for a couple of days, they tugged at her heartstrings. She knew all too well what Rose was feeling for Lily.

Virginia recalled when Shyanne's fallopian tube burst. She'd ridden in the ambulance with her sister, clutching her hand, trying desperately to hold onto Shyanne's life as if life was something tangible you could hold onto.

No matter how hard she'd squeezed, Shyanne had slipped away, like sand through her fingers, bleeding out.

Virginia cleared her throat. "You have a very minor fracture. You'll live, but you're not allowed to hang from the monkey bars again for a while. Now, why don't you tell me what color you want for your cast? I have lots of colors."

"I want pink, please."

"You really have a thing for pink, don't you?" Virginia teased.

Lily grinned. "Pink drives Uncle Gavin bonkers. Personally, I like blue."

"Why do you want to drive your uncle bonkers? I thought you guys loved him."

"Oh, we do, but it's just so funny."

Virginia bit back her chuckle and nodded. "Pink it is."

"Do you have any sisters, Dr. Potter?" Lily asked.

"I do."

"How many?"

Virginia bit her lip and hesitated. "I have two, but I did have three."

"What happened to the third?" Lily's eyes were wide.

"Promise you won't say anything."

"I do," Lily whispered.

"She died."

Lily's face fell. "Were you close?"

Virginia nodded. "Very close. She was my identical twin."

Lily nodded. "I was really close to my mom."

Virginia swallowed the lump in her throat. "I'm sure you were."

"Is your mom still alive, Dr. Potter?"

"Yep, someone has to take care of my other sisters and my two brothers." Well, financially anyway. She hadn't seen them in a long time. It was too hard. Virginia winked and continued finishing up the cast. "There, nice and pink. Do you think that'll drive your uncle bonkers?"

Lily smiled. "Yep."

"Good."

Gavin hung up the phone after his call to the girls' grandparents. They were relieved it was a minor fracture but they were hinting again about taking the girls, about suing for custody again. There were moments when he thought about it, not even bothering to fight it.

Moments like in the boardroom when he didn't even know something as simple as Lily's birth date. He knew generally when it was, he wasn't a total monster, but when Lily had been born he'd been in India.

Then it hit him and he remembered exactly when her birth date was.

Thank God.

Joss and Caroline had expressed again what kind of parenting they could provide the girls, but of course halfway around the world, and even then Joss could be transferred somewhere else until he planned to retire from the navy. He had no plans to take a commission in San Francisco.

That was not the life Casey had wanted for her daughters, even though she'd married a military man, they had bought the house outright and she had planned to stay there no matter where her husband was going to be sent.

Casey had been determined she wasn't going to drag her kids from pillar to post.

She'd wanted to give her girls stability.

"Why did you pick me, Casey?" he'd asked her. *"I'm not stable. Have someone else take the girls."*

"You're stable enough for me, Gavin. You took care of me when I was young. Please, I need you to do this for me."

There was no way he could've said no to Casey. He'd loved her so much, but right now with Lily in hospital, getting a cast on her arm, he felt like he'd let her down. Big time.

Perhaps he should just sign over custody to Joss and Caroline? Maybe that would be for the best.

He didn't know what to do.

He was confused.

He was lost.

Gavin headed back into the room and groaned when he saw what Virginia was doing to Lily's arm, but then he smiled and knew exactly what he was going to do.

There was no way in hell he was going to sign over custody of his nieces. He'd fight the custody issue again and again.

"It had to be pink, huh?"

Virginia grinned as she continued to wrap the cast and Lily shared a secret smile with her that made Gavin instantly suspicious.

"What's going on?" he asked as he took a seat next to Lily.

"Just girl talk," Virginia said absently, but winking at Lily, who giggled.

"If I didn't know better, I'd think you two were conspiring against me or something."

"Oh, please." Virginia snorted. "There, she's all done. I'll write up the discharge papers and you know the drill about cast care."

"Of course," Gavin responded.

"I'll write up a script for pain medication too. Take the

rest of the week off, Gavin, if you need to." She turned and left the room.

Gavin knew he should be appreciative that she was willing to give him the rest of the week off, but he wasn't a baby.

"I'll be right back, Lily."

"Okay." Lily closed her eyes and drifted off to sleep, her pink cast propped up.

Gavin chased after Virginia, who was at the charge desk, writing up the papers. "Hey, I don't need the rest of the week off."

Virginia's brow furrowed. "You don't? I thought with Lily…"

"No, she'll be fine with Rosalie. I have a job to do and the girls have to get used to it. Lily's fall wasn't a cry for help or anything."

Virginia's eyes widened, obviously stunned. "I never said it was."

"The implication was there." Gavin's voice rose.

"I really think you should bring your issues up with me later, in private," Virginia whispered.

"I don't need the week off."

Virginia shrugged. "Fine." She pullled the discharge note off the clipboard and handed both it and the script to Gavin. "We'll see you tomorrow. Keep her arm elevated."

Gavin regretted confronting her and he let out a sigh as he watched her walk away. What the hell was wrong with him?

I'm an idiot.

With another sigh of regret he folded the note in half and returned to Lily's room to take her home.

CHAPTER NINE

I SHOULDN'T BE here. What am I doing here?

Virginia had been having this argument with herself for the last twenty minutes as she'd sat in her car on the street outside Gavin's home, debating with herself about whether she should ring the doorbell.

This morning he'd been so irrational. Though she really couldn't blame him. He was under a lot of stress.

She was also a bit mad at him for accusing her of thinking Lily had broken her arm on purpose. The child was level-headed and mature, given her age and the fact she'd lost both her parents. Lily had fallen off the monkey bars. Greenstick fractures were the most common fractures in kids.

Heck, she'd sent money last month to her parents because her youngest brother, who was sixteen, had done just the same jumping off the roof of the trailer.

So why was she sitting in her car outside Gavin's house? He was a doctor, he could handle it.

He'd forgotten to fill out his patient forms, at least that's the excuse she'd used to rationalize her appearance outside his house.

Really, she need to get her clothes to the dry cleaner's, have some dinner and get to bed early because she'd managed to reschedule the board meeting until tomorrow.

But, no, she was sitting in her car, mentally arguing with herself.

When had life become so complicated?

The moment I hired Dr. Gavin Brice.

With a sigh she got out of the car and headed towards the door. The gate was locked so she rang the bell. The moment the bell rang, the curtains twitched and she saw little Rose standing in the living-room window in her pajamas.

Virginia smiled and waved and Rose waved back before disappearing, just as the door opened. Gavin opened the door in a ratty old T-shirt and pajama pants. There were dark circles under his eyes and his hair was sticking up on end.

"Dr. Potter?"

"I didn't wake you up, did I?" She glanced at her wristwatch. It was only seven o'clock in the evening.

"Yes, but it's okay. I must've dozed off during the movie." He unlocked the gate. "Come on in."

"No, it's okay. I just brought the patient forms. You forgot to fill them out and both our asses are on the line from Jo and my assistant Janice."

"Thanks." He took the forms and his gaze roved her from head to toe. "You're still in your scrubs?"

"Well, my street clothes are still covered with coffee."

Gavin chuckled and rubbed the back of his neck. "Again, sorry."

"I'll be going." She turned to leave, but he grabbed her arm.

"Come in for a few minutes and check on your VIP patient."

"I don't think that's wise, do you?"

"As friends. I promise, nothing else will happen. Scout's honor."

"I don't know, Gavin."

"Look, don't make me stand out here in these ridiculous PJs any longer. I don't want my neighbors talking. Come in and say hi to the girls. Lily hasn't stopped yammering about her visit with you today and I think Rose is a bit jealous."

"Okay, for a few moments." Virginia stepped inside and Gavin locked up. "So why are PJs so ridiculous? They look quite comfortable to me."

"I sleep nude." He winked and headed up the stairs.

I had to ask. Heat flushed her cheeks and she tried not to picture Gavin naked, though she'd done that very thing since Sunday, when he'd kissed her and she'd almost forgotten who she'd been kissing.

She squished something rubbery under her feet and Rose materialized again at the top of the stairs, arms crossed and giving them the look of death.

Gavin rolled his eyes and scooped down to retrieve the rubber giraffe out from under her feet, yet again. "Rose, you have to stop setting booby traps on the steps. Here, take Georgiana and stop subjecting her to such horrible torture."

Rose caught her giraffe and rolled her eyes as if to say *puhleze* and walked away.

"She's got a thing about that giraffe on the steps."

Gavin groaned. "Every time I go out. I swear that damn giraffe wasn't on the steps when I went down."

Virginia chuckled. "It's okay."

When she walked into the living room she noticed Lily in the corner of the sectional sofa, propped up with pillows.

"Dr. Potter, what're you doing here?" Lily asked, but her voice betrayed her joy, which made Virginia's heart squeeze with pleasure.

Don't get attached.

"I've come to sign your cast. I forgot to do that before."

Lily beamed. "Sure!"

Virginia pulled a marker out of her purse and sat down

next to Lily. She signed her name and drew a small cartoon frog. "There, now it's officially one of my casts. I always have to sign the casts I make. It's a rule."

"Thanks!"

Rose was frowning and Virginia could see a look of envy on her face. "Do you have a bear that needs a cast?"

Rose nodded and took off towards the back of the house.

"What're you doing?" Gavin asked.

"Saving you another trip to the hospital."

Rose reappeared with a bear and Virginia pulled out a roll of pink tape. "I presume pink, yes?"

Rose nodded vehemently and Virginia proceeded to apply a cast to her teddy's arm. When she was done, she signed the teddy's cast and drew the same goofy frog on it. "Now, make sure his cast doesn't get wet, keep his arm elevated and I'll see him in a month to get it removed."

Rose nodded solemnly and headed back to her bedroom.

"Nice move, Dr. Potter." Gavin grinned.

"Thanks." She put her pen away and stood up. "I should head for home. Long day of meetings tomorrow and I don't want to interrupt your…"

"We're having a sleepover pajama party tonight in the living room. Though we're not going to get to do manicures." Lily pouted for a brief moment and turned her attention back to the television.

Virginia cocked an eyebrow and eyed Gavin. "A sleepover. You're such a good uncle."

Gavin shrugged. "I try. I'm hoping her painkillers will kick in soon and I can carry them both back to bed."

Rose stormed back into the living room, wearing her pink tutu and curled up close to Lily. Virginia noticed it was really close, like Rose didn't want to let Lily out of sight for longer than she had to. Virginia knew how Rose felt. She missed Shyanne with every fiber of her being.

"Is Rose okay?" Virginia whispered.

"Yeah, I think she misses her grandparents. She was clingy when they went to the airport this afternoon." Gavin shrugged again.

Virginia glanced at the little girl in time to see an eye-roll and shaking her head in disagreement. "You think so?"

Virginia didn't think it was the grandparents' absence. "What else can it be?"

Virginia pulled him into the hallway out of earshot. "Lily mentioned your sister passed away at Bayview Grace."

Gavin's expression softened and he scrubbed his hand over his face. "Yeah, oh, hell. I didn't even think of that. Damn, and I go there every day to work. I never even thought of it. I started working there after Casey died."

Now it was Virginia's turn to feel guilty. She'd had no idea when she'd first hired Gavin that his sister had been an oncology patient and that she'd died in the hospital.

I'm the worst boss ever.

But, then, how could she have known? Gavin was such a private man.

"Gavin, I'm so sorry that I didn't know."

"No one knew, Virginia. I didn't want anyone's pity or condolences. I just needed the job. You know how I feel about the bureaucracy of my position."

Virginia nodded. "Still, if I had known…"

"Let's not talk about it. I'll mention this incident to Rose's counselor. Just another thing to add to the plate."

Virginia bit her lip and set her purse down on the hall table. "Why don't you have a shower or do something you like to do by yourself and I'll sit with the girls for a while? I'll give Lily and Rose a manicure, a nice-looking lacquer job."

"You don't have to do that. You have a busy day to-morrow."

"I insist. Besides, I'm not the only one. You took an unexpected day off and there was no head of trauma there to wrestle some of those residents in."

Gavin groaned and smiled. "Fine. I think I'll go have a shower or something. Thanks."

"No problem. Just bring me some nice pink nail polish."

He groaned. "Always with the pink."

Virginia laughed and headed back into the living room. The girls were watching a cartoon movie, something really annoying with terrible music.

"How about something a bit more fun? Something we can sing to? What movies do you have?"

"Mom's old DVDs are on the shelf there."

Virginia wandered over to the shelf and searched the titles, hoping Casey had had the DVD she was thinking of, and she almost shouted for joy when she pulled *The Sound of Music* out of the stack.

"Have you guys seen this movie?"

Lily and Rose shook their heads. "Isn't that Mary Poppins?" Lily asked.

Virginia grinned. "Yes, but this movie is awesome to sing to. I love singing to it. Whenever I was sick I would watch this movie over and over again."

She and Shyanne would sing the soundtrack at the top of their lungs. The last time she'd watched it had been a long time ago, with Shyanne right before she'd died. *The Sound of Music*, *Grease* and *Oklahoma!* to name a few had helped her while away many hours on the couch when she'd been feeling under the weather. It had also helped to drown out the sound of her parents fighting over money.

To this day, whenever she was feeling a bit rundown she'd pop on one of these old musicals and she'd feel like she was at home and comforted.

Julie Andrews had been more of a mother to her than her own mother had.

Gavin wandered in with the nail polish and, surprisingly, nail-polish remover, which caused Lily to squeal and Rose to jump up and down excitedly, because they knew what was about to happen.

He excused himself and Virginia put on the movie.

When the first number started Virginia took a seat between the two girls and started on Rose's nails first.

Gavin could hear the strains of the movie soundtrack drifting from upstairs. He retreated to the small basement and did some weights. Whenever he was stressed, he would work out. When he'd been traveling all over the world, working out had usually meant playing soccer, cricket or running. Exercising gave him the rush of endorphins he needed to put everything into perspective and he was still stressed about his run-in with the girls' grandparents when he'd brought Lily home.

They'd made it clear to him in no uncertain terms that they were going to petition for full custody of the girls.

Their reasoning was that he was a single man with no clue on how to be a proper father and they were the girls' grandparents, the closest the girls had to real parents.

He liked Joss and Caroline, but they had their faults.

Where had they been when Casey had been dying? Where had they been when Casey had been trying to fight the cancer that had claimed her life? When she'd been dragging herself to chemo appointments and raising two little girls on her own?

Then again, where had he been? He hadn't come back to the States until she'd called him to tell him she was dying.

Casey had been raising the girls on her own since Rose's birth and it broke Gavin's heart that he'd been halfway around the world, letting his sister fend for herself.

Joss and Caroline hadn't been there either.

When Casey had been dying they hadn't given up their lives, Joss hadn't retired from the service or tried to get a commission in San Francisco. No, but he had given up everything to be a father to these girls and he was damn well going to remain that way.

He'd fight Joss and Caroline tooth and nail to keep the girls.

Gavin continued to lift weights until he was exhausted and the sweat was pouring down his body.

After this he'd need to take another cold shower, because he couldn't get Virginia out of his mind.

He couldn't remember ever obsessing over one woman so much, but then again any woman he'd pursued for a brief dalliance hadn't brushed him aside and neither had he ever pursued his boss before.

Not that he'd really had a boss like Virginia before.

For a moment he fantasized that they were alone, that they weren't colleagues and were just two people who were attracted to each other. Two people who wanted one another and could give in to that passion.

He couldn't help but wonder what it would be like to take Virginia in his arms and make love to her. She was so prim and proper, but when he'd kissed her she'd melted just a bit and he couldn't help but wonder if she'd ignite under his touch.

Get a hold of yourself.

He was definitely going to need a cold shower and soon. First he had to get his mind off of her before he went upstairs in his current state, which was a hard thing to do, given the fact she was under the same roof as him.

When he set down the weights he realized the television had gone strangely quiet and he glanced at the wall and balked when he saw that it was close to midnight.

He'd let time get away from him.

He toweled himself off and headed back upstairs halfdressed. Everything was silent when he headed toward the living room.

"Virginia—" Gavin stopped when he noticed that Virginia was curled up on the couch, Rose was lying beside her and Lily was snoring in the corner.

The television was on, but the DVD was frozen on the scene selection menu. She looked so peaceful. They all did.

It surprised to him to see Virginia curled up with the girls, but it also pleased him. The girls' nails were the color of bubblegum and then he noticed Virginia's neat, well-manicured nails were also the color of bubblegum, and it wasn't a very tidy job.

Which meant she'd let one of the girls do it.

A smile tugged at the corner of his mouth. She was so tender, so beautiful.

Don't think about her like that. She doesn't want you.

Virginia had made it clear. Nothing could ever happen between them.

He moved to wake her up and then thought better of it. Virginia was exhausted; there were dark circles under her eyes. She'd had a pretty trying day herself.

Instead he shut the television off and then picked up the afghan from the recliner and tucked all the girls in.

Only two of them were his.

And the other one he wanted desperately to be his too.

The incessant squeaking in Virginia's ear alerted her to the fact she wasn't in her apartment. She cracked open one eye to see a silent golden angel holding a rubber giraffe by the name of Georgiana in her face.

Rose gave it another long squeak, which sent shooting pain up Virginia's neck and behind her eyeballs. Then she realized she'd spent the night on Gavin's couch. She bolted upright.

"Oh, my God."

Rose wagged her finger and squeaked Georgiana again.

"Sorry, I didn't mean to curse." She glanced around the

room until she spied the clock and realized she was going to be late for the board meeting.

Crap.

"I have to get to work." She stood up and realized she was still in the same scrubs she'd worn the previous day.

Double crap.

"Good morning," Gavin said, as he came into the room. He was dressed for work, coffee in his hand, and by the way his hair was glistening he'd obviously had a shower.

"Why didn't you wake me up last night?"

"You looked so peaceful."

Virginia groaned. "You should've woken me up. I need a shower and a change of clothes. I have an important meeting in an hour."

"There are some of Casey's clothes in the master bedroom and you can always borrow my shower."

"I don't think that would be appropriate."

Gavin took a sip out of his travel mug. "What's not appropriate about offering a friend some spare clothes and a shower?"

He had a point.

It wasn't ideal, but she really didn't have a choice. She hadn't become Chief of Surgery by attending meetings dressed as a slob.

"Point me in the right direction."

"Gladly."

She followed Gavin to the master bedroom. The room smelled distinctly like him. Masculine. A clean, spicy smell that she loved. The bed was made and she noticed a pile of blankets on the floor.

"What's going on here?" she asked as she stepped over the pile.

"Ah, I'm still not used to using a mattress. I've been sleeping rough for so long I find I can only get a good night's sleep on the floor."

"You've been in San Francisco for how long again?"

"Six months, but still no good. The bed is too soft and good for only one thing."

Virginia's pulse began to race, understanding his implication clearly.

"Clothes?" she asked, changing the subject.

He moved past her and opened up the closet. "Here's where Casey's clothes are."

"Why are you still keeping them?"

Gavin shrugged. "I haven't had the time to deal with her personal effects. Besides, they come in handy when I deliberately trap women here and force them to babysit my nieces."

Virginia rolled her eyes and snorted.

He opened another door. "There are towels in the closet. Feel free to use whatever."

"Thanks. I really appreciate this. I'll see you at work."

Gavin nodded. "See you."

When he left the bedroom Virginia peeled off the scrubs and climbed into the shower. The hot water helped work out the kinks in her back and neck.

She finished her quick shower and then dried herself off, towel-drying her hair. As much as she wished she had a straightener or a blow-dryer, she was just thankful she didn't smell like plaster or old coffee.

When she headed into the master bedroom she picked out a simple blouse and pants, which were a little big on her but at least she wouldn't be in wrinkled old scrubs. She jammed the scrubs in her purse after tying back her hair.

As soon as she left the bedroom Gavin was standing there, holding a mug of coffee out.

"Please, don't dump that on me."

"You might want me to." He winced. "Your car was parked in a no overnight parking zone and was towed."

Virginia closed her eyes and took a deep calming

breath. What she really wanted to do was let out a string
of profanities that would shake the very rafters of Gavin's
pink home, but there were children in the house, so she
refrained from uttering them out loud and kept them to
herself.

"How am I going to get to work?" she asked calmly.

"You can ride with me, but I hope you don't mind riding on the back of my bike. Rosalie needs the van for the
girls today."

"You ride a motorcycle?"

He nodded. "I do. What do you say, Virginia?"

Her heart beat a bit faster in anticipation at the thought
of riding behind the most stereotypical bad boy. She did
have a thing for motorcycles.

Instead of saying *I'd love that* and letting him know
how exciting the prospect was, she restrained herself.
"Sure, I really don't have a choice."

"Don't sound so enthused," he teased. "Well, let's go."

Virginia downed the rest of her coffee and followed
Gavin outside to the garage. He uncovered the Harley and
dug out an extra helmet for her. She was really excited to
ride behind him, but she also hoped no one from the hospital would see her arrive on the back of Gavin's motorcycle.

The gossip would be endless and she didn't want anything to get back to the board about it. It could put her career and Gavin's in jeopardy.

He secured her purse and his satchel in one of the pan-
niers, before climbing on.

She climbed on the back of his motorcycle and wrapped
her arms around him. The moment she did so, her heart
beat a bit faster and she hoped he didn't notice. What she
really longed to do was press her body tight against his,
but she kept her distance the best she could. Still, it felt so
good to be so close to him.

"Hold on." He revved the engine and the purr of the

bike drowned out the loud beat of her pulse. The vibrations rippled through her. He pulled out onto the street, parked and shut the garage door before climbing back on. "You ready?"

Virginia nodded and he turned on his signal and hit the streets of San Francisco. The moment he hit the road, she pulled him tighter as she held on for dear life. She'd lived in San Francisco for years, she learned to drive on its streets when she'd first moved here and had ridden the streetcars and trolleys up and down the hills, but until now those hills had never freaked her out.

She repressed the urge to cry out as Gavin maneuvered his way through the San Francisco streets towards Bayview Grace.

The ride terrified her, but it also thrilled her. As they crested a hill and raced down the other side she felt like she was on some crazy roller coaster.

For the first time in a long time she felt carefree and that feeling scared her. When they arrived at Bayview Grace Gavin parked in his reserved spot.

"What did you think of the ride?" he asked as she handed him her helmet.

Her knees wobbled a bit. "It was… Thanks for bringing me."

Gavin grinned. "Any time. If you want, I'll take you to the lot to retrieve your car after work."

"No, thanks, Dr. Brice. I'll take transit or a cab. I'm not sure how late I'll be working tonight."

"Sure. Thanks again for your help with the girls last night."

"My pleasure." She glanced at her watch and saw she was already five minutes late. "Look, I have to go. Thanks."

What she wanted to say was that it was no problem and that she would gladly spend another evening with the girls. She also wanted to tell him how much she'd enjoyed the impromptu sleepover party with them and how good it had felt to have two sweet little angels sleeping next to her on the couch, but she didn't.

It wasn't her place.

She turned on her heel and walked briskly towards the hospital. Her legs were still shaking from the ride and her heart was shaking a bit from the feelings that were threatening to overpower her common sense.

CHAPTER TEN

WHEN VIRGINIA CAME out of the board meeting a few hours later, she had a pounding headache. Janice was waiting for her in her office with some files.

"You look like you've been run over by a steamroller," she remarked.

"Haven't I?" Virginia asked as she took a seat behind her desk. "More budget cuts."

"Ugh," Janice remarked.

"My sentiments exactly."

Virginia was frustrated. The board had hired her to bring this hospital back from the dead, but how was she supposed to do that when they constantly cut her budget?

Because they wanted a private clinic, at least some of them did, and she wasn't going to let go of her ER without a fight. So she'd proposed a hospital benefit. A glitzy affair showcasing their brilliant attendings and the innovative strides they were making in order to receive funding.

Her suggestion had pleased the board no end, but it meant she had a big party to plan. So instead of spending time with patients, doing innovative surgeries or research she was going to be planning a big party.

"That's an interesting color choice and I don't mean to be disrespectful, but who did your nails?"

Virginia glanced down at her hands and groaned inwardly. Rose had painted her nails, and they were horribly mangled, messy and now the enamel was chipping. It was also pink. No wonder she had been getting weird glances from some of the members of the board.

"I'm not on the top of my game today."

Janice cocked an eyebrow. "No kidding. Wild night last night?" There was a hint of hope in her assistant's voice. Janice was always hoping that Virginia would live a little and she voiced her opinions quite loudly at times.

"You're young. Don't spend your youth locked away. Go out and live a little."

Why couldn't they just let her be? It was her life after all.

She knew one thing: planning benefits and schmoozing hadn't been part of the original plan. Virginia wanted to be in the OR or researching.

The internal dialog in her head was turning into a bit of a broken record.

"Well, what were you up to last night?" Janice prodded.

"A bit of an impromptu sleepover." She groaned inwardly, regretting the admission, because when Janice got a hint of gossip, she was like a dog with a bone. Virginia was usually more aloof with Janice, but lack of a good night's sleep had caused a lapse in judgement and she'd let down her walls a bit.

"Oh, do tell." Janice was grinning from ear to ear.

"You know, it's funny. I have all this work to do."

Janice snorted and dropped the last file on her desk. "Fine, I can take a hint. Before I go, though, A&B Towing called and they had information on where your car is being held. The message is the pink slip on the top."

Janice shot her a knowing but smug look as she left the office.

Virginia groaned. She'd forgotten about her car. She only had an hour before the impound lot closed. Her paperwork could wait until she got back. She needed her car.

When she left her office, Janice was smiling secretly to herself as she worked. Virginia just shook her head and left for the lot.

"I heard you were looking for this." Gavin dropped the patient forms onto Janice's desk. He'd meant to drop them off sooner, but he'd had a surgery to attend. He'd literally just got out of the OR. All he'd had time to do was scrub out, and he was still wearing his scrub cap, because Janice had been paging him about the missing forms since he'd arrived.

"Thank you, Dr. Brice, and very neat handwriting too."

"Sorry I didn't drop them off straightaway."

Janice cocked an eyebrow and looked at him over her horned-rimmed glasses. "Well, I can be persistent when I need something done. I know how distracted you surgeons get."

Gavin lingered and he didn't know why.

You know why.

"Is Dr. Potter out of her meeting yet?"

Janice's eyes widened and then she grinned and leaned forward. "Yes, but she had to step out. Her car was impounded last night. So unlike Dr. Potter."

"Right. I forgot."

"Really? You knew about her car being impounded? Do tell." Janice leaned on her elbow, propping her chin on her fist and fluttering her eyelashes behind her tortoiseshell bifocals.

Gavin held up his hands. "I don't think it's any of my business to tell you. If Virginia didn't mention it, then I won't."

"Virginia? Usually other surgeons refer to her as Dr. Potter or chief. Didn't realize you two were so close." Janice grinned like the cat that had got the cream, or like the Grinch when he thought of his evil plan. So smugly pleased with herself.

Gavin cursed inwardly. "You're a bit of a pest, aren't you?"

"One of the best, Dr. Brice."

Gavin backed away. He didn't want to make Virginia angrier at him. "Well, I'm being paged. I'd better go."

Janice gave him a skeptical look. "Of course, Dr. Brice. Of course."

Gavin made a mental note not to cross swords with Janice, though some of the nurses had already warned him of that. Janice was a force to be reckoned with. She'd been a charge nurse herself for years and was the keeper of the gates, more intimidating than Cerberus itself. Although it was Gavin's experience that women like Janice had barks that were worse than their bites. She had implied that there was something personal between himself and Virginia.

Though he wanted something more intimate, he knew if he went after Virginia it wouldn't be just a fling and he wasn't sure if he had anything to give Virginia because marriage and monogamy were something he had never pictured for himself.

When he headed back down to the trauma bay Dr. Rogerson popped out of a room.

Gavin liked independent, strong woman, but he didn't like being hunted down by overly forward women. To Moira Rogerson he was just a piece of meat and he didn't like it.

"How's your niece, Dr. Brice?"

Gavin frowned. "How did you know?"

He liked to keep his personal life just that—to himself. Especially with people he worked with.

"I was on duty yesterday. I was originally paged until the ice queen took over."

Gavin didn't like that nickname, knowing that was the

name the other surgeons used when referring to Virginia. Ice Queen was far from the truth.

She might be a bit heavy-handed when it came to running the hospital, but Virginia wasn't that way outside work. He'd seen the softer side of her.

"Well, Dr. Potter is a trauma surgeon and my niece broke her arm." Gavin pulled out his phone and pretended to check for text messages, though he had none. Moira didn't get the hint that he wasn't interested in talking.

"I didn't know you were guardian to your nieces. That's really sweet." Moira grinned at him, a smile meant to devour a man whole.

"I don't talk much about them. I like to keep my private life private."

He walked into the lunchroom and got himself a drink of water. Moira followed him and he groaned inwardly, wishing she would just go away.

"How old are your nieces?"

Swallowing the water was like trying to down a cue ball at the moment. "Why do you want to know?"

"Just trying to make small talk." Moira took a step forward and placed her hand on his arm, gently squeezing it.

"I'm afraid I don't do small talk."

Moira smiled. "What do you do, then?"

"Surgery?" he offered, and Moira just laughed, which was annoying and high-pitched, and she clutched his arm tighter.

"You're so droll, Gavin."

He ground his teeth, not liking the way she said his name. "I don't know what's so funny about stating the truth."

"So would you like to have dinner sometime? Maybe tonight?"

Gavin was about to answer and glanced up in time to see Virginia walk back into the hospital. His heart skipped a beat as he watched her walk through the entrance and he was taken back to that stolen moment on Sunday, down by the water, when time had seemed to stand still and he'd pulled Virginia into his arms and kissed her.

The scent of her perfume, the touch of her lips still burned in his memory, as did the pointed rejection, which still stung him.

Virginia and he were coworkers, maybe even friends, but that's all they could be.

She'd made that pretty clear.

"Gavin?" Moira turned to see what had caught his attention. "Oh, the ice queen."

"Sure, why don't we go out tonight?" Gavin suddenly blurted out, trying not to look at Virginia as she headed towards them.

Moira grinned. "Yes, I'd love that. I'll page you later for the details." Moira winked and finally left him in peace.

Virginia nodded curtly to Moira as they passed in the hall and then, as if knowing she was being watched, she glanced at him. Her dark gaze locked with his and he saw a faint pinkness tinge her skin as she walked into the room.

"You're still here. I thought your shift ended a couple of hours ago?" she said.

"Surgery. The closest hospital was packed and the ambulance rerouted here."

A brief smile flitted on her lips and he knew it wasn't because of the possibility that someone had been injured. Virginia was thinking in terms of business for Bayview Grace.

"I'm glad the ambulance thought to reroute here."

"We were the closest and the man was in no condition to wait for the ambulance to take him to the level two trauma. I don't think that's something we should be celebrating."

Virginia bit her bottom lip and gave him a quizzical look. "I'm not celebrating."

"Come on, I saw the brief smile that flitted across your face."

She pinched the bridge of her nose and sighed. He knew that response and he'd come to loathe it, especially after she'd had a meeting with the board of directors.

He moved past her and shut the door to the room then pulled the blinds to the room so they were in relative privacy.

"What's going on?"

Virginia shrugged her shoulders. "I don't know what you mean."

"I know that look. Very well."

This time she did smile and her shoulders relaxed from the tense hunch they'd had just moments before.

"It was just a long day and I didn't get the best sleep last night."

"What're you talking about? That couch is too soft."

Virginia cocked an eyebrow. "Says the man who sleeps on the hardwood floor."

"Did the meeting have something to do with me?" he asked. "You can tell me. I know for a fact you can tell me."

The smile disappeared and she sighed again. "Not you directly, just in general financial terms."

"That bad?"

"I have to organize a benefit for the end of the month. A real glitzy affair." She wrinkled her nose in disgust. "Not my most favorite job."

"I don't blame you." He rubbed the back of his neck. "Black tie, I suppose?"

"Yes, and mandatory for all Attendings. One month from today, so get yourself a sitter."

"Ugh."

Virginia chuckled and opened the door. "My sentiments exactly. Are you headed for home now?"

"I think so. I just dropped those forms off to Janice."

"Good."

They walked out of the room together.

"Hey, if you need help planning the gala or benefit, whatever you want to call it, just ask."

"You have hidden depths, Dr. Brice. I thought you were a roughneck sort of physician?"

"That may be, but I've attended many, many, many mandatory galas on behalf of Border Free Physicians."

"Well, maybe I'll take you up on your offer. I hate party planning. I never had a party when I was young."

"Never had a party?" Gavin asked, intrigued by this insight into her.

"No, my parents couldn't stretch to that luxury."

"What did they do?"

"Unemployed, for the most part. I grew up in a trailer in South Dakota with two brothers and three sisters."

"That's a surprise."

"Really? Why do you say that?"

"You don't seem the trailer type."

Virginia crossed her arms. "Is there a trailer type?"

Gavin rubbed the back of his neck. "Sorry, no, there isn't unless you count what's on television. I didn't mean to make assumptions."

"It's okay. I have hidden depths. Ugh, I hope someone can help."

"A surgeon as a party planner?" Gavin asked in disbelief. "Surgeons usually aren't social types."

"You'd be surprised around here." Virginia tucked a wayward lock of brown hair behind her ear. "I saw you talking to Dr. Rogerson. She's a bit of a social butterfly."

Is she jealous?

Gavin was amused, pleased she'd noticed, but he didn't want to talk about it. He'd let her stew a bit. "Well, I'd better head for home. The girls get anxious when I'm late."

"Of course. Have a good evening and send them my

best." Virginia turned and walked away from him towards the office.

Gavin watched her walk away.

And then a horrible thought crept into his mind. If the hospital needed to throw a benefit, one that would cause the chief of surgery a large amount of stress, how bad a shape was the hospital in and would he even have a job in the near future?

CHAPTER ELEVEN

GAVIN MANAGED TO finagle Rosalie into babysitting. He owed that woman a large Christmas bonus.

Now he was standing in the middle of Union Square, waiting for Moira to arrive. He glanced over and saw the place where Virginia had been waiting for him. When he'd seen her there, he'd been mesmerized by her simple beauty and he'd known he'd have a hard time keeping his hands off her.

Virginia occupied his mind constantly, made him think things he shouldn't.

Was that why he'd agreed on this date with Moira and suggested this location, re-creating the date he and Virginia had gone on? Was he trying to prove to himself that he could find that spark with anyone, that Virginia wasn't special?

He didn't have time to contemplate it further as Moira walked over to him. She was dressed nicely, different from her scrubs. She was dressed as prettily as Virginia, only the color was a deep emerald, which suited Moira's hair. It was also more seductive and instead of ballet flats she wore heels, which were impractical for the date he had in mind. Of course, Moira wasn't to know that.

"Hi," she said, her smile bright as she stopped in front of him. She leaned over and gave him a peck on the cheek.

Her perfume was a bit overpowering and floral. Not homey like vanilla and certainly not subtle.

"Hi, yourself."

"Where are we going? I hope it's not far." Moira pointed to her heels and then lifted the hem of her dress slightly, showing off her leg. "These are murder on my feet, but they're so pretty."

"I was actually thinking of the Fog City Diner."

"Oh." There was a hint of disappointment in her voice.

Gavin didn't know what she'd expected. Obviously something fancier as she was decked out to the nines.

"Is there something wrong with that restaurant? I've been told it's a San Francisco institution."

"For tourists, yes."

"I made reservations."

"Sounds good." Gavin could tell she was lying by the way she forced a smile. "Is your car nearby? I took a cab here as mine's in the shop."

"No, I'd thought we'd take the streetcar."

"You're kidding me, right?"

I guess I am. "No, I'm not kidding. I thought we'd take the streetcar and enjoy the sights."

"How about I pay for a cab? No offense, but these heels are a little much for a streetcar."

"Sure." What could he say to that, no? Gavin trailed behind Moira as she marched over to a taxi stand at a nearby hotel. It didn't take long before they were both settled into the back of the cab. Moira snuggled up next to him, her floral scent mixed with the spicy smell permeating the cab, making his stomach turn.

Virginia had had no problem riding the streetcar. In fact, it had seemed to enhance the experience of that night. It had been fun. Virginia wasn't high-maintenance. He had an inkling, going into this date, that Moira was high-maintenance.

Did he really want to date someone who was?

This wasn't for the long term, he reminded himself again. This was just a fling. Who cared if Moira preferred different things to Virginia? This wasn't a comparison between the two women. He wasn't looking for something long term.

Though maybe he was and that thought scared him.

On that short cab ride to the Fog City Diner, Gavin finally admitted to himself how lonely he'd been and maybe he did want to settle down and have it all. The thought was extremely unsettling. Having custody of the girls had changed his perspective entirely.

The conversation at the diner was one-sided and stilted. Moira chatted away, but Gavin just couldn't clear his head from his jangled thoughts. It'd been so easy to talk to Virginia.

"Gavin, are you listening?"

"Sorry, what?"

Moira frowned. "You're a bit out of sorts."

"A bit. What were you saying?"

"I was just telling you how some staff members think the ice queen is melting. That her demeanor is softening around her cold, hard exterior. Can you imagine? I wonder what brought that on, though I have my suspicions."

"Softening? How do you mean?"

"Well, she's been behaving differently lately. I think it's a man."

Gavin's heart stuttered, but then he shrugged, feigning indifference. "Maybe she has a lot on her mind."

"Who knows? But she's been more…I don't know… approachable. More relaxed and nice. Not so aloof. The nurses like the change."

"I don't quite see the problem, then."

Moira leaned forward. "I've heard talk of the ER getting the axe."

Now she had Gavin's full attention. He'd been sure something was up with Virginia planning that gala.

"Who told you that?"

Moira grinned. "Ah, so you've heard it too."

"Nothing concrete, just rumors. Especially rumors involving a certain fundraising event."

"The gala! Yeah, it had me worried too. My source is on the board of directors."

Gavin cocked an eyebrow. "Go on."

"There are threats to close the ER, but Dr. Potter is fighting tooth and nail to keep it open."

Gavin grinned, pleased to hear it. They called Virginia the ice queen. How little they knew when she was working so hard for them and they had no idea. "Is she?"

Moira sighed. "It won't do her any good. It's why I applied to another hospital and got a job."

"You're leaving Bayview?"

"Before it sinks, I have to protect myself and my career. If you're nice to me I can get you an interview." She slid her hand across the table, reaching out for his, and then her foot began to slide up his leg in a very suggestive manner. A move he would've welcomed six months ago.

"I think your thoughts on Bayview sinking are premature. I think Dr. Potter will save Bayview Grace."

Moira frowned, retracting her hand, and the game of footsie ended as well. "Why did you say yes to this date, Gavin?"

"What do you mean?"

She rolled her eyes. With a sigh she opened her purse and placed a twenty on the table. "You're clearly not interested in me. You're obviously hung up on someone else. I don't want to spend my evening talking hospital politics."

She slid out of the booth and stood. Gavin panicked and jumped in front of her, grabbing her by the shoulders and pulling her close to him before crushing her lips against his in a kiss. A kiss to prove to himself and her that he wasn't hung up on anyone.

Moira melted into his arms, a moan escaping from the back of her throat, then her tongue pushed past his lips.

Gavin felt nothing.

His kiss with Virginia had been so different. It had been gentle, sweet and it'd turned him on. This was rough, clumsy and evoked no response from him at all.

He didn't want Moira. He wanted Virginia.

Moira broke the kiss. She sighed and then frowned. "Goodbye, Dr. Brice."

Gavin didn't try to stop her this time as she walked past curious onlookers as she left the restaurant. He sank back down against the seat, before pulling out a couple of twenties to pay the bill.

When he walked outside a thick fog was rolling in and the sun was just starting to get ready to set, making the area glow orange in the haze. Gavin walked along the Embarcadero. August would soon be over. The girls would go back to school. He had to switch to nights so he could take them to and from school. Rosalie already said she'd take them during the nights he worked.

There would be no time for dating.

Not until the girls were older.

Only would it make a difference? Would he even have a job in a few weeks' time?

Was Moira doing the smart thing by jumping ship?

Gavin didn't know how long he walked, but he ended up in front of Bayview Grace. Virginia's car was still in the lot.

I need to know.

He had two little girls depending on him. He needed job security and stability in order to keep the girls. If he lost his job and had to move, the girls' grandparents would certainly sue for custody and possibly win. It would kill him to lose the girls now.

Virginia shuffled through more paperwork and glanced at the clock. It was almost eight. She should really go home, but what would she be going home to?

Nothing.

Then her mind wandered to Gavin. She knew he was on a date with Moira Rogerson. She'd heard it through the rumor mill—well, she'd actually heard it from Janice, who kept an ear to the grapevine.

It shouldn't bother her because she wasn't looking for a relationship, but it did. It made her feel jealous, just picturing him laughing and talking with Moira like he'd done with her.

If he started dating Moira she had no one to blame but herself. She'd pushed him away and it was for the best. She couldn't give him what he wanted because she was terrified to admit it was what she wanted as well, but she wouldn't put her heart at risk again.

She wouldn't lose anyone else she loved.

Virginia sighed and set down her papers. She stood up and stretched, deciding it was time to leave when the door to her office burst open. Virginia jumped and saw Gavin standing there, dressed in the same kind of clothes he'd worn when he'd taken her out.

"Dr. Brice, I thought you were out for the evening."

"I was, but I needed to talk to you."

The butterflies in her stomach began to flutter. "Oh?"

"I need to… I mean, I want…" Gavin rubbed the back of his neck and then shut the door behind him. "I need to switch to nights."

"Oh—oh, okay." Virginia took a seat, her knees knocking. She didn't know what she'd been expecting him to say, but it definitely wasn't that. She felt relieved and disappointed all at the same time. "Why?"

"The girls start school the first week of September and I want to be able to take them to and from school. It's Rose's first year there and I think it's important that I'm there."

Virginia nodded. "Of course. I would ask if you've talked to your superior but as you're head of that department there shouldn't be a problem. I'm sure someone will want to change."

"Jefferson is switching with me. He's young and he's looking forward to day shifts, even if it's only for the school year."

"Then it's all settled." Virginia watched him. He looked nervous and he stood there as if he wanted to say more. "Is that all you needed to talk about, Gavin?"

"No." His gaze met hers, those deep green eyes intense, riveting her to the spot. "Is the ER threatened?"

Virginia cleared her throat. "What're you talking about?"

"The gala. It's not just some fundraiser, it's to save the ER, isn't it?"

"It's a fundraiser for the ER, yes."

Gavin scrubbed his hand over his face. "Is my job safe?"

Virginia wanted to tell him the truth, but she honestly couldn't. She was sworn to a confidentiality agreement.

"The ER isn't in danger."

It was a lie, one that made her feel sick to her stomach. Gavin walked over to her desk and sat down in front of her.

"You're sure?"

Virginia looked away. "Gavin, I wish I could tell you otherwise, but I'm bound by a legal agreement to keep it secret." Then she looked back at him, trying to convey everything she couldn't say in a look.

"I see." Gavin nodded. "I understand."

"I would tell you."

"I know you would."

"I'll write you a recommendation letter if you want to leave. I understand why you wouldn't want to stay."

"I don't need a letter." Then he reached across the desk and took her hand in his. "I have faith that you'll keep this hospital from going under. I'm not ready to jump ship."

His hand around hers felt so good. It calmed her and made her wish that it wasn't just their bare hands touching. That it could be more.

Virginia took her hand back. "Where did you hear this rumor?"

"Dr. Rogerson."

"Ah, well, that makes sense. She handed in her resignation this morning." Virginia cleared her throat. "I heard you were on a date with Moira. How was it?"

Gavin grinned and leaned back in the chair. "Fine."

Virginia's cheeks flushed. "Oh, that's great. She's a wonderful surgeon."

"Are you jealous, Virginia?" Gavin asked, his green eyes twinkling mischievously.

"Don't be ridiculous. I just wanted to know where the rumor started so I could quash it before it got out of hand. I don't care who you see or don't see, Dr. Brice. You've made it clear that your personal life is no concern of mine and it isn't."

Gavin's smile disappeared and he frowned. "Well, glad that's settled."

Virginia nodded and turned back to her paperwork, effectively dismissing him. "I'd better get some more of this paperwork done and I'll schedule your duty shifts for the evening starting on your next rotation."

"Great. Thanks. I appreciate it." He stood and she watched him as he walked across the room and opened the door. He turned and glanced back. "Good night, Dr. Potter."

"Good night, Dr. Brice."

CHAPTER TWELVE

"YOU'RE DOING A fantastic job with the benefit, Dr. Potter."

Virginia plastered on her best smile as she walked through the Excelsior downtown San Francisco. "I'm glad you approve, Mr. Shultz." That was what she said, but what she really thought was, I hope this is worth it, because this benefit is already costing the hospital precious amounts of money.

Money that could be used to keep the emergency department open.

She'd been carrying around that information for a month and it was eating her up inside. This benefit had to go off without any kind of hiccup in order to save the emergency department. There were so many people in the department who depended on their jobs. Especially Gavin.

She let her mind wander to him for a brief moment. She hadn't seen him since they'd spoken that night in her office. Though it wasn't unexpected. He'd transferred to nights and she'd been so busy with the gala that there hadn't been a chance to catch up. There had been a few times when she'd caught a fleeting glimpse of him coming in as she was leaving, but that was about it. Although she'd see him soon because she had an appointment to see Lily in about an hour.

Virginia glanced at her wristwatch. "If you'll excuse

me, Mr. Schultz, I do have an appointment with a VIP patient."

"Of course, of course, but before you go I just wanted to confirm with you that Dr. Gavin Brice will be speaking at the event."

"Dr. Brice?"

"Yes," Mr. Schultz said. "Many of the attendees are quite interested in hearing him speak. He may have started as a bit of a rogue, but he's starting to fit in with our hospital. We'd love to have him talk about his experiences with Border Free Physicians."

"Well, I can certainly ask him, but he's not one of the attendings I asked to speak. He's on nights now and I may not be able to pull him away from his duties."

Mr. Schultz frowned. "Then you need to ask him, Dr. Potter, I would advise you to tell him to speak."

Virginia plastered another smile on her face and excused herself from the hotel ballroom.

"Tell him to speak."

Like she could order her surgeons to do anything like that.

Still, she had to try and get Gavin onside for the sake of the benefit.

Would it really save the hospital?

Or was it just a temporary patch on the shredded artery?

When she got to the hospital, she changed into her scrubs. When she came out of her office Janice stopped her typing.

"Lily Johnson is waiting for you in exam room 2221A. Dr. Brice is with her."

"Thank you, Janice. Hold my calls."

"Of course."

When Virginia entered the exam room Gavin was sitting with Lily. As were Rosalie and Rose. Gavin was in his scrubs because he was on duty tonight, and it pleased her that he was making time for the girls.

He always had time for his nieces. She admired him for that. First she checked out the X-rays waiting on the light box for her. "Well, it looks like that ulna is all healed. How about we take care of your arm and get that cast off? What do you say to that?"

Lily smiled. "I'm really looking forward to getting it off."

"I bet you are." Virginia readied her tools and smiled at Rose. "How are you today, Rose?"

Rose shrugged but didn't smile.

"Nervous about your sister?" Virginia asked.

Rose nodded.

"There's no reason to be nervous." Virginia picked up the saw used to remove the cast and started it. Rose's eyes widened, her little face paling. "This saw won't cut her skin. You want to know how I know?"

Rose didn't nod but watched the saw in fascination. Virginia placed it against her palm, running the saw over her hand.

"See, it just tickles."

"Cool," Lily said. "That's so cool."

Virginia winked at Gavin, who was hiding his laugh behind his hand. "Okay, Lily, let's get this tired-looking cast off." She slipped goggles and a face mask on the little girl.

"What're these for?"

"It'll protect you from the dust. I have my own pair too."

Lily held her arm still. Virginia slipped on her mask and goggles and set the oscillating saw down through the fiberglass, cutting away at the fibers.

Lily watched, her eyes wide from behind the goggles, until the cast fell away from her pale arm.

"Yuck, it's all weird-looking and it stinks." Lily pinched her nose.

Virginia set down the saw and palpated Lily's arm and

then moved it around, asking her if she felt any pain. "Well, your arm's been covered for a month. It hasn't seen the sun in four weeks. Your bone appears to be nice and healed, so I'm begging you, as your doctor, not to hang from any monkey bars at school. Promise me."

Lily grinned. "I promise. Can I keep my cast? I like all the signatures."

"Of course." She turned to Gavin. "Her skin is really dry. Bathe it in warm water for twenty minutes twice a day and dry it by rubbing gently."

"I know how to take care of a limb after a cast comes off."

Virginia chuckled. "Of course."

"Rosalie, can you take the girls home now?" Gavin asked.

"Of course, Dr. Brice. Come on, girls, you'll see your uncle tomorrow morning."

Virginia helped Lily down and handed her the cast. "Take care of that arm, Lily."

"I will, thank you, Dr. Potter." Lily took Rose's hand and they walked out together.

Virginia watched the girls leave with Gavin's housekeeper. "Dr. Brice, before you start your shift, there's something I need to talk to you about."

Gavin crossed his arms over his chest. "Of course, shoot."

"The board has asked if you would speak at the gala benefit next week."

"No."

Virginia scrubbed her hand over her face. She had half expected that answer from him. "Please, would you do it for the hospital? You offered to help me before with the planning."

"Yes, but that was organizing it. I don't do well with crowds. I don't like giving speeches and I'm sorry but I'm not going to give one for this hospital." He turned to walk away but Virginia stepped in front of him, blocking him from leaving.

"I don't think you quite understand what I'm asking you."

"I do understand what you're asking me, Dr. Potter. The board wants me to talk about all the great adventures I had with Border Free Physicians, but the thing is they *really* don't want me to."

Virginia was confused. "What're you talking about?"

Gavin let out a heavy sigh. "It's not that I don't like speaking to crowds, not really. It's just that I would write a speech, telling all those tuxedoed people exactly what I experienced, the nitty-gritty details of developing countries and how they should be pouring their extra money into helping those less fortunate. Even here, in this city, there are countless missions. There are people living in this city, not necessarily on the streets, who need medical attention. They just can't afford it."

Virginia was stunned. "And you're saying that the board wouldn't want you to talk about it?"

He nodded. "Precisely. I've written my speech countless times in my head. Each time it's edited. I'm not allowed to actually talk about what's needed. The people who buy these expensive plates and bid on the silent auction don't care about what's happening under their noses, let alone in the wider world."

"I will let you speak about that," Virginia said.

Gavin gave her a half-hearted smile. "You say that now, but your hands are tied, Virginia. Don't make a promise that you aren't able to keep."

"I don't think you understand what's really at stake."

"Tell me, then. Tell me what's at stake."

Gavin waited with bated breath for her answer. Though he knew. He'd heard enough rumblings in the hallways about

Bayview Grace bleeding out money like its carotid artery had been severed, that the emergency department would most likely be amputated, meaning that he would be out of a job. Moira had been right.

He wanted Virginia to tell him that. Though he knew she couldn't, he still wanted to hear it from her lips all the same.

The staff in the emergency department were stressed, worried about their futures, about their security, and when the staff were stressed, mistakes were made.

Gavin hated working in an environment like that.

What he wanted from Virginia, from his chief of surgery, was for her tell him that this benefit was a last-ditch effort to save the emergency department.

He wanted the truth.

So he waited, watching as Virginia thought of some kind of excuse or story to throw him off the scent.

He'd dealt with stuff like this in Border Free Physicians. He knew how to get around it and he wasn't going to back down until he had the truth.

"You need to speak at the benefit," she said, and straightened her shoulders, crossing her arms in that stubborn stance he knew all too well.

She was going to hold her ground, just as much as he was, and he admired her for that.

"I don't have to speak, Virginia. I'll attend the benefit, but I'm not speaking."

"Yes, you are."

He cocked his head. "I don't think you can force me."

"No, I can't and I really don't want to, but the board has made it clear that you will speak. Just like the other attendings who've been asked. You will speak at the benefit, Dr. Brice."

"Because my job depends on it?"

Virginia didn't utter a word but she nodded, just barely. *Damn.*

"How bad is it?"

Virginia glanced over her shoulder and then shut the door to the exam room. "It's bad."

"So the emergency department really is on the chopping block?"

"You know I'm betraying a confidentiality agreement. I could get sued."

"I won't breathe a word." And he wouldn't.

She sighed and her face paled.

"How bad is it? Is it just the ER?" he asked.

"A few departments, actually."

Gavin leaned against the wall. The last thing he wanted to do was uproot the girls, but the other hospitals weren't hiring attendings, and there was no way he was going to take up Moira's offer to put in a good word at her new workplace. Anyway, he'd burned his bridges with her after she'd walked out on their date.

"I'll give a speech."

Virginia relaxed. "Thank you. It means a lot to me."

"I'm doing it for the hospital, for all the people who depend on their jobs, but can you do one thing for me?"

"It depends," she said skeptically.

"Promise me you'll do it."

"I can't blindly promise, Gavin."

"Oh, but you expected me to blindly promise to speak at an event I don't agree with?" he snapped.

"You're an attending. It's your duty."

He snorted. "It's not my duty to watch the board try and make a bit of money by throwing away what little they have to try and save this hospital, by hosting some snooty benefit."

"Gavin, I really don't want to argue with you."

"Look, I just want you to tell my staff what's on the line. They know something is up and not knowing is stressing everyone out."

Virginia shook her head. "I can't tell, Gavin. They can't know. I can't afford to have some of my staff leave. Not just yet. You promised."

"That's unfair to them. To those who've given Bayview Grace their loyalty."

"My hands are tied."

"No. They're not."

"Don't you think letting them know that their jobs are on the line would be more detrimental to them?" Virginia's face turned crimson, her voice rising. Gavin had never seen her like this before but, frankly, at this moment he didn't care.

He was damn mad.

His staff deserved to know.

"Tell them."

"No, and you'd better keep your word to me that you won't either." She turned on her heel and stormed out of the exam room.

Gavin let her go and let out a string of profanities. He didn't want to fight with her. She was his equal and she rubbed him the wrong way, because she was just as pig-headed as he was.

Put yourself in her shoes.

Only at this moment he couldn't do that rationally. He didn't envy her her job or her position one bit, but the way he was feeling now, if he was chief of surgery he'd be warning his employees that this hospital was in danger.

He took a deep calming breath and then saw her logic.

If she did tell the staff, they'd all leave or not care any more about doing a good job, because what was the point if the hospital was doomed?

He was a jackass.

"Hey, I saw you were having some words with the ice queen," Dr. Jefferson said as he wandered into the exam room. "She was on a rampage, from what I saw. What did you say to her?"

"She's not an ice queen. Show some damn respect, Jefferson."

Jefferson frowned. "What has gotten into you?"

"Nothing."

"You're absolutely stressed."

You think? Only he didn't respond to him, he just paced back and forth, trying to calm his nerves. "Is there something in particular you wanted, Dr. Jefferson?"

"Yeah, there's been a major crash on Van Ness. A streetcar and a bus. All hospitals are being braced for trauma. We'll most likely be getting the less serious cases..."

Gavin didn't listen to him further. He pushed past Jefferson, grabbing a rubber gown from the closet and heading out the emergency doors. The moment he stepped outside onto the tarmac he could see a large billow of smoke to the west. Most likely from the accident.

The sound of sirens pierced the air.

He just hoped Virginia's decision to keep his staff in the dark was worth it, and he hoped they remained focused enough not to make any mistakes today.

CHAPTER THIRTEEN

"So, do you have a date?"

Virginia glanced up at Janice, who'd come into her office with a pile of files. "A what?"

Her lips twitched. "A date. You know, where you take someone out you're attracted to."

"No, I don't have a date."

Janice tsked. "I think the chief of surgery, who planned this event no less, should attend the gala with a hunky and gorgeous man on her arm."

Virginia shook her head. "This chief of surgery has been too busy trying to plan this gala and run a hospital to find a date."

"Well, I guess that's a good enough excuse." Janice dropped the pile of files on her desk with a flourish. "Your patient files to go over and report on. Records says you're behind on your reports."

Virginia groaned. "Can't you do it for me?"

Janice snorted. "Do I look like the doctor?"

"I'm not answering that on the grounds it might incriminate me." She grinned up at Janice, who looked unimpressed.

"However, if I was in your position I would be out wrastling me down some handsome hunk as eye candy for my arm."

"Thanks for the advice, Janice. I'll make a note of it."
She rubbed her temples.

"You could use a drink," Janice remarked as she left
the office.

I sure could.

Virginia checked her watch. It was almost seven in the
evening. She'd been at the hospital since four that morning.
Almost fifteen hours. It was then she realized how long
she'd been bent over her desk, planning a party.

Was this what she'd signed on for?

No.

She'd bought a beautiful dress yesterday. Royal blue,
but she hadn't gone out with anyone to get it, because she
didn't really have any girlfriends. There had been no one to
ooh and ahh over it. No one to tell her that her butt looked
too big or what shoes would go with it.

And now she'd be attending the gala alone. No one to
appreciate the dress, no one to dance with or make her
feel sexy.

She couldn't remember the last time she'd gone on a
date.

What about dinner with Gavin?

Her cheeks flushed at the memory of his kiss. The way
his hands had felt around her. The way his eyes had twinkled in devilment, but that hadn't been a date.

Had it?

Who was she kidding? It had been, but like most dates
she had, nothing had come of it. She and Gavin were
friends, or quasi-friends. She hadn't had a chance to speak
to him since she'd taken off Lily's cast and asked him to
do the speech.

She hadn't asked. She'd ordered him to and he'd asked
her to be up front with the staff, but she'd refused.

In her flurry of work Virginia had seen Gavin around
the hospital and she couldn't help but wonder what had

happened on that date with Moira Rogerson. Was he still seeing her? Before Moira had left it had been plain to everyone that Moira had had a thing for Gavin, and who could blame her really? Gavin was a handsome, accomplished and desirable man. Even if he was somewhat brusque.

Moira was a pretty woman and Virginia wondered if Gavin was interested in her.

A thought that irked her.

She had no claim on Gavin. He'd kissed her and she'd pushed him away. She'd made it clear that they could never be.

I have to get out of here.

Virginia closed her email and shut down her computer. She grabbed her purse and headed out. Janice had gone home for the evening, which was good because Virginia wasn't sure she could take any more teasing about "wrastling up" a man.

When she got outside she headed for her car and then stopped. There was a bar across the road. She'd never set foot in it but it looked like a respectable enough place.

What the hell?

She crossed the road and entered the bar. It was dark inside, even though it was still light outside for a quarter to eight. There were a few people in the bar, a couple playing darts, and she recognized a few people from the hospital, but they didn't acknowledge her and why would they? She was the ice queen of Bayview Grace.

Virginia took a seat at the bar.

"What'll it be?" the pretty blonde bartender asked.

"I honestly don't know."

She cocked an eyebrow. "Well, I've heard some strange things in here, but that's a first."

"Really?" Virginia asked. "I guess that fits as it's my first time in a bar."

"Wow." The young woman grinned. "You're a virgin, then."

Virginia noticed a couple of men down at the end of the bar perked up at the mention of the word "virgin."

"What would you recommend?" Virginia asked, changing the subject.

"How about a glass of wine? I have some nice local wines."

Virginia nodded and felt relieved. "That sounds good."

The bartender nodded. "I'll be right back with a nice red."

Virginia glanced around, not knowing where to look. There was a television over the bar, but it was on a sports channel and she had no interest in that.

"Here's a nice red from Napa." The bartender smiled at her brightly and set the glass down on a napkin. "I hope you enjoy it."

Virginia handed her some money. "I'm sure I will."

The bartender nodded and headed down to the other end of the bar. Virginia took a sip of her wine and read the labels on the bottles of liquor lining the back shelf.

"Now, I would've pegged you for more of a Shiraz type of girl." Gavin sat down on the barstool next to her.

"Fancy seeing you here."

He chuckled. "I could say the same about you."

Virginia shrugged her shoulders. "Janice suggested I should go out and have a drink. Among other things."

"Other things?" Gavin asked. "Now I'm intrigued."

"Janice likes her opinions, however inappropriate or personal, to be known."

"That's for sure."

"What'll it be, Dr. Brice?" the bartender asked.

"The usual, Tamara. Thanks."

Tamara the bartender nodded and pulled out and filled a glass with beer, setting it down in front of him.

"You come here often?"

Gavin nodded. "Lately. Rosalie is a lot like Janice. She felt I needed some release on my night off. Once a week for the last month I've been coming here. I have a beer and then head home."

"You've been coming here enough to know the bartender's name," Virginia remarked.

"See, that's the interpersonal skills I've been working on."

"Kimber in Trauma says you don't know her name yet."

"Who?"

"She says you call her 'Hello Kitty'."

Gavin laughed. "It's her scrubs. She wears a lot of scrubs that remind me of something Lily or Rose would be wearing. I like her, though, she's a good nurse."

"I like her too."

"Was she offended?" Gavin asked.

"You care?"

"Of course." He took a sip of his beer. "I need my staff on the top of their game. I want to prove to your board that the ER is worth saving."

Virginia's stomach knotted. "You haven't mentioned that to anyone?"

Gavin frowned. "Why would I? It's not my job to tell them their jobs are on the line."

Tension settled between them.

"No, you're right, it's not." Virginia set her wineglass down and stood. "I should really get going."

Gavin grabbed her arm. "Where are you going? You haven't even finished your wine."

"I came here to relax, Gavin. I don't want to talk about the hospital."

"I'm sorry. I didn't want to bring it up either. Don't go."

Virginia sat back down. "How is your speech coming along?"

"No work, remember?"

"Sorry." Virginia took a sip of wine. "It seems like work is all I have time for."

"That shouldn't be your priority, but who am I to talk?"

"How are the girls?" She'd missed them and it surprised her how often she thought about them.

"Good." She noticed tension there, something in the way he pursed his lips and the way his brow wrinkled. "Lily hasn't gotten into any more scrapes."

"I'm glad to hear it."

"Do you have a date yet?"

Virginia tried not to choke on the wine in her mouth. Had he just asked her what she thought he'd asked her?

"Pardon?"

"I asked you if you have a date for the benefit." Gavin watched her face for a reaction and he got the one he was expecting. Her eyes widened and pink crept up her neck to form a delectable little flush.

Virginia cleared her throat and began to fiddle with the stem of her wineglass. "I—I haven't had a chance to ask anyone."

Good.

"Neither have I, though I've been asked."

She looked up at him through her thick, dark eyelashes. "Oh, who asked you?"

"Does it matter?" he asked.

There was a flash of something which flitted across her face. Jealousy, perhaps. Gavin certainly hoped so.

"How nice for you."

"I'm not going with them, though."

Their gazes met. "Oh, why not?"

Gavin shrugged. "I'm not interested."

"She's pretty, smart, what's not to like?"

"Who are you talking about?"

"Moira Rogerson."

Gavin cocked an eyebrow. "Moira's left Bayview. I haven't seen her since that night I asked you to switch me to the night shift."

"Why? As I said, she's pretty, intelligent..."

Gavin grinned. "Are you trying to convince me to take Moira to the benefit?"

"Well, when all is said and done, it's someone to dance with."

"I don't dance." Gavin finished off his beer and signaled Tamara for another one.

"What's wrong with dancing?" Virginia asked.

"I don't know how to dance. Do you?"

"I do, in fact." She chuckled. "Don't look so shocked."

"And do you like dancing?" he asked.

"Of course. It's one of the perks of this upcoming benefit. I can't stand stuffy dinners but the dancing after the speeches should be quite enjoyable." Virginia smiled at him, making his blood heat. He loved it when she smiled at him, which wasn't very often.

"Then you should have a date."

Virginia groaned. "Not you too."

"Who's been bugging you to get a date?"

"Janice." Virginia snorted. "Something about being the chief, wrestling and arm candy."

Gavin chuckled. "Wrestling?"

"Her words, not mine." Virginia finished off her wine and set the glass down. "I really should go. I have a long day again tomorrow."

"I'll walk you out." Gavin dropped some money on the bar and walked outside with Virginia. The sun was finally setting in the west. It was brilliant, reflecting off the Golden Gate Bridge. Everything around them was warm and tranquil, but soon fall would be coming, though he'd been told that autumn in San Francisco didn't bring with it that fresh crispness as a lot of other places did.

When he'd first arrived a taxi driver had remarked that sometimes October was hotter than the summer.

He slipped his arm through hers and escorted her across the street, dodging a streetcar as they crossed the slow street.

Virginia pulled out her car keys. "Thanks for the company."

"You should come to the bar more often. It's a frequent haunt of staff members."

"I doubt they'd want the ice queen gracing the darkened doorway of their favorite watering hole, then."

"I wouldn't mind." Gavin cleared his throat. "The ice queen isn't such a harridan anymore."

Virginia blushed again and looked away. "I'll see you later, Gavin. Give my best to the girls." She turned to walk away but he stopped her again. "Is there something else I can help you with?"

"Go with me." His pulse was thundering between his ears.

"Pardon?" she asked, stunned.

"Be my date to the benefit."

"You're serious?"

Gavin nodded. "I am. You need a date, I need one and I can't think of someone I'd rather go with. I have a condition, though."

Virginia crossed her arms. "There's a condition to being my date? This I have to hear."

"Teach me to dance."

Virginia snorted and then laughed. "You're serious?"

"Well, I don't want to embarrass the chief of surgery by trying to whisk her around the dance floor with two left feet."

Her eyes narrowed. "You have a point, but I have to say I've never been asked out before and had to meet certain conditions."

"It's a date, but not really, you said yourself that you can't date someone you work with."

A strange look crossed her face and she appeared a bit disappointed. Just like he'd felt when she'd climbed into that cab after their dinner, but he wasn't doing this as revenge. Gavin wanted the blinders on Virginia to come off and see that it would be okay for them to date. He wanted to date her.

"You're right," she said, breaking the silence. "Of course."

"So is that a yes?"

"Perhaps." She grinned, a devious smile that made him cringe and wonder what he'd just got himself into. "I have a condition too, though."

"Are you in a position to demand conditions? I mean, I've had an offer."

Virginia punched him hard in the arm. "Hey, I can find a date."

"Okay, what's your condition?" Gavin rubbed his arm.

"I get to pick your tux."

"Tux?"

"It's a black-tie benefit. What were you going to wear?" There was apprehension in her voice.

"A nice suit."

Virginia rolled her eyes. "A tux and it'll be of my choosing. I'm not having you show up in your tuxedo shirt and jeans."

"Fine," Gavin agreed grudgingly. "So, do we have a deal?"

Virginia stuck out her hand. "We do."

Gavin took it, but pulled her close. "Since this is a deal on a sort of romantic notion, shouldn't we seal the deal in some other way?"

She was so close he could smell her perfume. Her body was flush against his, her lips soft, moist and beckoning.

"I think a handshake will do." Her voice was shaky as she took her hand back and stepped away. "Shall we go shopping for a tux after your next shift?"

"I'll check with Rosalie, but I'm sure it'll be fine."

Virginia nodded. "Good. Have a good evening, Gavin. I'll see you on Thursday morning."

Gavin watched her walk across the parking lot and he couldn't help but smile to himself. Sure, he'd manipulated her, but Virginia was a stubborn woman. She was a challenge and it'd been some time since he'd been challenged.

Now, if he could only deal with the other troubling aspect of his life and get the girls' grandparents off his case.

He let out a sigh and headed to his car.

Come hell or high water, he was going to get his life worked out.

One of these days.

CHAPTER FOURTEEN

"I FEEL RIDICULOUS," Gavin shouted from behind the curtain.

"I don't care." Virginia tried to suppress her laughter. "This is part of the deal." The salesman in the tuxedo rental shop shot her a weird glance from behind her, one he didn't think she'd see but which she saw clearly in the full-length mirror.

"I feel ridiculous."

"Shut up, you're just embarrassing yourself."

Gavin snorted and she laughed silently behind her hand. "I still don't understand what's wrong with my gray suit. It worked for other events I've attended in my career."

"It may have been fine for other events, but my benefit is black tie. It has to go off without a hitch." She paused and her stomach knotted as she tried not to think of the reason why her benefit had to go off without a problem.

The ER's head was on the chopping block.

She got up and wandered toward the curtain. "Are you going to let me see or do I have to come in there?"

"You could come in." And then he laughed from the other side of the curtain, which made Virginia's cheeks flush at the thought of him naked behind a thin curtain.

"I can get you a set of tails," she countered.

"No, thanks. I'm coming out."

Virginia stepped back as the curtain slid to one side. Gavin stepped out and her breath caught in her throat just a bit.

The black tuxedo suited him. Finally, she understood that expression "fits like a glove," because it was like the tuxedo had been made for him. It made her swoon, her stomach swirling with anticipation. He was a fine specimen.

"Well, how do I look?" Gavin straightened his collar a bit and turned. "Better than the scrubs?"

Much. Much better, was what she wanted to say. "You'll do."

He cocked an eyebrow. "Just do?"

"Well, I still think you should wear tails."

Gavin snorted. "No tails."

The salesclerk came over and took some measurements and Virginia watched, trying not to laugh. Gavin looked so unimpressed, but he looked so dashing. Like James Bond, but a more rugged Bond. Instead of the fancy British cars James Bond drove, this version of him drove a motorcycle.

"I'll get this order ready for you and you can change." The salesclerk rolled his eyes as he walked past Virginia.

"What did you do to the poor sales associate?"

Gavin grinned like a devil. "I coughed when he was doing my inner leg."

Virginia couldn't contain her laughter any more. "You're going to drive that poor man to drink."

Gavin shrugged. "I like having fun."

"Could've fooled me, the way you march around that ER."

His easy demeanor faded. "There's no time for frivolity there. If we relax even for a moment, a mistake might happen."

"I respect that kind of drive."

Gavin cocked an eyebrow. "It has nothing to do with drive, it's survival."

"Survival?"

"You've hinted in no uncertain terms that our department is poised to take the axe. We have to run like a well-oiled machine."

Virginia swallowed the lump that formed in her throat. "This benefit will change everything. If we raise enough money and get more investors on board, the ER won't close."

"Virginia, don't lie to me. The signs are on the wall. Mr. Schultz wants a private clinic to cater to the rich. He's just looking for an excuse to let the hammer fall."

She wanted to tell him he was wrong, but she couldn't because she'd thought the same thing more than once.

"Well, the tuxedo suits you. No pun intended." She hugged herself and walked away as he retreated back to the change room.

She wandered to the front window of the shop and watched the streetcars go by on Market Street. The light outside was getting dim and a fog bank was rolling in, but the fog bank was still high and wouldn't affect them as they were at the foot of San Francisco's many hills.

Gavin came out and paid his deposit and they walked outside together. The air was a bit nippy, but Virginia didn't mind this weather.

South Dakota, at this time of year, was a heck of a lot colder. She hadn't been back home in years. It was late September now and hunting season would be starting. De Smet was a sleepy town for the most part, except for the summer, when the Laura Ingalls Wilder pageants took over the town, and the fall, during hunting.

In a couple of months the temperature would drop and the snow would begin to fly and, boy, would it ever. The open vastness of the Dakota prairies would cause white-out conditions that rivaled those of Alaska and Canada.

San Francisco didn't get snow like that and for the first time in a long time she was missing it. They walked along Market and then headed uphill towards Union Square. The place where they'd met on their first date.

After that she'd sworn to herself she'd never let that happen again, yet here she was, walking with him back to that same place.

What am I doing?

"What're you thinking about?"

"Home," Virginia said.

"Where are you from again?"

"De Smet, South Dakota."

"Not far from Billings, where I grew up." He winked. "Although I've lived in many other places. My parents' jobs always forced Casey and I to be uprooted. I hated constantly moving around."

"Yet you worked with Border Free Physicians?"

"I liked what they represent and I didn't have a family I was uprooting. I would never move the girls. San Francisco is where I'll stay."

"Most army brats aren't so bitter about being moved around."

Gavin sighed. "My parents weren't very… They loved us, but their military careers were their priority and they weren't overly affectionate. Casey and I had no other family. I took care of my sister a lot."

"How did they die?"

"My father was killed in the line of duty the year I went away to college. My mother—my mother committed suicide a year later. She had undiagnosed post-traumatic stress from Iraq. My father's death caused her to snap. Casey was fresh out of high school and married the girls' father the year that happened."

"I'm sorry."

Gavin nodded. "Thanks. It was hard."

"I can understand your devotion to your nieces and wanting to give them that stability. I can see why Casey chose you over the girls' grandparents."

"Yes." Gavin's brow furrowed and she wondered if she'd touched a sore spot. "What about your family? Why haven't you gone home in a long time?"

Virginia hesitated. She never talked about her family to anyone. She didn't want people to know about where she came from. She'd made that mistake before and once people knew they judged her, and she didn't want that.

And she didn't go home because of Shyanne. Everything reminded her of Shyanne and it hurt too much, even after all this time.

The day Shyanne had died, a piece of her had died too.

"My parents live in a trailer, remember? There wouldn't be room for me to visit." Only her voice cracked with emotion she couldn't hold in.

"What's wrong?"

"It's too painful for me to go back."

They stopped in the square and she was glad for the bit of fog that rolled in as she blinked away the tears that were threatening to spill.

"What happened?" Gavin asked.

Virginia shook her head, but he wouldn't take no for an answer and he ushered her into a small café. The maître d' sat them in the back and Gavin ordered two coffees.

"What happened?" he asked again. "I've spilled some of my secrets so it's time for you to pay up."

She smiled, but barely. Her lips quivered slightly. "I'm a twin."

"Really?"

"Shyanne was my best friend, she was…" Virginia couldn't continue.

"How did she die?" Gavin asked, his voice gentle. His eyes kind.

"Ectopic pregnancy. Something so easy to take care of and diagnose, but I come from a very poor family. Shyanne got pregnant in the last year of high school. The guy took off and she didn't tell anyone because Dad couldn't afford health care insurance. He could barely afford to keep food on the table for the seven of us. Her tube ruptured and by the time they opened her up to do a salpingo-oophorectomy she was gone."

"I'm sorry. I'm surprised you didn't take up a job like I had, to help the underprivileged."

"Are you judging me now?" she snapped.

"No, I'm just curious."

"Who do you think pays for their health insurance now?" Virginia played with an empty packet of sweetener lying on the table. "Besides, my dad told me to get a job and work hard and keep it."

Gavin nodded. "I understand you a bit better."

Virginia snorted. "Should I be worried?"

"No, but I'm surprised your dad still doesn't have a job."

Virginia sighed. "He's disabled. He was a welder but was hurt on the job. He gets disability checks."

"So how many siblings do you have?"

"Two sisters left and two brothers. The sisters have moved out, but my two brothers are still in high school."

"Must've been nice, having a big family like that."

Virginia smiled. "It was. It is."

"Do you miss them?" he asked.

"I do, but I haven't been back since Shyanne died. Let me rephrase that. I tried once or twice, but it was too hard."

"Don't you get lonely around the holidays?"

"I could ask the same about you, Gavin."

Gavin gave her a half-smile. "It's hard to miss family when you're working."

"Exactly."

And that made Virginia a little sad. Kids and family had never been part of her plan, just working hard and making sure that she had a decent roof over her head and that none of her other siblings would have to die the way Shyanne had. That was what drove her.

She worked holidays and she didn't mind.

Holidays hadn't been extravagant when she was a child and she blocked most of her childhood memories, but one hit her.

Shyanne and her creeping out to the living room in the trailer to see if Santa had come, and that year he had. Their little stockings had had a bulge in the toe.

They'd curled up together on the couch, huddled together while a blizzard raged outside, and just watched the glow of the Christmas lights dancing off the old orange shag rug in the living room, waiting until everyone woke up in the morning and they could see what Santa had brought them.

Santa had brought her a toy pony, with pink hair.

She still had it in her apartment, packed away.

Last Christmas she'd run the ER and racked up a considerable amount of time in the OR. She'd been so happy.

Until she'd got the messages on her phone when she'd got home after a long shift at the hospital. Her mother begging her to come home, her mother wishing her a merry Christmas and telling her how much she missed her.

"Sorry for depressing you," Gavin said, breaking the silence as they finished their coffees. "Must be the fog."

"Must be."

"So, you said you were going to teach me how to dance?"

Virginia smiled. "I'm off tomorrow. I can stop by your place."

"The girls would be happy to see you."

"And I them."

Gavin grinned. "Good, it's a date, then."

"You weren't kidding. You seriously suck at dancing." Virginia winced as Gavin stepped on her toe again. Good thing they weren't wearing shoes. Even with the heels she had picked out for her dress, Gavin would still tower over her, which made her feel dainty. She was five ten and hardly ever met a man who towered over her.

"I'm good at head-banging if you put on some heavy metal." He moved away from her and selected a rock song from his music player, one that you couldn't dance to. At least, that's what she thought.

Virginia crossed her arms. "How am I supposed to teach you to dance to that?"

Gavin grinned and took a step towards her. "Maybe we should practice with a slow song?"

A lump formed in her throat, her mouth going dry, and he was just inches from her. She was suddenly very nervous about his arms around her, about being so close to him. They'd kissed, that memory was burned into her brain, but they were alone in the house, not out on the Embarcadero in public view.

His hands slipped around her waist, resting at the small of her back with a gentle touch, and he took her right hand in his left.

"I think this is correct?"

"Well, in proper ballroom dancing your right hand should be just below my shoulder blade."

"I like it where it is."

"You want to learn this properly, don't you?"

"My apologies, Ginger."

Virginia rolled her eyes and he slid his hand up her back. "Thank you."

"Where did you learn the proper stance for ballroom dancing?"

Virginia winked. "Google."

Gavin laughed and she began to lead him in a slow dance, but soon she wasn't leading and it was Gavin waltzing them around the room.

"I thought you said you didn't know how to dance?" she accused him.

"I have hidden depths, Dr. Potter." He grinned. "I don't know how to fast-dance, but I do know some of the basic slow-dance moves."

"And where did you learn these basic moves?"

"Junior high."

"Junior high, huh? So who was the girl?"

"You know me so well." Gavin winked. "Her name was Kirsten and I wanted to take her to the semi-formal and impress her with my mad skills. So I signed up for dance class, which was taught after school by the aging and venerable Ms. Ward, who smelled keenly like beef vegetable soup and heat rub."

Virginia laughed out loud. "And did Kirsten appreciate your efforts?"

Gavin sighed. "No, she decided to go to the semi-formal with Billy Sinclair."

"The hussy!"

Gavin laughed and then dipped her, bringing her back up slowly until their faces were just inches apart. Virginia's pulse thundered in her ears, being so close to his lips, so close but so far away.

"You're a fine dancer, Dr. Potter. A better teacher than Ms. Ward was, and you smell better too."

"I hope I don't smell like soup." She grinned and gazed up into his eyes, and her heart stuttered just briefly, being pressed so tight against him.

This was a dangerous position to be in.

"You smell a million times better." He touched her face, brushing his knuckles against her cheek and causing a shudder of anticipation to course through her.

Virginia braced herself for a kiss, one she wanted, one that she hadn't stopped thinking about for a long time, but he moved away when the front door opened. This was soon followed by loud shrieking and what sounded like a herd of wild elephants storming up the stairs.

They broke apart as Lily and Rose burst into the living room.

"Dr. Potter," Lily said with enthusiasm that matched the bright smile on her face.

Rose just waved but still didn't say anything.

Rosalie came up next. "Sorry, Dr. Brice. I didn't know you had company."

"No, it's okay, Rosalie. I should be going."

"Aww." Lily pouted. "Can't you stay for dinner tonight, Dr. Potter?"

Virginia glanced at Gavin and he shrugged his shoulders. "It's just hot dogs and hamburgers on the barbecue."

"Please stay, Dr. Potter," Lily begged.

"All right," Virginia said, capitulating. It had been some time since she'd had a real home-cooked barbecue.

Lily shouted her pleasure and Rose jumped up and down excitedly.

"Come, girls, let's get washed up for dinner." Rosalie ushered Lily and Rose from the room.

"Is there something I can help with?" Virginia asked.

"There's a plate of hamburgers and a package of hotdogs in the fridge. If you grab them, I'll get the grill heated up."

"Sure." Virginia made her way to the back of the house where the kitchen was. She opened the fridge and pulled out the hamburgers and hotdogs. As she bumped the fridge door shut with her hip a piece of paper fluttered down to the floor.

She cursed under her breath and set down the meat on the kitchen table so she could pick up the piece of paper.

Virginia glanced at it and did a double take when she saw it was a petition for custody. The girls' paternal grandparents, who were stationed in Japan, were suing Gavin for full custody of the girls. Or had. Virginia's stomach sank when she saw the judgment was attached and was momentarily relieved when she saw they'd been denied, but only on the grounds that Gavin had a good steady job in the girls' hometown and uprooting them would be cruel.

If that changed, according to the judgment, Gavin would lose custody of Lily and Rose. Virginia folded the paper up again, feeling guilty for prying. If Gavin had wanted to tell her this, he would've.

She placed it back on the top of the fridge and sank down in a nearby chair. His job was what kept the girls in his custody. If he lost it and had to uproot the girls, their grandparents would get them.

And his job depended on her, the benefit and her ability to keep Bayview Grace from turning into a private clinic. She couldn't bear it if she was responsible for Gavin losing the girls.

"Hey, the barbecue is ready," Gavin called through the open kitchen window. "Bring me those dogs, chief."

"I'll be right there." Virginia took a deep, calming breath and headed outside.

Lily and Rose were kicking a ball back and forth while Rosalie sat in a lawn chair with a glass of iced tea.

She handed Gavin the plate.

"Are you okay, Virginia?" he asked.

"What? Yes, I'm fine."

"You seem like you're in a bit of a daze."

"I'm okay. Really." She wandered over to the table and poured herself a glass of iced tea. The sun was setting, making the whole scene in the backyard glow with warmth. Virginia smiled. Everyone was so happy and she couldn't understand why the girls' grandparents would want to destroy this.

She would do everything in her power to convince the board not to close the ER. *It wouldn't be my fault.*

Only it would. She was Chief of Surgery.

There was no way she was going to be responsible for tearing apart this family. A family she desperately wished she was a part of.

CHAPTER FIFTEEN

VIRGINIA WAS STARING off into space again when her inbox pinged with a new email. She wasn't going to bother with it, except she saw it was from Boston General. An old colleague from her intern years was working there.

Out of curiosity she opened it and her breath caught in her throat when she realized it was a job offer.

It was for the head of their level-one trauma center. It wasn't Chief of Surgery, but the salary was good and there would be an extensive amount of research money at her disposal. Her friend had recommended her for the job. Boston General wanted her. They were impressed by how she'd managed to salvage Bayview Grace and it was a tempting, tempting offer.

And then guilt assuaged her. Her career path was secure, but Gavin's and those of the rest of the ER staff were not.

"You're still here?" Janice asked, barging into Virginia's office.

"Of course. Why wouldn't I be?"

Janice raised her eyebrows. "Have you seen the time?"

Virginia glanced at her phone and realized it was a quarter to three. "Darn." She was running late for her hair appointment. The benefit was tonight, the very benefit that was going to make or break this hospital.

"Thanks for the reminder, Janice." Virginia grabbed her purse.

"So, you still haven't told me what piece of hot man flesh you managed to wrangle up to take you to the benefit."

Virginia rolled her eyes. "Sometimes I think you take too many hormones."

Janice snorted. "Cheap shot, Ice Queen. Now, come on and spill the beans."

Virginia tried to suppress her smile. "Dr. Brice is accompanying me to the benefit."

"As in Dr. Gavin Brice?" Janice's mouth dropped open like a fish gasping for air. "You're joking, right?"

"No, I'm not. Dr. Brice is my date for tonight. Why is that so hard to believe?"

"I guess because of how many times he's been hauled into the principal's office." Then she grinned. "Perhaps that's *why* he has been."

Virginia shook her head. "I'm going to be late."

"Please, tell me you're wearing something drop-dead sexy."

"What is up with you?" Virginia asked as she put on her coat.

"Just living vicariously. Now, tell me about the dress."

"You're the one who told me I was going to be late."

"I guess I'll have to wait to see it tonight." Then she grinned, one of those grins like the Cheshire cat in *Alice in Wonderland* would give.

Virginia shook her head. "I'm going to send you for a tox screen. I swear sometimes you're dipping into the sauce."

Janice laughed. "Hey, as I said, just living vicariously. I'm glad for you."

"Glad?"

"I like you and I want to see you happy." Janice shrugged.

"Now, go on, get out of here and get all made up. Knock his socks off."

Virginia smiled and left. Janice may be all up in her business at the best of times, but the woman really was the closest thing she'd had to a friend since she'd become Chief of Surgery and the closest thing to an overbearing and overprotective mother since she'd moved out here.

The next shift of physicians was arriving. Physicians who were going to work the night shift while a lot of the department heads were at the benefit.

Virginia avoided making eye contact with anyone. She was tired of being stopped and asked questions about the future of Bayview Grace and whether this benefit would help.

As far as she was concerned, she didn't believe it would. She felt like she was delaying the inevitable, but the board was very keen on the idea and she knew it was for them. The rich investors who liked to have a good party. Having this benefit and raising money would make them feel good later when they dropped the axe on the trauma department of the hospital.

"*Que bueno,* Dr. Brice!"

"Yeah, you look handsome," Lily gushed. "And I bet she won't recognize you since you shaved off your scruffies."

Rosalie laughed and Rose grinned.

"Why are you laughing, Rosalie? Uncle Gavin's scruffies were weird and patchy. He looks good with a shaved face."

Gavin sighed and straightened the black bow tie. He felt like an overstuffed penguin in this tux, but when he'd tried it on, Virginia's face had flushed and he'd known she approved.

"I'm uncomfortable," he muttered.

"Of course you are, Dr. Brice, but just think how your *querida* will light up when she sees you."

"Dr. Potter is *not* my *querida*." Though he wanted her to be.

Rosalie cocked an eyebrow in disbelief. "Sure. Lily, don't you have a present for your uncle?"

"Right!" Lily leapt down from the bed and ran out of the room. Gavin heard the fridge door open and Lily came running back with two clear boxes and handed him one. "It's your boutonniere."

"My what?"

Rosalie stepped forward and took the box from him, opening it and then pinning the spray on his lapel. "I did this for my son when he was going to prom."

"I'm not going to prom," Gavin said. "It's a benefit."

Rosalie tsked under her breath. "Let them have their fun. They were so excited to buy you one."

Gavin felt a bit goofy with the small white carnation and spray of baby's breath pinned to his lapel, but overall he felt uncomfortable. He was used to jeans and a T-shirt, not this penguin suit. He glanced at Rose, who was sitting cross-legged on the floor in front of the full-length mirror.

"How do I look, Rose?"

Rose grinned and gave him a thumbs-up, before scrambling to her feet and leaving the room.

"I'll take that as a compliment," Gavin murmured. "What's the other box for?"

"It's for Dr. Potter," Lily said, holding it out. "It's a wristlet."

Gavin ruffled Lily's head. "Thanks, I'll tell her it's from you."

"No, you can't do that, Uncle Gavin. You have to tell her it's from you." Lily handed him the box. "You look worried."

"I'm a little worried that you're getting so excited about this. It's a work thing really."

"Don't worry, Dr. Brice. The girls just aren't used to you getting all dressed up and going out." Rosalie straightened his tie. "You look good. Go and have some fun. Don't come home until after your shift tomorrow."

"Fun is not something I'm planning on having."

Rosalie shook her head. "Dr. Potter is a very attractive woman."

Gavin cleared his throat and patted his jacket. "Shoot, have you seen some cue cards? My speech is written on there."

"On your dresser," Rosalie said. "Now, come, Lily, let's leave your uncle in peace to finish up and we'll watch for the limo."

"Limo?" Gavin asked. "I didn't order a limo."

Rosalie grinned deviously. "I know, Dr. Brice. You were going to pick up the chief of surgery in the minivan. I think not."

"Rosalie, you're going to be the death of me."

Rosalie just laughed and shut the door to the bedroom. Gavin let out a nervous breath he hadn't realized he'd been holding and smoothed down his hair again. His usual cowlick of hair wasn't standing on end. It was actually tame tonight. It was weird that he'd shaven off his "scruffies," as Lily so eloquently put it, but he wanted to make a good impression.

And not on the board.

Everything he was doing was for Virginia.

"The limo is here, Uncle Gavin!" Lily shouted down the hall.

"Thanks." Gavin picked up the wristlet Lily had picked out for Virginia. It was a bright bubblegum hue of pink.

Always pink.

The limo had better not be pink.

He said his quick goodbyes to the girls and headed outside, breathing a sigh of relief when he saw the limo was black. It was sleek and sophisticated. Even though he planned to give Rosalie a stern talking to for hiring a limo, he decided that it had been a smart thing to do.

He gave the driver Virginia's address and climbed into the back.

It was a short drive to Virginia's Nob Hill apartment and he realized he'd never been to her place before.

Her apartment was in a modern-looking building halfway up the steep hill. He pushed her buzzer.

"Who is it?"

"It's me. Gavin."

"Come on up."

The door unlocked and Gavin entered the lobby. Her apartment was on the third floor, so he didn't bother waiting for the elevator. Instead he took the stairs, trying to calm his nerves. Virginia's apartment was at the end of the hall. He took a deep breath and knocked.

Virginia opened the door and his breath was taken away at the sight of her. He'd known she was going to be dressed up, but he hadn't mentally prepared himself for what he was seeing. Her hair was swept up off her shoulders in a French twist at the back, but it wasn't the hairstyle that caught his attention. It was the creamy long neck that was exposed to him, thanks to the dress she was wearing.

The color was a deep royal blue, which set off her coloring perfectly. It was a one-shoulder dress, but it had lace across the shoulder and the bodice. There was beige fabric underneath to hide any nudity, but you couldn't tell there was fabric there. The intricate lace flowers looked like they were painted on her skin.

There were a few sequins that made the dress sparkle in the light. The dress hugged her curves, clinging to her in all the right places, and there was a slit up the left side, almost to her thigh.

Her legs were long, lean and he had a mental image for a brief moment of them wrapped around his waist.

His breath was literally taken away and he knew he wouldn't be able to mumble any two words together co-herently.

What he wanted to do was scoop her up and take her to the bedroom to show her just how much he liked her dress.

"How do I look?" she asked, and did a spin.

"Wow." It was all he managed to get out.

Virginia cocked an eyebrow. "Wow? That's it?"

"I—I don't know what else to say." *I could show you exactly what I think about you wearing that dress.* "You look stunning."

She blushed. "Thank you."

"The color is becoming."

Virginia gave him a strange look and then shut and locked her door. "So, should we take my car?"

"No, I have that taken care of."

Gavin held out his arm and she took it as they walked to the elevator.

"Well, I guess no one will see us arrive in the minivan."

Gavin snorted. "It's not the minivan."

"The motorcycle?" She frowned. "I don't want to ruin my hair."

He shook his head. "You'll see."

As they walked into the elevator she cocked her head to one side and then touched his face gently. "You shaved! I don't think I've ever seen you without…"

"Scruffies, as Lily calls them. Yes, she was quite im-pressed I'd shaved my scruffies off."

Virginia chuckled. "You do clean up nice, Gavin."

"As do you."

They rode the elevator down to the lobby and she gasped in surprise when she saw the limo. "Oh, Gavin. Wow."

"Now who's using wow?" he teased, and opened the door for her. As she climbed inside, Gavin caught another glimpse of her creamy-white leg and took another deep breath. He slid in beside her and shut the door.

"Can you take us to the Excelsior on Market, please?" Gavin asked.

"I will, sir, but I was told to take you on a small little drive first. There's some complimentary champagne in the bucket. We'll arrive at the Excelsior at six-thirty." The driver put up the privacy screen.

Gavin looked at Virginia apologetically. "Are we going to be late?"

She shook her head. "No, the happy hour is from six to seven and it's only five-thirty. Let's enjoy ourselves."

"Okay. Oh, but first I have something for you." He reached for the clear box. "I'm sorry, it's bright pink."

Virginia giggled. "The girls?"

"I'm not supposed to say. You don't have to wear it."

"No, I love it. Pink goes with blue." She held out her hand. "Besides, I didn't get to go to prom. This is fun."

Gavin opened the box and then slid the wristlet onto her, but before he let go of her hand he brought it up and pressed his lips against her knuckles.

"Gavin," she whispered. "You know…"

"I know." He knew her feelings on dating, but he couldn't help himself. He was falling in love with Virginia, in spite of everything. He'd never thought he'd feel this way about a woman, but he was falling head over heels for her.

"How about we have some of that champagne? It might take the edge off for your upcoming speech."

"Good idea." Gavin found the champagne and handed Virginia a flute. He popped the cork and poured them both a glass. "To a successful benefit tonight."

"Cheers."

He hated champagne, preferring beer, but he downed it
as quickly as he could. He wanted the alcohol to numb him
from the nervousness he felt about his upcoming speech,
about the security of his job at Bayview Grace, and to keep
him from pressing Virginia down against the leather seat
and taking her, like he desperately wanted to.

Tonight was going to be a long night.

The limo driver took them up the long figure-eight
length of Twin Peaks Boulevard. Gavin didn't really enjoy
the twisting and turning. They were gripping the seat of
the limo tightly, jostling back and forth from the drive up
the Eureka North Peak.

"Whose idea was this?" Virginia asked.

"Most likely Lily's. She said Casey used to speed up
this hill and it was like being on a roller coaster."

Virginia chuckled. "I can see why."

One sharp turn caused her to slide across the seat and
fall against his chest, her hand landing right between his
legs.

"Gavin, I'm so sorry." She moved. "I wasn't expecting
such a sharp turn."

"Don't apologize. I understand." What he wanted to tell
her was he didn't mind in the slightest. It was nice having her so close, even if her hand had landed dangerously
close to possibly injuring him.

The limo driver took them to Christmas Tree Point,
which had the best vantage point over the entire city and
the bay. The driver got out and opened the doors. Gavin
grabbed the champagne glasses as Virginia wandered over
to the railing. The wind, surprisingly, was not strong and
there was no fog rolling from the Pacific to obstruct the
view.

There was a breeze and it whipped at Virginia's dress,
making it swirl and ripple like deep blue waves. A smile

was on her face and she sighed as he handed her a full glass of champagne.

"Whatever happens tonight with the benefit, you should be proud. It's quite a feat for a prairie girl."

She grinned and took a sip of her champagne. "Lily's idea was good. You'll have to mention it to her."

Gavin chuckled and moved closer. "I will."

"I love this view." She sighed again. "So different from vast prairie."

"I've been through South Dakota, there are some rolling hills."

"The Wessington Hills. Yes, to the west, but where I come from it's just prairie. Don't get me wrong, I love it but I think I love this more."

Gavin leaned on the railing. "It is quite beautiful. I can see why my sister chose to settle here."

"Have you ever been up here before?" Virginia asked.

"No, this is my first time." He straightened and took her empty glass from her, setting it down on a bench so he could cup her face. "I'm glad I could share it with you."

"Me too," she whispered. Her cheeks were rosy and he wasn't sure if it was the nip in the air, the champagne or whether she was feeling something for him.

Gavin hoped it was the latter.

He tipped her chin so she was forced to look at him. Her eyes were sparkling in the fading sunlight. The sun was going down behind her, giving her the appearance that she was glowing.

"Gavin..."

"I know what you're going to say."

"You do?"

He nodded. "I do, but I'm going to do it anyway."

Before she could interrupt him again he kissed her, gently. Though it took all his strength to hold back the passion he was feeling for her right now. There was something so right and perfect about this kiss and he hoped it wasn't going to end up as badly as the first one had.

Virginia moved in closer, her hand touching his cheek and then sliding around to the nape of his neck, her fingers tangling in his hair. It made his blood heat.

He wanted her. Right here. Right now.

Virginia broke off the kiss and leaned her forehead against his. "I think—I think it would be wise if we head back downtown."

Gavin nodded and fought the desire coursing through him. "You're probably right."

She grinned, her eyes still twinkling. "I know I'm right. You're a dangerous man, Gavin." Then she blushed again and moved past him towards the limo. The driver, who'd discreetly returned to the driver's seat while they'd been making out, jumped out and opened the door for Virginia.

Gavin watched her climb back into the limo, catching just a glimpse of her bare leg through the slit in her dress.

What does she mean by saying I'm a dangerous man?

A grin broke across his face as he thought about the possibilities, but the one that excited him most was that he affected her just as much as she affected him.

He wanted her. More than that, he was almost sure that he was falling in love with her. Maybe he wasn't the only dangerous individual here tonight.

Virginia was just as dangerous as he was.

CHAPTER SIXTEEN

VIRGINIA COULDN'T TAKE her eyes off Gavin. When she walked in on his arm, she saw the looks of envy and admiration from the other women in the room. Gavin cleaned up nicely. She liked him all rough and rugged, but she liked him this way too, in a tuxedo, looking svelte.

When Virginia caught Janice's eye from across the room, Janice winked and gave her a thumbs-up, which made Virginia blush, but Janice was right. Gavin was a fine specimen and it was taking all her strength not to jump into his arms like some kind of teenage girl.

And that kiss up on Christmas Tree Point was burned into her lips. And into her mind. And it was all she could do to keep her wits about her. All she wanted to do was drag Gavin out of the room and have her way with him.

Which shocked her.

Get a hold of yourself.

Instead, she made sure they were mingling, that they weren't alone together, and she was pleasantly surprised at how charming and affable he was to the board members and investors. Even Mrs. Greenly, who'd nearly been trampled by Gavin on a gurney just a couple of months ago, was conversing with him and then checking him out when he wasn't looking.

Though she couldn't blame Mrs. Greenly one bit.

Gavin looked so fine.

He was up on the stage now, talking to the board about his work and how important trauma medicine was to Bayview Grace, but Virginia couldn't make out a word. All she heard were muffled sounds like Charlie Brown's teachers would make on the old cartoon specials.

It has to be the champagne.

The stuff they'd had in the limo was top-end champagne and she'd had a couple of glasses. Well, more than a couple. She'd had four and she was feeling happy at the moment. Not drunk, just relaxed. She hadn't planned on drinking so much before the benefit, but being trapped in that limo with Gavin as they'd gone on a little scenic drive up the twin peaks had been more than Virginia could handle.

The whole time she'd just wished that the driver would make himself scarce so they could make out in the backseat. Like teenagers.

She'd fallen in love with Gavin. She didn't know when or how, she just realized it now, but she really didn't have any chance with him because every time he'd tried with her, she'd shot him down.

The sensible side of her, the chief of surgery side, had turned him down flat.

As long as they worked at Bayview Grace and she was chief, there was no way they could date.

Unless she took that job, but that new job was across the country and Gavin had already stated he wasn't going to uproot the girls and she didn't blame him one bit.

There was applause and Virginia realized the speech had come to an end. She clapped in enthusiasm and moved up on the stage to give her little spiel and thank the people who had spoken this evening.

Gavin passed her on the stairs and flashed her an encouraging smile, one that made her knees knock together and her blood heat.

She only hoped no one would see her blush up on stage.

"Thank you, Dr. Brice, for your impassioned speech about trauma care at Bayview Grace. I want to thank all my esteemed colleagues for taking time out of your hectic schedules and speaking here tonight about our hospital. I also want to thank the board of directors and their guests. Bayview Grace runs on the generosity of caring individuals such as yourselves. Our hospital has come a long way in the two short years I've been Chief of Surgery and I know with your continued support we can go much further. The dance floor is being cleared and our band is ready. Please, enjoy your evening here and thank you all again." Virginia smiled and acknowledged the applause as she left the stage.

"You're very good at PR, Dr. Potter," Gavin teased as she took a seat beside him.

"It's all part of the job." They were alone at the table, as everyone was getting up to mix and mingle as the band warmed up.

"Do you enjoy it, though, or would you prefer to be in surgery?"

"That's not a fair question, Gavin."

He cocked an eyebrow. "Why not?"

"I like being Chief of Surgery," she stated, and only because no one else was sitting at their table at that moment. "I would like it even more if I had more OR time. Are you happy?"

Gavin grinned. "Very."

"I find that hard to believe."

"Why?" he asked.

"Because you're not off trekking around the world. You made it very clear to me several times you'd rather be anywhere but here."

Gavin hung his head in defeat. "That was before."

"Before what?"

Gavin opened his mouth to say something else but Mr.

Schultz approached the table. "Excellent speech, Dr. Brice. I didn't think you had it in you."

Gavin plastered a fake smile across his face. "Neither did I, Mr. Schultz. If you'll excuse me for a moment, I think I'll check on the girls."

Virginia watched Gavin leave the room and wished she could go with him, but Mr. Schultz took his empty seat.

"You did a fine job, Dr. Potter."

"Thank you."

Mr. Schultz sighed. "I hope you'll be able to do the same when we transform Bayview Grace into a private hospital."

Virginia's stomach knotted. "You can't have made the decision already—we haven't even tallied any of the donations and the silent auction isn't even finished."

Mr. Schultz shrugged and downed the glass of Scotch he had in his hand. "The board wants what it wants."

"I think you'll be pleasantly surprised by what we achieve tonight, Mr. Schultz."

He gave her a petulant smile. "We'll see, Dr. Potter. We'll see."

Virginia shot him figurative daggers as he got up and left to schmooze with some rich potential investors.

She was annoyed.

Mr. Schultz didn't care how much money they brought in. In his eyes, the ER was deadweight and he wanted it gone.

A private hospital specializing in plastics and sports medicine would bring in so much more money and all Mr. Schultz saw was the dollar signs. He didn't care about the poor people on the street who came into the ER every day.

Those without insurance or funds to pay for the medical help they needed. Like Shyanne.

What am I doing?

Having a good job and security was one thing, but not living by your principles was another. If the ER closed, she would quit. There was nothing else for it. There was no way she could work at a private hospital, treating only the privileged few. That's not why she'd become a doctor and she couldn't help but wonder when her course in life had left that path.

"Are you all right? You look a little pale." Gavin sat down and then poured her a glass of water from the carafe. "Here, have a drink."

"Thanks. It's a bit hot in here." She took a sip of the water, but the lump in her throat made it hard to swallow.

The band started up by playing an old rock ballad from the eighties. One she'd always liked as a child.

"Come on." Gavin took her hand and pulled her to her feet. "Let's dance. You look tense."

Virginia didn't argue as he pulled her out onto the dance floor. Only he didn't hold her in the proper stance she'd lectured him about only a couple of nights ago. His hand rested in the small of her back and this time she didn't argue. She liked the feeling of his strong hand there, guiding her across the dance floor.

"What's wrong?" he asked.

"I told you, it's the crush of people. I'm not good with large crowds."

"You live in the city," he teased.

"I grew up on the prairies." She laughed. "It's so silly."

Gavin shook his head. "No, it's not."

"And you're used to a mad crush."

"I traveled across India by train, remember? This is nothing compared to that."

Virginia shuddered. "I wouldn't like that."

"I wouldn't let you do that. Not dressed the way you are." He leaned in close, his hot breath fanning her neck. "You look good enough to devour."

Her pulse quickened. "Devour?"

"Yes, it's what I've been fighting all evening."

"The urge to d-devour me?" Her voice caught in her throat. Even though she shouldn't press it further, she wanted to. Badly. "Tell me how."

Gavin moaned and held her tighter, her body flush against his. She could feel every hard contour of his chest through their clothes and she wondered what it would be like to feel nothing between them. What it would be like if they were skin to skin, joined as one? The thought made her knees tremble and her stomach swirl with anticipation.

"I would take out the pins in your hair so I could run my fingers through it." The words were whispered close to her ear, making her skin break out in gooseflesh. "Then I would kiss you. I want to taste your lips again."

Virginia closed her eyes and recalled the way his lips had felt pressed against hers. She wanted him. What did she have to lose?

"Go on," she urged.

"Virginia, I don't think I can. Not in decent company." He pulled her tighter and she felt the evidence of his arousal pressed against her hip.

"Come on." Virginia moved away and pulled him off the dance floor.

"Where are we going?"

"I was offered a gratis suite for booking the function at the hotel." She pulled out the key card the hotel had given her this morning when she'd finalized details. Virginia swiped it in the elevator and then glanced nervously at Gavin.

"Are you sure?" he asked.

Virginia kissed him then, showing him exactly how sure she was. She was tired of being alone and for once she wanted to live a little. Take a chance, and Gavin was worth the risk.

The elevator doors opened, but they didn't break their kiss. She just dragged him in, letting her fingers tangle in the hair at the nape of his neck. His tongue pushed past her lips, twining with hers.

The elevator doors opened with a ding and they broke off their kiss. Virginia was glad no one was waiting on the other side, but even that wouldn't have stopped her from her present course.

"Which way?" Gavin asked, his voice husky and deep, rumbling from his chest.

Virginia took his hand and led him down the hall to the suite. She swiped the keycard and opened the door, but before she could cross the threshold Gavin scooped her up in his arms, claiming her mouth again. He kicked the door shut with his heel.

The room was dark, except for the thin beam of city lights through the blackout curtains. Gavin set her down on the floor, her knees back against the edge of the bed. It made her feel nervous, but exhilarated her all the same. It felt like the first time all over again.

If only it was. Her first time hadn't been all that memorable and the guy hadn't made her feel the way Gavin was making her feel right now.

She wanted Gavin.

All of him.

She wanted him to possess her. For once she didn't want to be the boss and she was giving it all to him.

Gavin reached up and undid her hair from the twist, letting it fall against her shoulders. He ran his fingers through it.

"I've been longing to do this since you opened the door to your apartment and I saw you in that dress."

He kissed her again, just a light one, then he buried his face against her neck. His hot breath fanned against her skin, making goose pimples break out. A tingle raced down her spine and she let out a little sigh.

Air hit her back and she realized he was undoing the

zipper in the back of her dress. She shivered, from nerves and anticipation.

His lips captured hers in a kiss, his tongue twining with hers. Gavin's fingers brushed against her bare back before he trailed them up to slip the one shoulder off. Her dress pooled on the floor. All she was wearing now was her bustier, lace panties and heels.

It was so risqué.

It thrilled her. Virginia's heart was racing.

"God, you're beautiful. More beautiful than I imagined."

Virginia kicked her heels off and sat down on the bed. "Come here." And she reached out and pulled him down.

"You'll wrinkle my suit."

"I do hope so." She undid his bow tie and tossed it away. Then helped him take off his tuxedo jacket.

"No throwing that." He stood up, laying the jacket neatly on a chair, and began to undress for her. Her body was awash with flames of desire. She leaned back to watch as he peeled away the layers.

His chest was well-defined and bare. Then he toed off his shoes and socks before he undid his trousers, stepping out of them and hanging them over the chair as well. He was wearing tight boxer briefs and Virginia could see the evidence of his arousal.

Gavin approached the bed and Virginia pulled him until she was kneeling in front of him. His eyes sparkled in the dim room. "I wanted you the moment I saw you, Virginia."

"Even with all my nagging?"

Gavin moaned and then stole a kiss, his fingers tangling in her hair, pulling her closer. "Especially with the nagging."

"Me too," she whispered. Reaching for him, she dragged him into another kiss. His hands slipped down her back, the heat of his skin searing her flesh and making her body ache with desire. Gavin made quick work of her bustier.

Knowing that she was so exposed to Gavin sent a zing of desire through her. He cupped her breasts, kneading them. Virginia let out a throaty moan at the feel of his caresses against her sensitized skin.

Even though he was a surgeon, his hands were surprisingly calloused. Probably from all his years in Border Free Physicians.

Virginia ran her hands over his smooth, bare chest, before letting her fingers trail down to the waist of his boxers. He grabbed her wrists and held her there, before roughly pushing her down on the bed, pinning her as he leaned over her. He released her hands and pressed his body against hers, kissing her fervently.

"Virginia, you drive me wild."

She kissed him again, letting his tongue plunder her mouth. Her body was so ready for him.

Each time his fingers skimmed her flesh, her body ignited, and when his thumbs slid under the sides of her panties to tug them down, she went up in flames.

He pressed his lips against her breast, laving her nipple with his hot tongue. She arched her back, wanting more.

"You want me?" he asked huskily.

Make me burn, Gavin.

His hand moved down her body, between her legs. He began to stroke her, making her wet with need.

"I want to taste you. Everywhere."

Virginia didn't even have a chance to reply. His lips began to trail down over her body, across her stomach and down to the juncture of her thighs. When he began to kiss her there, she nearly lost it.

Instinctively, she began to grind her hips upward; her fingers slipping into his hair and holding him in place. She didn't want him to stop. Warmth spread through her body like a wildfire across the prairie.

She was so close to the edge, but she didn't want to topple over. She wanted him deep inside her.

"Hold on, darling."

Virginia moaned when he moved away. He pulled a condom out of his trouser pocket and put it on. She was relieved. Being with him had made her so addle-brained she'd completely forgotten it.

"I see you've planned for all contingencies," she teased.

"Honestly, I just remembered it was in there. Thank goodness, it is. It's a force of habit from my wilder days."

"I'm glad that's a habit you haven't broken."

"Damn straight. Now, where were we?"

He pressed Virginia against the pillows and settled between her thighs. Gavin shifted position and the tip of his shaft pressed against her folds. She wanted him to take her, to be his.

Even though she couldn't be.

He thrust quickly, filling her completely. She clutched his shoulders as he held still, stretching her. He was buried so deep inside her.

"I'm sorry, Virginia," he moaned, his eyes closed. "You feel so good." He surged forward and she met every one of his sure thrusts.

"So tight," he murmured again.

Gavin moved harder, faster. A coil of heat unfurled deep within her. Virginia arched her back as pleasure overtook her, her muscles tightening around him as she came. Gavin's thrusts became shallow and soon he joined her in a climax of his own.

He slipped out of her, falling beside her on the bed and collecting her up against him. She laid her hand on his chest, listening to his breathing.

"That was wonderful," she whispered.

"It was."

As Virginia lay beside Gavin in silence, the only sounds the city of San Francisco and his breathing, she couldn't help but wonder what she'd done. She'd made a foolish mistake. She'd slept with a fellow employee. Something on her no-no list, but right here, right now she didn't regret it.

This was where she wanted to be and for the first time in a long time she didn't care what happened to her job, and that thought terrified her.

CHAPTER SEVENTEEN

INCESSANT BUZZING WOKE him from his slumber. When Gavin opened his eyes a crack, the light from the rising sun filtered in through a gap between the hotel room's curtains, blinding him, and he winced. The buzzing continued and he reached over for his phone. He glanced at the clock. It was only five in the morning. It took him a few moments to focus enough to read the words.

"Large incoming trauma. Please report to hospital stat."

Damn.

He sent off a quick text to Rosalie about being called in for a trauma, but Rosalie wouldn't mind. She'd take the girls for the whole weekend, she'd said so last night.

It was as if Rosalie had known what was going to happen. He usually hated it when she was right, because she loved to lord it over him, but in this instance he didn't mind.

Not in the least.

Gavin placed his phone back on the nightstand and let out a groan. He rolled over and looked at Virginia, sleeping with her dark hair fanned out over the thick pillow. She looked so peaceful nestled amongst the feather pillows and the feather top. A tendril of her brown hair curled around her nipple and he groaned inwardly as he ran his knuckles gently over her arm.

He remembered every nuance of her. It would be burned

on his brain forever. Virginia had been so responsive in his arms.

So hot.

Being buried inside her had been like heaven. He hadn't realized how much he'd wanted her until he'd been joined with her.

When everything else had been pulled away and it had only been them.

Vulnerable. Naked.

Exposed.

Just thinking about her made his passion ignite again. He was so hard and ready for her. Gavin groaned and moved away.

As much as he wanted to spend the morning in bed with her, he couldn't.

A trauma was coming in. All part and parcel of being head of Trauma and he didn't want to give Mr. Schultz any more reason to close the ER.

He'd do anything to help Virginia and make her job easier.

He leaned over and pressed a light kiss against her forehead. Virginia stirred and opened her eyes, but just barely. There was a pink flush to her cheeks. She looked very warm and cozy.

"What time is it?" she mumbled.

"It's five. I have to go to the hospital." He kissed her bare shoulder, groaning inwardly again, not wanting to leave.

She sat up quickly. "What's wrong?"

"A trauma is coming in and they need all hands on deck." Gavin cupped her face and kissed her again. "I'm sure if they need the chief of surgery, they'll page you. For now, why don't you just lie back and rest?"

Virginia snorted. "As if. If there's a trauma coming in, I'll be there."

Gavin watched as she scrambled out of bed, the sheet

wrapped around her. "You know, you don't have to be so coy with me in the morning. Not after last night."

Virginia's cheeks flushed pink. "It was dark last night."

"You're a prude." He winked.

"Not at all." Then, as if to prove her point, she dropped the sheet, showing off every inch of her naked body to him.

Gavin's sex stirred and he groaned. "You're killing me."

"You're the one who called me a prude." She slipped on her lace panties and then pulled on her dress. "Are you going to just lie there with a trauma coming in?"

"Turn around."

"Now who's the prude?" she asked, teasing him.

"Fine." He stood up and her eyes widened at the sight of him, naked and aroused. Her blush deepened and she turned away.

"A little warning would've been nice."

"I warned you." He waggled his eyebrows when she glanced back at him.

"Get dressed and I'll meet you downstairs." She grinned at him as she collected her purse and left the room.

Gavin quickly pulled on the necessary components of his tux and carried the rest. Virginia was downstairs and was just finishing with the check-out.

A cab was hailed by the doorman and they slid in the back together. The atmosphere became tense and Gavin couldn't figure out why, but Virginia was barely glancing at him and she was sitting ramrod straight almost right against the opposite door.

"Are you okay?"

"Fine," she said, but there was a nervous edge to her voice.

"What changed between the hotel room and here?"

"The taxi driver." Virginia winked and then she lowered her voice. "Last night was wonderful, Gavin, but right now there's a huge trauma coming in and we need all our wits about us."

"I think coffee is in order. I didn't get much sleep last night."

The cab driver smirked in the front seat and Virginia shot him a warning look.

"This is me being a prude again. Seriously, we can't have people gossiping."

He was tempted to say, "Who the heck cares?", but he didn't. He knew Virginia as the chief of surgery had a professional image to keep up.

"Okay, you have my word. I'll be good...for now." And then he snatched her hand and kissed it.

Virginia smiled and touched his face. "Your scruffies are back."

Gavin laughed. "Well, I didn't have time to shave."

When the cab driver pulled up to the emergency room doors at Bayview Grace there were already four ambulances pulled up out front.

"Go," Virginia said. "I'll take care of this. I have to swing around to the front to change. You'd better change into scrubs too. That's a rental."

Gavin nodded and jumped out of the cab. He ran into the emergency room and headed straight for the locker rooms. He peeled off his tux, jammed it into his locker and pulled out a fresh set of scrubs and his running shoes.

Once he was suitably dressed he headed back out into the fray.

"What do we got, people?" he shouted over the din.

"Multi-vehicle accident on the freeway." Kimber, the charge nurse on duty, handed him a clipboard. "The less critical cases are being sent here as the nearest hospital is full up."

Gavin nodded. A gurney was coming in and he ran to catch up to the paramedics. "Status?"

"Jennifer Coi, age thirty, was a restrained driver in a multi-car pileup. Vitals are good, but she's complaining of tenderness over the abdomen and pain in her neck."

"Take her to pod one," Gavin ordered.

He glanced around the emergency room, which was humming with activity. This was nothing as traumatic as the other hospital was probably getting, but he couldn't see how the board could or would close this department down.

Bayview Grace's ER was needed in this end of the city. Only truly heartless, greedy people would shut it down. He shuddered because that was the impression he got from Edwin Schultz. Greedy. If that man had been a cartoon character, he'd have permanent dollar signs in his eyes.

Dollar signs Gavin wanted to smack off his face.

Lives mattered more than the almighty dollar. That was what he'd learned in the field. Only more dollars would've brought better medicine to a lot of those developing countries.

It was a vicious cycle.

Focus.

Gavin shook those thoughts from his head. There was no time to think about budgets and politics. Right now, Mrs. Coi was his priority.

Life over limb.

Mrs. Coi needed him to be alert and in the game.

This was why he'd become a doctor, to save lives.

This was all that mattered to him.

Before he ducked into pod one to deal with his patient he caught sight of Virginia coming from the direction of her office, in scrubs and with her hair hastily tied back, examining individuals on the beds in the main room. They hadn't paged her and she could've just stayed in bed, but she'd jumped into the fray without complaint.

It was just one more thing he loved about her.

Mrs. Coi's condition was a lot worse than original triage at the accident site had indicated. Her spleen had been on the verge of rupturing, so Gavin and Dr. Jefferson had wheeled her into emergency surgery.

Gavin had got to the woman just in the nick of time. He'd removed her spleen and was now closing up.

"How was the benefit last night?" Jefferson asked as they worked over Mrs. Coi. The question shocked him. He was not one for idle chitchat in the operating room.

"It went really well." He cleared his throat. "Why?"

"I heard your speech was something to hear, that's all," Jefferson said offhandedly.

"Clamp." He held out his hand and the scrub nurse handed it to him. "I don't know about that."

Jefferson's eyebrows rose. "I've heard nothing but great things about your speech, Gavin. I only wish *I* could've been there to hear it personally."

Gavin just shot him a look of disbelief as he really couldn't frown his disapproval behind a surgical mask. He wasn't going to get into this with him.

"More suction, please, Dr. Jefferson."

Jefferson suctioned around the artery and Gavin began to close the layers.

"I did hear something very interesting last night, though." The way he'd said "something very interesting" made Gavin's hackles rise.

What had he heard? Had anyone seen him and Virginia going to the elevator or had someone seen them this morning, leaving in a cab together?

"Did you?" He was hoping his tone conveyed that he

wasn't in the least bit interested in pursuing this topic of conversation.

"Yes, according to Janice, the ice queen is leaving Bayview Grace."

"What?" Gavin paused in mid-suturing. "Sorry. Dr. Potter is leaving Bayview Grace?"

Jefferson's eyes narrowed. "Dr. Brice, are you going to continue to close?"

He shook his head. "Yes, but continue what you heard. I'm all ears."

"Ice Queen was offered a job at some fancy Boston hospital. They're offering her a huge salary and lots of research grants. It's also a level-one trauma center."

Gavin's stomach dropped to the soles of his feet and his head began to swim. How many times had Virginia reiterated that her career was important to her? Her job was everything, and if a Boston hospital was offering her a heck of a lot more, why would she stay?

Maybe that's why she seduced me.

That thought angered him, but it made sense. She'd constantly rebuffed him, telling him they couldn't be in a relationship because she was essentially his boss, but last night she'd been the one to drag him upstairs to the room.

The one who'd kissed him. She'd been the one who'd wanted him last night. Oh, he'd wanted it too, but he hadn't been going to press her. He hadn't wanted to scare her off, especially after how she'd made it so clear that they couldn't be together in that way.

"Did she accept the job?"

"I don't know, but I heard Janice talking about it to another nurse last night. Janice was gushing to anyone who would listen about how proud she was of Dr. Potter and how she was going to miss her." Jefferson snorted. "Well, I'm not going to miss the ice queen. Good riddance, as far as I'm concerned."

Gavin gritted his teeth and took a deep calming breath, because he was suturing up the subcutaneous layer and because he didn't want Jefferson or any of the other staff to know this news affected him.

Only it did.

After what they'd shared last night, Gavin was positive something was going to come of it, but if she was going to move to Boston…

You don't know that. It's all hearsay.

"Would you finish closing for me, Dr. Jefferson?"

"Of course, Dr. Brice."

Jefferson took over the suturing and Gavin left the operating room. He tossed his gloves in the medical waste and jammed his scrub gown in the laundry basket. After he'd finished scrubbing out he headed straight for Virginia's office, hoping she'd be there.

What Jefferson was saying could be just idle prattle. The only one who could confirm it was Virginia. He hoped it was just a rumor.

He hoped she hadn't just slept with him because he was one last fling and that it was okay to have sex with him because she was going to leave Bayview Grace and San Francisco.

There was no way he could go to Boston. He wasn't going to uproot his nieces on the off chance Virginia wanted more from him.

And he wasn't going to go through another custody battle with their grandparents. The only reason he'd won the last one had been because he planned to remain in San Francisco and give them the stability Casey had so desperately wanted for them.

Gavin wasn't going to risk all of that for idle gossip, or for someone who'd just used him. Who didn't really want him.

Janice wasn't at her desk, but he could see that Virginia was in her office, bent over her desk and working on files.

He didn't knock, he just barged in. She looked up at him, momentarily surprised, but then grinned. "Gavin, I heard you were in surgery for a ruptured spleen. How did it go?"

"It went fine," he snapped.

"Is something wrong?" Virginia frowned and set down her file.

"Are you taking that job in Boston or what?"

Virginia's mouth dropped open. "What're you talking about?"

Gavin shut her office door. "I heard you were offered a nice job in Boston. One with lots of nice research funding."

She frowned. "Where did you hear that?"

"Dr. Jefferson."

"And how did Dr. Jefferson find out?"

Gavin's stomach twisted. "So it's true. You've been offered a position."

"I'm not going to deny it, so yes. Yes, I have, and it's a very nice offer."

Gavin crossed his arms. "I see."

"A friend recommended me for an opening."

"So it's a good offer?"

"Yes," Virginia said. "It's tempting."

"Did you accept?"

Her mouth opened and she was about to answer but her office phone rang. "Dr. Potter speaking. Yes, Mr. Schultz. Of course, I'll be up momentarily."

"The board?"

"Yes, they want to meet with me." Virginia didn't look at him as she picked up her white lab coat and slipped it over her scrubs. "I have to go, Gavin. Can we talk about this later?"

"I think I have all the information I need."

Gavin left her office. She hadn't denied or confirmed anything, meaning that she probably was going to take the job and move across the country. He was angry at himself for letting her in when he'd known he shouldn't. Virginia was career driven, but mostly he was angry that he'd allowed the girls to get to know her.

And that rested solely with him. It was his fault and the guilt of allowing that to happen was eating him up inside.

"First off, Dr. Potter, we'd like to thank you for organizing such a great benefit last night. Even though it was a huge success, the investors still feel like their money would be better put to use if we turned Bayview Grace into a private clinic." Mr. Schultz gave her a pat on the back and then returned to his seat at the end of the long table. "We're cutting the trauma department. We've decided to turn the emergency room into a plastic day-surgery suite."

"Plastic day surgery?" she said.

"Botox and skin-tag removal. Clinics like that prove to be the most lucrative." Mr. Schultz grinned and started going on and on about his plans for turning her emergency room into a spa.

Botox and skin tags? Virginia had to repeat the words in her mind again because she couldn't get a grip on the reality of it.

Was that what her emergency room was being reduced to? Two years of hard work, late nights and sacrifice to salvage a wreck of a hospital, to bring it up to national standards, and it was all being wiped clean. Excised like a blemish on the face of San Francisco.

Virginia's heart sank, but she was also angry. She didn't know why she bothered wasting her time and wasting the time of all those surgeons who had given such excellent speeches. It had been an exercise in futility. Just like she'd feared it would be. "I see, and what other departments will be cut?"

"Just the emergency department. It's the one that bleeds the most money. We have people just wandering in off the streets and there's no guarantee that billing could track them down and get them to pay."

"And what of the staff in the trauma department?"

Mr. Schultz tented his fingers, the sunlight filtering through the slatted blinds reflecting against his shiny bald head, making him look like one of those evil villains from an old cartoon or an old James Bond movie. "They'll be given a generous severance package as per their contracts. We really don't have the spots for them. We're planning to recruit some of the top plastic surgeons in the country. We are aware you're primarily a trauma surgeon but we'd like you to stay on as Chief of Surgery."

Virginia closed her eyes and all she could see was Shyanne's face in her casket. She couldn't afford the health care she'd needed and it had cost her her life. Then she thought of Gavin and the girls. What would become of them?

She couldn't work for a hospital like this, for a board of directors who only wanted to help people who had the money to pay. Growing up in a poor family—well, she'd been a victim of such exclusivity before and she wasn't going to work for an employer who believed in it.

It went against everything her father had taught her, but she knew for the first time she was going to have to quit without the promise of another job, because she wasn't going to take that job in Boston either.

She wanted to stay in San Francisco with Gavin. Maybe she'd open up her own urgent-care clinic somewhere down in the Mission district, where she could give help to those who needed it. It frightened her, but also gave her a thrill.

"I'm sorry, Mr. Schultz, but I'm going to have to decline."

"Pardon?" he said. "What do you mean, decline?"

"I mean I'm quitting. I'll give you my six weeks' notice, but after that I'm done. I can't work for a private hospital."

Mr. Schultz shrugged. "Very well, but before you go you have to tell the trauma department what the board's decision is. We want the ER closed by the end of this week."

Virginia's stomach twisted. She'd never had to fire so many people in her life, but she had little choice. The axe was dropping on Bayview Grace and there was nothing she could do about it. "Fine, I'll tell them tomorrow. They're still dealing with a large trauma that has come in."

Mr. Schultz wrinkled his nose. "Yes, I'm aware of that."

Virginia nodded and left the boardroom. Mr. Schultz didn't thank her for her years of service, or anything else for that matter, and she didn't care. She never had liked the head of the board.

Janice was at her desk when Virginia returned and she looked anxious.

"Well, what's the word, Dr. Potter?" she asked in a hushed undertone.

Virginia just shook her head.

Janice's face paled. "No."

"I'm afraid so."

"When?" Janice asked, her voice barely more than a whisper.

"By the end of this week. I have to tell the staff tomorrow."

"That's—that's crappy."

"Your words, my sentiments."

"I'm sorry, Dr. Potter. Truly I am. I wouldn't wish that job on my worst enemy."

"Thanks, Janice." Virginia scrubbed her hand over her face, feeling emotionally drained and exhausted. She let out a long sigh. "If anyone wants me, I'll be in my office. I need some time to think."

"Speaking of enemies, Dr. Brice is in there. He's been waiting since you went up to your meeting. He looks quite agitated."

Virginia groaned inwardly. "Thanks, Janice." She opened the door and Gavin spun around to face her. He'd been looking out her window, the one that overlooked the garden courtyard.

"What did the board say?"

"If I tell you, you can't say anything to your staff until I make my announcement to them tomorrow. I mean it, Gavin."

His brow furrowed. "You can't be serious. After everything that happened last night, they're going to axe the trauma department?"

Virginia scrubbed her hand over her face. "Yes."

Gavin cursed under his breath. "You're going to tell the rest of the staff tomorrow?"

"Yes, everyone is being let go in that department. The board wants to start fresh and they want the budget to hire top-of-the-line plastic surgeons to come to Bayview Grace."

Gavin snorted. "Plastic surgeons?"

"They're going to turn the ER into a plastic day-clinic/spa thing."

"Just what the city needs, more botox clinics. Of all the stupid, moronic… It's just plain dumb. What a bunch of heartless money-mongers."

Virginia sat down in her chair, suddenly completely exhausted. "Your words, my thoughts exactly. I'm sorry this had to happen to you, Gavin. Hopefully, you won't lose custody of the girls."

"What?" he snapped, his eyes narrowed and flashing with anger. "What did you say?"

Virginia cursed inwardly, knowing she'd overstepped

her bounds by reading that document, but there was no going back now.

"The custody battle with the girls' grandparents. I saw the judgment stipulated that you had to remain in employment here in San Francisco or you could lose custody of the girls."

"How do you know that?" Gavin demanded, his voice rising in anger.

"I read the judgment."

"How dared you read that? That was private."

Virginia stood up. "It fell off the fridge and I picked it up. If you wanted to keep it private you shouldn't have left it in your kitchen, where anyone could see it."

"It doesn't matter where it was, that was none of your business."

Virginia pinched the bridge of her nose. "Why are you making such a big deal about it?"

"Because it was private. You're not part of my family or the girls'. You had no right to go prying."

"I'm sorry."

Gavin snorted. "Sorry doesn't cut it."

"I thought we meant something more to each other."

"Yeah, well, that was before your job offer in Boston and you prying into things you had no business to." Gavin strode across the room and opened the door. "I won't say a word to the staff, but I hope you enjoy the east coast, Dr. Potter."

"I'm not taking the job, Gavin. I want to stay in San Francisco."

"You should take that job in Boston. There's nothing left here for you." And with those parting words he slammed the door to her office and to her heart.

Virginia didn't sleep well. When she dragged herself into the hospital she saw that the notice was already taped to the ER's doors. Last night when they'd had a slow period she'd called Ambulance Dispatch and told them that Bayview Grace was closing its emergency room. Then she'd asked Security to lock all the doors and tape the notices up.

The nurses and doctors on duty had been dumbfounded.

When all the patients had left, she'd told them she'd speak to them in the morning when the morning shift came in.

She hadn't even gone home that night. Instead she spent the night on the couch in her office, but sleep hadn't come to her. Her mind had just kept racing. Two thoughts plagued her. The layoff speech and Gavin's dismissal of her.

"You should take that job in Boston. There is nothing for you here."

It had stunned her and broken her heart.

Why did I read that judgment?

She kept chastising herself over and over again. In the early hours of the morning she'd finally realized she had been in the wrong for reading the custody judgment, but Gavin had totally overreacted. He'd won the judgment. There was nothing to be ashamed about.

Closing her out and ending what they'd had was immature. Especially without giving her the benefit of an explanation.

She deserved to have her explanation heard after all they'd had.

What had they had?

That was the crux. There had been no firm commitment in their relationship. All they'd had was one night of wanton abandon and the odd pleasant discourse.

No. Not just the odd conversation. Virginia had thought at the very least they were friends. She didn't have many girlfriends, but from what she understood, friends gave friends the benefit of the doubt.

Virginia shook her head in the bathroom mirror and then finished brushing her teeth. She'd thought Gavin had at least been her friend, but apparently she'd been wrong.

It was just better for her when she had no connections. When it was just her and the pathetic cactus in her apartment.

Relationships were messy and needy. Virginia didn't have time for all this stuff.

Only she'd never felt more alive or happy as she had these past few weeks that she'd been with Gavin, and now it was all gone.

Janice knocked on the door and opened it. "Dr. Potter?"

Virginia rinsed her toothbrush and walked out of her office bathroom. "Yes, Janice."

"The trauma department staff are waiting for you in boardroom three." Janice gave her a weak smile and turned to leave, but then stopped and walked toward her.

"Is there something you need, Janice?" Virginia asked, confused by Janice's demure manner.

"I just wanted to tell you that I'm going to miss you, Dr. Potter. I've enjoyed working with you."

Virginia was confused. She hadn't told Janice about her decision to leave. She had been planning to tell her after she dealt with closing down the ER. She didn't want the trauma staff to think she was playing the martyr for them.

"Where did you hear that I was leaving?"

"Mr. Schultz asked me to post an advertisement for your position amongst the other senior attendings who are staying."

Virginia pinched the bridge of her nose. "I was going to tell you."

Janice nodded. "I know, and I understand why you were keeping it a secret, but now the staff know."

Virginia sighed and then two arms wrapped around her. It was Janice hugging her. Just that simple act of human contact caused Virginia to break down in tears. She'd never mourned her sister properly. She'd never had time, but even that was coming out of her.

It was like a dam had exploded and everything she was feeling, that she'd pent up inside for too long, came gushing out of her, washing her clean.

Janice just held her, patting her back and whispering soothing words to her. How everything was going to be okay and that she understood Virginia had to do it.

When the sobbing finally ceased, Janice let go of her firm grip on Virginia and smoothed back her hair.

"I know it's not my place, you being my boss and all, but I do think of you as a daughter, Virginia."

It was the first time Janice had really used her name. Virginia returned the wobbly smile. "Thanks, Janice."

"No, I mean it. I remember when you came in for your interview as a resident. You were so aloof and like a robot. That's where you earned the nickname Ice Queen. You displayed no emotions, no empathy, but these last couple of months…" Janice shook her head and smiled. "You're not an ice queen any more. You don't deserve that name. The Dr. Virginia Potter who first started here wouldn't be as compassionate about what she has to do now. I like you so much better this way and I'm really going to miss this woman."

"Janice, I don't think I can do this. I fought so hard to bring that department up to level-one standards and now I'm pulling the plug on it. The board signed a DNR and I'm unhooking it from life support."

Janice's brow furrowed. "That's the corniest thing you've ever said to me."

Virginia laughed and brushed away a few errant tears with the back of her hand. "Sorry, my brain is a little fried."

"I noticed, but something else is going on."

"I slept with Gavin."

Janice's eyes widened and then she nodded. "I thought so. The way he looks at you and the way you look at him. Look, I don't think he'll be angry at you, he'll understand why you have to lay him off. He's a bit of an ass and clueless when it comes to social interactions with the staff, but I don't think he's cold-hearted."

Tears stung Virginia's eyes again. "It's over; it was over before it really got started."

"I don't understand."

"Gavin overreacted to something I did and basically rejected me."

Janice cocked an eyebrow. "What did you do?"

"I can't say what it was. It was nothing bad. I just read something private that I shouldn't have. It fell off the fridge at his place and I picked it up and read it. He was livid."

Janice snorted. "Then he shouldn't have left it on the fridge. What is wrong with men? The next time I see him I'm going to give him a piece of my mind."

"No, don't do that," Virginia said. "Then he'll get angrier that I told someone about it. Just let it be. It was never meant to work out anyway. I can see that now."

"Okay," Janice said. "You know, you really look wiped."

"I didn't get much sleep last night and I feel like I've aged about ten years."

"You've got some deep shadows around your eyes. I'd put on some concealer if I were you." Janice winked. "It won't be smooth sailing today, I'm not going to lie to you, but don't let them bully you."

Virginia gave Janice a peck on the cheek. "Thanks."

"You're welcome." Janice opened the door and turned. "If you set up another practice somewhere I can be bought for the right amount of money and vacation time." Janice winked and left.

Virginia scrubbed her hand over her face and headed back to the bathroom. Her face was blotchy and red. Her eyes were bloodshot. She looked and felt like she was a hundred years old. She couldn't help but wonder how many gray hairs from this ordeal she was going to get.

At least it would soon be over. The ER doctors and staff would get their severance packages and they'd be gone.

All she would have to do was paperwork and tie up some loose ends. Then she could walk away from Bayview Grace.

And go where? She didn't know.

She had no interest in going to Boston.

She felt like she was in limbo and it terrified her.

Virginia splashed some water on her face and pulled her hair back into a ponytail. She held her head high when she left her office, Janice giving her an encouraging smile, which she appreciated immensely.

Shoulders back and head held high, Virginia.

Her hand paused on the knob of the boardroom door. She could hear the rumbling murmurs from those who were about to lose their jobs, through the door.

You can do this.

Steeling her resolve, she pushed open the door and stepped into the room. The large boardroom was full. All the seats were taken and there were several people standing along the walls. In the crowd she picked out Gavin right away. He was looking at her, but there was no warmth to his gaze.

It was like she was looking at a stranger. A cold, distant stranger, and that made her heart clench.

The room fell silent and every eye in that room was on her. She could feel them boring into her back. She walked up to the front of the room.

"I'm glad you could all make it. I want to discuss the reasons I closed down the emergency room last night. The board of Bayview Grace Hospital has decided to turn Bayview into a private hospital. One that doesn't have a trauma department."

"What?" someone shouted, and an explosion of angry voices began to talk amongst themselves and at her.

Virginia held up her hand. "I know. I understand your frustrations."

"But what about that benefit?" Kimber asked. "I don't understand. I heard that it went well."

Virginia nodded. "It did, Kimber, but the investors who signed on agree with the board's decision to turn this into a profitable private hospital."

"So what's going to happen to the ER?" Dr. Jefferson asked. "Is it just going to be wasted space?"

"It will be turned into a plastic surgery-day spa."

"What does that mean?" someone shouted angrily from the back.

"It doesn't matter what it means. It's done. The board is hiring plastic surgeons this minute and Dr. Watkinson from Plastics is being made head of that department."

"What's going to happen to us?" Kimber asked, her voice tiny in the din.

Virginia glanced at Gavin. His eyes looked hooded and dark from across the room, but then she saw a momentary glimmer of sympathy.

She looked at Kimber. "I'm afraid, effective immediately, you've all been made redundant here at Bayview Grace."

Kimber's face fell and she looked like she was on the verge of tears. Tears Virginia herself was trying to hold back. The angry voices increased, but she kept her focus on Kimber.

Or, as Gavin had referred to her, Hello Kitty. She was wearing those scrubs now. Virginia had always liked Kimber. She was one of the many staff Virginia liked and was sad to see go.

"Tomorrow you may all pick up your severance packages. You will each find a letter of recommendation from me."

"You tried, Dr. Potter," Kimber said.

Virginia paused as she tried to leave the room and met Kimber's gaze.

"We know how hard you worked to save our jobs."

Virginia glanced at the faces of her staff and, except for the odd irate doctor, all she saw was sympathy and compassion. Even gratitude for what she'd tried to do. It made tears well up in her eyes, but when she looked for affirmation from Gavin, the one person she cared about, she found none.

Gavin had left the room.

What did you expect?

Virginia then knew it was definitely over. He was done and so was she.

CHAPTER EIGHTEEN

Six weeks later

"YOU NEED TO get out of this funk, Dr. Brice," Rosalie chastised him. "You're seriously starting to depress me. I don't understand what you're so upset about. Your urgent care clinic is running smoothly and you have more hours now to spend with the girls."

Gavin sighed and poured himself another cup of coffee. She was right. He'd been in a funk since his *stupid* fight with Virginia.

He'd thought about calling her but hadn't. He'd been such an idiot.

"You're right, Rosalie. I'm sorry for bumming you out."

Rosalie *tsked* under her breath. "It's Dr. Potter, isn't it? Have you talked to her?"

"No. I haven't spoken to her since I was handed my severance package." Even then it hadn't been Virginia who'd handed him the severance package, it had been Janice, who'd given him the stink-eye when she did it.

"I still don't understand what happened." Rosalie shook her head. "I could've sworn that woman cared for you. I'm usually never wrong about these things."

"I overreacted. I was tired, emotionally drained and I overreacted. I blew my chance because of my temper." And then he proceeded to tell Rosalie the entire story of what had happened between him and Virginia the last time they'd spoken.

Rosalie let out a string of Spanish curses, all of which he was sure were aimed at him and were probably different words for idiot.

When her tirade subsided she crossed her arms over her ample bosom and glared at him. Her dark eyes were flinty. "You need to go and see her before she leaves San Francisco and you never see her again."

"She won't want to see me."

"Ah, you're so stubborn. It drives me crazy." Rosalie began to curse again and then marched over to him and pinched his cheek, shaking him hard. "You need to apologize to her. So what she read the judgment? She was right. You left it in a stupid place and, frankly, I think it meant she cared."

"She was offered a job in Boston and slept with me on the same night. Don't you find that suspicious?"

"No, I don't. I saw the way she looked at you and the way you looked at her. The job offer and you two finally getting together were just coincidences. I know she cared for you. It's just you're a man, you're *stupido*."

"*Stupido* I will take. You could've called me worse."

A smile cracked on Rosalie's lips. "Believe me, I want to."

Gavin groaned. "I miss her."

"So do I."

Rosalie let out a shriek and Gavin spun around, spilling coffee down the front of his shirt. Rose had climbed out of bed and was standing in the doorway of the kitchen. In her hand was Georgiana.

"Rose, what did you say?" Gavin asked as he knelt down in front of her.

"I miss Virginia." Then she gave Georgiana a little squeak right in his face. Gavin pulled his niece tight against him, hugging her. She'd spoken. The last time he'd heard her voice had been just before Casey's death.

"I want my mommy."

"I know you do, Rose."

It was the last thing she'd said. It had haunted him daily since she'd gone silent. He'd been worried she'd forget how to talk or, worse, that they'd forget what her voice sounded like.

The doctors called it selective mutism, but no matter what Gavin had done, he hadn't been able to coax Rose to talk.

Right now, her voice had a lilt of a thousand angels.

"I'm hungry and you're squishing me." She squirmed out of Gavin's arms and climbed up to the table.

"What do you want for breakfast, *querida*?" Rosalie asked through some choked sobs.

"Cereal."

"Then that's what you shall have." Rosalie covered her face with her hands and sobbed silently, her back to them, her shoulders shaking.

"What's wrong, Rosalie?" Rose asked. "Why are you sad?"

Rosalie laughed. Her voice was wobbly. "I'm not sad, *querida*. You make me so happy. Now, what kind of cereal?"

"Chocolate!" Rose's eyes twinkled as Rosalie grabbed a bowl and poured Rose a bowl of chocolate puffs.

Gavin brushed away a few of his own tears as he stood up.

Rose had made perfect sense and had stated the obvious. And Lily had been in a foul mood for a long time, as had he.

Virginia had brought a light to their lives. One he couldn't deny any more.

He'd never thought he'd find someone he wanted to settle down with, but then again he'd never thought he'd be raising children. When he'd pictured his life, he'd imagined that he'd be working until he died in some far-flung country.

Now that life was not one he wanted.

He wanted the stability that Casey had achieved. He wanted family and someone he loved to come home to.

He wanted Virginia.

"I'm going out."

Rosalie grinned. "Are you going where I think you're going?"

Gavin nodded. "Yeah, I'm going to go make things right."

Virginia worked her last shift at Bayview Grace in the evening, only because she didn't want to face Janice and all the others during the day. She didn't want them to see her cry. She tied up the loose ends she needed to in the peace and quiet of the night shift. There was no one in the trauma department. All of the staff were long gone.

Word about her leaving Bayview Grace was actually met, for the most part, with sorrow. No one wanted to see her go.

The board had hired Dr. Watkinson as their chief of surgery and he was already out ordering people around and making changes, all with Edwin Schultz's glowing affirmation.

Even though, technically, Virginia was still Chief of Surgery, she just let Dr. Watkinson have his way, because she'd emotionally disconnected herself from the hospital the moment she'd laid off all those employees.

Dr. Watkinson had hired some of them back, nurses he was fond of, but not everyone. Kimber, for instance, was gone. There was no smiling face down in the ER any more. No more "Hello Kitty" scrubs directing paramedics where to go.

Of course there was no ER.

And as she walked through it on her last day the scene with Mr. Jones and the board replayed in her mind and now she could laugh about it.

She could see it all so clearly. Gavin cracking that man's chest with such skill and precision. Not caring that the board and a handful of investors were watching with horror on their faces.

"Life over limb."

It was his motto and it was a good motto. Mr. Jones had survived.

Maybe if Shyanne had got herself to a hospital when she'd first started having shoulder pain she would've come across a trauma surgeon like Gavin and her life might have been spared by a simple operation. They just would've removed the fallopian tube.

Virginia sighed and left the ER. Heading back to her office, or rather Dr. Watkinson's office. When she got up there she could see him in her old office, measuring something.

She just shook her head.

Janice stood. "I couldn't keep him out of there a moment longer. I took your box and purse out. I figured you wouldn't want to go in there and talk to him."

"I appreciate that, Janice. I've talked to him enough this week about the job." Virginia rolled her eyes.

"What're you going to do now? I know you turned down that job in Boston."

Virginia shrugged. "I don't know. Maybe I'll open a private practice somewhere, but first things first. I'm going to go home and visit with my family."

"South Dakota?"

"Yep." Though it was not really home to her anymore.

San Francisco, Gavin and the girls felt like a real home to her, but that was all gone. She hadn't seen him in weeks. Not since the layoffs and their gazes had locked across the room. She'd thought she'd seen a glimmer of sympathy there, but she must've been wrong.

"How long have you been away?" Janice asked.

"I haven't been back there…" She hesitated like she always did when she came close to mentioning Shyanne. "I haven't been home since my sister died. It was too painful, but now I feel resolved. I feel like a huge weight has been lifted from my shoulders."

Janice hugged her. "I'm really going to miss you, Dr. Potter."

"I'm going to miss you too, Janice."

Janice nodded and smiled. "Don't worry. I won't make things easy on Dr. Watkinson." With the mischievous glint in Janice's eyes, Virginia was prone to believe her.

"Well, I'd better be going. I'm officially no longer an employee here." She handed over her hospital ID and key card. "I'd better leave and make this less painful. The exit interview was bad enough. Goodbye, Janice."

Virginia picked up her box of belongings. Throughout the week she'd taken larger items home. All that remained were the few things she'd needed to get her through until the end.

And now it was here.

As she walked through the halls of the hospital that had been her passion, the very center of her being for so long, she didn't feel sad.

When she stepped outside an unseasonably warm breeze caressed her face and she sighed.

She turned back, only once, and looked up at Bayview Grace, staring the hospital she'd tried to save. A few months ago she would've been sad to walk away, but now she just felt resolved to Bayview's fate. In retrospect there was nothing she could've done.

She'd done everything right.

She'd done her best.

She felt nervous that she didn't have a job yet, but she was sure she could find something in San Francisco. In the interim she'd booked a trip to return to De Smet and visit her family.

It was something that was long overdue; she had to put the ghost of her sister to rest.

And she wouldn't mind having the company of her large family in a confined space for a bit. It would be better than staring at the walls in her apartment. She hadn't realized how much she'd miss Gavin until he was gone.

She wasn't angry at him any more, she just missed him.

They were both too stubborn and settled in their ways to be together—at least, that's what she told herself.

Kids and a husband hadn't ever been in her original plans, but life could change in an instant. Something she'd learned from working in trauma her whole career, but she hadn't really understood it until Gavin Brice and his two nieces had come barging into her life.

The box under her arm was heavy and she shifted it, pulling out her car keys. With a sigh of resignation she turned around to head to her car and froze in her tracks.

Gavin was in the parking lot, leaning against his motorcycle and dressed in his leathers. He was parked right next to her sedan.

Her knees knocked with nervousness, while the rest of her body was excited to see him. She wanted to throw herself into his arms, but after his parting words to her she refrained from making such a fool of herself.

Instead she walked over to him, opened her car and shoved her box of belongings inside. "Hello, Dr. Brice."

"Dr. Potter," he acknowledged. "Coming off the night shift?"

"Yes."

"I'm glad it was the night shift. I didn't really relish waiting here all day."

"What are you doing here?"

Gavin took off his sunglasses. "I've come to apologize."

Her eyes widened in shock. She leaned against her car. "I'm listening."

"I'm sorry, I was just angry about losing my job and... well, I wasn't angry that you read that judgment. I was angrier about the fact that I could lose you."

"To the Boston job?"

"Yes, but by the time you told me you weren't taking it my temper had gotten away with me. I was an idiot."

A smile quirked her lips. "I agree with that."

Gavin chuckled. "I've been trying to apologize for a couple of weeks now. I just... As I said, I was an idiot."

"Yes, so you said. I'm sorry too, Gavin. I shouldn't have pried, but I care for you and the girls. So much."

"They care for you too. Rose said she missed you."

"What?" Virginia was stunned. "Rose spoke?"

Gavin nodded. "This morning. She said she misses you, and Lily has been in a foul mood for weeks."

A lump formed in Virginia's throat. "I miss them too. I never thought kids liked me too much and vice versa, but I do miss your girls."

Gavin took a step forward, taking her hands in his. "Is that all, just the girls?"

Her heart began to race. "I've missed you too, Gavin. So much."

He cupped her cheeks and kissed her. Virginia's knees went weak and she melted into him, her whole body feeling like gelatin, almost like the earth below her feet was shaking, but it wasn't an earthquake she was feeling. She was feeling relief, love and joy.

Gavin broke off the kiss and leaned his forehead against hers. "I've missed you, Virginia. I fought my feelings so many times. I didn't want to settle down, but I can't help it. I love you."

"I love you too, Gavin...against my better judgment," she teased.

He laughed and kissed her again, holding her tight against his body. "Why don't we head back to my place? We can come back for your car later. That is, unless you have any other plans?"

"No, nothing. Even though it terrifies me to the very core, I'm unemployed."

"I have an opening at my clinic."

Virginia cocked an eyebrow. "Your clinic?"

He nodded. "I took my severance money, got some investors and opened an urgent-care clinic not far from here. I hired as many staff members from Bayview's trauma as I could. Kimber is head nurse now!"

Virginia was pleased. "That's—that's wonderful. Kimber is an excellent nurse. What else do you have at your clinic?"

"We have an OR and can do most minor surgeries. I also have a generous enough budget to do pro bono work. So, what do you say? Would you like a job?"

This time Virginia kissed him. She couldn't remember the last time she'd felt so happy, so free. The job he was offering wouldn't pay as much as Bayview or the Boston hospital would, but she'd be doing a job that would help out people like Shyanne and that was worth its weight in gold.

"When do I start?"

"I'm headed there right now." Gavin handed her a helmet. "But you're just coming off the night shift."

Virginia took the helmet and jammed it on her head.

"I'm a surgeon. I'm ready. Although I will have to cancel my trip to De Smet next week."

"You were going to visit your family?"

"Yeah, but I can cancel it."

"No, you're going, and Lily and Rose could use a bit of a holiday. Don't they have a Laura Ingalls Wilder museum there?"

"They do."

"Then I think we should all take a trip out there."

"Are you sure? It'll be cold this time of year."

"Positive. I want to meet your family, because all I want is you, Virginia. Just you."

She wrapped her arms around his neck and kissed his scruffy face. "Did I tell you how much I love you and your scruffies?"

"Yes, but tell me again."

Virginia grinned and kissed him again. "So much."

Gavin nodded. "Ditto. Let's go check out your new job, Dr. Potter."

Virginia climbed onto the back of his motorcycle, wrapping her arms around his chest. "I'm ready, Dr. Brice."

And with him, she was. She was ready for anything.

* * * * *

RESISTING
HER EX'S TOUCH

BY
AMBER McKENZIE

Published in Great Britain 2014
by Mills & Boon, an imprint of Harlequin (UK) Limited,
Eton House, 18-24 Paradise Road, Richmond, Surrey, TW9 1SR

© 2014 Amber Whitford-McKenzie

ISBN: 978 0 263 90749 0

Harlequin (UK) Limited's policy is to use papers that are natural,
renewable and recyclable products and made from wood grown in
sustainable forests. The logging and manufacturing processes conform
to the legal environmental regulations of the country of origin.

Printed and bound in Spain
by Blackprint CPI, Barcelona

Dear Reader

It is my true belief that at the heart of every woman is a romantic. In some way or another we all envisage our hero, and the moments that will perhaps change our lives for ever. My parents, however, raised a very practical young woman who was taught from a very early age not to look for a hero to complete me, but instead to complement and enrich a life I had built for myself.

Throughout my prolonged fourteen years in post-secondary education I gained that partner, and a further respect for my parents' teaching. I have been privileged to have met and worked with some of the finest, most beautiful and most dedicated female physicians around. By the end of my training, when life was moving away from textbooks and on to ways to maintain a decent work/life balance, a spark began to burn.

As a lifelong reader of Harlequin Mills & Boon® I always had dreams of what I considered the perfect book. And then I realised. Who would be better heroines than my friends? Women who are gorgeous, smart and by all means successful, but maybe have some unconsidered challenges when it comes to finding love. Meet Kate, a combination of many of my friends, and aptly named as thirty per cent of my colleagues at one time were named Kate. Her story is completely original, though, featuring some of my most favourite romantic gestures—from emotional torment in the rain to forehead-kisses.

My debut novel, RESISTING HER EX'S TOUCH, is the first of hopefully many forays into the perfect romance. I hope that you fall in love and gain the same admiration that I have for the men and woman who devote their lives to the world of medicine.

Amber

There is nothing better in life than the people
who love and support you and inspire you to
be better than you ever thought you could be.
My love and gratitude to my mom Linda, my ultimate
best friend Jennie, and my amazing husband Kyle.

CHAPTER ONE

HER HEART POUNDED against her chest, keeping cadence with the rhythm her heeled boots made against the linoleum floor. She had everything to lose and little to no control over an outcome that was going to decide her future. Some people would take comfort in knowing they were in the right and hadn't done anything wrong, but not Dr. Kate Spence. She had learned early in life that bad things happened whether you deserved them or not.

She walked through the corridors of Boston General with reluctant determination. For the first time in five years she felt out of place in the hospital. She was used to being in her element, dressed in surgical scrubs with her entire focus on her job as a general surgery resident. Today was different. Every fiber of her being was on alert and she was conscious of waiting for the intense foreboding sensation that had come over her in the past several weeks to be fulfilled.

After years of school and sacrifice, Kate had almost made it. She had made it as a doctor, as a surgeon, and in three months' time would be starting a fellowship in New York, in one of the most acclaimed hospitals in the country. She had three months left of residency and then she was done in Boston and on her way to New York to complete her final training and have a second chance at a new beginning.

They had called it a strategy meeting, whatever that was supposed to mean. The only thing that had registered with Kate was that they were going to have to talk about "that night" and the guilt was overwhelming.

Kate took a deep breath and tried to gather her mind and her facial expression into that of the composed professional she was widely regarded as being. She was the chief resident of general surgery in one of the nation's top five surgical programs. She arrived at work no later than five-thirty every morning and was never home before seven—and that was on evenings when she got home, because most nights she stayed and operated. Being in the operating room, fixing people, had become her salvation in life. She loved the feeling of working meticulously at something, never knowing what challenges lay inside and pushing herself to overcome all the difficulties and limitations that could arise.

In a place where things could easily get out of control, Kate felt the most in control, confident in her ability to get the job done and do what was needed for her patient.

Kate pushed through the frosted glass door leading to the conference room and took in the scene. Sitting at the large wooden conference table were all of the expected people. The hospital's chief executive officer, lawyer, chief of staff, and Dr. Tate Reed, Vascular Surgeon, her co-defendant and ex-boyfriend as of six months ago.

She knew this wasn't going to be easy, but it still hurt more than she had prepared herself for. No one liked facing their own mistakes and Kate rarely made mistakes. She had taken an oath to do no harm and had promised herself years ago that she would never be responsible for causing someone she loved pain, and she hadn't until Tate. It had been six months and every day she regretted what had happened between them. She had never fallen in love with him and that horrible night she had been forced to accept that he wasn't the man for her no matter how hard she had tried to feel otherwise.

When she walked in, every face peered up at her with acknowledgement, except for one, who refused to acknowledge her presence.

"Good afternoon Dr. Spence, please take a seat," Dr. Williamson, the chief of staff instructed.

Then and only then did he look up and their eyes meet. The same combination of hurt and anger that had been there six months earlier stared back at her. The worst part was that she knew she deserved it. She felt every muscle in her face strain as she struggled to maintain a neutral expression and conceal the feelings of hurt and regret she felt every time she thought of Tate.

Kate walked towards one of the two empty places at the conference table, choosing the one farthest from Tate. She sat down in the leather chair and wished she could just keep sinking. She looked away and focused her gaze towards the other men, reminding herself that she needed to stay confident and collected. She was the only woman in a room full of the hospital's most prominent male leaders. There would be plenty of time for guilt and remorse to torture her thoughts later, without an audience.

Jeff Sutherland, the hospital's lawyer, started the meeting. "As you all know, four weeks ago Boston General, Dr. Reed, Dr. Spence and several other hospital personnel were served with a multimillion-dollar lawsuit for wrongful death on behalf of the Weber family. The lawsuit alleges that there was a critical delay in Mr. Weber reaching the operating room, which lead to his death, and that had he received more timely medical and surgical attention he could have survived his condition."

"They're wrong," Tate responded unequivocally.

Jeff looked up briefly, but continued. "In their affidavit, the Weber family alleges there was a twenty-minute delay and critical time lost between the diagnosis of Michael Weber's ruptured aortic aneurysm and Dr. Spence's ability to locate Dr. Reed and communicate the findings. Mr. Weber subsequently did not reach the operating room until fifty-five minutes following diagnosis, and by that time was so unstable that he did not survive attempts made by Dr. Reed to repair the aneurysm."

"He was never going to survive," Kate said. She replayed the images of the night in her mind, as she had a countless number of times. That night the happiness then the devastation, the genuine love, followed by pain and loss, had been heartbreaking. It had been the first and only time she had ever wanted out of a case, not to be in the operating room. Working across the table from Tate, knowing it was hopeless, knowing there was nothing left for Mr. Weber or for them. For the first time in her career she had felt like a coward because she hadn't been able to bring herself to confront Tate with the futility of their actions. She didn't know if it had been because of what had happened between them or if it had been because on that night she had been unable to bear the prospect of telling Mrs. Weber the man she loved was gone.

Dr. Williamson spoke. "Tate, I have reviewed this case, and in my medical opinion and in the opinion of this hospital you acted in an appropriate and timely manner in your complete care of Mr. Weber. His condition was such that even with immediate surgical intervention he was unlikely to have survived such an extensive rupture. Most vascular surgeons would not have even attempted surgical management, and unfortunately because you did you are now the target of the family's grief."

Kate exhaled for what felt like the first time since she

had entered the room, grateful for a small reprieve from the nightmare.

"Thank you, David. I appreciate your support," Tate replied.

She glanced up to look at Tate, her first instinct to share their sense of relief, but he wasn't looking at her. Her relief that the chief of staff was on their side quickly left her when she remembered there was no "their" any more and that had been her choice.

She focused her attention on the chief of staff, once again mentally trying to separate her professional and personal lives. The problem was that Tate had been both. Between the demands of the hospital and the need to study whenever she wasn't at the hospital she didn't have time for a social life, but Tate had come as the complete package. They had become colleagues, then friends, and eventually lovers. Everyone had thought they were a perfect match, everyone except Kate.

Kate was forced to refocus when Dr. Williamson began speaking again.

"Unfortunately, Tate, it is more than my opinion that counts in this matter. The Weber family has been able to document and produce several witnesses who verify a twenty-minute delay in your response to Kate's repeated attempts to make contact that night. It is this evidence that has led the family to believe they have a case, and despite several medical experts, who all agree that Mr. Weber's condition was medically and surgically futile, they are bent on having this matter argued in court."

Kate could not think of anything she wanted less and felt her stomach heave with the implications of a court hearing. The events of that night were completely entwined with every personal and private detail of her life. The thought of her personal life being discussed and examined in public, when she could barely face the details in private, was unfathomable. Kate had had six months to think about that night. Professionally, in her heart and her brain she knew that the delay had not caused Mr. Weber's death.

"In response to the legal action, the hospital has retained outside counsel to represent all parties named in the lawsuit," Jeff announced. Kate's defensive body language and Tate's unusual silence must have said more than words could express.

"Drs. Spence and Reed, this hospital expects your one hundred percent co-operation with our attorney and in all matters relating to this lawsuit," Quinn Sawyer, the chief executive officer, announced with finality. "I do not need to impress upon you the risk this hospital and your careers face if this does not go in our favor. I trust your personal relationship, whatever it may be, will not interfere with your ability to protect those interests."

"I no longer have a personal relationship with Dr. Spence."

An uncharacteristic flush burned up Kate's neck, coloring her entire face. She focused on the window, unable to face the humiliation of having her personal life referenced so openly among the most important men of the hospital. She had kept everything about her relationship with Tate private. She had never wanted anyone to think she was getting ahead by any means other than her natural surgical ability and strong work ethic, so it hurt and embarrassed her to think just how un-private things had become and what questions people would have about her now that the relationship had come to light, even if it no longer existed. She barely noticed the door open and close as she fought for control of her emotions.

"Mr. McKayne, I would like to introduce you to our senior management." Jeff's voice echoed in the background.

Kate felt her heart stop and then everything around her

seemed to be suspended in time. There was no way she could have heard that correctly and she quickly turned to the door, looking for reassurance.

In as long as it took for their eyes to make contact, Kate went from pink to white. She felt a sharp pain hit her chest and tasted bile in the back of her throat. She closed her eyes, hoping for someone different to be standing at the head of the table when she reopened them. Please, not him, anyone but him, she thought, but the man standing at the front of the room was the same. He had not changed in the past ten seconds and, for the most part, not in the past nine years.

Kate was vaguely aware of introductions being shared around the table. She was falling, her mind was in free fall, overwhelmed with flashes from the past and desperately trying to reconcile what was happening in the present. Nothing that was going on inside her was in her control.

"Dr. Spence."

"Kate."

"Katherine." It was Tate's voice biting out her name for the first time in months that brought her back to the table. Tate was staring at her with a new look of confusion. She had a well-earned reputation for being focused and unshakeable, even in the worst circumstances, until today. Everyone was standing and staring at her. She rose to her feet, praying her legs would support her, and turned to face the group.

"Dr. Kate Spence, this is Matthew McKayne. He will be representing you, Dr. Reed, and the hospital in this matter."

Kate turned towards Matt and saw that his hand was outstretched towards her. The gesture was appropriate in the circumstances but completely inappropriate given their past. She didn't want to shake his hand, look at him, or want any part of him in her life. Shock evolved into anger as she once again met the eyes of the one man she never wanted to see again.

Katie was still the most beautiful girl he had ever seen, though any hint of "girl" had been replaced by a very grown-up and striking woman. Matt struggled to keep his expression neutral as he studied her. She had always been taller than most women, with both a long body and legs to match. Her figure had changed. Gone was the softness from her body and from the expression on her face. The new "Kate" that was standing before him had more of an athletic build. Her legs appeared well toned beneath her fitted dress pants and her waist was more defined, making both her hips and breasts appear more prominent and sensual. Her light blue shirt was tucked in and the top two buttons were undone, only hinting at the curves underneath.

Discomfort tore through Matt's body as he remembered the old Katie and took in the sight of new Kate. Her hair appeared darker, like a rich dark chocolate, though he couldn't tell if her hair had changed or merely now appeared darker in comparison to her pale complexion. Her skin still appeared perfect, though, with the pattern of beauty marks he could have drawn from memory.

Then he met her eyes and whatever track his mind had been on, it was sharply derailed. Katie had changed a lot in the last nine years but his enjoyment of those changes was halted by the look in her eyes. It was the same look he had seen the day he'd left, the look that had tortured him for almost a decade.

"Dr. Spence," he greeted her, the formality of calling Katie by her full title necessary but awkward on his lips. She placed her hand in his and his hand wrapped around hers as though every muscle remembered the feel of her, before she snatched it away and sat back down at the table.

Everyone else followed and Matt took the last remaining chair. That chair was next to Kate, and with his first breath he smelled the familiar scent of her rosemary and mint shampoo, which brought back more memories than the sight of her had.

His position beside her spared him from the look in her eyes. He had known he had hurt her, badly, but he had never imagined that Katie could hate him and what that would feel like face-to-face for the first time.

"Mr. McKayne, Matt, Drs. Reed and Spence have been briefed regarding the details of the lawsuit. They are aware that this hospital and its medical staff are completely behind them and their actions. They are in turn willing to work with you and your team as much as needed to resolve this matter," the CEO stated. "They have been informed that we expect an honest, full disclosure regarding all the details of that evening, so that we can resolve this lawsuit for both the hospital and the Weber family."

Matt studied the other men at the table and his focus landed on Tate Reed. In turn Tate appeared to be studying both Matt and Kate with what appeared to be hostile curiosity. He wasn't the only person who seemed to have noticed the change in her since his arrival.

"We will leave you three to co-ordinate your schedules and work on your response. Matt, if there any difficulties, in any regard, I expect to hear about them sooner rather than later," the CEO remarked to Matt, with a message that was obviously more for Kate and Tate. The group of men left and the room fell silent.

Kate and Tate remained seated at the table. Tate was looking at the pair of them intently and Kate strongly refused to look at either man. "Do you two know each other?" Tate asked.

"No," Kate responded firmly, before he could even turn to see her response to the question. When he did turn to-

wards her, her back was straight, her head was high and she
was entirely focused on Tate, dismissing Matt completely.

Tate stood from his chair and for the first time since
he'd arrived, Matt took a long look at the man he was representing. Tate Reed was tall, similar in height to Matt's
six feet three inches. Where Matt had dark, thick hair and
the constant appearance of shadow along his jaw, Tate was
dark blond and clean-shaven. Tate was well built; if paired
against each other they would both probably be able to do a
significant amount of damage before a victor was declared.
Tate's green eyes appeared to similarly be evaluating Matt
before he turned his attention back to Kate.

"I wish I could believe you, Katherine." Tate spoke, and
the comment was directed only to her.

"Mr. McKayne, here is my card. I can be available to
meet you when you are ready to discuss the medical facts
of the case." He passed Matt the card and then shook his
hand with obvious strength and power in his grip.

When the two broke apart, he turned to Kate. "Katherine, try not to make things any worse for me than you
already have."

Tate left the room and Matt turned to look at Kate,
who was staring intently at the door Tate had just walked
through. Her gray eyes looked stricken and he felt equally
struck. He recognized that look in her eyes—it was one
that reflected her feelings of pain and love.

"Katie," he said softly a few moments later, his inherent
need to comfort her taking precedence over the jealousy
was that simmering inside him.

She flinched and turned to meet his eyes, not bothering to hide her fury. "Do not call me Katie. It's Kate or,
better yet, Dr. Spence."

"Not Katherine?" He couldn't resist it, his compassion
turning to jealousy and anger.

She stood from her chair and glared down at him. "I

meant what I said to Tate. I don't know you and I don't want to know you. I don't know what you were thinking when you came here today, but I don't need you or your help."

"I am not sure you have a choice in that. The hospital has hired me to defend you and Dr. Reed, who, in case you haven't noticed, doesn't care what happens to you, Katie," he delivered coldly from his chair, waiting to see if he hit his mark.

He watched her response. Her gray eyes widened, initially looking hurt, then narrowed. She straightened her back and drew her shoulders down to focus on him and he felt instant unease.

"Like I said, it's Kate, and I guess that makes two of you. The difference being that I care what happens to Tate and you can go to hell." She turned and walked out of the conference room, seemingly controlled, apart from the slamming of the door behind her.

Too late, Katie, or Kate, he thought, I'm already there.

CHAPTER TWO

SHE WANTED TO run. Run to escape the confines of the hospital and her professional reputation. Run until she was so exhausted that there was no chance of being able to think about the lawsuit, Tate, or Matt. Run as far and as hard as she could until the only pain she could feel was the burning in her lungs and the tightness in her chest and not the emptiness in her heart. As she entered the hospital hallway the only other thought in her head was how to get out of the building as quickly as possible without having to talk, see, or take care of anyone else. She needed to be alone, needed to gain control of her thoughts before she risked sharing them with anyone.

"Kate!" She looked up to see her best friend, Chloe Darcy, leaning against the hallway wall, waiting for her. Chloe had been her best friend since the first day of medical school when the two women had sat next to each other, and they had been constants in each other's lives since. Chloe had chosen emergency medicine and was almost as busy as Kate. The fact that the two women still found time for each other was a tribute to the strength of their relationship. When Kate reached Chloe she felt her friend's assessment. "Do you want to talk about it?"

"No," she replied, turning her head in dissent, her eyes shut against the scene that had just unfolded.

"Okay. Is there anything I can do to make it better?" Chloe offered, not pushing Kate, as usual. Kate couldn't help but smile at her best friend. Chloe was the most beautiful person Kate had ever known, both inside and out. When they had met in medical school Kate had been an emotional disaster and most of her classmates had not made the effort to befriend her, but not Chloe. She had sat by her side daily, never prying, never pushing, just being there for the little things, until Kate had realized that she had found a true friend.

With a sense of horror Kate felt her resolve begin to crumble. Kindness at that very moment had been enough to push her over the edge. Chloe read her friend perfectly.

"Kate, let's get you out of here before you ruin your macho surgical reputation." She felt her friend's strong grip on her arm as she led her down the hall. Moments later they were in the women's change room, away from at least half of the prying eyes that filled the hospital.

"Kate, I know how private you are but sometimes it does help to talk about things." Chloe spoke quietly, her voice intentionally no louder than necessary.

Kate stared back at Chloe and knew she could tell her anything. She wanted to pour out every thought and feeling inside her in the hope that the purge would rid her of the maelstrom of emotion tormenting her. But how could you explain to someone something you couldn't bring yourself to face? "I can't, Chloe, I just can't."

It was the truth. She couldn't explain what had happened, how she was feeling, what she was going to do, what she should do, and she couldn't talk about Matt and Tate without completely breaking what little of herself she felt she was still holding together.

Chloe stepped back and Kate could tell she wanted say something and was choosing her words carefully. "Kate, you are one of the strongest women I know and there is nothing you cannot do or overcome. You just need to remind yourself of that more often."

Perfection, thought Kate. Chloe was always perfect in her words and in her support and her friendship. At that moment Chloe felt like the only secure thing in her life and more than she deserved. "Thank you. You're not so bad yourself." She smiled weakly at the understatement.

"Keep that in mind, Kate. You can't keep living your life holding everything on the inside and hidden from those who love and care about you." It was the closest Chloe had ever come to confronting her and she recognized the truth and sentiment behind her friend's words.

"I know." Her acknowledgement surprised even herself. It was another truth to add to the avalanche rolling through her mind and threatening to bury her. "But I can't, not here and not tonight."

"I know, Kate. I knew it wasn't going to be easy for you to see him today and I don't expect you to change overnight."

Kate blanched. How did Chloe know about Matt? She had never talked about Matt to anyone.

Chloe noted her friend's pallor and lowered her voice even further to ensure complete privacy. "Kate, are you sure you are okay with Tate and I still being friends? You need to be honest with me and tell me if you're not."

Kate felt relief wash through her and then guilt for focusing on Matt and forgetting the significance of today's meeting with Tate. Chloe had been talking about Tate. There was no one other than she and Matt who knew about their past together. Matt was her past and even though he was forcing himself back into her present, what had happened between them was something she had never told anyone about, and she only hoped he had done the same.

Chloe was staring, waiting for a response, and she had to think hard to remember the question.

"Chloe, you are an amazing friend to me and to anyone else you decide to be friends with. If feeling worse about what happened with Tate was possible, thinking that I ruined your friendship with him would make it so."

She reached over and hugged her friend, trying to convey her emotions with the uncharacteristic action.

"I need to get out of here. Thank you, Chloe, for being my friend and knowing me better than I know myself sometimes."

"Always." Chloe smiled.

It was raining and she didn't care. She didn't even attempt to avoid puddles as she ran along the trail parallel to the Charles River. She let her feet strike the wet pavement as music blared in her ears and she tried to free herself from the memories that had been flooding her mind since the initial shock of seeing Matt again had worn off. The cold spring rain hit her face and blended with the warm tears that streamed from her eyes. Classic Kate, she chastised herself. Hold everything in as though nothing is wrong and then cry alone so no one can see that you are hurting, so no one thinks you are weak. The irony was that it made her feel even weaker.

As the miles passed she forced herself to accept that Matt McKayne was back in her life and she had no idea why or what he wanted. All she knew was that it was going to be hard, maybe impossible to be around Matt again. For their entire relationship she would have sworn that she knew Matt better than anyone else in the world. Then he had completely proved her wrong and now he was a familiar stranger. A stranger whose motivations and actions she couldn't predict and didn't understand. That alone terrified her, but not as much as the feelings she experienced, seeing and being near him again.

She could still describe every inch of Matt—except after today she couldn't tell if her mind had downplayed his features or if he had become even more beautiful in the intervening years. She hated it that she'd noticed, even in that brief time she had seen him. Hated it that when he'd sat next to her she had recognized his scent. But what she really hated was that when Matt had been sitting next to her, her body had remembered him in all the wrong ways. While the sharp pain in her chest had resurfaced, so had the flood of heat and spasms of attraction that had rippled through her body, the latter being responsible for her shortness of breath.

Even now in the cold rain she could still remember what is was like to be with Matt, and the combination of desire and pain associated with the memory kept her running.

She was being punished, that was the only conclusion she could settle on. This was karma because she had done to Tate what Matt had done to her, and now she was being served up the consequences. She could remember every second of their breakup, recognizing Tate's look of disbelief and hurt as the one she had worn after Matt had walked out on her. It felt hypocritical to feel this much anger towards Matt, knowing that she wasn't any better than he was, but it didn't matter. It didn't stop her from feeling like there was not enough air and that what was left of her heart was going to die. It didn't stop the desire to rip into his chest to confirm the heart she'd thought had loved her was not actually there.

She pushed forward, harder, resolving to herself that even though she had hurt Tate, at least the reason she had broken up with him was because it had been the right thing to do for Tate. Matt had broken her heart because it had been the right thing for Matt.

It was dark when Kate started to make her way home. Her apartment was a one-bedroom in a brownstone that had been divided up for rental. It was small and cheap, but it was one of her favorite places in the world. It was the place where no one put demands on her and she could let herself be who she needed to be and not what people expected of her.

Kate had spent a lot of time making her apartment the home she craved and needed. She had chosen the soft cream paint that adorned the walls. Over time she had saved and slowly put together the furniture that made her house a home. The antique wood that filled the space was precious both because of the money it had taken to purchase it and because of the time, her limited time, it had taken to find it at markets and small town shops nearby. Her favorite spot was the deep, wide, soft yellow couch that she probably slept on more than her bed. It was where she felt at peace and that thought propelled her forward to home as her body screamed at her to stop running.

The cold had finally started to set in as she rounded the final corner to her apartment. She knew her clothes were soaked through and she felt the squish of her feet in the watery soles of her shoes. All she could think of was a hot shower and curling up on her couch with her favorite charcoal throw, away from all the memories that were tormenting her.

She didn't see him in the darkness until she started up the brownstone's stairs. Her first reaction was fear at the sight of the large man tucked under the staircase awning out of the rain; her second thought was still one of fear when she recognized that man as Matt.

Stay away, her mind screamed at her. She refused to

acknowledge him as she reached the door and tried to free her key from inside the wristband she wore for running.

"Katie." He said her name, asking her with his tone to acknowledge him.

"I can't talk to you right now. You need to leave," she said, not looking at him and trying to focus on the task at hand.

"I'm not leaving, Kate," he replied with a firmness that left her little doubt of her inability to dismiss him.

"Yes, you can, and you did," she said flatly, staring ahead at the door and refusing to give him any more notice. She didn't trust herself to look at him so instead looked away. Her attention was drawn to her hands, which were shaking. Her whole body was shaking and the key, which she had managed to get out, dropped onto the concrete step.

"I'm cold," she declared, hoping he would believe that was the reason for the tremors that were starting to over-take her body.

He didn't reply. Before she had a chance, he bent down and picked up the key and used it to unlock the building's front door. He walked through and held the door open, waiting for her to follow. She didn't. She stood under the awning, staring at him with a sense of panic that was build-ing at the thought of him in her home.

"Kate, you are wet and probably freezing. Please, just come inside. I promise you can despise me just as much from in there." His new position in front of her forced her to look at him for the first time and she was immediately drawn to his face and eyes. She recognized his expression of concern and it brought her back to all the other times she had thought Matt cared for her. Familiarity propelled her forward.

Once she was inside the building, the warm air and

bright lighting brought Kate back to the present. Matt was tall and overpowering in the small entryway. His hair was damp and had started to curl slightly at the ends. The angle of his jaw and the rigid way he held his shoulders gave Kate some indication that he shared her tension. He had changed out of his business suit but was no less stunning in an open leather jacket and dark blue striped shirt that he had left untucked from the jeans, which hugged low on his hips. His sexual power was breathtaking, and she struggled to get her breath back and gain control of the situation.

Never before had she felt self-conscious about her running clothes. But at this moment she desperately wished to be wearing anything other than the black tights and fitted heather-blue base layer top that provided her protection from the cold, but no modesty, outlining every curve of her body. She crossed her arms across her chest and held out one palm.

"Keys?" she asked, trying to adopt the same tone she used in the operating room when calling for an instrument.

He didn't yield and her sense of discomfort was replaced by anger. "Not until I'm sure you are okay."

When had it started to matter whether she was okay or not? It hadn't mattered to Matt nine years ago, and even though she felt far from okay, she resented his concern.

"I'm not your responsibility, Matt. You don't get to worry about me," she ground out. She tilted her head upwards, trying to make up the six-inch difference in their height, and held his gaze.

"Easier said than done," he sighed, and started climbing the stairs towards the second floor. His long legs took the stairs two at a time and before she could react he was at the top.

Not in her home, she thought. Matt could not go into her

apartment, her home. It was her refuge, her place where no memories of Matt existed.

She reacted quickly to this thought, running up the stairs and without thinking, wedged herself between him and the apartment door. He wasn't ready for her movement and his body followed through on its planned course, causing him to fall against her.

She was pressed between Matt and the door, and she didn't know which one felt harder against her. She started to shake and felt warmth spread through her, his warmth. She could feel every contour of his chest through his open jacket, his shirt slowly dampening from her wet body. He instinctively widened his stance and braced himself with a hand on the door behind her to keep himself from falling any further forward into her. She ended up nestled between his legs, pelvis to pelvis, his upper body bracing over her.

Instinctively, she pressed into him and felt the hard ridge that was increasing in prominence. Beyond the slow roar that was filling her head she heard a small gasp but couldn't tell if it came from him or her. She wasn't sure how long they stood pressed against each other, until she felt him pull away at the same time he brought his forehead down to rest against hers, his eyes closed.

"Why?" he demanded quietly.

"Why what?" she whispered, confused and trying to block out the sense of loss his body's retreat had caused.

"Why don't you want me in your apartment? Is it about him? Is Tate Reed in there, waiting for you?" His voice was accusing, each new question seeming more condemning than the next. But he kept asking, not pausing, as though not wanting to hear her actual response.

Tate. Every warm enticing feeling she was having left her and she felt cold again as guilt washed over her. She tried to move even further back but felt the wood of the door against her. Tate loved her, Matt had never loved her, and she felt empty inside, thinking about both men.

"I'm not discussing my relationship with Tate with you and you have no right to ask me," she whispered, not being able to bring her voice above the intimacy his question had possessed but still containing the outrage she felt. "You need to leave."

He didn't reply. He simply lifted his forehead, replacing it with his lips. She felt both heat and memories surge through her before he backed away and pressed her key into her hand. She remained against the door as she watched him leave, not trusting herself to move until he was gone.

She wasn't sure how long she stood against the door even after he left. She felt like part of the wood, except for the small spot where her forehead burned with the memory of his soft lips pressed against her. It took hearing the beat of her shivering against the door to force her into action. She walked through the apartment in the dark, removing her clothes and leaving them in a wet trail behind her.

She stepped into the shower consumed by the cold inside and out. She had loved Matt then she had hated him, and now she had no idea how to feel. Part of her wanted to act out for the first time in her life and force him to tell her why. Why had he done it? But her instinct for self-preservation was stronger. No matter what she had told herself about why Matt had left, it would hurt more to hear him say it aloud. Seeing him today had not only brought out her anger but also unleashed every painful question and feeling of self-doubt she had tried to bury away and forget.

It took the water transitioning to cold before she thought of leaving the shower. She changed into scrub bottoms and a cotton tank top and ate the only thing she had the energy to prepare for supper— toast. It wasn't long before she was lying on the soft yellow couch cocooned within the gray blanket, trying to focus on her medical textbook and not the memories that kept replaying in her mind.

As a child she had been outgoing and bright, ready to tackle and succeed at every challenge presented to her. She had been fearless with the knowledge that her parents had always been behind her, supporting her and loving her. Then things had changed when she was eleven. Her mother had been diagnosed with breast cancer and for two years everything had focused on her mother and the disease. Kate had watched helplessly as nothing had worked, nothing had made things better, for her mother or her family.

She'd died when Kate was thirteen and from then on her family had no longer existed. She remembered one of their last moments together at the hospice. Her father had been sobbing and with what little energy she'd had her mother had stroked her hair and told her not to cry. And she hadn't.

Without her, Kate had felt lost, but not as lost as her father had. Kate's parents had been the loves of each other's lives, and without her mother Kate's dad had withdrawn from life and from his daughter. She had lost both parents, one to cancer and the other to depression, which as a thirteen-year-old she'd had no capacity to understand.

Kate's memories of middle and high school were not normal ones, something she had realized but didn't have time to care about. She spent those years trying to be the perfect daughter, student, homemaker, and friend to her dad, anything to make him happy, to make him come back to her. She hid every feeling of unhappiness and loneliness away, afraid that her pain would make her father worse and ruin what little they had together. She never discussed her mother and carried her grief alone. Every new womanly feeling or change she experienced she ignored, because it hurt too much to miss the mother she wanted to share those moments with.

Kate was terrified to graduate from high school, knowing that it meant she would have to leave home and her dad. It wasn't until she arrived at Brown University and had some time on her own that she realized how different she was from the other students, especially the other girls. They all seemed so beautiful and confident and, next to them, she felt completely inadequate and unprepared for life as a woman. She went home every weekend, not just to see her dad but also to escape the weekend social gatherings where she felt so out of place.

This eventually became a comfortable routine that lasted three years, until one weekend she came home and her dad introduced her to Julia. Her father had found love again and for the first time since her mother's death he was happy. Kate shared his happiness and at the same time felt her feelings of loneliness hit rock bottom.

Watching her father and Julia made her feel even more alone than she had before because they were together, a team, and she had no one. It was no longer necessary for her dad to be her focus in life, and she was now being forced to focus on herself and she didn't even know who she was or who she wanted to be. All her anxieties and feelings of inadequacy battered her every solitary moment while she continued to play the role of the perfect daughter, stepdaughter and student. Her dedication towards a career in medicine was her only life raft in the storm in which she found herself.

She met Matt three months later and her world changed. She had been studying at her favorite coffeehouse when she glanced up and saw the most attractive man she had ever seen in her life. The glance had easily turned into an irresistible stare. He was tall and broad shouldered with thick dark hair and piercing blue eyes. He was standing beside her table and it took her an embarrassing amount of time to acknowledge to herself that he was talking to her and to figure out what he had said. He asked to share her table, because it had an electrical outlet in the wall beside it for his laptop computer.

Previously, she would have just offered him the table, making some excuse as to why she needed to leave, but she was so drawn in by everything about him that she just managed to say yes and slide her own computer toward her to make space. He thanked her and while he started studying, her mind completely shifted, thinking only of him. He was perfection. His strong jaw was covered with a shadow of stubble that screamed masculinity to her. A gray T-shirt spanned his broad chest so that she could see the outline of every muscle group she had just been studying attentively in her textbook before he'd joined her. His shoulders led to muscular tanned arms and hands that were twice the size of hers. She could imagine the strength in his hands and what it would feel like to be held by him, to feel his jaw brush against hers, to press against his strong frame.

She started and blushed when his voice broke through her thoughts with an offer to buy her coffee. She barely managed to tell him her order without stammering, feeling completely stunned by the most outrageous thoughts she had ever had and insecure with her inexperience.

When he returned to the table with their drinks he didn't reopen his computer. He introduced himself and she was drawn in by the kindness and genuine interest she saw in his eyes. There was something about Matt that had made her feel instantly safe, and with that feeling grew the confidence she had been lacking. They spent the rest of the afternoon talking and Kate felt more important in those few hours than she had in years.

In the course of their conversation she learned about his long-distance girlfriend and on hearing that felt crushed and disappointed, but still intrigued by the man who already had someone special in his life and was still interested in her, even if she wasn't girlfriend material. The more they talked the more she liked him and the more she wanted him in her life, no matter what he had to offer.

And that was exactly what followed. At first they would see each other casually, both studying. Matt was pre-law and she was pre-med, which meant they studied a lot. She got used to him joining her on Saturday and Sunday afternoons at the coffee shop, and even had the confidence to join his table when he arrived there first. The only time she didn't see him was when he went back to New York for a weekend with his family and girlfriend, though he never talked about the visits and she didn't ask. They eventually started meeting outside of the coffee shop and beyond studying, until they were together several times a week and spoke on the phone daily.

It was hard for her to understand her feelings. Matt was her first university friend, her first male friend, and eventually her best friend. She didn't know how to sort out what she felt for him as her friend from what she assumed were normal feelings of attraction any woman would have in Matt's presence. Part of her was actually relieved to be having the same thoughts and feelings about a man that she had heard other women talking about; it made her feel normal.

One Saturday she didn't show up at the coffee shop, like she normally did. Even though they didn't have formal plans to meet, Matt came to her apartment early that afternoon to check on her and see why she had been absent from the routine they had perfected over months. She hadn't expected that. If she had she wouldn't have an-

swered the door. Instead she answered the door in jogging
pants and an oversized sweater, her face red and swollen
from hours of crying. He didn't let her turn him away and
on the eighth anniversary of her mother's death Kate allowed her emotions to show and cried in front of someone
else for the first time since her mother had died.

She couldn't have asked for more in Matt's response.
He held her until her tears subsided and then listened as
she talked about her parents and what she had lost. For the
first time her feelings didn't make her feel weak and helpless. Matt made her feel he understood in his responses
and desire to listen. They talked for hours and he discussed
his own father's death, which helped her feel normal and
less like the poor orphan she had perceived herself to be.
When she was finally spent of emotions and words, she
fell asleep on her couch, Matt still sitting at the end. She
could remember the strength of his arms around her as he
picked her up and carried her to her bed, the tenderness
and caring as he laid her down and covered her, and the
weight of his lips against her forehead as he kissed her
good-night. And her last thought as she drifted to sleep
was that she was in love with her best friend.

Kate woke to the darkness of the living room lit only by
the soft glow of the end table lamp. She struggled to adjust
her eyes to the lighting and the reality of her surroundings.
She wasn't in her old college apartment and the dreams
she'd had of her past had been just that, dreams, followed
by a harsh reality. She glanced over at the clock on the mi-
crowave—four o'clock in the morning. No hope of getting
back to sleep, she thought.

She stretched; her neck had a kink in it from falling
asleep on the arm of the couch and her legs ached from
pushing too hard on her run, but she was also acutely aware

of the deep ache and warmth in her pelvis. She could still feel the memory of Matt's lips against her forehead, his body pressed against hers, and the feel of him wanting her, both past and present. It made no sense. She cringed, thinking about the last time she had felt that need from him and the disaster and complete and utter devastation she had felt afterwards.

Anger overtook her as her feet hit the cold wooden floor and she walked towards her bedroom. She didn't want to remember every detail of their relationship and that night. She didn't want to still feel what it was like to be touched by him. She didn't want to still feel the pain of rejection and betrayal. She didn't want to feel anything for Matt McKayne.

CHAPTER THREE

THIRTY HOURS INTO her shift Kate's pager blared through her dictation as she described the detailed steps she had taken to resect the necrotic bowel and anastomose the viable segments. She paused in mid-sentence, her usual rhythm interrupted by the reminder tone that followed. She pressed the pager's recall button and the hospital switchboard extension flashed back at her.

Dread filled her. She was between surgical cases and had two consultations in the emergency department to review. One more interruption and there would be no chance of getting to the washroom between cases. She had long ago given up the hope of eating any time soon and sleep was like a mirage in the desert to her.

She signed off the dictation and dialed the digits she knew by heart.

"It's Dr. Spence from General Surgery. I have an outside call."

"Yes, Dr. Spence, I'll put him through."

"Kate, it's Matt, we need to talk." She had been correct with her feeling of dread. Years ago those words would have changed her world, but now they left her with a sense of foreboding.

"Why are you calling me?" The question didn't make sense as he had already stated his intentions, but it was the first thought that came to mind. Why? Why was he back?

He sighed and she sensed his impatience. Tough, she thought. "Kate, we need to discuss the details of the case, the sooner the better."

The case, of course he wanted to talk about the case. How could she have forgotten the lawsuit? It was threatening to destroy her career and now was wreaking havoc on her personal life as well. She had received notification from the New York Medical Board that her medical license for the state was on hold and would not be granted until the lawsuit was resolved. No license meant no hospital privileges, which meant no fellowship for Kate. Everything she had worked for was now in Matt's hands. Even with that in mind, she wasn't ready to face Matt again. She couldn't guarantee he would stick to the script of the present, and the past was too much to add to her fragile state of mind.

"I don't have any spare time, Matt." It was true.

"Make time, Kate, or I'll make it for you." It didn't sound like a threat, more like a fact, and something she knew he was capable of following through on. If they lost the lawsuit she was going to find it next to impossible to find employment anywhere else and she couldn't afford to burn her bridges with the hospital administration who had already warned her they expected her full co-operation.

"I'm not working this weekend." She dragged the words from herself like a confession.

"Let's meet Saturday afternoon. Do you have a preferred café you go to?"

No, she thought. There was no place she would prefer to meet with Matt. She needed to keep focused on what his new role was in her life, and the lawsuit. "We can use one of the hospital boardrooms." She had perfected her professional veneer within the hospital and if she had any hope of maintaining it with Matt, it would be here at the hospital.

"I'll see you Saturday at two. Goodbye, Kate." Such a simple word, but it wasn't goodbye.

Matt strode through the halls of Boston General on his way to meet Dr. Reed. Half of his attention was spent looking for Katie, Kate, the other half trying to decide whether he could truly represent Tate Reed. As a lawyer his job was to act in the best interests of his clients, but how could he do that for the man who had the one thing in life he wanted—Kate. One thing he did know, legally, if not personally, was that Tate and Kate were in this as a pair, and if he wanted to represent her then he had to agree to defend Tate Reed as well. And he needed to defend Kate.

Matt found the department of general surgery and made his way towards Tate's office. Along the wall of the main corridor hung the yearly photographs of everyone who had been in the residency training program. Matt stopped and examined the last five years. Kate was in all the photos, each year changing just slightly, but enough that between the first and last photos she appeared to have become not only more beautiful but more confident and mature.

He moved to the closed door with Dr. Reed's name on it and knocked louder than he'd intended. It also took longer than he expected before Dr. Reed opened the door. As he stepped into the office he was surprised to see a beautiful red-headed woman standing in the center of the room.

"Matt McKayne, this is Chloe Darcy. Chloe is in Emergency Medicine here at Boston General," Tate said by way of introduction. "Chloe, Matt is a lawyer specializing in medical defense and has been hired by the hospital to represent Katherine and I in the lawsuit."

Chloe looked at him appraisingly. "Nice to meet you." She reached out and shook his hand. "Are you any good?"

Matt was surprised by the question and instantly liked her. "I'm very good, Dr. Darcy."

"Call me Chloe, and I am very happy to hear that. The last thing Kate needs is for this to drag on."

"You know Dr. Spence?" he asked, trying to sound professional while struggling to understand the network of relationships going on around him.

She smiled. "I know Kate probably better than anyone. I've been her best friend for the past nine years."

So Chloe Darcy was Kate's best friend and she knew her better than anyone, but apparently knew nothing about him. He assumed that because she showed no signs of hostility towards him. Tate, who, it seemed, had replaced him in Kate's life, also didn't seem to have any knowledge about their past together.

"Chloe, Matt and I have an appointment. I'll talk to you later."

"Don't worry about it. I'm not going anywhere," Chloe stated flatly. Both men watched as she left the room, closing the door a little too forcefully for it to have been accidental.

"Have a seat." Tate gestured to one of the two chairs opposite his large wooden desk and returned to his position behind the desk. He was taking charge and Matt let him. The more in control Tate felt the less likely he was to be defensive and hold things back from him. He had a lot of questions and not all of them were professional.

"I won't waste your time or mine, Dr. Reed," Matt opened, looking at him directly.

"I appreciate that. Call me Tate." He returned the challenge in his gaze, and Matt grudgingly respected the man for not backing down.

"I have thoroughly reviewed the file, as have our medical experts. The unanimous opinion is that Mr. Weber's condition was not survivable. He would not have survived even with immediate medical attention. My concern is that if this case goes to a jury they will not appropriately focus on that fact." Matt waited for his reaction.

"What is it exactly you think will be distracting them?" Tate questioned, examining Matt as intently as he was being examined. Tate was trying to gauge what Matt did and did not know, and in that moment Matt knew he was right about the nature of the relationship between Tate and Kate.

"Your relationship with Kate Spence," he responded and then in silence waited for the other man to give him the details he unwillingly craved.

"I don't have a relationship with Katherine Spence," Tate stated coldly.

Matt recognized the defensiveness in Tate's tone and decided to change tactics before Tate completely shut down. "Why do you refer to her as Katherine when everyone seems to call her Kate?"

"Old habit, I guess. The rhyming of Kate and Tate is too nauseating. Either way, it won't be an issue for much longer."

"Why not?" Matt asked, still searching for answers and what Tate was not saying.

"Katherine, or Kate, will be moving to New York in the summer to start her fellowship in breast oncology and reconstruction."

Matt processed the information. He remembered the afternoon he'd found her crying in her apartment. He had never before felt so helpless. It hadn't been that he had never seen a woman cry—his mother and sister were known for their histrionics—but Kate had been crying from a genuine feeling of pain and not as a means of manipulation. Her career choice made perfect sense and he wondered if it was the one thing she needed to be able to finally make peace with her mother's death. If it was, he wasn't going to let anything stand in her way.

"Is there anything else you would like to tell me about you and Kate?" Matt asked directly, determined to find out the details of their relationship.

"No," Tate snapped. This time Matt was sure there was something to tell.

"Tate, I'm going to be honest with you. With expert medical opinion on our side, the hospital has no intention of settling this lawsuit. Which means that the Webers' attorneys are going to start digging, if they haven't already. They are going to talk your friends, nurses, residents, your colleagues, anyone, in the hope of finding something seemingly improper in your and Kate's actions that night. So if your goal is to protect your privacy, the best way to do that is to tell me exactly what your relationship with Kate Spence is and what happened that night. If you tell me the truth, I can find a way keep this out of court." Matt seemed to have gotten somewhere with his direct attack, because Tate grimaced and leaned forward in his chair, his arms on his desk. Matt recognized the haunted look in his eyes.

"Katherine and I had been involved in a personal relationship. It ended six months ago," Tate stated flatly. Surprising how a statement, which revealed next to nothing and contained what he already knew, still felt like a sucker punch. Once again his feelings towards Tate shifted. Any burgeoning thoughts of liking the man came to an abrupt end and he felt a masochistic need to know more.

"You are going to need to do better than that," Matt replied, unable to keep his tone neutral.

"Fine. Katherine and I had been seeing each for a year and a half," Tate answered, still barely budging on what Matt needed to know, more personally than professionally.

"Was it serious?" That was as close as he could get to asking if they had been lovers.

"For one of us." Matt didn't want to hear any more. He had made some very hard decisions years ago with regard to Kate. Decisions he had justified as being the best for her. Now to hear that instead of living the perfect life he had hoped for her, Kate had fallen in love with a man who hadn't loved her back was a bitter pill to swallow. More so when he thought of the way she had reacted when the two men had been introduced; she still loved Tate even though he didn't love her.

Matt studied the man sitting across from him, but then realized, to be honest; he had let Kate go too. So he wasn't any better, despite his intentions. He then straightened in his chair and began a new resolve to remain professional and get through this meeting before he said or did something he would regret.

"Six months ago. So the time your relationship ended was the same time of Mr. Weber's death? If the two events are linked, I need to know." Matt noticed Tate's attitude change from adversarial to sad; maybe the man realized what he had given up. Tate's shoulders had fallen and he no longer looked at Matt. Time passed and Matt thought Tate wasn't going to answer. Then he heard a deep breath and a less assured voice started.

"Kate and I broke up the same night Mr. Weber died. We saw each other earlier in the evening and later that same night she was called into the hospital to cover for one of the other senior surgery residents who had to leave with the transplant team. I was on second call for Vascular Surgery."

"What was her state of mind?" Matt asked, his worry for Kate, even past Kate, taking precedence.

"I think you should ask her that," Tate answered.

"I'm asking you. I need to know the impression she gave that night."

"She had been surprised. She said she hadn't seen it coming." He was nodding, as if remembering the evening and confirming to himself how it had been.

"Then?" More and more this felt like watching a car accident in slow motion when you knew it was not going to end well but you couldn't look away.

"She was the most upset I had ever seen her and she left." Was that regret he heard in Tate's voice? But before he could examine the thought further, Tate was continuing. "However, when I saw Katherine later in the operating room and throughout all of our medical interactions that night she was one hundred percent professional and composed."

So Tate was going to back and defend Kate. That was going to make the case easier to defend, but Matt wondered about what was motivating the gesture. Was it professionalism, honesty, guilt from breaking off their relationship or part of a plan to win her back?

"Can you explain the time lag between her first attempt to contact you and the response?" Matt asked. Gone was any desire he had to continue this conversation. He actually wanted to leave and get away from the memories of Kate that were filling his mind. Kate with that look of shock and pain filling her eyes. Had she looked the same for Tate?

"Katherine had been surprised. I honestly don't think she had expected anything that happened that night. After she left my loft and things started to sink in, she wanted to talk. She called and I told her there was nothing more to discuss. She called a few more times shortly after that and I ignored her calls. A few hours later when she called on my cellphone to discuss Mr. Weber, I didn't realize her focus had shifted and I again ignored her attempts to talk to me. It wasn't until the hospital operator contacted me and patched her through that I learned about Mr. Weber."

"Does anyone else know the details of that night?"

"The only close friend Katherine confides in is Chloe Darcy."

"So Chloe is a friend of both of yours?" Matt asked, trying to understand what role Chloe Darcy had played.

"I met Chloe through Katherine. We used to spend time together as part of a social group prior to the breakup."

"And now?"

"She is Katherine's best friend. Chloe and I have never talked about that night. I'm not sure what Katherine told her, but Chloe would never do or say anything to deliberately hurt Katherine, that I'm sure of." Matt believed him. Chloe was obviously protective of Kate and he had instinctively liked and trusted her. At least Kate had one person in her life she could depend on.

"Do you think Kate has any reason to want to hurt you?" Matt pried.

"I don't understand your question, Mr. McKayne."

"Please, call me Matt. The other day Kate seemed very concerned about you and your well-being. Do you think she will vouch for your actions as clearly as you are for her?"

"Absolutely. Katherine is nothing if not honest. That night she told me she wanted desperately to be with me, to be in love with me, and I believed her. I don't think any amount of time will change that." He didn't sound arrogant and that disheartened Matt much more than the statement had.

"I would appreciate it if, when you talk to her, you could spare her the same discussion we have just had. I think the only reason this situation has developed is that the hospital gossip mill put together the timing of our break-up and Mr. Weber's death. We were both completely professional in our behavior that night and the hospital switchboard reached me within appropriate professional standards." Tate was ending their conversation and stood from his chair.

Matt conceded and stood. He paused and studied Tate's face, but the other man gave nothing away. The meeting had only generated more questions for him than answers. It had confirmed what he already knew, that Kate and Tate had been a couple. For a year and a half Tate had had Kate, and even though they had now broken up, he still had Kate. The fact that, after breaking up with her, Kate was still defending him spoke volumes about the type of man Tate was. He wanted to hate the man but couldn't, despite the jealousy that was growing inside him.

The sane part of his mind also recognized that Kate still loved and trusted Tate, and Kate didn't do either of those things easily. She was introverted and cautious, which made her actions towards Tate even more telling. What would happen when this was done? Would they find their way back to one another? Would Tate realize what he had given up and want her back? He needed to talk to Kate and he couldn't wait one more day for his answers. The one thing Tate was definitely right about: Kate and Tate was a nauseating combo, and not just the rhyming names.

It took Kate another ten hours to complete her mental list of tasks. She had worked one of the hardest shifts in her career and she hadn't cared. She'd wanted to work, to stay busy, to avoid everything, including her own thoughts.

After going to work an hour early the previous day at five a.m., she had worked through the day, the night and well into the next evening, and it was nine o'clock on Friday night before she was ready to finally leave the building. She was exhausted, and it actually felt a relief to have that as her primary state of mind.

She yawned as she pulled off her scrubs and pulled on the same jeans and fitted long-sleeved blue shirt she had arrived in the previous day. She pulled her hair out of its ponytail and put her watch on. If she hurried she could force herself to eat something and be asleep by ten. If she slept well she might actually have the focus to study tomorrow and not think about her impending meeting with Matt.

Kate walked out of the women's locker room and literally ran into Tate leaving the men's change room. She bounced off his lean frame and had to grasp the wall for support. She didn't realize whom she had hit and he looked equally surprised as she caught the moment when he recognized her. "Sorry," she said awkwardly.

He reached out to steady her, grasping her forearms and holding her until she regained her balance and straightened. "Katherine. I heard you did well last night." His tone was genuine, without the anger or hurt she had come to expect. She couldn't disguise the surprise she felt. For the first time since *that* night, the tension between them was gone. He wasn't the warm Tate she had loved, but this was better than it had been, and probably better than she deserved. She blushed, embarrassed by his kindness.

"Thank you. Your opinion means a lot to me," she replied shakily. Her exhaustion made it hard to control the feelings of relief and loss she associated with her new and old relationship with Tate.

"I spoke with our lawyer, Matt McKayne, today."

No! her mind screamed as she reached out and grasped the wall for support. She studied his face and saw no signs that he knew about her past with Matt. He would be hurt and disgusted with her if he knew. It was sickening to think about the two men together. For different reasons, she hadn't been good enough for either of them, and the thought of them discussing that fact was like a hot poker ripping through her chest. They had both been witness to her greatest inadequacies and she would rather die than have either man share their "Kate Spence" story.

"It's okay, Katherine. I told him the truth. That you are a professional, competent surgeon and that nothing in your actions that night was negligent. He knew about us, though, and was asking the details of our relationship and breakup."

She went from panic, to relief, to anger, to fear within seconds. Matt had no right to ask about her relationship with Tate. He really had no right to ask Tate about her at all. What questions would he have for her? "What did you tell him?" She gulped.

"As much of the truth as he needed to know, while protecting both of our personal lives and reputations." She didn't need to know more. Tate would keep the personal details of their breakup to himself, for his own sake as much as hers.

"Thank you."

He stared at her, his thoughts hidden as he looked at her for an unknown answer. "Goodnight, Katherine. If it's okay by you I think I'm going to use Kate from here on in, like everyone else."

She smiled a little sadly. "I'm just happy you are planning to talk to me."

"Good night, Kate." The conversation was definitely over and Tate walked away. She wondered what had changed for him, but honestly didn't care what the impetus had been for what felt like the forgiveness she didn't deserve.

She walked through the halls of the hospital lost in her thoughts. The overhead fluorescent lights reflected off the linoleum floors as she made her way towards the glass-walled lobby. Her head felt as full as her body felt exhausted. She was grateful that she had put Matt off, even if it was only for a day. She paused at the entryway, threading her arms through the sleeves of her black wool jacket and slowly working the buttons closed to protect her from what appeared to be a cold spring night.

"Kate." In what felt like slow motion she turned towards the voice she recognized. Matt was walking towards her. He was dressed in a dark gray suit with a blue tie that matched his eyes perfectly. She felt her breath catch and a flush spread through her, her body recognizing his with appreciation. She reached up and ran her fingers through her hair, trying to tame the mess that had been tied back and stuffed under an operating-room cap all day, then stopped, catching herself in the action. It didn't matter to Matt how she looked and she no longer cared what he thought, she reminded herself.

"Matt." She forced his name out.

"We need to talk."

He looked agitated. If you didn't know him you wouldn't be able to tell, but she had known him well and recognized the subtle force in his voice and his rigid posture.

"Yes, I believe we have a meeting for tomorrow at two." She didn't have the energy to play this game. Whatever Matt had come to say to her tonight, he needed to say it and let her go home.

"I met with Tate Reed today." The statement reminded her of old legal dramas where the prosecutor baited his witness into revealing information without even asking a question.

"Yes, I know. I already talked to Tate. It appears he has already answered many of your questions about the circumstances behind the lawsuit, and other than that we have nothing to talk about." She tried to sound like her professional, confident self and force out the exhaustion and pain that made her feel unprepared to deal with Matt. He needed to know her boundaries and now was as good a time as any to make it clear what was off-limits for discussion. He didn't seem pleased with her answer.

"I don't care about Tate Reed," Matt said. Now he was definitely angry. Part of her told herself to walk away, that she wouldn't win, not against Matt and not when she was this tired. Unfortunately, the same exhaustion allowed her emotions to take over.

"You seemed to care the other night. You also seemed to care enough when you talked to Tate and asked him questions that are none of your business," she responded, matching his anger in her tone.

"Like it or not, Kate, you are my business." Mistake. She had made a critical mistake in challenging him. Now they were on a path she didn't want to be on. She didn't want to talk about them, about their past, yet couldn't hold back her reaction to his statement or the look in his eyes. He was looking at her with passion and the irony made her want to cry.

"It has never mattered what I thought or felt, has it?" She was done with being professional as she felt her personal pain seep through. She met his look and saw that she had wounded him, and it didn't make her feel any better.

"That's not true, Kate." His hands were jammed in his pockets, his shoulders pulled back, his whole stance masculine and set.

She looked at Matt and briefly remembered the girl she had been and the man she had thought he was. For the second time that night she smiled sadly then regained control of the woman she had become. "I'm not going to do this, Matt."

"Do what?" he asked, but she kept talking.

"I'm not going to talk about the past. It happened a long time ago and it doesn't matter, I've moved on with my life, without you."

"I don't believe you." And then he reached out and took

her hand in his and held it hard. The touch was electric. Warmth spread through her whole body and she felt her heart start to race. She stared for a long time at his face, meshing in her mind the two versions of him. Old Matt and this Matt.

"Believe what you want, it doesn't matter to me," she sighed, pushing away the memories that statement brought forward. "Please, let go of my hand, I'm tired and I want to go home." He didn't look like he was going to let go, he just kept staring at her as if she was a puzzle he could figure out. "Please, Matt."

He released her hand. "I'm parked out front. I'll drive you home."

"No, thank you." She'd had about all the quality Matt time that she could handle and would rather walk the entire length of Boston than risk spending more time with him.

"Kate, if you don't want a scene, just get in the car and let me drive you home." It was a statement more than a threat, but coming from Matt it got her attention.

This was not the Matt she had known. She had never seen Matt lose control. He had always been calm and in control of everything, but not now. One look at his face told her to listen. His eyes were boring into her, his jaw was clenched, and she saw the small tremor that seemed to be traveling through his body. She looked around the lobby, the fluorescent lights creating an unnatural contrast to the darkness that seeped in through the glass wall from the outside. The atrium was still well populated with hospital staff, sufficient that if a scene did occur, she would be back as the number-one topic for the hospital gossips. That, combined with the look on Matt's face, that said he just might do it, and her overwhelming fatigue forced her to give in. "Okay."

She had lost the fight, and her resignation kept her from pulling away when he placed his hand on the small of her back and led her out the hospital's front entrance. His hand spanned almost the entire width of her back. Even through her coat and sweater she could still feel his warmth and the sense of protection she had always felt around Matt. She was surprised that feeling hadn't vanished from its association with him.

A car door was being opened in front of her and she got in, barely registering the car's luxury name and features. Once inside, she sank into the deep pocket of the leather seat. Matt got in the driver's side and started the engine. The air from the heating system was like warm milk to her exhaustion. He reached over and turned on her seat warmer. She didn't fight the strong urge to close her eyes, it seemed the better option to having to look at or make conversation with Matt.

She rolled over, her mind barely registering the soft pillow under her head. It wasn't until she felt the friction of the sheet against her bare abdomen and the weight spanning her body that she realized something was wrong, very wrong. She opened her eyes and found herself looking at an unfamiliar ceiling. It was a high ceiling, white, crossed with dark wooden beams. She didn't need to look to her side to know what she would find. She had always been able to sense his presence before she actually saw him.

How had she ended up here? She felt vulnerable; she was still incredibly tired, and couldn't remember how she had ended up at what she knew must be Matt's apartment. She moved again and processed that she was naked, apart from her bra and underwear. She flushed, both embarrassed and angry that Matt had taken it upon himself to undress her, that she had slept through it all, and, worst of all, that Matt had seen the dark purple lace thong and matching bra that had never been intended for anyone else's eyes.

Anger became her dominant emotion as she turned to look at Matt, who was asleep on top of the blankets with one arm extended across her. That explained the weight. He was wearing a ragged university T-shirt and jeans and looked too much like the old Matt, her Matt. As if on cue, he opened his eyes, and a few inches away she saw the familiar blue eyes that looked softer than she had seen them since their reunion. Her heart fluttered and she forgot her anger.

He didn't say anything, and she was too overwhelmed with memories of the past to tear her eyes from his, still trying to understand the man she'd once thought she knew. His eyes didn't have the answers, only more questions that he seemed to have for her. She watched as he propped himself up on one arm and his other hand moved from her waist to the side of her face, his wide palm spanning her cheek, his fingers in her hair. His eyes changed then, darkening as his pupils widened and his mouth came down on hers.

It started as a soft kiss, his lips brushing against hers. Then he pressed deeper and the pressure of his lips, the stubble brushing against her face, his hand pulling her towards him, was all-encompassing. She opened her mouth in shock and felt his tongue slip inside as he deepened the kiss. Instantly she was on fire, she could feel, smell, taste everything about him, and it inspired a passion that she hadn't felt in so long. She felt alive. She felt like herself.

Her arms reached up to wrap around him, her sudden movement causing him to move on top of her and crush her. The weight of his body on hers heightened her desire; he felt incredible and she responded to his kiss, her tongue matching his with an increasing sense of urgency. Her fingers were in his hair, pulling him closer and closer, desperately wanting to have no space, no air, nothing between them, nothing that could stop this feeling. She felt a sense of panic when she felt him lift himself from her slightly, but was rewarded when he pulled away the blankets that covered her and came back down on her.

Every part of her body yearned to be touched by him. Her breasts felt heavy and a steady throb pulsed between her thighs. She moved her hands down his wide shoulders and muscular back, feeling his hard muscles tremble in response. She grabbed his shirt in her fists and struggled to pull it over his head, until he sat up and removed the offending garment. She couldn't stand to be separated from him even for that moment, and sat up to press herself against his kneeling form. He hauled her onto his lap, her legs straddling him. She wrapped her arms around him again, feeling her breasts crush against his chest as much as they could within their constraint.

His hand swept her hair to one side as his mouth came down along the side of her neck. He licked, kissed and tasted the low part of her neck just above her collarbone and she arched her head back in response. She needed more, wanted more, wanted to ease the large ache that was growing inside her, and she moved her pelvis forward and ground into his. She was rewarded as his hard ridge pressed into her. Then she felt a new release as her bare breasts collided against his chest, her bra having been unfastened and pulled away. One hand closed over her breast, his thumb stroking the already erect and sensitized nipple.

The other hand grasped the bare bottom that her thong exposed, trapping her against him and echoing her need to push into him. It quickly became not enough, and he pulled away and bent his head to kiss her breasts, his tongue reaching her nipples, taking time to encircle and draw each into his mouth. She pulled open his jeans, the zipper falling from the pressure of him. Her hand reached in to touch him, and she felt him contract against her.

Two hands then grasped her hips and she was moved

from her straddled position. She looked up in shock but the same heat that she felt was mirrored in his eyes. She watched as he removed his jeans and boxers, leaving just him. He was fully aroused and everything about him was masculine perfection. He rejoined her on the bed and gently pushed her onto her back against the pillows. She bent her knees and spread her legs, wanting him between.

His hands tangled in her hair as he returned to kissing her, the head of his shaft now rubbing against the damp purple lace between her legs. It was the best form of torture, one where you wanted to stop because the pleasure was too intense, but at the same time knew the release would be more than worth the progression, and that was what made it unforgettable. His hand skimmed her body and ventured towards her inner thighs. She felt the lace move slightly, as his finger caressed her crease and pushed inside. She knew she was wet, and even though the penetration was not the part of him she desperately wanted inside her, she still contracted her muscles around him, both for her satisfaction and to tempt him.

It worked, and for the first time since they had awoken, words were spoken. "Oh, God, Katie, I want you so badly," he whispered against her cheek, breaking from their kiss.

His words, however softly spoken, had the opposite effect on her. Katie, she wasn't Katie any more. Katie had been the foolish girl who had fallen in love with her best friend and had had her heart broken. Katie was the girl he had walked away from and ignored. The memory of that feeling was the only emotion powerful enough to break her from the path to ultimate fulfillment that she had been on. Instantly she felt vulnerable and weak, and very exposed, which technically she was. Her hands pressed against his chest and she shoved as hard as she could.

"Stop."

He made eye contact with her, and she wasn't sure

what he saw, but he moved. She scrambled off the bed and headed for the nearest door, praying it was the bathroom.

She closed what thankfully was the bathroom door and pressed her back against it. The dark, empty room calmed her growing sense of panic as she gulped for air, trying to hold back her tears. She looked around, her eyes adjusting to the city night's light filtering through the frosted window. She was in Matt's bathroom, virtually naked, only a door separating her and Matt. What had she been thinking? She hadn't. She had completely lost control; she had almost lost herself in Matt. Again. Self-loathing rose up inside her. She knew better. If anything had come from their last time together, it had been the hard truth that in life the only person she could depend on was herself, and tonight she had let herself down.

Her hand found the light switch. She blinked rapidly at the brightness and studied the reflection looking back at her in the large bathroom mirror. Her hair was wild, her lips were swollen, her cheeks showed the marks of Matt's five o'clock shadow, there was a faint mark on her left breast, and she was naked except for her purple thong. She shuddered, looking around the room for something to cover up with, needing to hide the evidence of her mistake. Her eyes fell on Matt's robe. She hated it that that was her only viable option, but nothing else in the room would provide her the coverage she desperately wanted so it would have to do. The brown terry-towel robe smelled like Matt, but she blocked that from her mind, ran the cold water and splashed it on her face.

Now what? she thought to herself. Naked Matt was on the other side of the door, waiting, probably, for an explanation. He would be waiting a long time for that, because she couldn't explain how tonight had started and had no intention of telling him why she had put an end to it.

It took another ten minutes before she was ready to

leave the room, holding her breath as she opened the door. Folded up in the doorway were her clothes. Her eyes darted around the room. She saw the bed and the tangled sheets, but there was no sign of Matt. She took the clothes back into the bathroom, closed the door and dressed quickly, pulling her hair back with the extra hair tie she found in her jeans pocket. She took a final steadying breath, trying to summon the strength she was going to need to face him.

She found him in the living room, sitting on the couch, his attention fixed on the gas fireplace in the center of one of the walls. He looked up as soon as she came in. He too was fully dressed, not that it mattered as she could still see every contour of his naked body in her mind. It was a battle in her mind between the need to be with him, feel him against her, and the memories that told her to run as fast as she could and never look back. Before she could say anything he was walking towards her, reaching out with her coat and bag in his hand. He passed them over carefully so as not to touch her and gave the impression of not even wanting to be near her.

"I'll drive you home." He didn't sound like himself, but she couldn't figure out much beyond that. This was not the reaction she had expected, and while she was grateful not to have to replay the details of their encounter aloud, she was also hurt by his dismissal and couldn't control the accusation in her eyes when she looked at him again.

He misunderstood the look. "I did drive you home earlier, but when we got to your apartment I couldn't wake you up and couldn't find your keys to carry you inside. So I brought you home so you could sleep here. That's it; that's all." He sounded defensive and angry. Well, so was she.

"Thank you." The words were terse. She put on her coat and snatched her bag from his outheld hand. He grabbed his own jacket and unlocked the apartment door.

They traveled in silence down the elevator, into the

parking garage and during the entire car ride back to her apartment. At three in the morning traffic was minimal, so the drive was mercifully short. Normally silence like this would be uncomfortable, but she knew talking about what had just happened between them would take discomfort to a whole new level.

Her hand was on the door handle as he pulled up in front of her building and she had the car door open before the vehicle had even come to a full stop. She needed to get away from Matt, she needed time to figure out what tonight meant, if anything. Her foot was on the curb, half-out of the car, when she heard his voice.

"He's not going to change his mind." She would have missed the words if it had not been for the dead silence of the night.

It made her pause, settling her body back into the seat. She looked back at Matt, whose hands were still gripping the steering wheel, his gaze focused straight ahead, not looking at Kate. What was he talking about? She slumped further back into the passenger seat, too thrown by his statement not to voice the thought in her head. "I don't understand."

"Tate Reed." By now he had turned to look at her, and she still didn't understand. The mention of Tate, though, brought a comparison to mind. She hadn't ever felt with Tate the way she had tonight with Matt. Never so out of control, never so desperate for release, so passionate.

"He doesn't love you," Matt stated, almost apologetically, like he was breaking bad news to a client.

It felt like a slap in the face, a reminder of another time long ago. Okay to have sex with but not worthy of love. No wonder he hadn't wanted to talk about what had almost happened between them tonight. It was no big deal for Matt, just as it hadn't been the last time. She could feel a lump start to form in the back of her throat and focused her eyes into a hard glare in effort to control the tears of humiliation that were forming at the edges.

"No, he doesn't love me any more. But he did love me and he still respects me and would never hurt me, which makes him a better man than you." She had meant to hurt him, to wound him, to have him feel some of her pain, and when she looked over and saw that she had succeeded, it didn't make her feel any better. What was she doing here with Matt? Wasn't the definition of craziness repeating the same actions again and again and expecting a different result?

"I'm a complete fool," she muttered to herself, and completed her departure by slamming the car door and not turning back to look at Matt, who remained parked outside as she entered her building. She was locked safely inside her apartment and lying in bed before she heard his car start up again and leave.

He sped through Boston's underground tunnels too angry to return to the memories that now awaited him at home. He looked at his now-empty passenger seat, remembering her in it curled up, sleeping, looking no different than she had almost a decade ago. When he had lifted her out of the car and carried her to the apartment, she had curled her arms around him and he had remembered what it had felt like when she'd been his.

When she had woken up he had seen the same trusting eyes of the past and he had been unable to resist kissing her. He didn't know what he'd meant by the kiss, he'd just felt a need to be closer to her, to regain the intimacy they had lost. The instant he had felt her lips, tasted her, he had lost all control. He shifted uncomfortably in the sports car seat, his erection returning painfully with the thought of Kate and her passionate response. The Kate he had been with tonight was not the same Katie he had known. The new Kate was no longer tentative. She had grabbed at him, moaned beneath him, had eagerly lain back and opened herself to him. Or so he had thought.

It had been a complete and sudden change, a moment of recognition. The moment she had heard his voice she had pushed him away and run. It had felt like a cold knife had stabbed him in the chest as he had felt the full impact of her rejection. He had wanted to go after her, to make her face him, but pride had held him back. He hadn't wanted or needed to hear that the reason she had stopped was because he was not the man she wanted or loved. He hadn't wanted to hear her reject him aloud, to tell him that she only wanted and loved Tate. That in her sleep-deprived state she had fantasized that he was Tate, right up until his voice had broken the illusion.

Her rejection tortured him. He never expected Kate to live a life of celibacy, but he had also deliberately chosen not to think about the alternative. Now he was faced with a reminder of the facts, what she looked like, what she felt like, how she would react and respond to the most intimate of touches, in essence how she would make love with the man she loved. And in acquiring that knowledge he was also faced with the fact that he was no longer that man.

CHAPTER FOUR

THE LOUD KNOCK brought Kate out of the darkness and forced her to open her eyes. She had been awake until six a.m., thinking about Matt, being torn between painful memories of the past and her body's frustration at its lack of fulfillment. The knock came again and Kate grabbed her bathrobe and made her way to the door.

Chloe was standing on the other side, smiling, her hair down and straightened, her casual yoga pants and V-neck shirt nicely outlining her figure. She looked perfect, and Kate shuddered at the contrast to her own disheveled appearance. Chloe must also have recognized the difference because her smile quickly vanished and her green eyes began to evaluate Kate as she would a patient. "Oh, my God, I woke you up. Are you okay? Are you sick?"

It would be so easy just to agree and send her friend away, but Kate felt like she had lied, even if by omission, more in the past few days than she had in years, and she was tired of it. That wasn't her; it wasn't who she was. "No, Chloe, I am post-call and had a late night. Come in so I can stop standing in the doorway half-naked."

Chloe stepped through into the small kitchen and perched on a stool at the kitchen bar. Kate shut the door and joined her, starting to make coffee. "It's okay, I actually brought coffee for both of us, though by the looks of things you could use both."

Kate smiled ruefully at the comment, wondering how she could have missed the tray and bag in Chloe's hands but grateful to not have to make an effort and at the accuracy of Chloe's assessment.

"I brought the coffee and muffins in case you wanted to study together; I didn't think you would be post-call today," Chloe said.

"I'm not technically post-call. I'm post-post-call, which is normally fine except that I didn't get much sleep last night so it still feels like the day after." Kate was normally very disciplined in her post-call routine—she needed to be or the fatigue would drag on for the entire week.

"Did you have an extender shift yesterday?" Chloe asked, obviously puzzled. Kate had worked as a physician extender after her first two years of residency had ended and she had passed her basic boards. The shifts involved her being on call and available for medical emergencies in various rehabilitation facilities and nursing homes. The shifts paid well and she had needed the money to help with the massive interest payments on her student loans. Kate had had to stop taking the shifts once she had become Chief Resident because of the added workload of her new role and needing to study for her final board exams.

Kate's expression faltered at the immediate vision of Matt naked and pressed against her. She blinked, holding her eyes shut against the memory. When she opened them Chloe's face had transitioned from surprise to disbelief.

She couldn't face the look or the questions that were about to follow, so she turned and left the kitchen, moving to the soft yellow couch, curling her legs beneath her and covering herself with the throw blanket. Chloe read her friend correctly and said nothing as she moved to follow Kate, taking a place on the opposite end of the couch. She brought her offering with her, handing Kate a muffin and pressing a coffee into her other hand. Then to Kate's surprise she didn't say anything else. She just sat, and waited.

The silence was calming. It helped Kate regain her composure and gave her time to think as opposed to react. She absently picked at the muffin, thinking through the events of the last few days, and realized that Chloe was right, she did need to learn to talk about her feelings. She needed to tell someone, needed to say the words and thoughts in her head aloud before she went crazy, rethinking, reanalyzing, reliving the same moments over and over again.

"Have you ever been in love with someone when they didn't love you back?" Kate asked, more as an explanation than a question. "When I was at university, completing my undergraduate degree, I fell in love with my best friend and in the end he didn't love me back."

"I'm sorry, Kate, but I don't understand how that connects to now."

"Tate and I broke up because he asked me to marry him. When I looked down and saw him on one knee, holding out an engagement ring, the first thought in my head was that it should have been Matt. And that was when I knew I didn't love Tate in the same way, not enough to be his wife."

"Oh." Chloe's face was beyond shocked. They had never talked about why she and Tate had ended, just that they had. She hadn't told her about the proposal or about Matt or the role he had played. "Kate, that was months ago. What happened with Tate last night?"

"Nothing. We talked and it was nice. For the first time since we broke up I actually think he and I might be okay."

"If nothing happened with Tate, why are you tired with what appears to be stubble burn on your cheek?" Chloe asked pointedly.

Kate felt heat rise through her as her hand reached up to touch the mentioned area, feeling the change in her sensitive skin. "That's from Matt. He kissed me last night and for a few minutes I forgot about our past."

"Are we talking about the same Matt? The Matt I met yesterday? The lawyer who was meeting with Tate to discuss the case?"

"Same Matt. As luck would have it, the hospital hired my old ex to defend my new ex and me. Horrible, isn't it? The only two men I have ever been with in my entire life in a room together. I never told Tate about Matt. I didn't want to hurt him any more than I already was, and I couldn't explain how and why I still had feelings for the man who broke my heart."

"Does Matt know about your relationship with Tate?"

"Yes, but how much I don't know. He keeps making comments about Tate that I don't understand."

"Is he jealous?"

"No, of course not, he has no reason to be jealous. If he wanted me he could have had me, but he didn't. He told me to my face that he didn't love me and then walked away, back to his girlfriend, and never looked back. Jealousy implies wanting something someone else has, and Matt made it perfectly clear he didn't want me."

"If he doesn't want you, how do you explain his marks on your body?"

"I can't. Maybe he's lonely and I'm convenient, again," she sighed.

"That sounds really harsh, Kate."

"No, what's harsh is walking out on someone who maybe you didn't love but at least should have cared about enough not to obliterate her existence from your life."

"When did all that happen?"

"Right before medical school started. As you recall, I wasn't exactly coping well with life when we first met."

"Makes sense now. I wish you had told me then, though."

"Talking about it would have made it worse. As it was, it took me a long time to realize that he wasn't who I'd thought he was and we weren't what I'd thought we were."

"I'm sorry, Kate."

"Me too."

"Are you going to tell Tate about your past with Matt?" Chloe asked.

"No, it's in the past and I refuse to give Matt any more importance in my life and humiliate myself again by explaining it all to Tate."

"You're being pretty hard on yourself over this, Kate," Chloe said sympathetically.

Kate shook her head and stood from the couch. "I made a huge mistake with Matt and I refuse to risk ever repeating it."

"So if you don't have any feelings for this guy then what the hell happened last night?"

"Insanity and fatigue happened. I woke up and it was like how it used to be and for a moment it was the old Matt and the old Katie. But I guarantee you that will never happen again. I know too much about Matt. I'm not the naïve girl I once was. I have my own life now and I know that I don't need him. Even better, seeing him again has helped cure me of any lingering images I had of the guy I once loved. I know for sure that he doesn't exist and I can move on with my life."

"Kate, I hate to point out the obvious, but you do need Matt. He's your only hope for settling this lawsuit and getting your fellowship and career back on track."

"I know. I guess that is one small bright side to this situation. I know Matt and some things never change. If there's a way to win this case, he will. Matt is driven to succeed at all costs."

"That doesn't sound like the type of man you would fall for."

"It's not. The Matt I fell in love with was giving and kind. It just happens that that part of him wasn't as important to him as it was to me."

Matt walked back into the hospital the following day for his meeting with Kate, and for the first time in his career he felt completely unprepared. It was not a feeling he enjoyed. He didn't know how he would react to her, or her to him, if she would even show up after their night together.

He walked into the boardroom five minutes before their scheduled meeting and was surprised to see her already seated at the table. She was reading from a large textbook, her hands tangled up in her long brown hair. She stopped reading the moment he entered the room, her eyes rising to stare up at him.

It reminded him of their past. She had been sitting exactly the same way the first time he'd seen her. She had easily been the most beautiful woman in the café but, compared to almost all the other women he'd known, she hadn't seemed to notice or try to use it to her advantage. He had seen her in the same spot every time he'd gone to the café, until one afternoon he could no longer resist the temptation she'd presented.

Within a few hours of talking to Kate he'd known that his instincts had been dead on. She had not been like any other woman he had ever met. Matt had never been without a woman from a young age. His appearance, confidence and social status had been enough to ensure a willing and ready woman on his arm and in his bed. The fact that he'd had such a woman already in his life had not been enough to keep him from exploring Kate.

Soon she had become his favorite person, his best friend, and Matt had liked himself most when he'd been around her. He would sometimes stand back across the coffeehouse and just watch her. The intense look of concentration on her face, the way she would abstractedly run her fingers through her hair, and then she would look up and see him and smile. She had made him feel welcome and like he belonged. But that had been then, and today Kate was not smiling.

He took the seat opposite her across the table. He needed to remind himself that his purpose was the lawsuit and sitting too close to her was a distraction from that purpose.

"My firm has acquired and reviewed all the documents related to the case. There are a few depositions we need to talk about."

"Your firm?" she asked, the question holding more censure that he'd expected from her. She was still angry and he needed to do his best to calm her down if they were ever going to be able to discuss the case in a constructive manner.

"I'm a partner at my grandfather's law firm. I started and head up the medical defense division."

The McKayne family was rich and powerful and known for their prominent presence in the New York legal community. His grandfather had founded a law firm decades earlier that had grown to be one of the best, making his family very wealthy. Matt's father had been in line to succeed his grandfather until he'd died suddenly of a heart attack when Matt had been four, leaving the family's dynasty and future firmly on Matt's shoulders. Matt often wondered how different his life would have been if his father had lived.

The medical defense division was his creation and he was involved in every aspect of its operation. He represented clients but also oversaw the operations of all the firm's satellite offices, which was how he'd ended up back in Kate's life.

He had been reading the monthly client reports at home one evening when he'd seen her name. A combination of fear and desire had broken through his whole body. He'd called the Boston lawyer assigned to the case and confirmed it was his Katie being described. Without hesitation he'd released the other lawyer from the case and arranged to handle it personally. He had never once considered the ramifications of their reunion.

"Did you pick this case because of me?" she asked, her shrewd intelligence piecing together what he wasn't saying.

"Yes." He knew better than to lie to her but also wasn't willing to offer her any more of an explanation for his actions.

Matt had been raised to be responsible, with the high expectations and demands of his family behind his every decision and action. He hadn't realized he resented it or what a heavy burden it was until he'd met Kate.

She'd never asked him for anything and in return she had been the first person in his life that Matt had wanted to do things for, simply to make her happy, to make her smile. This was in stark contrast to his family, who had been blatant and demanding in their needs, wants and expectations. Kate had got more joy out of simple things than Matt had known was possible. Remembering how she took her coffee or asking about how her exam went had seemed to mean the world to her, and had been a far cry from the over-the-top and lavish gestures his family had expected.

He had been the best version of himself during his time with her. It hadn't been anything she had done or said, it had been all the things she hadn't done that had made him feel a sense of freedom and a willingness to give of himself that he had never experienced. She'd had no expectations or demands of him and had never pushed for more than he'd offered.

It was that part of Kate that was driving his need to personally defend her, not his guilt, he told himself. She seemed to take in his answer, an internal debate apparent in the emotions that crossed her face before she let the matter drop.

He took her cue and refocused on the case. "Kate, I want you to think back to that night and the interactions you had with Mr. Weber and his family. Can you think of anything you said or did that would make the Webers believe there was negligence involved in his death?"

She was silent across the table, but her nonverbal cues made up for the lack of words. She tangled her hair into a knot, pulling it from her face as her perfect posture slouched in defeat. "Yes."

"What happened?" He knew the answer. He rarely asked a question without knowing the answer but he needed to hear it from her, even though he knew it would kill her to say it.

"I cried." No emotion was in her words, just a statement of fact. But the look on her face told a different story.

"When did you cry, Kate?" Memories of the two times he had ever seen Kate cry revolved in his mind. Both instances had been extreme, when she had been pushed to her limit.

"When I was talking to Mrs. Weber after her husband died." Still no elaboration. He hated this. Hated that his job was to force her to discuss something she had no desire to share with him. It went against everything they had once been.

"I need you to tell me exactly what happened." She stared at him and he couldn't tell what she was thinking. Minutes went by and he started to worry she would refuse him. Not for the first time he reconsidered whether he should be representing Kate, or whether the past between them was too much to overcome.

Finally she sighed, obviously resigning herself to the situation. "After Mr. Weber died, Tate, as the attending surgeon, went to talk to Mrs. Weber to disclose his death.

When he was done I joined her in the operating room's family room. I had met her earlier in the night and felt compelled to see her. She already knew her husband was dead and was crying alone in the room when I got there. When she saw me she reached for me and I let her embrace me, and she didn't let go. The more she cried, the harder she held me. Eventually I started to cry too and I told her I was sorry."

"What were you sorry for, Kate?"

"I was sorry that she had lost the love of her life. That she was going to have to go on by herself and try to make a life without the one person she was meant to be with."

"Do you think it's possible that she misinterpreted your empathy as guilt?"

"Given that we are talking about it, I would say yes, wouldn't you?" Her derision was very clearly focused on herself, despite the sarcasm in her response.

Yes, he would. Kate crying and saying she was sorry would definitely raise suspicions when reflected on after the fact.

"Are there any other patients, nurses, or colleagues that would speak for a pattern of behavior? That you frequently empathize with your patients and their emotions?"

"No. That was the first and only time I have lost my composure at work."

"Is there anyone else in your life who can testify to your emotional nature?" He was reaching, looking for some way to get her out of a situation that now seemed partially her own making.

Her face changed. Gone was the steely armor and replacing it was the same softness he recognized from the past. "You."

"Me what, Kate?"

"You are the only person who has ever seen me cry." Her words were a painful confession, but the information was just the opposite. It highlighted to him what he had always known. They had been something different, something special, something he should have held onto at all costs. He couldn't let those thoughts take over; he needed to keep his focus. He knew bringing up the past would be a sure way to make Kate retreat and he wasn't willing to lose another minute with the real her.

"What was different about that night?"

"I'm not sure." She raked her hand back through her hair and looked down at the table as if she would find the answer she was looking for in the grain of the wood. "She really loved him and he loved her. I saw it between them in the emergency department, true love. Then within hours it was gone and I couldn't put together what would happen next. She was so lost without him already and all I could remember was what it felt like to lose the person you love. I remembered that feeling and knew that my love and pain were only a tenth of what she was experiencing, and I didn't know how to help her."

The most remarkable woman he had ever met looked defeated and it was enough to break his resolve. He didn't stop to question whether she was referring to her mother, him, or Tate Reed in her memories of pain and loss. He rose from his chair and crossed around to her, the drive to hold her in his arms breaking through his common sense. She looked up as he drew her up from her chair, her lips parting in shock. He didn't mean to kiss her, his intent, brief as it had been, had been to comfort and hold her, but one look into the depths of her eyes and the sweet fullness of her lips was enough to change his mind.

It was an experience in contrasts. The softness of her lips to the hardness of his mouth; the surprise in her reaction to the deliberate intent that drove him; the sweetness within her to the ruthlessness of the man he had become. She didn't pull away and the small surrender drove him harder. He explored her, reminding his mind and body of the places he had once been and had never forgotten. His tongue teased hers while his hands roamed her body in his embrace. Her hands clung to him, grabbing handfuls of the fabric of his shirt until the moment was broken and he felt her step back from the kiss and push him away.

She was staring at him, her eyes wide. "You want me."

His arms were still holding her and he was unwilling to let her move further away. He also wanted to make it clear to her who she was with and who was responsible for the dilation of her pupils, her parted moist lips, and the points of her nipples, which were pressing against the fabric of her long-sleeved cotton shirt.

"Why?" she whispered, the word coming at the end of a gasp to find her breath.

"Why what?" His brain had been robbed of its blood supply and his ability to comprehend her question was inhibited by the physical desire he was struggling to restrain.

"Why are you really back?" It was the question that had been in the background of their every interaction and had remained unasked and unanswered between them.

"Code Orange. Code Orange, Emergency Department. All available personnel." The hospital intercom sounded within the room, the intrusion startling both of them. His arms dropped and she moved away. He had no idea what the announcement meant, but as he watched her face change from the intimacy of her question to immediate business, he realized it was serious.

"That's a mass casualty code. I need to go." She went back to her spot at the table, shoved her textbook into her shoulder bag and then left without another look at him.

He was torn between anger at the interruption and relief that he didn't have to answer the question he didn't have an answer for.

He knew why he had left her but had no explanation for

why he was back. He paced around the room, the motion helping him to organize his thoughts. It wasn't the first time he had thought it through. It was an argument he had had over and over again, and never once had he come to a different conclusion. Kate was special. She was beautiful, selfless, and genuine in her feelings and actions. She was everything he wanted and he had loved her enough to let her go before his world ruined her and robbed her of everything that made her the woman he loved.

Why was he back? He had asked himself a thousand times since coming to Boston. Why, after nine years of being apart, had he finally given in to the temptation to return to her? It wasn't that he had forgotten her. In the beginning it had taken every ounce of his willpower to break away from her. When she'd called and emailed he had forced himself to erase the messages before listening to or reading her words.

He had begun filling his life with women and alcohol, neither providing any comfort. For a time he'd actually thought he was losing his mind, because out of the corner of his eye he would think that he saw her across campus or heard her voice in a crowd. One afternoon he had walked into a campus coffeehouse and seen a woman that could have been her. The long brown hair, the way she had been bent over a textbook, intensely concentrating, reminding him so much of Katie that when she had started to look up he'd had to turn and leave. He had been unable to face the crushing disappointment that would have come when he discovered it was not her.

After that he realized he needed something in his life that reminded him of her without being with her. That was when he discovered medical defense law. It brought out the best in him, just as Kate had. The ability to defend and protect physicians who dedicated their lives to caring for others brought a purpose to his life that he desperately needed. It was also the first step in breaking free of his family's self-serving dysfunction.

After finishing law school, it had been understood that he would join the firm and he did, but with one condition—he wanted to specialize in medical defense. When faced with the prospect of having his grandson work for another law firm, his grandfather relented and let him start a separate division for medical defense within the family firm. Matt was the best at everything he did, but as a medical defense lawyer he excelled. Within two years the firm's value had tripled and Matt was made a partner. By twenty-eight, Matt was a millionaire, having channeled his share of the firm's profits into successful investments.

Despite being born into privilege, Matt became a self-made man, and with that came insight into the family dynamic that had dominated his life. He loved his family, but that feeling was marred by the sense of responsibility he felt toward them and disdain for their way of life. They judged and treated people entirely according to wealth and background with no regard for true character. They would have eaten the old Katie alive, and Matt knew that, despite his best efforts to protect her, his family's resentment of who she was and her position of importance in Matt's life would have slowly eroded her spirit and the small amount of self-confidence she had.

But now things were different. New money was no longer vulgar, not when Matt had accumulated more wealth than the rest of his family combined. He had also learned to draw some hard lines surrounding his personal life and they no longer dared to interfere in his relationships or other choices.

If his ability to control his family was the reason he was back in Kate's life, he would have found her years ago. He could more easily explain why he'd stayed away than why he'd returned. He'd stayed away out of guilt. No matter how noble his reasons had been for ending their relationship, he had done it horribly, his mind reacting instead of thinking.

To avoid her sacrificing who she was and wanted to be for him, he had sacrificed his own character. He had stayed away because after all these years he knew he couldn't offer her what they had once had—trust. If she asked him again why he was back, he would be honest. He was back because she needed him and after nine years apart he finally had something to offer her, and he wasn't going to let her refuse.

CHAPTER FIVE

KATE REACHED THE emergency department within minutes of hearing the overhead call for help. A code orange was one of the most rare codes and in her entire career she had never heard one called. A code blue was called when a patient stopped breathing. A code red when there was a fire in the hospital. A code orange was reserved for when some sort of disaster occurred and the emergency department was overwhelmed and unable to cope with the patient load.

She wasn't working, she wasn't even supposed to be in the building, but that didn't matter. She had been trained to care for the sick and no office hours applied to that duty.

She threw her bag into the locker room, exchanging her shirt for a scrub top, not so much to protect herself but more to identify her in the sea of people that would be filling the department.

She walked to the trauma bay, coming alongside Chloe and her attending physician, Dr. Ryan Callum. They showed no surprise at her arrival.

"What's going on?" she asked, her eyes darting around the department, evaluating.

"Multiple vehicle collision in the tunnel, including a city bus, with an unknown number of casualties. The Boston fire department and medics have been on scene for at least fifteen minutes but they are having trouble extracting some of the passengers. We are the closest and the first-response site for all trauma cases, with County and other surrounding hospitals as overflow."

"What would you like me to do?"

"The operating room has been notified and all nonurgent cases are on hold until we evaluate how much surgical trauma there is. Chloe and the other emergency residents are going to triage the victims according to their injury severity score. If you could be on hand for the critical and severe patients and work with the trauma team to decide who goes to the operating room and in what order, that would help immensely." He didn't elaborate further as the team poured into the ambulance bay to meet the first arriving victims.

Within an hour, fifteen patients had been classified with severe and critical codes. Kate mentally ordered the surgical cases for the operating room, taking into account both the severity of their injuries and their readiness for the operating room. She picked up the phone and asked to be put through to the attending surgeon responsible for the trauma team.

"Jonathan Carter," the surgeon answered, obviously waiting for this call.

"It's Kate Spence. I have seen the critical and severe tracked patients from the tunnel accident. Nine are presenting as clear surgical cases and four need to go immediately. There is an obstructed airway, a rib fracture with flail chest, a compound femur fracture, and a penetrating trauma to the abdomen."

"The operating room has four rooms available with nursing and anesthesia. Orthopedics has a team in place and can start with the femur and work through the orthopedics cases. I'm here and so is Dr. Reed, but we don't have a third surgeon in-house on a Saturday and the nearest person is one hour away because of the tunnel closure."

"Are you asking me which two of the three non-orthopedic cases we should take first?" she asked, knowing the wrong choice could lead to a patient's death.

"No, I'm telling you that you are taking the penetrating abdominal wound to the OR without an attending surgeon."

Her train of thought changed from patient triage to shock. She didn't need him to repeat himself; he had been clear and his words were echoing in her mind.

"Dr. Spence, you are three months away from being a board qualified surgeon. I've worked with you, Dr. Reed has worked with you, and we both agree that you are more than capable of acting alone. The patient is better served with you now than waiting around for someone else."

"Thank you." She felt humbled and terrified and neither emotion was she going to allow to show in her voice.

"Don't thank me. You've earned this. I've already notified the operating room that you will be doing the case solo. They are just waiting for the patient details and then will send for the patient immediately."

The team moved quickly. She made the necessary call and then went upstairs to change into her surgical attire. Within ten minutes the patient was on the table, being anesthetized. She moved to the left-hand side of the table and waited for the signal from the anesthetist to start. She could hear the monitors firing, her patient's heart rate racing, just as hers was. She knew she could do it. Knew they wouldn't have let her if she couldn't. But there was something about being the most qualified person in the room, with no one to help her if she got in over her head, that was terrifying.

She needed to set the tone. Everyone in the room was on edge because of the severity of the situation. The only way to bring people down was to lead by example, to stay calm. She could do that. She held out her gloved hand. "Knife."

She worked meticulously, creating an incision extending

from either side of the metal shard that was plunged into
the center of the man's abdomen. She couldn't just pull it
out, she needed the shard in place to act as a tamponade
for the bleeding until she could identify which organs and
vessels had been damaged. She worked through the layers of the abdominal wall until she was able to place a re-
tractor to hold open the wound and give her the complete
visualization she needed.

Damn, she thought to herself. The metal was extending
into the transverse colon and the abdomen was completely
contaminated, placing the patient at high risk for postoperative infection. Thankfully, the shard had stopped before reaching the aorta, which lay two centimeters below
the tip.

Typically this was when her attending would ask her
what she wanted to do. Did she want to repair the bowel or
remove a segment of the damaged bowel, and if she chose
the latter, did she want to do a primary or secondary repair? She knew the answer, but this was thefirst time she
was taking one hundred percent ownership of the decision.

She called out to the circulating nurse and requested the
necessary staplers and devices. Within an hour she was
sitting in the recovery room with her patient, completing
her postoperative orders and dictation.

Her emotions were mixed. On one hand she was proud
of her surgical accomplishment; on the other, she felt for
her patient, who still had a long road ahead of him to full
recovery.

The automatic doors swung open and Dr. Carter walked
in alongside the stretcher on which his patient was being
transferred to the recovery room. He approached Kate,
and she prepared to defend her decision to resect the bowel
with delayed anastomosis.

"Dr. Shepherd has just arrived and is going to take over
the third room until things are clear. Thank you for your

help today. Your patient has been formally admitted under my care, but you should consider him yours until he goes home."

"Thank you again."

"Don't thank me. You proved yourself long ago."

She retraced her steps through the hospital, collecting her belongings from the various locations she had been. She had never questioned her decision to become a surgeon but in that moment she had never been more certain that she had made the right choice. She felt like the doctor and woman she wanted to be, confident and in control, and it was time for her to take control of all aspects of her life.

She dug through her bag in search of her phone and the business card the hospital's lawyer, Jeff Sutherland, had left her after the initial meeting. She dialed the number and waited as it rang.

"McKayne."

"It's Kate. We need to talk." It was the understatement of the year, but what she needed to say she needed to say in person. She wasn't going to take the easy way out over the phone.

"I won't dispute that." His assuredness irritated her and she tried to stay on track.

"Where are you now?"

"I'm at my apartment—do you need the address?" Yes, she would need the address. Leaving a man's apartment at three in the morning after an unexpected sexual encounter did not typically lend itself to remembering logistics, but it did remind her of the dangers of entering a lion's den.

"No. I mean I don't need the address because I'm not coming over. Can you meet me at Gathering Grounds on Beacon Street?" She held her breath, waiting for his response.

"I can probably be there in about an hour."

"Okay. I'll see you then." She pushed the off button, not

wanting to prolong the conversation. She needed to keep every ounce of the confidence she had gained this afternoon for when she met Matt.

Almost exactly an hour later Matt entered the coffee shop. She knew he was there the moment he walked through the door, and she watched him get a coffee and then join her at her table.

"We need to speak quietly while we're talking about the case."

"I don't want to talk about the case," she said, still quietly, her personal life just as confidential to her as the details of the lawsuit.

"Okay, so what do you want to talk about?"

"Us."

"You said you didn't want to discuss the past."

"I don't. I want to make things clear now."

"Kate, nothing is more clear. You want me and I want you."

He was right. She wouldn't deny it. How could she when he had witnessed her response to him? Even as he spoke the words her body flushed with the memory of him. She swallowed hard and forced herself to remain focused. "That doesn't matter."

"How can it not matter that every time we touch, neither of us can keep control?"

"Because I can keep control, Matt. I don't know you, I never did. But I remember what it feels like to be hurt by you and those memories are way stronger than any physical attraction that still lingers between us."

His face, which had been heated describing the passion between them, cooled, and she faced a steely expression before he spoke. "Do you want a different lawyer?"

"No. You need to fix this for me, because I know you can. But while you are doing that I want you to forget everything else that is between us. The only relationship we have is of lawyer and client."

"The attraction between us isn't going away, Kate, no matter how hard you try to control it or tell me to ignore it."

"But you are, Matt. When this case is done you are going to move on back to your high-society life and you'll forget that I ever existed."

"And what if I can't?"

"You can, Matt, and you have. You just need to do it again."

Kate spent the remainder of the weekend trying to get caught up with life. Her work schedule made even basic life tasks seem like monumental challenges. Cleaning her apartment, doing laundry, shopping for groceries, and sorting her mail were all luxuries saved up for a rare day off. Her student-loan statement was a grim reminder of the ruin she faced if they lost the case. She had no way to pay back that amount of debt, not to mention the money she owed her father, unless she was employed as a surgeon, and that was dependent on the case. Not to mention the pain of losing her chance to devote her career to women with breast cancer, women like her mother.

She moved through the apartment, trying to restore the same order to her home life as she had her personal life, and eventually she felt more herself than she had since Matt's return. She had done it. She had taken the steps she needed to protect herself and her heart. She would never let him hurt her again, because if she did she knew she wouldn't survive it.

Her sense of peace remained with her until Monday afternoon. Matt's office called and scheduled a meeting for Thursday. The receptionist didn't provide any details about why they were meeting. She could only assume it was to continue the conversation that had been cut short on the weekend. Two feelings filled her and neither was welcome. One was a sense of dread at having to relive the night of Mr. Weber's death and her time with Mrs. Weber. The other was hurt that Matt hadn't called her himself. The latter she resented deeply, despite it being what she wanted: lawyer and client, nothing more.

She operated all day Tuesday and took a call shift on Wednesday in order to be able to leave early for the meeting on Thursday afternoon. By that time her sense of peace had long left her. It was just fatigue, she lied to herself. That was why she felt so on edge about meeting Matt, because she was in control and had every intention of staying that way.

"Kate, are you okay?" Tate's voice interrupted her thoughts as she made her way through the hospital atrium towards the building's exit. It was jarring to hear his voice when she was thinking about Matt. She looked up to find him walking beside her, and she hadn't even noticed.

"I'm sorry, Tate, what did you say?"

"I asked if you were okay."

She wasn't going to lie to Tate. "No, but I am going to be," she said, with enough conviction to convince both of them.

"So where are you headed?" she asked as they left the hospital, his early departure as uncharacteristic as her own.

"I'm guessing the same place you are, to a meeting with Matt McKayne."

She shook her head from side to side, the momentary lightness now gone. Who was she kidding? The only person in control was Matt. He had always been in control, it was one of the things that had drawn her to him, but now she was terrified. If he was in control then she wasn't, and the small whisper of doubt she had over her ability to keep her emotional distance from him blossomed into fear.

"I don't think you have to worry about the lawsuit interfering with your fellowship. McKayne seems to know what he is doing."

Tate had assumed her anxiety was related to the lawsuit. She should have felt relieved at his assumption but instead she felt insulted. It felt like Tate was choosing Matt over her and it hurt. She couldn't help her bitter response. "Looks can be deceiving, Tate."

"You don't trust him," Tate replied, more as a statement than a question. Kate was glad they were walking, wanting to hide her face and blame her expression on the feel of the cold spring chill on her face.

"You do?" she countered, unwilling to divulge any information about whether or not she trusted Matt, because truthfully she still didn't know herself.

"Yes, I do. I am not sure what it is about him. He's arrogant and he likes to be in charge, but I can tell it comes from a driving need to succeed and do his job well. He probably should have been a surgeon."

"Ha," Kate scoffed, thinking about how Matt's family would have taken a departure from the legal profession.

"What is it you don't like about him?" Tate asked.

He broke my heart and abandoned me, Kate said inside her head. Out loud she simply said, "I think we are here."

They walked into the lobby of the downtown high-rise and took the elevator to the top floor. Tate walked to the receptionist's desk to check in while Kate took in her surroundings. Matt had done well if the office was anything to go by. There were floor-to-ceiling windows with a view of the water. The office reception area was beautifully furnished with comfortable seating and a granite coffee bar. Tate handed her a warm mug. "I thought maybe you should avoid any more caffeine. It's lemon tea."

Kate looked down and noticed the small tremor in her hand that Tate had already taken note of. "Thanks."

"Dr. Spence and Dr. Reed."

She looked up and saw a middle-aged woman looking at her expectantly. Tate rose with Kate and they followed the woman through the open office area towards a corner office. "Mr. McKayne, Dr. Spence and Dr. Reed."

They walked into the office and sat in the two large leather chairs across from Matt's desk. Once seated, Kate took her first real glance at Matt. He was dressed in a charcoal-gray suit with a blue shirt and steel-gray tie that matched the cold look in his eyes. His jaw was clean-shaven and clenched. She couldn't read him and that bothered her on multiple levels.

"You went to Brown?" Kate turned to look at Tate, who was looking past Matt at his framed degree hanging on the wall behind the desk.

"Yes, I did my undergraduate degree there, before going to Columbia Law." She was watching Matt intently, waiting for him to change the focus and start discussing the case, but instead he was staring at Tate like she wasn't even in the room. He wouldn't, there was no way he would.

"Tate, as your lawyer, I need to disclose to you a potential conflict of interest I have in regard to this case."

"Go ahead, I'm listening."

Kate tried to speak, to stop Matt from saying whatever he was going to say, but no words came out.

"Kate and I knew each other during our undergraduate degree at Brown. We were lovers."

Everything was slipping away. She couldn't focus. Not on Matt, not on Tate, not even on her own thoughts and feelings that were racing through her. Cruel. This was cruel to her and to Tate. After what seemed like an eternity Tate's voice broke the silence.

"I would have appreciated that information much earlier. From Kate," Tate said in a monotone, turning his head towards her as he spoke. It was the same look he had worn the night they had broken up, one of shock and disappointment. She wouldn't look away, he deserved her attention, but maintaining eye contact did nothing to assuage her feelings of helplessness and shame. He was right: he had deserved the truth from her.

"Tate, I can explain," she said, knowing nothing was going to make this better. She had already destroyed their relationship once, and just when they were finally getting back on track with being the friends they always should have just been, she had lied to him and allowed him to be made a fool of in front of Matt.

"You don't need to explain anything to me, Kate. Your sexual relationships are no longer relevant to me, but I thought we were going to be honest with each other from here on in. I guess I was wrong." He rose from the chair and turned, focusing his attention on Matt.

"Matt, at this point there is only one thing I want from you. I want this case and my connection to Kate over." Then he walked out of the room, and the sound of the door slamming behind her made her jump.

"Kate, I had to tell him," she heard Matt saying from across the desk with an air of authority and conviction that she didn't appreciate. His tone only helped to fuel the deep sense of hurt that had been close to the surface since their reunion and now was ready to boil over.

"You have to do a lot of things, Matt. You have to be the perfect son, the perfect grandson, and now the perfect lawyer. But what you really are is the perfect coward, taking the easy way out, hiding behind all the grandiose responsibilities of your perfect, rich, high-society life, ignoring the real things in life you have to be responsible for."

"What are you talking about, Kate?" He hadn't yelled, but he might have, to look at him. Still, the look of Matt, his jaw clenched, his hands gripping the arms of his chair was not enough to stop the words that she had screamed in her head for years.

"That's just it, Matt, you are so screwed up that you still haven't bothered to figure out what is really important to you."

"And Tate Reed? That is who's important to you these days, is it, Kate?" He had left his chair, his hands bracing his body as he leaned across the desk towards her. Even though they were still feet apart, she felt him, his anger, his fire, and she drew back in her chair, pressing herself into the back of it.

"Yes, Matt. My friends are important to me and they deserve to be treated far better than what Tate got today."

"You don't think Tate deserved to know we were lovers?" His words were sarcastic, and everything about him reminded her of a hunter about to go in for his final attack, but she wasn't about to concede to him now.

"We were never lovers, Matt. You never loved me. You may not remember that, but I do."

She stood from the chair and was happy that she had kept her coat with her, feeling more than ready to leave this conversation and Matt's office. She had turned towards the door when she felt Matt grab her hand and spin her back towards him.

"Kate, don't go, we're not done," he ordered.

Grief tore through her and settled low in her stomach. "I didn't go, Matt, you did. I trusted you once and I was wrong, and I have had to live with that. But we are done, Matt. You decided that years ago." She backed away and he let her go.

She walked into the dimly lit establishment that was filled with the rich smell of wood and the sound of fiddle music playing in the background. Her eyes scanned the room until she found what she was looking for.

She went to the bar, ordered two eighteen-year-old single malt Scotches, and walked over to Tate's booth, sliding in on the leather padded bench opposite and passing over the tumbler before he took notice.

"I should have told you about my past with Matt. I was wrong and you have every right not to forgive me, but I really hope you do because you are one of the few people in this world that I trust and I respect so much more than my actions have shown." Her words tumbled from her with unmistakable sincerity.

"You have always had more guts than any other surgeon I know." He picked up the glass she had brought him and took a fortifying mouthful. "That night six months ago you were right."

"I know. We both did everything we could to save Mr. Weber but it was futile."

Tate shook his head. "No, Kate, you were right about us. We were great friends and we loved each other, but we were not *in love* with each other. It took me a long time to admit that to myself. My pride was hurt when you rejected my proposal and the anger I felt towards you made it hard for me to realize that I was more angry than sad at what should have been the loss of the love of my life but wasn't."

"And now?" Kate asked tentatively, not knowing where the conversation was going.

"Now I should probably thank you and apologize to you for being an ass for the past several months, including my part in what happened today."

"You have every right to be angry about what happened today. I'm angry. I should have been honest with you from the start when you asked if Matt and I knew each other. But it wasn't like how he made it sound."

"It doesn't matter. For the most part, what happened in your past is none of my business."

"For the most part?"

"Unfortunately, he is our hospital-appointed lawyer, and requesting a change in counsel might bring to light this little love triangle that I think we all would like to keep under wraps."

"The hospital rumor mill would love that. It would give the operating room nurses something to gossip about well after my departure. Kate Spence, surgical slut."

"Don't." For the first time in the conversation Tate's anger returned. "You and I both know you are absolutely anything but."

"Thank you," she replied, embarrassed. Despite her level of comfort with Tate, it was still awkward to discuss her sexual history, particularly as he represented half of her total number of partners. He must have felt the same, because he drained the remainder of his glass.

"He still has feelings for you." Kate's eyes flew wide and landed on Tate. "It took me a while to pick up on it because things were so tense and uncomfortable between us, but today at his office I think he was clearly marking what he considers his."

"I'm not his, he never wanted me. He made that very clear, repeatedly clear."

Tate's face quirked sarcastically and he changed his voice to a slow,, explanatory drawl. "Kate, I think we have already delicately established that at one time he wanted you very much, and I'm not wrong about him now. Finish your drink and let's get out of here. We both have early mornings."

Outside the bar he hailed them a cab and rode with her back to her apartment. When the cab stopped she immediately saw Matt sitting on the front steps of the brownstone, waiting.

"You have company. Do you want me to leave?" Tate asked as the cab pulled to a stop.

"No," she responded, not sure what she wanted to happen but knowing she was in no state to be alone with Matt. Outside his office, out of his expensive suit, he looked more like the Matt she'd known, and she still didn't trust herself, angry or not, to be with him.

Without further words, Tate paid the driver and exited the vehicle, coming around to her side to open the door and secure an arm around her waist both for support and as a statement.

"McKayne," Tate greeted Matt.

"Reed," Matt replied, before turning his burning stare directly to Kate. "I need to talk to you."

"We have already talked today and we both said what we wanted to say. Nothing has changed since then."

"By the looks of things, a lot has changed since then."

"Not between you and I. Now, if you will excuse us, it's late." Kate avoided any further eye contact as she brushed past him, but felt his anger. She opened the door to her building and eventually the one to her apartment, with Tate still behind her. She didn't look back when the door closed.

"He's gone." Tate answered her unasked question. "And I'm not wrong. Matt wants you. Badly." There was no jealousy in his words.

"'Night, Kate. Take care of yourself." Then he turned and left. Kate walked over to the door and locked up for the night. If only keeping her heart safe from Matt McKayne was that easy.

CHAPTER SIX

KATE WAS BACK with Tate. Again the sound of their names together and the very thought of it was sickening. Apparently competition was all Tate had needed to see the light and reclaim Kate as his own, and she had been ready and willing. He walked to the kitchen bar and poured himself a drink. He took a sip, allowing the feeling of the cool liquid flowing down his throat to replace the taste of bile the image Kate with another man brought forth.

It didn't help. He reached for his keys on the entry table but then common sense returned. Nothing good would come of going back to Kate's tonight. It would probably have the opposite effect of pushing Kate further into the other man's arms. But he needed to do something. Something to take his mind away from the jealousy he felt towards Tate and the anger he felt towards himself for ever letting her go. He dropped the keys back onto the table, peeled off his shirt and went towards the punching bag in the den. Not bothering to change out of his jeans, he hit the bag, once, twice, and then again and again. No matter how many times or how hard he hit the bag, nothing changed. He wasn't the man in Kate's life any more, and he was entirely responsible for that.

He stopped punching and ran his hand through his sweat-drenched hair, feeling his chest rise and fall with the force of his exertion. He needed to cool off his body and his temper so he walked outside onto the penthouse balcony, letting the cold night air hit the bare skin of his chest. He rested his hands on the cement ledge, looking out into the night and without thought in the direction of Kate's apartment. He couldn't escape it. Tonight was going to be another night where he relived their ending and the choice he had made.

Kate had always been a temptation he couldn't resist. From the moment he'd seen her, to every time he had spent time with her, he had told himself he needed to walk away, until he finally had, but not until after the damage had already been done.

If he had known how they were going to end, maybe that would have been enough to keep him from her. But from the moment he'd met her she had became like a vice, a secret addiction that he felt powerless against. He had known that it would never last, couldn't last. Kate hadn't fitted into his world, and the way they had been together wouldn't have lasted once his real life had intruded.

The end was supposed to be graduation. Kate had applied to several medical schools, but of all the Ivy League schools that had accepted her, only Boston had provided her the scholarship she had needed to be able to attend. She'd had no choice: if she wanted to be a doctor then Boston was it. For the complete opposite reasons he'd had to go to New York. Every man in his family had attended Columbia Law and despite his ever-increasing resentment towards his family and their demands, he hadn't been able to abandon the tradition his own father had been a part of.

Their end came more spectacularly and painfully than he ever could have imagined. It was Kate's last night at Brown before she moved home for the summer. It was also their last night together. They had talked about visiting each other, staying in touch, but both knew their workloads and schedules were likely to make that impossible, no matter how much they wanted it to happen. He also knew that Kate was an indulgence he couldn't afford to keep, not with the life that was planned for him.

So that last night she came over to his apartment, like she always did, and they settled in for a night of the "usual." Take-out, beer and a movie that was meant to serve as a distraction from the inevitable goodbye. As the movie droned on in the background, as she had many times before, Katie cuddled into his side, her naturally cold hands tucked into the warmth of his body. Despite his attraction to her, he had never let their "friendship" become closer than this. What had become torture for him months ago now felt like a lifeline slipping from his grasp.

He was never going to have this again, be with her again, and as he looked down at her, she tilted her head up to meet his gaze. Her eyes said everything he was feeling. This was it, this was their end, and her lips started to part. She was going to say goodbye, and he didn't want to hear it. He needed to stop her and instinct took over as he brought his mouth crashing down on hers.

Never in a million years would he have imagined the instant explosive desire he felt on contact with her lips. They were soft and pressed against his. Still partly open, he slid his tongue across them, tasting her; she gasped and he slid his tongue into her mouth, wanting more. He encircled her with his arm, his hand weaving into her hair to hold her against him. Then he felt it, the tentative motion of Katie tasting him back. He slowed for a moment, enjoying the feeling of her exploring him, before his desire was once again demanding more.

He pushed them both back across the couch, her body fitting perfectly beneath him. He moved from her lips to her cheek and down her neck, his body supported on one flexed arm, while his other hand dipped underneath her shirt and pressed into her bare abdomen. He heard her moan, felt her arch against him. More, he need more, and he rose from her long enough to pull both their shirts over their heads before coming back to her.

He continued where he'd left off, kissing her neck, her shoulders, her collarbone, and then the tops of her breasts, which were pushing out of her black lace bra. He brushed his hand over her breast, feeling her hard nipple jutting for attention. Then he cupped her and let his thumb trace the nipple's outline. More, his lips found the other nipple, and Katie gasped as he kissed and suckled through the black lace. She arched again and he reached behind her and undid the clasp. She grabbed the front of the bra and tugged herself free.

She was perfect. Her brown hair fanned over the couch, her eyes a sultry gray he had never seen before, and her creamy-white skin pink with a flush he now knew extended beyond her face.

He returned to her mouth and kissed her as deeply as he could. Her hands traced up his chest, then curled as she clung to him. She wanted him and he had to have her. He didn't stop kissing her as he reached for the button on her jeans, pulling them open. His hand slipped inside and he used the heel of his hand to grind against her. She gasped and then moved against him. It was all the encouragement he needed as he slipped his fingers inside to feel her. She felt like hot silk and for the first time Matt thought he might not be able to hold on as he felt himself getting harder than he had ever felt.

Opening his own jeans for relief, he then removed both pairs, pulling her small black panties with her jeans. He was staring at the most beautiful naked woman he had ever seen when Katie reached up and touched him. Her fingers first brushed against the length of him and then encircled him. Her thumb rubbed against the moistness at his tip. He couldn't wait or last any longer. He moved between

her legs and reached behind her thigh to draw one leg up
to open her to him and then plunged into her as deep and
hard as he could.

He heard her cry out at the same time as he registered
the exquisite tightness and muscles clamped all around
him. He looked down and saw the pain across her face
and a small tear coming from her eye. Oh, God, what had
he done? He started to withdraw when her hands came
up and grabbed his shoulders to hold him in place. "Don't
move," she whimpered.

"Katie, I'm hurting you."

"Please, Matt, just don't move."

"Katie."

"Please," she begged.

Katie had never asked him for anything before this moment and he shuddered at the thought of this being her
first request. He closed his eyes and buried his face in her
neck as he tried to block out the reality that she was a virgin and he had hurt her. He took a deep breath, inhaling
the rosemary and mint scent of her shampoo. He couldn't
face the tears in her eyes right now, so instead he spoke
softly into her ear.

"Katie, do you trust me?"

"Yes." The honesty in her response was heartbreaking.

"Okay, wrap your arms around my neck and hold onto
me." She complied, and Matt reached behind her other
thigh, holding her to him as he lifted them both into a sitting position, keeping himself deeply embedded within her
but now with her in control. He ran his fingers softly up
and down her bare back, trying to soothe the pain.

"I'm sorry," she cried softly.

"Shh… I'm the one who's sorry, Katie." His hand
cupped her face and his thumb brushed away the few tears
that were there. Then he kissed her softly and was rewarded with her kissing him back. How long they stayed

locked together, kissing, exploring each other's mouths, tasting and trailing paths across each other's necks he didn't know, but he did notice the first small rise and fall of Katie against him. His body had not forgotten where it was and her small movement was enough to make him harden further.

"Oh," she gasped.

Before he could beg her to let him let go so he could stop hurting her, she moved again, a little more this time. This time the expression on her face was far from one of pain. She was mesmerizing as she moved up and down against him. Her hands anchored on his shoulders as he reached around and cupped her bottom. Each movement was slightly more than the last, her breathing becoming more erratic.

He removed one hand from her bottom and gently spread her, letting his fingers brush her swollen nub at the same time she moved against him. This time her cry was not of pain, and Matt felt her lean into him and increase her pace and depth. She was so tight that every time she moved he felt himself push into a new hot, wet place. Her movements also caused her breasts to brush against his chest with every stroke. Her bottom was firm beneath his hand and his other hand confirmed the wetness he was feeling from the inside.

It was only his fascination with watching her that kept him from losing control. Gently, Matt lifted his hips to meet her downward stroke. Then with each subsequent stroke she came down a little faster, a little harder, a little deeper as Matt continued to rise up to meet her. Then he heard her start to hold her breath, little cries escaping her throat, until she raised herself to his tip and came down as deep and hard as his first thrust, crying out, and he felt her shudder and pulsate against him. He gripped her hips, pulling her as hard to him as he could, and cried out with equal satisfaction as he emptied into her still pulsating body.

She was collapsed against him, panting and slick with sweat, when he heard her whisper, "I love you."

His heart had been pounding and his mind racing, trying to take in everything that had just happened. It was an impossible situation to avoid, with Katie wrapped around him, him still inside her. He had played with fire and had gotten burned. After over a year of resisting his attraction to her they had gone over a cliff together, past the point of no return. He tried to think rationally, which was almost impossible in the circumstances, but one of them had to, and apparently it wasn't going to be Katie. He had heard of women becoming emotionally attached to their first lovers, overwhelmed by the experience. Was that what she was feeling? Surely if Katie loved him she would have told him before this.

He wrapped his arms back around her and stood, still clutching her to him. He strode through to the bedroom, where he laid her on the bed, finally separating them. He was pained at the small stain of blood on her thigh, recalling the force that had put it there. He lay down beside her, drawing the duvet over both of them. Katie backed against him, her curves tucking against him, and without thought he wrapped his arm around her. "I'm sorry, I didn't know. Are you okay?" he asked quietly.

"I'm perfect," she responded softly, taking his hand in hers and nestling further into him. Minutes later she was asleep, her breathing the only sound in the dark quiet night.

He didn't sleep. He lay there tortured by the naked reminder of what they had done and tried to figure out where they would go from there. He stared at the night's lights through his bedroom window and played the arguments in his head over and over again. They had passed the point of no return, and the impossible task of saying goodbye to her had just gotten infinitely harder. It had been a night of firsts for both of them. Kate had lost her virginity and he had actually felt like they had made love, unlike his previous physical encounters. With the added emotion he had become out of control with desire and need. He couldn't think straight. Not with Katie naked, pressed against him. Not while he was hard and using all his energy just to resist waking her up to make love to her all over again.

When morning had come, he awoke to find Katie facing him, her eyes watching him intently. "I'm not going to Boston." She had been definitive in her statement and Matt felt the ramifications of their night together growing beyond what he had lain awake imagining.

"Of course you are. I'm going to New York and you are going to Boston, Katie. You know that." He tried to keep the panic from his voice and match her decisiveness.

"I don't want to go to Boston, Matt. Not without you." The situation was spiraling out of control. Did she know what she was saying? Medical school, her scholarship, everything she had worked for, she was going to give that up? For him? No way in hell was he going to let that happen. He had spent his life not being able to have his own dreams or plans and he would be damned if Katie was going to give up hers. He got out of the bed and grabbed the nearest pair of jeans on the bedroom floor, wincing slightly as the denim covered his body's response to her nakedness.

In a single moment he knew what he needed to do and didn't stop to think before the words came from his mouth. "Katie, last night was a mistake." She recoiled and he could tell that he had hurt her, but if that was what it took to keep her from throwing her life away then so be it.

"I don't believe you." He could tell that she was trying to be brave with her tone and eye contact, but he also saw that she was now clutching the sheet in her fist as she clung to it. She was still so innocent and he wasn't going to let his family take that from her.

"I told you last night that I was sorry it happened." Even he wasn't sure at that moment whether he was telling the truth or not. Would he trade last night not to hurt her this morning? The only thing he did know was that he would not let her sacrifice her dreams for him.

"And I told you last night that I love you. And I think you love me too."

She was so brave and so beautiful, and at that moment he knew that he did love her, was in love with her, and loved her enough to do the right thing and let her go, by whatever means necessary.

"Katie, you don't love me. You just think you love me because of last night, because of it being your first time."

"Don't tell me what I think or how I feel, Matt. I loved you before last night, during last night, and even now."

"Katie, I'm sorry. I don't love you." And he turned and left the room, but not before he saw the look of pain strike as his words hit her. When he entered the living room, re-minders of the previous night were all around. The half-eaten pizza, the couch cushions on the floor, their clothes haphazardly scattered across the room. He had to leave. He couldn't face any reminders of what they had shared, reminders that might make him weaken and change his mind, go back to her, tell her he loved her, let her sacri-fice herself to be with him. He picked up his shirt, grabbed his keys and left without looking back. When he returned hours later the apartment was empty and Katie was gone.

CHAPTER SEVEN

A SLEEPLESS NIGHT turned into a painful morning as Matt arrived at his office. For the first time in his life he had arrived after eight and already regretted the time spent in self-recrimination over a past that he could not change. He walked through the waiting room on a direct route to his office and saw Tate stand and walk towards him.

"We need to talk," Tate said bluntly. He was looking him directly in the eye and was obviously not going to back down or be dissuaded.

"Not here," Matt replied, aware that there was potential for this conversation to end in the two men coming to blows, and wanting to keep that event out of the office. "I need a cup of coffee."

The two men walked out in silence and remained that way for the ten minutes it took them to reach a local coffee shop. They each ordered and sat down at a table, sizing up each other. Tate was not backing down in his gaze or the hard line of his jaw.

"Are you here to tell me to stay away from Kate?" Matt asked bluntly, challenging the man sitting opposite him.

"No. Kate is a grown woman who is capable of making her own decisions," Tate answered calmly. The man was confident, but Matt would be too if he had just come from Kate's bed.

"Apparently," he replied sarcastically. "So what do we need to talk about, then?"

"Whether you are the best person to be representing us," Tate answered in the same calm tone, unfazed by Matt's barb.

"I'm the best," Matt stated definitively. Through the long hours of last night he had questioned that very issue, wondering if he could stand being with Kate and the man who had taken his place throughout the duration of the case. In the end he'd decided to stay on the case because he still wanted the best for her, and he was still the best.

"I don't doubt that. My problem is that your former relationship with Kate and the unresolved issues between you are not compatible with working well together. You also probably do not have my best interests at the top of your list of priorities either." Tate was faintly smiling at his last comment.

"So you want me to resign from the case?" Matt asked, feeling no patience for whatever game the other man was playing.

"That was my first instinct. Then I realized that your resignation would lead to a lot of questions. The last thing I want is for anyone else to know about you and Kate." Any trace of a smile was gone and Matt saw anger in his eyes for the first time since his initial disclosure of their past together.

"Why is that? You don't like the comparison?" Matt knew he shouldn't be pushing, but he couldn't help himself, his burning resentment overtaking his well-practiced interview skills.

"What I don't want is the hospital administration rumor mill circulating the exploits of Dr. Spence's sex life. She'll be portrayed as something we both know she's not."

Matt hated Tate at that moment, hated and respected him for putting Kate first. It was sickening to think that she might have replaced him with a man who was better and more worthy of her than him.

"So what do you want?" Matt finally responded.

"I want you to do your job. I want the lawsuit against us dropped so that we all can move on with our lives."

"And Kate?"

"I've said what I came here today to say. You can figure out the rest." Then he walked out, leaving Matt at the table.

How many casualties did an event have to involve before it was considered to be a mass trauma? Kate wondered. She was sitting in the café near her brownstone, studying for the board exam, and unfortunately drawing parallels between the state of her life and emergency states. Factor A, the man who had broken her heart. Factor B, a lawsuit threatening her career. Factor C, the risk of failing the board exam due to stress from the aforementioned factors A and B. For the first time in years she was distracted; the words she read fleeing her mind as soon as she read them.

She felt overwhelmed. This was not a new state for her as she was constantly overwhelmed by the physical and emotional strain of her job. But now, for the first time, she felt guilt towards Matt, and the mere presence of the new emotion was enough to push her past her tipping point. It was a struggle, feeling anger towards him and his nerve at coming back into her life as if he belonged there and on the other hand feeling guilt for misleading him about the status of her relationship with Tate. She didn't want to be the bad guy; she didn't want to be anything. She wanted to let go of her relationship with Matt; she just didn't know how to do that.

As if on cue, she lifted her eyes away from her textbook for the hundredth time that afternoon, but this time they fell on Matt. He was walking towards her in jeans and a black polo shirt, which made him look younger than his expensive tailored suits did. The effect was still the same, though, and she watched as several female heads turned and admired everything he had to offer. It was odd that she never stopped being taken in by his pure physical beauty. It wasn't just his tall stature, powerful build, or the face whose features aligned perfectly, from his deep blue eyes to the perfect faint pink lips that sat between the masculine jaw and nose. It was him, his presence, the effortlessness he exuded.

This was not a made-up appearance, this was who he was—a man like no other. She couldn't look away, even when parts of her reacted treacherously, still apparently remembering the feel of and taste of him from nights earlier.

Aside from unwanted attraction, she couldn't move past the astonishment of watching Matt walk up to her table and take a seat opposite her, so much like years past that it hurt, and she swallowed the pain she felt rising within her. She waited, speechless, to hear what was going to come next. What else did they have to say to each other? How much more pain could they cause each other?

"Ask me how I found you?" It was more of a challenge than a question. He was resting on his forearms on the table, his body leaning forward, his entire focus on her.

"I don't know," she replied honestly, confused with where the conversation was going.

He reached over and pushed a lock of hair behind her ear, twirling it in his fingers before he uncovered her face. "Because, Kate, I know you."

"No, you don't." She lacked his conviction. His single touch had been less physically intimate than most of their contact since his return, but emotionally it tore at her resolve. He seemed to believe every word he was saying, but she still felt the need to contradict him, to protect herself from the temptation of him.

"Yes, Kate, I do. I appreciate and respect everything

that you have accomplished, but that doesn't change who you are."

"Who am I, Matt?" She couldn't resist the question. It was a question that had plagued her for years. Who was she in his eyes?

"You're mine." His eyes flashed with the same possession his words held. She should have been offended, she should have been afraid, but what she felt was want.

"No." The word escaped her lips, but in truth it was more a reminder to herself of what she could not have.

"Yes, you are, Kate, you always have been. You and I both know that."

She had been his. She couldn't deny that she had been one hundred percent in her feelings towards him, so much so that the memory of their coming together still brought with it as much a memory of completeness as it did emotional pain. She had also never given him up, not completely, not enough to move on and fall in love with someone else. Enough was enough, though. She wasn't going to let him keep playing whatever game he was playing.

"What do you want, Matt?"

"Isn't it obvious? I want you."

"It's too late, Matt, you can't have me." Nothing changed in his demeanor, except that he appeared even more focused and more all-encompassing. He had heard her, but obviously didn't believe her.

"I already have you, Kate, and this time I have no intention of walking away. The sooner you accept that, the sooner we'll all be better off."

Then, without warning, he stood over the table, leaned down and pressed his lips to her forehead. This time he lingered. She could smell his cologne, breathed in his scent, and felt that heat of his body, before he pulled away. Then, just as he had joined her, he turned and left.

Shock seeped through her from her forehead, which he had kissed so sweetly, to all the muscles inside her that contracted at his touch. Several parts of their conversation competed for attention in her mind. Had he remembered the night she had cried about her mother and he had kissed her on the forehead after carrying her to bed, the night she had realized she was in love with him?

Then there were his words, not just the words but the way he had said them. He had left no room for doubt that he had meant everything he had said. But would she know if he hadn't? She had spent her career learning to trust herself and her instincts, but with Matt she couldn't trust herself, her feelings, or him. All the words, declarations, and touches couldn't change the words that had been carved into her soul. "Katie, I'm sorry. I don't love you."

The offensive wail of her pager broke through her thoughts and provided temporary respite. She dialed the hospital operator and was patched through to the emergency department. Within a minute she was gone from the shop, her focus back where it needed to be and the past left behind.

CHAPTER EIGHT

SHE REACHED THE hospital within fifteen minutes and was in the trauma room gowned and shielded before the ambulance arrived. Chloe was standing next to her, both women waiting. This time their entire interaction was succinct and directed towards patient care.

The ambulance attendants rolled a gurney into the trauma room and the patient was transferred to the hospital bed. The young man appeared to be in his early twenties and was strapped to a backboard with full C-spine precautions. Chloe took the head of the bed and assessed his airway and level of consciousness while he was hooked up to monitors, and Kate and the trauma-team nurses completed a full body survey, assessing for areas of maximal trauma and prioritizing injuries for care.

"His airway is compromised and GCS is six—we need to intubate," Kate heard Chloe order. And for a window of ninety seconds the team stood back while Chloe intubated the young man. After the endotracheal tube was in place, she and Kate auscultated the lung fields. She didn't hear any breath sounds on the right, and Chloe confirmed the finding.

"Set up for a chest tube," Kate called. A sterile tray of instruments was opened and after quickly prepping the skin and changing into sterile gloves, she made a stab incision above one of the man's ribs and inserted the hard plastic tube until she felt a loss of resistance and heard the trapped air escaping, allowing the man's lung to reinflate.

"Breath sounds on the right established. Good job, Kate," Chloe said.

Once the patient's airway, breathing and circulation had been stabilized, Kate continued. "Details," she called to the paramedic team, who remained in the room.

"Unknown male, traveling by bicycle when he was hit at moderate speed by a mid-sized SUV. The patient was found several yards from his bicycle, with his helmet still in place but cracked in multiple locations."

"Has he been conscious since your team arrived?"

"No."

"Chloe, once you're happy he's stable for movement, we need to move for a full-body CT. I need to know what to worry about first, blood in his brain or blood in his chest and belly."

"He should be stable enough in five minutes. He needs more volume so that he can maintain his pressure and make up for any ongoing losses prior to going to the operating room."

"Okay. I'm going to call the OR now and have them set up. Have the team page me once his scans are done so I can review them immediately with the in-house radiologist."

"Will do."

"Thanks."

Four hours later, Kate was finally leaving the intensive care unit, where she had just dropped off her patient direct from the operating room. She was still strapped to her pager as the trauma team leader for the week, but now had a momentary reprieve. The cyclist's helmet had saved his life. His brain had fared okay in the collision.

Unfortunately, the same could not have been said for his spleen, which had suffered a massive laceration after he had hit the curb. The young man had needed an emergency laparotomy and splenectomy, along with several units of blood and blood products, but was going to recover.

Kate walked back to the emergency department to find Chloe finishing up the paperwork from a shift that should have ended an hour and a half earlier. Kate hadn't bothered to change out of her scrubs and the clogs she'd worn in the operating room and felt exhausted from the fast pace and physical demands of the procedure. Chloe looked like she felt the same, appearing pale in contrast to her bright red hair and the dark blue of the hospital scrubs the emergency doctors also wore. Kate slumped into the chair beside her friend, losing her normal good posture.

"He's okay. It was a spleen trauma, but it's out and he's stable in the intensive care unit," Kate reported, knowing Chloe's desire to follow all of her patients.

"Thanks for coming back and letting me know."

Chloe stood from her chair and wavered before reaching down to the desk for support.

"Are you okay, Chloe?" Kate asked.

"Yeah, just tired, stressed, busy, the usual. I think I might have some low-grade virus or something that has pushed me over the edge."

"Is there anything I can do?" Kate asked, concerned that for the first time her perfectly put-together friend was actually admitting to struggling. Chloe had always made everything seem effortless, which made Kate worry that she was feeling a lot worse than she was admitting.

"Don't you think you have enough on your plate?" Chloe asked, one eyebrow arching upwards, in a friendly, teasing tone.

"More than I ever wanted, but I'm sorting through it the best I can." She stared at Chloe, knowing what she should say but fighting a lifelong instinct to keep things inside.

"I know that you're tired, but I was wondering if I could drive you home and maybe we could talk a bit."

Chloe stopped all the other tasks she was trying to finish and looked Kate in the eye. "That would be more than okay. Give me ten minutes to hand over my patients and I'll meet you by the parkade elevators."

True to her word, Chloe met her and they managed their escape without further interruption. "Are you hungry?" Kate asked, realizing she had missed lunch and supper while dealing with the trauma.

"A little bit. Do you have anything at your house?"

"No. Do you?"

"No. Eating out, it is."

Creatures of habit, Kate and Chloe tucked themselves into the back of the small Italian restaurant where the staff knew them by name. Kate waited to order and for their drinks to arrive before she drew in a breath and took the plunge. "Matt wants me."

Chloe didn't appear surprised. "What does that mean exactly?"

"I have no idea. At first it seemed purely physical and I thought you were right about it stemming from jealousy over Tate, and I told him that I wanted nothing more than a lawyer-client relationship. Then he told Tate about our past and we had a huge fight, which didn't seem to deter him at all because he showed up again today."

"And?"

"He said I was his and that I always have been and I always would be." She shivered, saying his words aloud having no less impact than hearing them from him hours earlier.

"Is he right?"

"I don't know. I don't understand what happened between us all those years ago and I don't understand what's happening now."

"So stop trying to think through and understand everything. How do you *feel*, Kate?"

"Terrified."

"What are you terrified of?"

"Of trusting him. Of making the same mistakes, getting hurt and losing myself all over again."

"Okay, that's a start. If you could trust him and weren't going to get hurt, would you want to be with him?"

"Yes."

"Are you still in love with him?"

"Yes." She was surprised at how quickly the words left her, but knew in the instant she heard her own answer that it was the truth.

"Can you talk me through what happened last time?"

"He was my everything. We met in my third year of undergraduate studies at Brown and became friends. He still had a long-distance girlfriend back in New York. During our friendship I fell in love with him, but never told him or acted on my feelings. After graduation he was going to law school in New York and I had a full scholarship to medical school in Boston."

"So what changed things?"

"Our last night together was unbearable. It was the end: he was going to go on with his life and me with mine. I spent the evening torn between telling him I loved him and just saying goodbye. Then before I said anything he kissed me."

"And?"

"And I thought we made love."

"I'm confused."

"We had sex. I told him I loved him and fell asleep in his arms happier than I had ever been in my entire life. The next morning I knew I couldn't say goodbye and I told him I wasn't going to."

"And?"

"He said he didn't love me and it had been a mistake. Then he went back to New York to be with his girlfriend and I never heard from him again."

"Oh, my God, Kate, I'm so sorry. I can't even imagine how devastating that must have been."

"What's worse is that I didn't believe him at first. After he left I waited for him to come back to apologize, to tell me the truth, that he loved me and things were going to be okay. But he never came back. I sat in his apartment for hours, waiting, hoping, and he never came back. Even after I left his apartment, I still thought he just needed time, that there was no way he could touch and hold me the way he had and not be in love with me too."

"So what did you do?"

"I held on as long as I could. I gave up my scholarship to Boston and managed to secure a place at Columbia in New York. I begged my father to take a second mortgage on our house to cover the lost scholarship and I left messages for Matt to tell him I was in New York when he was ready to talk."

"He never tried to contact you?"

"No, he never looked back. I believed in him so much that I lost all faith in myself."

The waitress arrived with their order and Kate was grateful for the interruption. As cathartic as it felt to finally talk about what had happened, it also brought to the surface how she had felt.

Both women were silent as they began to eat. Kate's mind kept telling herself the story. Matt's abandonment had left her with a small seed of self-doubt that had germinated over months of loneliness. She hadn't been able to resist following the coverage of his life in the society pages, and seeing him with other women had intensified her loneliness.

It had been a cold, windy day in November when she'd seen him again, walking across campus. She hadn't seen him in five months but had recognized him instantly in the crowd. She'd called his name and he'd turned to look and then kept walking. She'd convinced herself that he hadn't seen her. The second time she'd seen him she'd called his name more loudly and he'd moved his head slightly in her direction but hadn't turned around.

The final rejection had come in March. She had been sitting in a local coffee shop, studying, determined to make the dean's honor list so she would qualify for a scholarship the following year. She had been deep in thought when she'd had a sense that she hadn't felt in almost a year. She'd looked up and seen Matt, the same old Matt, in jeans and a cream sweater, with his brown leather tote bag slung across one shoulder. She'd seen him as he'd been looking at her and turning away.

That time she hadn't been able to say anything, she hadn't called out his name or even moved from her seat. She'd watched in horror as he'd walked away from her and out of the shop. In an instant all her fears had been confirmed. She had no longer been able to deny that he knew she was in New York and he'd wanted nothing to do with her.

She looked up to see that Chloe wasn't eating. She glanced at her own plate, which was almost full with her favorite pesto linguine that she had no appetite for. "Do you want to get this to go?"

"Yes, please. I'm exhausted," Chloe replied. As they waited for the check it was Chloe who broke the comfortable silence.

"Kate, can you think of any reason why Matt walked away from you?"

"I've thought of every reason. The only one that justifies his actions is that he really didn't love me."

"You're sure?"

"Yes."

"So what do you want now?"

"I want the impossible. I want to trust the man I love to love me back and not break my heart again."

CHAPTER NINE

IT WAS ANOTHER week before she heard from Matt again. A whole week to replay their entire relationship from their friendship to the night they'd made love, and the repercussions that had followed.

Kate was once again in the emergency department, reviewing consultations with the junior residents, when her pager went off. She looked down at the little black box that seemed forever attached to her and didn't recognize the number.

She reached for the nearest phone and dialed the displayed number. "This is Kate Spence. Someone paged?" she answered once the person on the other end picked up.

"It's Matt."

She paused, not sure what to say. Her conversation with Chloe had helped her understand her feelings towards Matt and it felt even harder to talk to him knowing she still loved him.

"Kate." Matt said her name.

"I'm here." She had lowered her voice, not sure where the conversation was headed but knowing she didn't want it overheard.

"We need to get together to talk about that night," Matt stated, in what Kate considered to be an overly business-like tone for something so intimate, something so personal. She arched her back in defense and looked around the crowded emergency department to ensure that no one was within earshot.

"I gave you more than enough opportunity to talk about that night nine years ago, Matt. I don't want to talk about it now." She waited and heard him exhale slowly.

"I meant the night that Mr. Weber died, Kate. I need to finish your statement to help with the case. But, for the record, a talk about the other night is long overdue."

It was her turn to sigh now. She felt embarrassed and could feel color flooding her face. She looked down and studied the linoleum floor as if the more intensely she stared, the more she could avoid Matt's presence on the other end of the phone.

"I can meet you after you're done working," Matt offered, saving her from having to respond to his earlier statement.

"Okay, but not at the hospital." She actually didn't know where the best place to talk with Matt was. Nowhere, she thought. She wanted to avoid a public scene but it would be worse to be together in a private place.

"I'll pick you up at nine—will that give you enough time to finish up? You can tell me then where you want to go." He was giving her control, but the gesture did little to put her at ease.

"Yes, that's fine. I'll be waiting outside my place at nine. See you then." And she hung up before she could embarrass herself further.

Matt was becoming more of a contradiction each time she talked to him. Everything she had believed about him was changing. She'd thought he didn't want her, but now he did. She'd thought what they had been together had been a lie, but he'd said she'd belong to him always. Now, after nine years, he thought they needed to talk about that night, after he had done everything possible to avoid doing that.

Kate returned to the waiting resident and did her best

to focus on the patient's history. After examining the middle-aged woman together and then arranging her admission for management of a partial small bowel obstruction, it was eight p.m., and Kate found herself sprinting home.

By the time she entered the brownstone apartment she was breathless. She had twenty minutes before Matt would be arriving, and she knew she had just enough time to shower and change. Years of rushing to and from the hospital at a moment's notice had taught her to be efficient.

She showered and washed her hair, toweling it dry and twisting it into a knot on top of her head. She rubbed in the lotion her skin desperately needed after long days spent in the dry, non-infectious conditions the hospital maintained. In her bedroom, she managed to find a pair of clean jeans and a long-sleeved black sweater. She was just bending to put on socks when the front buzzer rang. She slipped her feet into tall black leather boots, grabbed her wool coat and applied lip moisturizer as she locked her apartment and proceeded down the stairs to meet Matt.

He was waiting in the entry. He had obviously been home since the office, because the business suit was gone and in its place was a pair of dark jeans with a dress shirt and blue sweater layered over the top. Despite the layered look there was no mistaking the broadness of his shoulders and the build of his chest. The chest she had seen, had felt pressed against her. Damn, this is not what she needed to be thinking.

Matt didn't say anything. He held open the front door to her building and followed her out to his car, where he opened the passenger door for her as well. Once she was settled he closed the door securely and circled to the driver's side. It felt like being taken care of, it felt nice, and she didn't want to be feeling that again with Matt.

"Where do you want to go?" Matt asked, turning towards her with his full attention.

"I don't know," Kate answered honestly, too off balance by the situation to think properly.

"We should probably go somewhere private where our discussion can't be overheard if we're talking about the case. That leaves out public restaurants. So the options are my office or my apartment—"

"Office," Kate answered, before Matt had even finished. There was no way she wanted to be back in his apartment with him. Things had gotten way out of control the other night and she would be a fool to think that couldn't happen again.

"Okay, as you wish." He shifted the car into gear and they entered traffic. Kate avoided small talk, not knowing what to say, what it was safe to say, in this new weird dynamic between them. They wove down the streets of Boston towards Matt's office.

They arrived and Matt parked in the underground garage. He used a swipe card to open the door and unlock the elevator that carried them up to his top-floor office. Once inside, he led her through, not to his office, where she would actually have been uncomfortable given their last interaction there, but to a conference room.

The view was beautiful. Floor-to-ceiling glass windows highlighted Boston at night. The sight of the whole city spread out in front of her made her feel less important and actually calmer about the impending discussion.

"Sparkling water okay for you?" Matt asked, breaking her attention from the beauty of the city.

"Sure." She took her place in one of the chairs opposite him. "Where do you want to start?" she asked.

He nodded at her and took out a pen and pad of paper. "What was your official role the evening of Mr. Weber's death?"

"I was the chief surgical resident. I serve as backup in all situations—resident illness, difficult cases and high patient volumes. That night the on-call resident, Dr. Jensen, had been called away to do a retrieval with the transplant team, and I was called in in his absence." Okay, so maybe this was going to be okay, clean, surgical. She relaxed back into the leather conference room chair.

"What was Dr. Reed's official role?"

"Dr. Reed was the second on-call vascular surgeon. We have a backup system for all the major surgical disciplines so that in the event a surgeon is tied up in a prolonged surgical case, another patient can still receive timely care and surgical management."

"How often is the second on call needed?"

"About once every three months, but Tate might be better able to answer that question."

"Dr. Reed," Matt stated firmly.

"Pardon?" Kate asked, not understanding what the question was.

"Refer to Tate Reed as Dr. Reed in all your discussion of the case. Referring to him as Tate implies you know him beyond your professional relationship."

Kate couldn't tell if this was just Matt the lawyer talking or if it was personal. She decided she didn't need to know and waited from him to ask another question.

"When were you asked to consult in Mr. Weber's care?"

"At about ten p.m. I was already in-house, dealing with some issues in a postoperative patient, when the emergency room doctor called me."

"How soon after did you see him?"

"I went downstairs to the emergency department immediately and started my assessment. While I was examining him, the radiologist called and notified me of the CT scan findings."

"When did you first try to contact Dr. Reed?" Matt lowered and softened his voice for this question. They were getting into the part of the evening that was less clinical and more personal.

"I called Dr. Reed on his cell phone immediately after I finished on the phone with the radiologist."

"How many times did you try to call Dr. Reed?"

"I didn't count, I just kept redialing when I didn't get through."

"Did you leave any messages?"

"Yes."

"Was it unusual for Dr. Reed not to answer his cellphone?"

"Yes." She wasn't elaborating on her responses or providing any additional information. The lawyer in Matt actually seemed pleased about that.

"Were there any other occasions when Dr. Reed did not answer his phone?"

"Not prior to that night."

"Did you have any reason to believe that Dr. Reed was purposely ignoring his calls?"

Here it goes, time to get personal. She took a deep breath and straightened away from the chair, sitting upright and focusing her eyes directly on Matt's.

"After trying to contact Dr. Reed for twenty minutes, I concluded that he was probably unaware that the attempts being made to contact him were for patient care and subsequently asked the switchboard to reach him."

"Was his primary contact number for patient care his cell phone?"

"Yes."

"Then why would he not answer it in his role as second call?"

"That is a question for Dr. Reed. I cannot speak to why he would or would not do something."

"You were always too smart for your own good, Kate." He reached down and pulled his sweater off, leaving the dress shirt behind. Then he unbuttoned the cuffs and rolled the sleeves up, exposing his muscled forearms. He leaned on them and stared at her across the table. "I have a copy of Dr. Reed's phone records from that night, as does the plaintiff's attorney. They show several calls from your cell phone to Dr. Reed's, all lasting less than a minute."

"As I stated, I tried to call Dr. Reed for twenty minutes before relinquishing the responsibility to the switchboard."

"The calls from you start at eight-thirty p.m., well before your interaction with Mr. Weber."

"Yes." She wasn't going to give more detail. She had no intention of describing to Matt, Tate's proposal and the reasons behind her rejection.

"If Dr. Reed had not answered your earlier calls, do you think it was appropriate to spend twenty minutes using the same form of contact that had been ineffective up until that point?" He wasn't enjoying this, she could tell, and that was at least something.

"I was using the form of communication listed by the hospital as Dr. Reed's first contact. When that failed I appropriately moved on to the switchboard as second contact and focused on Mr. Weber, pending Dr. Reed's contact and arrival."

"Your attempts to contact Dr. Reed earlier in the evening, were they related to patient care?"

"No."

"You have a personal relationship with Dr. Reed?" It was more of a statement than a question. She knew where this was going.

"Yes."

"What is your relationship with Dr. Reed?" He was agitated now. He ran his fingers through his hair. It was going to be a mutually uncomfortable conversation.

"We have worked together for several years and are friends." Honest, she was being honest.

"Do you have a romantic relationship with Dr. Reed?"

"No."

"What was your relationship with Dr. Reed the night of Mr. Weber's death?"

"I was the chief resident and Dr. Reed was the staff surgeon."

"What was the nature of your personal relationship with Dr. Reed the night of Mr. Weber's death?" Matt asked pointedly, his entire attention fixed on Kate.

"We had been dating for one and a half years."

"Was there anything about your personal relationship that night that would have led Dr. Reed to not answer your calls?"

"Once again that is a question for Dr. Reed. I cannot speak to why he would or would not do something."

"Did you and Dr. Reed end your romantic involvement that night?" His jaw was clenched and she could see the muscle tense as it extended towards his temple. She hadn't seen Matt angry a lot when they had first known one another, but she recognized it now.

"Yes."

"Kate," he sighed, and ran his fingers through his hair again, "you are answering like you are talking to the enemy, which I'm not. If this ever gets to court then, yes, this is the exact way you are to testify, but tonight, with me, you need to open up. I need to know what happened if I'm going to help you."

"Are you sure that's the only reason you want to know?" It was direct and she didn't back down with her question or when she held his eyes. What she'd had with Matt in the past had been a lie and she damn sure wasn't going to continue to let anything but the truth be between them now. He didn't answer.

"It's not the only reason." She looked up as he started his response and saw heat in his eyes. They were locked on hers and she felt her whole body flush and pulse in response. What had seemed like a good idea, to call Matt out, now seemed an obvious, horrible mistake. The detached tone of their earlier conversation had left and everything personal was flooding in. She didn't know how to respond, couldn't respond, as her lips parted and she struggled to breathe in and out.

"Kate, are you sure you're ready to hear more? Are you ready to ask me about the things you want to know?" He was being gentle in his voice, the same soft whisper that had once been in her ear, the same careful handling when she was clearly in over her head.

"Why now, Matt? What's changed?"

"Everything, and nothing, Kate. I'm not the same man you knew, just as you aren't the same woman, but what's between us hasn't gone away and never will." He reached out and covered her hand with his. It felt warm, and strong, and all-encompassing.

"There wasn't anything between us." She pulled her hand from under his and tucked both hands under her legs, away from the temptation to touch him. She couldn't let herself get drawn back into the belief that their love was mutual.

"How can you say that, Kate? How can you speak to how I felt about us?" He was lawyering her now, using her own argument about not speaking for someone else against her. It left her cold and brought out the clear, precise, objective words and voice she used as a surgeon.

"Because you told me. You looked me in the eye the morning after we made love and you said, 'Katie, I'm sorry. I don't love you.' Then you proved it by walking out and not coming back, not answering my calls, my e-mails, my letters, and running from the sight of me. That's how I know how you felt about us." The ache in her throat was intensifying but she was not going to cry, despite the burning feeling that was pooling behind her eyes.

"I lied to you."

Her eyes flew to his.

"Why? Why would you do that? Was I that disappointing? That bad in bed that it was worth throwing everything else that was good about us away?" Gone now was her composure and with it her pride, and out came the most painful thought she had buried deep within her and avoided voicing at all costs.

She placed her elbows on her legs and buried her face in her hands, unable to face him any longer, unable to hear his response and horrified that she had asked the question. Within seconds she was being lifted from her seat. Matt had reached for her beneath her arms and raised her out of her chair. Startled, she wrapped her arms around his neck for balance and he wrapped his arms around her further, gathering her to him.

Then he crushed his mouth to hers. It wasn't soft, it wasn't gentle, it was possessive. The pressure of his lips parted hers and he began to taste her and explore her mouth as if he was a dying man searching for his last drink of water. She was angry, surprised, and entranced all at the same time, until the same urgency and passion from the other night took hold.

She ran her tongue across his lower lip, her response escalating the passion between them. At some point he walked them up against a wall and pressed her against it, shifting her to place himself between her legs and holding her by her bottom, his hands firm and solid. Warmth was spreading through her body until she felt like she was on fire. When they finally broke apart, both were gasping and he slowly slid her down his length to the floor, his erection prominent in the journey.

He cupped one side of her face and brought her gaze to

his, and it was the same old Matt. He put his finger against her lips and silenced her before she could talk. "You are the most perfect woman I have ever met, both in bed and out. No woman before or after has ever compared to you. Not a day has gone by in the last nine years that I haven't wanted to be with you, to hold you, to kiss every inch of your naked body and move inside you until you scream out my name over and over and over again."

"No." She shook her head against his words, looking away from the man who was confusing her mind and body.

"Yes, Kate," he said as he cupped the side of her face again, bringing her eyes to his.

"I don't believe you," she said. Actions were more important than words, and his actions had spoken so loudly.

"I did it for you, Kate, I walked away for you, not for me. You were going to throw away medical school, everything you had worked for. You were the most perfect, selfless woman I had ever met and I wasn't going allow anything to change you or take away your dreams."

She was stunned by his claim, both by the audacity of the lie and how truthful and heartfelt he seemed to be while making it. She took a deep breath and very clearly and slowly spoke to Matt, looking him in the eye and searching for the truth. "So what you are saying is that if I had been strong enough and gone to medical school in New York, you wouldn't have broken my heart and walked out on me without looking back?"

"If you had been in New York, I wouldn't have been strong enough to stay away from you, even if I thought it was for your own good." The passionate statement fueled her own passion and she reached out and slapped him across his cheek. The sound echoed across the conference room and she was shocked silent by her own action, drawing her hand up to touch her own cheek, mirroring his reaction. She was horrified by her response yet unwilling to apologize.

"It's been nine years, Matt, you don't need to bother lying to me any more."

She didn't let him reply. He seemed shocked by the turn of events in the last few minutes. She grabbed her jacket and purse and left the conference room, searching for the quickest way out. She didn't have a keycard to access anything, so instead she headed for the fire stairwell and fled down the twenty-five flights into the building alley. Her heart was pounding as the sound of her boots echoed on the cement stairs. In the dark, in the cold, she caught her breath, her chest heaving. He wanted her. He wanted her enough to lie to her to get her back.

CHAPTER TEN

SHE WAS FROZEN. The wind was blowing strongly off the harbor and the wet coldness was seeping through every inch of her body. She walked quickly through the cobble-stoned old roads of Boston that wound their way through the city's core from Matt's office back to her apartment. Why had Matt lied to her? What purpose did it serve? Nothing made sense, and she couldn't tell what hurt more, Matt's lies or that for a moment she had believed him.

It had taken so long to learn how to trust herself again, but she had, and a lot of that feeling had come from her confidence and success in medicine. She had even felt happy and contented with her life, leaving the past and Matt behind, until Tate had proposed.

Tate on one knee in front of her with a ring, and she had seen Matt. Pain didn't begin to describe the way she had felt when she'd realized she wasn't in love with the man in front of her, and that deep inside Matt was still trapped in her heart.

When were those feeling going to go away? Matt wasn't the same man she had known back at Brown, but that didn't seem to make a difference. The way she sensed him when he walked in a room hadn't changed. The way she felt when he touched her had changed, but unfortunately had increased a thousand times over in the intensity she felt go through her the moment his lips or hands touched her body. It was the only time her mind forgot about everything that had happened between them.

Thoughts of the passion tempered the cold she was feeling and she quickened her pace. She could have hailed a cab, but the clear, cold night air was a needed contrast to the storm she was feeling inside. Forty-five minutes later she reached the steps of her apartment, not failing to notice the large expensive sports car and the man behind the wheel a few doors down. So it was not over for tonight, she thought to herself.

She let herself into her apartment and turned on the kettle. What she really wanted was a glass of bourbon, something to warm her through, but she would have to settle for tea, begrudging the responsibility of the pager she carried. She brought her cup to the couch, curled into the charcoal-gray throw blanket and waited. It was ten minutes before the buzzer sounded and she walked to the intercom, buzzed him in and propped open the door. She resigned herself to another conversation that would hurt and bring her no answers or closure.

He walked through the door without words. She watched him expectantly as he closed and locked the door, took off his jacket and made his way towards the couch. He still didn't say anything as he picked up her legs, which had been running across the cushions lengthwise, and redeposited them on his lap, taking the time to wrap her feet in the blanket-ends to make sure they didn't get cold.

"We don't have anything more to say to each other," she finally said.

"We have a lot more to say to each other and you know it, Kate. The problem is that you don't believe what I'm saying." He was subconsciously stroking the sole of her foot with his thumb but didn't look at her.

"What's in this for you, Matt? I don't understand what you want. Why are you saying and doing all these things?"

"I want you," he said simply, finally turning to look at her, his gaze unwavering.

"Now," she stated flatly as she pulled her knees to her chest, and her feet and legs away from his touch. "You want me now," she said. "What has changed your mind? It is Tate?"

If jealousy was what was fueling this, then she was going to call him on it. There would be no more lies or words left unsaid between them. She watched as he reacted to her words: his jaw tightened and his fingers clenched into his palms. He stayed like that for what seemed like an eternity but must have only been a few seconds.

"Tate Reed is a good man, but you don't belong with him, Kate, you belong with me, you always have."

"No, Matt, I don't. Our past together has proved that. We had our chance together and it wasn't enough for you, and this change of heart isn't enough for me." She hadn't even known herself that was how she felt until the words were out of her mouth. She looked at him and understood that part of him was right, she would always be his, but she couldn't trust him, and without trust they couldn't move forward.

"Kate, when was the last time you trusted me?" He knew her too well. He also probably knew the honest response. That night when he'd asked her if she trusted him and then made love to her. She was going to be honest, even if he wasn't.

"Our last night together at Brown."

"When was the last time you believed I loved you?"

"The same."

He didn't say anything. He reached over and lifted her towards him as though she weighed nothing. He placed her astride him, and she had to place her hands on his shoulders to stop herself from colliding with him. He gently pushed her hair away from her face and pressed his lips to hers. It was them, as they had been.

His lips were soft, the only soft part of a hard man. He didn't make any move to deepen this kiss, to open her to him. She felt him pull away and opened her eyes with surprise. He had tangled his hand in her hair and from her position on his hips she could feel the hard bulge pressing into the core of her. But he wasn't moving any further and treacherously she wanted him to.

"Kate…" He quickly touched his lips to hers again before continuing. "Let me prove to you that I love you." He swept her hair away from her neck and started pressing his lips against its length.

Did he love her? She didn't know, just as she didn't know if she could ever trust him enough to believe the words she had waited so long to hear.

"What if you can't?" she whispered, her sense of reason managing to escape before it was completely lost to his touch.

He stopped and cupped the side of her face, returning his eyes to hers. "I will, Kate. This desire, this passion between us is there for a reason, and it's not going away. I'm not going away."

Of all the words he could have said, the promise not to leave was the most important thing for her to hear.

He wanted her. She believed that from his touch and the physical pull between them. He'd said he'd lied, but when? Had it been nine years ago or tonight? Did it matter? The only truth she knew was that she wanted him too and that feeling was not going away. Risks versus benefit, she thought to herself. She was pretty sure he couldn't break her the way she had been broken before, but maybe being with him again would help heal the wounds that had been left between them. Or maybe it would simply cure her burning need to experience again what had been physically and emotionally so nearly perfect that night all those years ago.

She moved her hands from his shoulders and ran her fingers through his hair as she returned her lips to his. She tugged gently at his lower lip, a physical act of agreement, and he responded. The pressure from his lips increased and she felt her lips part as his tongue swept their thin line. She opened her mouth to him and savored the feeling of him exploring and tasting her, responding with equal fervor. He broke from her mouth and moved along her neck as his hands swept under her shirt along her bare back.

Moving forward, his thumbs brushed the sides of her breasts, and her need increased a hundred times over. She reached down to the hem of her shirt, pulling it over her head and off her overheated body. Then she did the same to Matt, wanting to feel their bare skin touching. He kissed her again as their bodies pressed and she instinctively ground her throbbing core against him.

She sighed with relief when she felt the clasp of her bra unhook and the weight of her now heavy breasts drop. She pulled away slightly and Matt threaded the black lace bra off her body. She experienced satisfaction, watching and feeling him cup her breasts in his hands. His thumbs traced the outline of her nipples before rolling them gently between his fingers. It was torture, sweet, sweet torture. She moaned the word "More" and watched Matt smile a very familiar smile as he took the nipple into his mouth. His other hand never left the other breast and it was hard to cope with all the different sensations of pleasure running through her body. She needed something to focus on or she thought she might actually faint from the intensity of his touch.

She ran her hands down the hard, flat plane of his abdomen to the waistband of his jeans. She tugged open the belt, button and zipper, releasing him into her hand. He

was so hard that he easily slipped through the fly opening in his underwear, allowing her to touch and caress his
naked length. Her hand stroked his entire length, fantasiz-
ing about the moment when all of him would be inside her.
Her thumb circled his tip, slick already with desire. She
felt his hold on her breast and the intensity with which he
was sucking her nipple increase as he groaned against her.

"Kate," he moaned, as he released her breasts so that
he could use his hands to gently remove hers from him.
Gray eyes met blue as they stared at each other with looks
of agreement about where this was headed.

She pulled herself up off his lap and led him down the
hall towards her bedroom. She didn't turn on a light but
the uncovered window allowed in the city's night-light
glow, which reflected off their bodies. She finished what
she had started and while standing in front of Matt, facing him, she removed the rest of her clothing. He stepped
towards her and she removed his as well, until they were
both naked.

His hands returned to her face and hair and he pressed
his lips against hers again, like ex the calm before the storm.
Kate gasped as he lifted her from her feet and deposited
her on the bed. She felt a shiver course through her body
and couldn't tell if it was from the night air against her
naked skin or from anticipation.

She didn't stay cold for long. She watched Matt study
her before he joined her, covering her body with his own.
She savored the feel of the weight and the heat of him
against her. She opened her hips as each leg wrapped
around him until he was positioned perfectly, as much
her doing as his.

He didn't enter her. He stayed motionless below the
waist, even though she was arching and pushing against
him. He started kissing her again, her lips, her neck, her
breasts and nipples. His body weight was held on one arm

and as Kate writhed beneath him she unconsciously absorbed the beautiful architecture of the muscles in that arm and shoulder. His free hand caressed down her side towards the inside of her thigh. She had never wanted something so badly and she grabbed his hips in an attempt to pull him forward, but again he resisted.

She felt his lips and the stubble of his cheek return to her neck when he again moaned against her. "Kate, I'm trying really hard to take things slow this time and make love to you the way I should have, but you're making it really, really hard."

"Please, Matt," she begged, still struggling towards his final possession. She could see the change in him. His resolution faded and the small upward turn of a smile appeared at the corner of his mouth.

He stroked her leg one last time from her bottom to the knee that was crooked around his back. His hands went to either side of her head as he pressed forward and she felt the tip of him at her entrance. The slight touch after the agony of waiting caused her to catch her breath and close her eyes with pleasure.

"Kate, open your eyes and look at me."

She did so and the moment they made contact he pushed into her so deeply that she didn't know where he ended and she began. He moved slowly at first, his eyes never leaving hers as he stroked within her. There was no pain this time, just pleasure and a sense of completeness that she didn't want to examine. With every touch of him she couldn't imagine being able to stand the exquisiteness of another touch, and then he pushed in again. She could feel her body working with his as her muscles tightened against him, and he responded by moving more deeply inside. She felt panicky as the surges of pleasure started to build and she couldn't stop them, couldn't stop the release that was coming so quickly. She teetered on the edge, trying to hold on, trying to prolong the intimacy and connection between them.

"Kate, trust me, let go." His words, accompanied by almost complete withdrawal and a deep thrust, sealed her fate as she finally broke eye contact, closing her eyes and arching her back as she climaxed and tears of release streamed down her face. Her first aftershock was almost as powerful as her orgasm and was joined by a growl from Matt as he buried his head against her and cried out as she felt him spill into her.

She struggled to catch her breath, but equally calmly savored the weight of him collapsed against her. His lips brushed against her cheek, tasting the saltiness of her tears. She wasn't sure how long they remained that way, contented and too spent to move.

The shrill of her pager startled them both. Matt pulled out and away from her and she felt instantly bereft. The second beep focused her attention on the little black box that was still clipped to her jeans, lying discarded on the bedroom floor. She moved off the bed and unclipped the device, pushing the solitary button and registering the number of the emergency department.

"I'm sorry," she murmured. She found the portable phone and dialed the number, her back turned towards Matt.

"It's Dr. Spence. I was paged to this number."

"It's Ryan Callum." Dr. Callum was one of the senior emergency attending physicians, and if her alarm hadn't been raised before, it was now.

"Kate, I'm calling about Chloe Darcy. During her shift tonight she was found unconscious in the doctors' change room." Any self-conscious feeling she had about standing naked answering a page faded in place of fear as her heart started pounding in her chest and the blood seemed to drain from her body.

"Oh, my God." She slumped down onto the edge of the bed. "Where is Chloe now?" It was hard to contain her panic. This wasn't a patient, this was her best friend.

"She's in Section A of the emergency department. Kate, I'm calling because you are listed as her emergency contact on her health forms."

"I'll be right there." Section A was not good. If Chloe had just fainted from exhaustion or low blood sugar she would be in a lower acuity part of the department. Section A was reserved for critical patients requiring continuous monitoring and one-on-one care.

She stood, turned and collided with Matt, her naked body flattening against him. He had pulled on his underwear and jeans, but his shirt was still in the living room. His arms reached around to steady her and then quickly released her. He handed her a robe, which she batted away, and then he left the bedroom as she searched for new clothing. In less than thirty seconds she was ready and in the living room, where Matt stood holding the front door of the apartment open.

"I'm driving you." It was not a request, it was a statement, and she found herself grateful for his decisiveness as she was feeling more panicky than she could ever remember feeling.

She was gripped with fear as Matt sped towards the hospital. She couldn't talk, her thoughts stuck on repeat in her head. Chloe was her best friend, her rock. Chloe had gotten her through Matt's abandonment. Chloe had supported her through the breakup with Tate. But where had she herself been when Chloe had needed her? She had been self-destructing with Matt. Guilt coursed through her, thinking of the pleasure she had been experiencing while Chloe had been lying unconscious, waiting to be found.

Her friend had not been herself the other day. Kate had noticed that she had looked tired and pale, but Chloe had reassured her that it was just a virus. Kate had been so wrapped up in her own problems she hadn't taken the time Chloe had needed, like a good friend, like a good doctor, should have. Her mind raced as she established the differential diagnosis for viral illness and syncope. For a healthy woman to be in a critical condition it either had to involve her cardiac, respiratory or neurological systems, or a combination of them. If it was her heart, that would mean myocarditis and inflammation of the heart, leading to abnormal rhythms or, worse, a cardiomyopathy or valve damage, leading to permanent disability. If it was respiratory, then it would be an aggressive coronavirus like the SARS outbreak a few years back that had led to the deaths of many health care workers. If it was neurological, then it would be meningitis, which could lead to permanent neurological impairment.

"Stop." Matt's voice broke through her thoughts. She turned and looked at him, though his eyes didn't leave the road. "She's going to be okay."

"You can't know that," Kate replied in a scared whisper. She wanted in her heart to believe what Matt was saying, but rationally she knew that there was no way to predict sometimes what would happen. She had been in medicine long enough to understand that bad things happened to good people for no reason at all, and Chloe was the best person she knew.

Before they could talk more, Matt pulled into the emergency room loading dock. She took one glance at him, and heard him tell her to go as she jumped out of the car. She raced through the automatic doors and through the emergency department to Section A. She reached the large, wall-mounted computer screen that tracked patients, searching for Chloe's identifier. She saw 30F listed under room four, thirty-year-old female—that would be Chloe.

She controlled the desire to keeping running, and walked quickly to room four.

She wasn't prepared for the sight that greeted her. The room was empty but not cleaned. Her eyes darted around as her mind pieced together the information her eyes were processing. The stretcher was gone, so that meant that Chloe was somewhere in the hospital, having been transported on said stretcher. The floor was smeared with blood, not a lot of blood but enough. The rapid transfuser was in the room, a sign that Chloe had required a blood transfusion. In the sink she saw several empty IV bags, more evidence of vascular collapse. The scene before her was compatible with only two scenarios. One was a severe viral infection, leading to hemolytic anemia and septic shock. The other was hypovolemic shock secondary to acute blood loss. Either way, Chloe was very, very sick.

She left the room and her eyes searched the unit for Ryan Callum, but she couldn't see him. When she didn't immediately see anyone who would be useful in helping her locate Chloe, she left the department with a list of three possible locations in mind. Radiology, Intensive Care Unit, or the operating room. Chloe had to be in one of those locations.

She went to the main floor radiology unit first. The one benefit of doing nothing but work for the past four and a half years was that everyone in the hospital recognized her, even out of scrubs, and was quick to provide her with the information she wanted. Chloe wasn't in Radiology, neither was she in the intensive care unit. That left the operating room and Kate's fear increased. She went to the OR change room, put on scrubs and covered her hair to allow herself access to all areas.

It was after hours, which meant that only a few of the operating theatres were still running. She walked the hall, looking for activity and lights. She stopped dead in her tracks when she saw Tate staring through the small rectangular window of an operating-room door.

He didn't notice her. He just stared, transfixed, through the window.

"Tate," she said quietly, as she placed a hand on his shoulder.

He didn't turn to look at her, keeping his eyes glued on the window. "I think she's stabilizing. They kicked me out of the room, so I can't tell for sure. But they have stopped calling for blood and I can see the anesthesia monitors and her heart rate has come down to the one-twenties and her blood pressure is back up."

"What happened?" Kate asked, desperately wanting to see for herself.

"I don't know, they won't tell me anything. The usual patient confidentiality, etc. I only got here about fifteen minutes ago. I was checking the operating-room board to see how many cases were lined up for tonight at the front desk when the porter from the blood bank came to drop off blood. I overheard him verifying Chloe's name and blood-bank number with the unit clerk."

"Who is in with her?"

"Gynecology," he said, his resentment coming through clearly.

"Oh." Kate felt some understanding drift in. The department of obstetrics and gynecology was a separate surgical department from the department of general surgery. While both groups worked in the same operating rooms, the two disciplines kept to themselves with little understanding of the ins and outs of each other's fields.

"Is it a hemorrhagic ovarian cyst?" Kate asked, still needing answers.

"I don't know, Kate. Like I said, they won't tell me anything." She stopped asking questions.

It was right that they were guarding Chloe's privacy,

but at the same time it was intensely aggravating. Being in the health care field, she had become used to having access to people's confidential information. Only this time she and Tate were not responsible for Chloe's care, so they had no need to have access to that information other than for their personal interest, which did not entitle them to it.

She and Tate stood there for another twenty minutes before Kate had had enough. Let them throw her out, let them reprimand her even for her inappropriate behavior. She was already being sued. This, at least, would be worth the consequences.

Without words, she gently pushed Tate to the side and went through the operating-room door. She wasn't ready for what she saw, despite it being an everyday scene. It felt completely different when the person on the operating table was someone you loved. Chloe was lying there, surrounded by the surgical team. There were two anesthetists at the head of the table, two scrub nurses, and what looked like three people from the gynecology team. She looked at the faces and recognized Erin Madden, the chief gynecology resident, whom she had met on several occasions over their years in training.

"Hi, Kate." Erin acknowledged her presence, though her eyes didn't deviate from Chloe's abdomen, which was open on the operating room table.

Part of Kate wanted to get closer, but she wasn't sure she was ready emotionally to see Chloe so exposed. She also didn't want to push her luck and risk getting thrown out, as Tate had.

"She's going to be okay. We have evacuated the hemoperitoneum and have stopped the bleeding. We are going to be closing in the next few minutes and then she will be going to Recovery, followed by a short stay in the intensive care unit in case she runs into any massive transfusion complications."

"Uh-huh." Kate nodded, trying to process the information she was being given.

"I'm sorry we had to open her, Kate. We tried with the laprascope but she had too much blood in her abdomen and was too unstable to tolerate it."

"But the bleeding has been stopped?" Kate asked, unable to keep herself from surveying the room, her eyes focused on the evidence of what looked like a massive blood loss.

"Yes."

"What happened?" Kate finally asked.

"That's not for me to disclose to you, Kate. Chloe will be able to tell you herself later, if she chooses to. I think you should go now and take Dr. Reed with you. She is stable and we'll take good care of her. You can see her in the intensive care unit in a couple of hours, once she's settled in."

"Okay," Kate said, resigned, knowing she would get no more from Erin. "Thank you," she said to the team that had obviously saved Chloe's life.

She left the room, gently pushing on the door to make sure it didn't hit Tate. He hadn't moved.

"She's okay. They won't tell me what happened, but they opened her, stopped whatever was bleeding, and she's stabilized. She's going to go to the intensive care unit for a short while because of the large amount of blood products she received."

"Thank you, Kate," Tate replied. His eyes were still trained on the window and he didn't budge from his spot outside the door.

"Tate, they have asked us to leave the operating room and I think we should. She's stable and there is nothing we can do for her except get in the way and distract the team."

"I'm not leaving her."

"We're not leaving her, Tate. We are helping her by getting out of the way and letting them do their jobs. The same thing we ask other people to do for us." She grabbed his arm and pulled him a little to ease him away from his spot.

"Tate, we need to go. You know Chloe would never want us to see her like this." It was true, but she still felt mean, using guilt to move Tate away.

"Are you in love with Matt McKayne?" he asked, with no reproach or anger left in his voice.

She was shocked both by the abrupt change in the conversation and the directness of the question itself. So much so that she answered without thinking about her response. "Yes, I think I always have been, even when I hated him."

"Then you should be with him. Forget everything that has gone wrong between you and be together."

"It's not that simple, Tate. I can't trust him."

"Kate, that's not simple," he replied, pointing towards the door. Then he took one last look through the window and walked away from both Chloe and Kate.

CHAPTER ELEVEN

AFTER DROPPING KATE off at the emergency entrance doors, Matt waited. The admitting office had informed him that Dr. Darcy would be going to the intensive care unit and Matt found his way to the unit's family waiting room and waited. In the three hours he waited for Kate he replayed all the scenes of the past, including the one tonight.

She had known it was him. For the first time there was not a single doubt in his mind about whom Kate wanted. She had used his name and kept her eyes open as they had made love and it had been the most powerful sexual experience he had ever had. She really was the most perfect and beautiful woman he had ever met.

The hard waiting-room chair he sat on and the coffee-machine brew he sipped were a stark contrast to the earlier events of the evening. He cringed both at the coffee and at his unfair resentment and anger towards her pager and her job. It was irrational to feel resentful when Chloe Darcy was fighting for her life, but he still had the feeling. He had finally been getting through to Kate. Physically they were on the same page and he was angry that they were not going to have the rest of the night to work towards resolving the remaining distance between them. There was still some part of the picture he was missing, something that was holding Kate back from opening up to him completely.

Ever since he had returned he had assumed that something had been Tate. The pair's past relationship, that first night together when they had almost made love and she had stopped suddenly, the night he'd seen them together at her apartment, and the obvious continued connection and trust between them had left him with little other explanation. But he had been wrong. He was certain now that they were not together romantically. Kate was Kate and she would never have made love with him if she was in love and involved with another man, he was certain of that. So what explanation did he have for her refusal to believe the truth and her violent reaction towards him and his long-ago reasoning?

He shifted uncomfortably in his seat, having to purposefully steer his mind from the graphic images from earlier tonight that were etched in his mind. The site of Kate and Tate walking through the intensive care unit's automatic doors helped his cause.

He studied them, looking for signs of how Chloe was and also in an attempt to define their relationship. There was a familiarity, a trust between them that he envied.

Kate had changed into her hospital scrubs, the dark blue matching the smudges under her eyes.

"How is she?" he asked. Tate took a moment to look at Kate, though Matt had no idea what meaning was meant to be expressed.

"Excuse me," Tate said, before he walked away down the hall of the busy unit.

"She's going to be okay." Kate's voice brought his attention back to her.

"What happened to her?" He knew enough about medicine from his work in medical defense to know that healthy young women did not end up in the intensive care unit without a serious reason.

"We don't know. Well, the doctors who worked on her know, but they are maintaining her right to confidentiality," she replied, her frustration and despair obvious. She pulled the elastic band from her hair, allowing it to tumble around her shoulders in an effort to release tension. He reached out and drew her to him, wrapping his arms around her, and was comforted when she relaxed into him. He didn't say anything, didn't want to break this moment of respite between them. He moved his hand up to the base of her head and gently massaged the tense muscles beneath his fingers.

He didn't know how long they stood together, but he savored every second. She finally pulled away and stepped back to look at him. "I need to check on Chloe, shower, and get to work."

He placed his hands on her upper arms, not wanting to break their connection. "What can I do, Kate?"

"Nothing, there is nothing you can do. I have a change of clothes and toiletries here so I don't need to go home. Tate is on nights this week, so between us one of us can always be with Chloe. I need to focus on her, Matt. She needs to be my priority." There was a clear message in her statement, and Matt knew better than to try to change her mind. Kate would spend twenty-four hours a day at the hospital if that was what it took to do her job and be with Chloe. She had ranked her priorities, Chloe and then work. He wasn't on her list, despite what had happened between them.

"Promise me you'll call me if you need something, Kate. I would also like to know how Chloe does. She seems like a good person."

"Yeah, she really is." She sighed and then drew a deep

breath and squared her shoulders. "I need to go. Thank you for being here." Then she broke free and walked away.

Matt left the hospital just as the sun was rising in the cold spring air. He stopped at his apartment to shower and change clothes and was in the office by seven. He knew that there was nothing he could do to help with Chloe's recovery, but he could do the one thing he had been hired to do, and get Kate out of the lawsuit.

He had reviewed the file and after talking to Tate and Kate he had a clear understanding of the events of that evening. Tate and Kate had been together, and that night Tate had ended their relationship. Kate had been upset and had made several attempts to talk to Tate and he had ignored her calls to his cell phone. Kate had then been called back into the hospital, where she had been when she'd been consulted on Mr. Weber's care. After the results of the CT scan had established the diagnosis, Kate had organized Mr. Weber's care and made attempts to contact Tate Reed as the second on-call vascular surgeon. She had reached him via the switchboard within twenty minutes and Mr. Weber had been in the operating theatre within twenty minutes of that contact. All the medical experts agreed that Mr. Weber's aortic dissection had not been survivable, based on the extent of damage seen on the CT scan images.

There was no way the Webers' attorneys had not had the same medical opinion. It was the most consensuses Matt had ever had on a medical opinion, with all five of the firm's retained experts plus an additional two independent consultants reaching the same conclusion.

So what was fueling this lawsuit? Was it Kate's conversation with Mrs. Weber after her husband's death? Was it greed? He didn't think so. He had learned a lot about Mrs. Weber in his preparation and she didn't seem like the type of woman who would sue for the purpose of undeserved financial gain. Was it love? The couple, by all reported accounts, had been devoted to each other, but, that being said, being in love and losing that loved one alone didn't typically lead to multi-million-dollar lawsuits. That left guilt. Guilt could lead to just about any action, as he could attest to, based on his own past actions.

The question he had to answer now was what was there for Mrs. Weber to feel guilt about to the point she would want Mr. Weber's death legally proclaimed the fault of Boston General and the medical staff responsible for his care?

Typically, this was the point in the case where the firm's private investigators would take over and within one to two months would produce the report he needed. But he didn't have that kind of time.

He read the file again and then picked up the phone. "Hello," the voice of a woman answered on the other end.

"Mrs. Weber, this is Matt McKayne. I represent Boston General in the lawsuit that has been brought against them. I was wondering if we could meet? You are welcome to bring your attorney along, of course, if that would make you feel more comfortable." Matt waited as there was no response other than the sound of her breathing.

"Why should I meet with you, Mr. McKayne?" she asked tentatively.

"Because I want to do the right thing, Mrs. Weber. For your sake, as much as that of everyone else involved in this case." He was being sincere. Mrs. Weber would eventually lose this case and the longer it went on the more legal expenses she would have, with nothing gained except for more unresolved grief.

"I need to discuss it with my attorney."

"Of course. Ask him to contact my office and we can meet whenever you are ready. I appreciate you talking to me today." He had no anger towards this woman, despite that fact that she was responsible for the lawsuit that could destroy everything Kate had worked for. If the lawsuit was successful, everything he had given up would have been for nothing. But Mrs. Weber was also a widow. She had already lost her husband, the love of her life. She had lost enough. Matt couldn't be angry with her, however misguided her actions had become.

"We'll be in touch, Mr. McKayne. Goodbye."

Forty-five minutes later, her attorney called and an appointment was made for the day after next. That gave him forty-eight hours to find the real reason behind the lawsuit and get the case dropped.

He was missing something. There were facts somewhere that didn't add up, with the case and with Kate herself. For the first time in his career he felt inferior to the task at hand. His feelings and involvement with Kate had led him to change his approach, and his focus had been on her and not on the facts of the case. Not that he was succeeding with Kate. Physically, they connected. Emotionally he still felt like they were living two parallel stories.

He picked up the desk phone again and dialed his assigned paralegal. "Andy, it's Matt. I want every piece of information we have on the Boston General case. I also want the security video from the emergency department waiting room and the triage area for the night in question."

He didn't wait for a response and hung up immediately. He needed to focus on the case and find the small thread that would lead him to the answer. Would getting the lawsuit dropped win back her trust? He didn't think so. She wanted something more from him and he didn't know what that was. He had already confessed to her the truth about his lie and why he had done it, but that hadn't been enough for her.

Damn, he couldn't think about the case without thinking about Kate and last night. He pulled at the tie around his neck and ran his fingers through his hair, squeezing the tense muscles at the back of his neck. Even with her preoccupation with Chloe's illness, it was going to be impossible to stay away from her. Every part of him wanted to be with her again. It wasn't just the physical desire. It was her letting him hold her that morning in the intensive care unit lounge and for the first time relaxing and not pulling away. It had been a small return to the way they had once been. He passed his hand over his face and straightened his posture. He needed to separate himself physically from her if he had any hope of finding out the truth.

Kate shifted uncomfortably in the bedside chair. It was nine in the evening and the toll of the stress and lack of sleep was building by the hour. She felt new compassion for the family members who "slept" in the chairs every night to be close to their loved ones. Her neck and back ached from the awkward positioning and her heart ached from last night.

So much for closure, she thought to herself. Making love with Matt had done anything but provide closure. It had brought her back to the way they had once been, the way she had once felt, and afterwards she'd had no doubts that she didn't just love him, she was in love with him. Again. Still.

The monitor rang and a white tape was ejected from the machine. She looked at Chloe and her guilt was enormous. It seemed so wrong to be thinking about Matt when Chloe was lying in the intensive care unit intubated and unconscious while her body slowly recovered from the massive insult it had been dealt.

Her red hair made a sharp contrast to the pale hospital linen and the sterility of the room. Hours earlier Kate had brushed it and braided it to the side, trying to maintain some of her friend's dignity in such exposing circumstances. Her face, on the other hand, blended in perfectly, her pallor severe despite all the blood she had received. Kate reached out and curled her fingers around Chloe's. She was surprised at the small twinge she felt in response to the action, a reflex she hadn't expected yet but was grateful for.

"Chloe, it's Kate," she said, though even if Chloe had been conscious she would be physically unable to answer her with the breathing tube in place.

"Chloe, I'm so sorry I let this happen to you. I should have been a better friend to you when you told me you weren't feeling well, instead of focusing on myself and my problems. I promise I'll make it up to you."

She understood family members more at that time than she ever had in her career. The ones who asked the same questions over and over again, so much so that she was late every morning on rounds, the ones who pushed and demanded for more testing and intervention than was being recommended, and the ones who never left the building, despite your assurances and recommendations to do so. She understood perfectly now that they did those things out of love, guilt, and fear; all in a desperate attempt to bring that person back to them the way they had once been.

The alarm rang out again and Kate's focus shifted back to the monitor. Chloe's heart and respiratory rates were elevated beyond the machine's set parameters. She was breathing on her own above the ventilator. She looked back and saw Chloe start to move subtly, her head moving back and forth and her arms and hands testing their strength. The alarm had also triggered her one-on-one nurse to come into the room.

"She's waking up and starting to fight the tube," the nurse assessed quickly.

"Page the doctor on call and ask him to come and see if she can be safely extubated," Kate ordered, temporarily forgetting her role as a friend and not as the physician giving orders.

She reached out and stroked Chloe's hair away from her forehead. "Chloe, it's Kate. Try to stay calm. You are okay. You are intubated and in the intensive care unit but, I promise you, you are okay. You just need to hold on for a few more minutes and I'm going to see if they will take the tube out. If you start panicking they are just going to give you more drugs and leave it in, so you need to stay calm with me for the next few minutes, okay?"

Kate hadn't been sure how conscious Chloe was until her eyes slowly opened and they looked remarkably clear, like she had understood every word Kate had spoken. Kate reached out and squeezed her hand, in part as reassurance and in part to prevent Chloe from instinctively reaching for the tube.

She didn't break eye contact with her for what seemed like hours, but was actually only minutes, before the on-call intensivist arrived.

"Dr. Spence, I'm going to ask you to step out while we go through our extubation check list to make sure it is safe to do so."

She still didn't turn to look at the voice, not wanting to break her connection with Chloe. "Chloe, you heard that. I have to leave for a few minutes while they evaluate you. No room for big dumb surgeons on these occasions. I'm not going to be far away, though, and I'll be back here as soon as they let me, okay?"

She waited for a sign of understanding and felt relieved as Chloe slowly moved her head up and down on the pillow. She squeezed her hand one last time and then let go, leaving the room quickly before she changed her mind and tried to force them to let her stay.

Back in the family waiting room she dug into her bag

for her cell phone. She needed to call Tate and tell him about the change in Chloe's condition.

"Tate Reed," he answered instantly, as though his phone had never left his hand.

"It's me. I was just with Chloe and she has regained consciousness and is looking appropriate to extubate. They kicked me out, but the ICU doctor is with her now, so I'm hopeful that they'll take the tube out and she'll be well enough to leave the ICU."

"Is she in pain?" he asked, and Kate was impressed that he seemed to have more surgical sense than she did. She had almost forgotten about the six-inch incision that spanned Chloe's abdomen and which had remained well covered beneath the bed's sheets.

"No, Tate, she didn't seem to be in any pain. She actually seemed just like Chloe, surprisingly beautiful and understanding, even intubated with all the other tubes and wires all around."

"When do you think we can see her?"

"I think these things take about an hour by the time they assemble all the equipment and appropriate staff in case she doesn't do well. But I really don't think she is going to run into a problem."

"I have to start another case in the operating room and it's too late to find someone to cover for me. Can you let me know how she is as soon as you see her again?" Tate was a meticulous and in-control surgeon. He had to be. As a vascular surgeon, his target was everything from the largest to the smallest of blood vessels, with many of his cases being the difference between life and death.

"Of course, but, Tate, I'm really sure she is going to be okay. It's Chloe. I mean, who else goes directly from work to the intensive care unit? I wouldn't be surprised if she tried to take a shift tomorrow," she tried to joke.

"That's not going to happen." Her attempt to lighten the conversation hadn't worked.

"I know, Tate. Go and do your case. I'll call you as soon as I know anything."

"Thanks, Kate."

She glanced again at the phone in her hand, thinking of Matt. A sense of déjà vu passed over her and it was not a welcome one. No messages and no missed calls. Nothing to reassure her she had not just made the same mistake twice.

"Kate." Her thoughts were broken by the sound of her name. Erin Madden was standing in front of her. She glanced at her watch and was surprised to find that an hour had passed and it was almost eleven o'clock. Her fellow resident was dressed as though she had just come from home, in jeans and a casual long-sleeved shirt.

"The intensivist paged me to let me know that Chloe had regained consciousness and had been safely extubated. I need to do her assessment and talk to her and then you can see her."

She had never respected gynecology as much as she had learned to in the past twenty-four hours. It wasn't the roses-and-sunshine specialty the other surgeons thought it was. They really did save lives, this time her best friend's life, and she would be forever grateful. "Okay. Thank you, Erin, for everything."

"It's our job. Kate, I'm probably going to be at least a half an hour if not more. Why don't you get something to eat or take a nap in one of the call rooms? I'll page you when I'm done."

Kate nodded, appreciative of Erin's concern for her well-being and also for the time she was spending on Chloe's care. She watched the petite blonde walk away and decided to take her up on her advice. She walked from the intensive care family lounge to the operating room and found Tate in the recovery room, writing postoperative orders.

He noticed her instantly and she smiled warmly at him, trying to convey the good news before she reached him. "She's been extubated and is doing well. They paged Gynecology as her attending service and Madden is in with her now. It will be another hour before she can have visitors."

"Thanks, Kate."

"Don't thank me. I should have known something was wrong when I saw her the other day and she complained about feeling unwell. Instead, I was too distracted by Matt to notice what was going on with my best friend."

"Kate, you are one of the most important people in Chloe's world. She knows how much you love her and how important she is to you, just as you are to her. You two are inseparable. So stop feeling guilty about a situation you had no involvement in or control over. You know that she would hate that, even more than I do."

"You're right. You know us both really well."

"Yeah…" He paused. "I need to get these orders done and the operative note dictated. I'll go and see Chloe in a few hours after you two have had some time together."

"Thanks, Tate. I'll see you later."

She hurried downstairs towards the hospital coffee shop, happy to have made it before its midnight closing. Too many nights confined to the hospital's vending machines had made their contents completely unappetizing. After getting a cup of tea and a sandwich prepared earlier in the day by the hospital's ladies auxiliary, she made her way back to the intensive care lounge, knowing that she would be more disoriented after thirty minutes of sleep than she would be after none.

She ate the sandwich quickly, having failed to notice how hungry she was until she actually had food in her stomach. She sipped the cup of tea slowly. It was almost a full hour before Erin Madden emerged.

"At least you went for something to eat," she said, smiling and gesturing at the wrapping. "Chloe's doing well. They are going to move her to the obstetric ward in the morning."

"The obstetric ward?" Kate repeated, her confusion clear in her tone.

"Chloe and I both agreed that that would offer her more privacy than any of the other surgical wards, where she might have known or interacted with some of the patients," Erin answered, unfazed by being questioned about her medical decision-making.

"Do you think the nurses there are experienced enough to handle her postoperative care?" Kate asked, still feeling wary of the choice of ward. She had rarely been to the obstetric ward and felt anxious about Chloe being somewhere she didn't know.

"Kate, if there is one thing Obstetrics is good at, it is management of bleeding."

"Okay," Kate agreed. She couldn't dispute the quality of care Chloe had already received and had to trust the team taking care of her. Particularly as she still didn't know what exactly had happened to Chloe.

"I'm sure I'll see you tomorrow. Try not to totally exhaust yourself, Kate. I promise you, if anything changes you'll know as soon as I do."

"Thanks, Erin. Have a good night."

She walked back to Chloe's room and found her asleep in her bed. She no longer had the breathing tube and without the sound of the ventilator, the room was much quieter. Chloe opened her eyes as Kate moved back towards the bedside chair.

"Hey," Chloe croaked, her throat still raw from the irritation of the tube.

"Hey, yourself," Kate replied, unable to keep herself from smiling at the joy of just being able to have this conversation.

"I'm sorry I scared you," Chloe whispered.

Kate reached out and took her hand, fighting for control of her emotions as she said the words that had been repeating in her head since the call. "I'm sorry that I wasn't there for you."

"Kate, there was nothing you could have done."

"Do you want to tell me what happened?" Kate asked gently.

"Not tonight. It's too complicated and I'm too tired and sore to understand the situation myself. Is that okay?"

It was a complete role reversal. Chloe was asking for understanding without explanation, the same thing Kate had wanted when they had first met.

"Of course it's okay, Chloe. Anything you want."

"Anything I want?" she replied. A little flicker of her usual self in her eyes, as one eyebrow arched upwards.

"Anything you want," Kate reaffirmed. She was ready and willing to agree to anything for Chloe.

"Go home, Kate, you look almost as bad as I must." She laughed and then had to brace her stomach because the movement caused her pain. Then laughed again at her action.

"Nice, Chloe." Kate laughed quietly. "Are you sure? I don't mind staying."

"I know. And you also know that all I'm going to do tonight is sleep, so you should go home and do the same."

"I hate it that you are so selfless and reasonable, but I'll do as I'm told. Tate is working nights this week. He's going to stop by in a couple of hours to check in."

"Thanks for the warning."

"Behave yourself while I'm gone. Can't have you cheating on me with any other surgeons, now, can I?"

Chloe laughed again, clutching her stomach. "Get out of here before I need more pain medication just for the laughter."

"'Night, Chloe. I love you."

"'Night, Kate. I know you love me and I love you too."

Kate got home shortly after midnight, exhaustion seeping through her the moment she opened her apartment door. Her eyes immediately fell on her black sweater and bra, which were still strewn on the living-room floor. The ones she had pulled off herself the night before.

The bed wasn't made. The sheets were tangled and she could still see Matt lying there, the memory strong in her mind. She changed quickly into her pajamas and walked out of the room back to her couch. She curled up on its familiar comfort, shut her eyes, trying to block out the events of the past thirty-six hours, and begged for sleep.

It didn't come and she lay exhausted, her mind refusing to quiet or slow down and think rationally. She oscillated between anxieties at not being with Chloe, to pain from not hearing from Matt. Why hadn't he called?

She officially gave up hope at around four in the morning and went back to the hospital. Quietly she retook her place at Chloe's bedside, assuaging at least once source of torment. At exactly eight in the morning she couldn't take the waiting any more and called Matt's firm. The main receptionist put her through to Matt's office.

"Hello, Matt McKayne's office, this is Andy." Disappointment ricocheted through her as she realized it was not Matt himself answering.

"It's Dr. Kate Spence, I'm looking for Mr. McKayne."

"Mr. McKayne has returned to New York. Can I pass on a message?"

She felt her breath leave her but was incapable of taking in more air. This wasn't happening, this couldn't be happening, could it? Would Matt really leave? Now? After everything? After they had made love? Her mind and her heart both knew the answers to her questions.

"No message, thank you."

CHAPTER TWELVE

MATT SAT IN his New York penthouse, the normally minimalist look of his home now overwhelmed with papers strewn across every surface. He didn't usually work from home, but with only a few days to find the missing piece of the puzzle he didn't want to risk any interruptions or distractions from other cases.

He had started with the medical reports and the reviews by the medical experts. Nothing appeared amiss. Mr. Weber had had a Stanford A aortic dissection. It had involved the major branches of the aorta and was a lethal state; there had been no hope of saving him and unfortunately no warning signs of the condition prior to him presenting to hospital that would have alerted him or his family to the impending crisis. The delay in reaching Dr. Reed had been unfortunate, but in no way had it led to the man's death. The attempt at surgical intervention had been an exercise in futility from the beginning.

The firm's legal assistants had taken depositions from every health care worker involved in Mr. Weber's care that night. The plaintiff's counsel had done the same. Matt's junior colleagues were charged with reading and summarizing them, highlighting any points in their favor or causes for concern. He had complete faith in the people who worked for him. He had selected each team member himself and had overseen enough of the cases they had worked on to know he could trust the quality of their work. But this case was different. Something wasn't adding up and it wouldn't stop nagging at him until he could reassure himself that he had looked over every fact and piece of information personally.

He glanced at the clock that was perched on the fireplace mantel. It was two in the morning. He had to leave to go back to Boston the following day and felt like he was running out of time. He flexed his back and shoulders, trying to ease the tension that was building knots in the muscles. Kate hadn't called. He hadn't expected her to, between Chloe and her job, but it still bothered him that she hadn't. He wondered what she had said in her messages all those years ago.

He rose from the kitchen table that he had never used for eating and walked into his state-of-the-art granite and stainless-steel kitchen, also rarely used for its intended purpose. His only appliance on its smooth stone counters was an espresso machine that he had never been as grateful for as he was tonight. As he waited for the machine to produce the espresso shots to top with brewed coffee, he fixated on Kate. What was she doing right now?

He tried again to block her from his mind and resisted the temptation to call her. It was late and if there was the small possibility she was sleeping he did not want to be the cause of disturbing that precious sleep. Instead he took his coffee and the pile of depositions to the comfort of his leather couch. It was the only piece of furniture he had never changed no matter where he lived, much to his designer's dismay. It reminded him of where he had been and his mind and body relaxed as he sank into the cushions and began to read.

Three hours later he was only halfway through the pile and he was getting sloppy. The last deposition had taken him twice as long to get through as it should have and he finally surrendered to the need for sleep. He rose from the couch and went to his bedroom, climbing into the king-size bed. Time was running out for him and for Kate.

He was awoken from sleep later in the morning by the sound of his cell phone. It took him a few seconds before he remembered where he was and was able to answer the call.

"McKayne."

"Are you really gone?" Kate's voice wavered over the phone and he didn't miss the hurt or the accusation in her voice.

"Kate."

"It's an easy question, Matt."

"Yes, I'm back in New York."

"I'm a fool."

"No, Kate, you don't understand. I'm trying to help you."

"That's what you said about last time, Matt. It didn't make it okay then and it doesn't make it okay now."

"Kate, when are you going to trust me again?" He was tired of this; he had been honest with her and there was nothing else he could do. He waited as time passed in silence.

"How can you ask me to trust you after everything?"

"I thought we had gotten past that."

"No, Matt. Another night together hasn't fixed our past. I still remember you leaving. I still remember being discarded and replaced."

"Replaced?"

"Your sexual exploits were very popular in the New York society pages your first year in New York, Matt."

He cringed. He wasn't proud of his behavior that year, but he wasn't going to defend it now, not so many years later and definitely not over the phone, when Kate was clearly trying to use it as an excuse to drive a wedge between them.

"Where is this coming from, Kate?" He waited again for her answer, all of his senses alert now and focused on her.

"I can't believe you left. I feel so stupid for everything. I won't let you hurt me, Matt, not again. You may not be able to say it, but I can. Goodbye."

The click was unmistakable. He phoned her back and the call went straight to voicemail. He didn't try again: her message had been loud and clear.

He showered but skipped shaving, not wanting to waste any of the time he had left. He returned to the stack of files and worked steadily for the next ten hours, his focus unwavering. Nothing was out of place or suspect. The overwhelming sentiment in all of the depositions was of support for Drs. Reed and Spence. All their actions were deemed not only professional as per the standard of care but also excellent in their quality. Those who had worked with the two together that night had seen nothing in their interaction that had even hinted at a change in the personal nature of their relationship.

His stomach growled and he realized that he had neglected to eat any of the delivered food from earlier. He went to the brown bags and brought them into the living room, where he prepared to watch, while he ate, the emergency department surveillance tapes his assistant had retrieved. He inserted the first disk into the DVD player and noted the time on the bottom of the screen. It was five-twenty in the afternoon, several hours before Mr. Weber had presented. He reached over to grab the remote to fast-forward the tape to later in the evening when something caught his eye.

He watched as Mr. and Mrs. Weber entered the emergency department and checked in at the triage desk. They spoke with the triage nurse and then after several minutes left the department and the hospital itself through the main doors. Matt was stunned. Nowhere in any of the medical charts was this interaction described. He didn't move from his spot for the next several hours, watching every second of footage in real time, afraid that something else might be hidden in the tapes.

Mr. Weber and his wife arrived back in the emergency department at nine twenty-three that evening by ambulance. The ambulance bay bypassed the main triage desk so the nurse who talked with them earlier would have had no knowledge of their reappearance in the department. From that point on every moment of his hospital care had been documented and was recorded accurately in the case files.

Matt picked up the phone and called Jeff Sutherland's cell phone, disregarding the time of day. "Jeff, it's Matt McKayne. Does the hospital track patients who present to the emergency department and then leave without being assessed by a physician?"

"Yes. Those charts are kept in a separate area, to be used for future needs assessment and capacity planning."

"But do they have the patient's identifying information on them?" Matt asked, wanting more than just the video to back his argument.

"Yes. They also have the presenting complaint as listed by the triage nurse and any other information collected during the encounter."

"Good. I'm flying back to Boston tomorrow morning and will meet you at eight. I need you to take me to where the files are stored so we can get access to a file. I also need you find the nurse who was working the emergency department triage desk the late afternoon to early evening of Mr. Weber's death. I want to speak with her tomorrow at eight-thirty."

"Are you going to tell me what's going on, Mr. McKayne?" Sutherland asked, obviously not used to being on the side of accepting orders.

"Not yet, but if things work out, by this time tomorrow I should be able to tell you everything."

"Okay. I'll see you in the morning. Good night."

Matt stood in the large conference room, staring out the windows, waiting for Mrs. Weber and her attorney to arrive. He hadn't felt this level of pride in his work for years. He hadn't tried to call Kate again, knowing that he needed to bring something different to their circular conversations of the past.

His eagerness faded when Mrs. Weber entered the conference room with her attorney. She was the same age as his mother. Her once blonde hair was peppered with gray and she had a kindness to her face that shamed Matt. The problem with winning a case was that it meant someone else had to lose and today that would be Mrs. Weber. He smiled politely and genuinely at her, taking no joy in what he was about to do.

"Thank you both for coming today. Please, take a seat. Can we get you anything, tea, coffee, water?"

"A glass of water would be nice," she answered, looking nervously around the room.

He gestured to his assistant and took a seat on the opposite side of the table, trying to do everything in his power to make Mrs. Weber feel comfortable for the conversation they were about to have. He had purposefully kept the number of people from his firm down to only him and his assistant, guessing it was probably going to be a painful discussion for her.

"What did you want to discuss, Mr. McKayne?" her attorney asked confidently. Matt glared at the opposing counsel. He was in his mid-forties and had dressed in an overpriced suit that was designed to be recognized for its brand and not the cut and quality of the design. His hair was receding and he had a hungry look in his eyes as he surveyed the scale of the boardroom.

Half of Matt's passion for medical defense stemmed from his hatred of men like Mrs. Weber's attorney. They were vultures who preyed on the misfortune of others for their own gain. There were a few who represented those who were truly victims of malpractice, but the vast majority were opportunists. Mrs. Weber's attorney was a pure opportunist. No malpractice attorney worthy of the title would have taken this case, and Mrs. Weber's money, with all the expert opinions so in favor of the hospital's care. If the man thought Matt wanted to discuss a settlement, he was going to be sorely disappointed.

Matt completely disregarded the other attorney and focused all his attention on Mrs. Weber. "Mrs. Weber, the night your husband died you brought him to the emergency department yourself earlier in the evening." It wasn't a question; it was a statement, delivered as gently as he could in the circumstances.

Her eyes widened and Matt knew in an instant that everything he'd uncovered was indeed correct. He didn't wait for her to answer.

"I had our medical experts reexamine your husband's death. Even if you had convinced him to stay that night when you first came in, he would still have died from the aortic dissection."

"I tried to get him to stay, but when the triage nurse said it was up to a six-hour wait, Michael refused. I thought because the nurse had checked his blood pressure and pulse that he wasn't that sick." It was the panicked explanation of a woman who still didn't understand what had gone wrong.

"Stop talking, Marion," her attorney instructed her harshly. Matt turned and glared at the creep and within seconds he shrank back into his chair. Matt directed his attention back to Mrs. Weber, who was crying and trying to wipe away the evidence with the sleeve of her cardigan.

"I know," he started gently. "The triage nurse remembered you from that night because of how strongly you tried to talk him into staying. You did your best, Marion. There was nothing the triage nurse, you or Michael could have known or done that night to prevent what happened. Just as there is nothing that Drs. Spence and Reed could have done, but they tried—just as you did."

The woman crumpled before him and Matt could feel no joy at discovering the truth. He passed her the box of tissues he had left on the conference-room table and waited for her, not wanting to diminish her grief by interrupting.

"I just needed it not to be my fault. I wasn't interested in the money. I just wanted the court to say 'Yes, it was the doctors' fault' so that I would know for sure it wasn't mine. I miss him so much."

"It wasn't your fault, Marion," he said, as clearly and firmly as he could. She looked at him and he maintained eye contact. "It wasn't your fault."

The sympathetic tone in his voice faded when he shifted his attention to Mrs. Weber's attorney. "I expect you to file the papers to drop the case before the end of the week. I also expect your firm to cover the entire cost of this case. It should never have gotten this far and you and your firm are going to take the blame and shoulder whatever costs have been incurred. I'll be keeping in touch with Mrs. Weber and if I hear that she has received any type of invoice or attempt to request payment from you I will personally represent her *pro bono* in actions against you for negligence and misrepresentation. Do I make myself clear?"

"Perfectly," the man remarked snidely. Although it annoyed him, Matt let it go as he was certain the lawyer had gotten the message.

"You can leave now. I'll make sure Mrs. Weber gets

home." The man rose from the table and left the room without even addressing Marion Weber. Matt motioned for his assistant to leave and he walked around the table to sit at Mrs. Weber's side.

"I'm so sorry for my actions, Mr. McKayne. Can you please let Dr. Spence and Dr. Reed know that? I was so lost without him, I couldn't tell right from wrong. I think even if the lawsuit had been successful I still would have always wondered if I had really been responsible. At least I know now there was nothing I could have done. Maybe I can start to move past that night and focus on the forty-two wonderful years that came before it."

"That sounds like an excellent plan, Mrs. Weber. I'll definitely pass that along to Drs. Reed and Spence. They know how much you loved your husband and have no hard feelings towards you. Can I arrange for our driver to take you home?" He rose from the table and helped her to her feet, wanting to make sure she was steady before he let go.

"Yes, that would be very nice. Thank you, Mr. Mc-Kayne, for everything today." Matt was startled when she put her arms up and hugged him, but he instinctively hugged her back, her blonde head barely reaching his chest.

"Let's get you home," he said, gently waiting for her to let go before letting go himself and walking her back to his assistant to make the necessary arrangements. Once he was sure she was safely taken care of, he went back to the conference room to pick up his files. He paused and glanced out over the Boston skyline. He had been the type of man he wanted to be today. Kate had done that.

CHAPTER THIRTEEN

SHE STILL WASN'T answering her phone. Matt walked through the lobby of Boston General, searching for Kate. He didn't want to page her in case she was operating, but he also wanted to see and talk to her as soon as possible. The past days without her had seemed almost as long as the nine years they had been apart. He had discovered the motivation behind Mrs. Weber's actions and now he was determined to do the same with Kate.

If she wasn't with a patient, she would be with Chloe, he thought to himself. He went to the admitting office and turned on the charm to get Chloe's room information. He was surprised to be directed towards the obstetrics ward and verified the information twice, before departing for the fourth-floor unit. The pink and blue pastel walls of the unit were different from anywhere else he had seen in the hospital. He made his way towards the front desk and the unit clerk seated at it.

"I'm looking for room 4501."

"Dr. Darcy is not having any visitors," the clerk replied, not needing to reference the room number with the patient bed list. This was obviously not the first time she had delivered this news.

"Can you please ask her if she would be willing to see Matt McKayne?" He smiled warmly and smoothly at the clerk, using his charms again, and she seemed to have a change of heart, rounding the desk to go check with Chloe.

'I know Kate better than anyone,' Chloe had said the first and only time they had met. Maybe if he couldn't find Kate, he could start searching for answers with Chloe.

"Dr. Darcy said you can go ahead—last room on the left at the end of the hall."

He walked into the room and was taken aback at the sight of Chloe. The feisty redhead he had met in Tate's office had been replaced by a fragile-looking woman in a hospital bed.

"It's not contagious." She laughed, attuned to his reaction. The action made her grab at her stomach and groan with regret.

She's still there, he thought to himself, and walked into the room, shutting the door and taking the chair by her bed. "How are you feeling?" he asked.

"Like I got hit by a bus, thank you for asking. Why are you really here, Matt?" She was direct and completely disarming.

"I was looking for Kate, or at the least some information about Kate." Chloe would see through anything other than the truth and he had nothing to lose or hide.

"Do you really think that's a good idea?" she asked without scorn. Chloe had obviously gained some knowledge about his and Kate's past together since they'd first met a few weeks ago. He wanted and needed to know what Kate had told her, how Kate was seeing things.

"What do you mean, Chloe?"

With not insignificant effort she pushed herself up on the hospital bed until she was sitting upright and staring him directly in the eye. "I mean that Kate was really messed up when we first met at Columbia and I won't let that happen again."

"Columbia?" Matt felt all the air leave the room and he stared at Chloe, waiting for her to correct her error.

"Yes, Columbia. We both went to medical school at Columbia University in New York City. I believe you are familiar with the institution, given that's where you apparently went to law school?"

Chloe was staring at him, eyebrows arched, waiting for a response. He didn't have one. Kate had gone to Columbia for medical school. She had been there the entire time. When he'd thought he'd heard her voice or seen her on campus, he had. When he'd seen the woman in the coffee shop who had reminded him so much of her that he'd had to leave, it had to have been her. She had found a way for them to be together and he had taken the now seemingly easy route and ruined it. She had been stronger than he had given her credit for. She had also probably been strong enough to survive his family, he just hadn't believed in her the same way she had obviously believed in him.

The other night he had vowed to her that if she had been in New York, nothing would have kept him from her, but she *had* been in New York, at Columbia. He had deserved that slap. He actually deserved much worse and he now completely understood why Kate didn't trust him.

"Matt? Matt?" Chloe's voice broke through his thoughts. "Hello-o-o, are you all right?"

"I didn't know," he responded absently. He had come for answers and he had gotten them. He looked at Chloe and felt grateful for her help amidst his shock. "Thank you, Chloe."

He walked out of the hospital room while a maelstrom of thoughts and emotions charged through his mind. He would never forgive himself for what he had done, so how could he expect Kate to?

Kate walked through the corridors of Boston General with more foreboding than she had the afternoon Matt had walked back into her life. Once again she was being summoned to a meeting with the hospital's senior administrators and this time she didn't waste what little energy she had left worrying about the reason behind the last-minute request.

She reached the corridor outside the main boardroom and saw Tate leaning against the wall, looking equally as unimpressed with the circumstances.

"Do you know what this is about?" he asked, apparently having received no more information than she had.

"No idea," she sighed, coming to a stop beside him.

"Well, I guess there's only one way to find out." He led the way into the room where it had all begun. The conference room was filled with all the same men, except that Matt wasn't there. She immediately felt crushing disappointment. Her heart and mind were still trying to relearn to live without him, while at the same time she felt angry at herself for loving someone so deeply who had proved repeatedly how little he loved her back.

"Take a seat, Drs. Reed and Spence," Jeff invited them both. This time they took chairs side by side, united in whatever was about to occur. "We have some information we would like to share with you."

She held her breath and braced herself for whatever was about to be said. Her personal life was in a shambles and she felt like her career was hanging by a precarious thread.

"Tate, Kate," Dr. Williamson started. "I am pleased to inform you that the Weber family has dropped the lawsuit against Boston General and yourselves. They have also agreed to sign an agreement against any future legal action."

Kate felt her jaw drop and quickly looked at Tate for confirmation. He looked equally as surprised and she knew then she had not been wrong in what she had just heard.

"Why the change of heart?" Tate asked the group.

Sutherland answered, "Mr. McKayne discovered some information that helped him understand Mrs. Weber's motivation behind the lawsuit. He met with her this afternoon and after discussing the events of the evening and the medical expert reviews, she no longer felt there was any negligence involved."

Matt had done this. Pride and pain filled her at the same time. He had saved her from what would have been a permanent mark on her career and he hadn't even bothered to tell her himself. Maybe this was his goodbye?

"Thank you all. We appreciate your support throughout this matter," Tate said to the group. She should probably say something similar but no words came to mind and she sat there mutely.

"We value both of you and the work you do for this hospital. We strongly hope, Kate, that you'll consider returning to a staff position once you have completed your fellowship." Dr. Williamson's attention was directly focused on her.

A staff position at Boston General was the job she had wanted for the past five years but in the past six months she had forced herself to give up dreaming about it. After her breakup with Tate she had ruled it out as a possibility. She had been crushed, knowing she was going to have to leave Boston General, the city itself, and especially Chloe, who had accepted a staff position in the emergency department.

"There is nothing I would like more," she answered, but in her heart she knew there was something she wanted much, much more.

"Then consider it a done deal. Now, if you'll excuse us, I think we all have work to do." Dr. Williamson rose and the other men followed suit, leaving the conference room. Kate stood from her chair, her mind still reeling from the events.

"Congratulations, Kate." Tate was smiling at her, but

she was still trying to process the developments of the past ten minutes.

"Thanks," she mumbled in return. The lawsuit was over and she had received the job offer she had desperately been working towards, but it wasn't enough. With Matt she remembered what it was like to be happy, even for one night, and nothing felt as it should without him.

When she looked back at Tate his expression had changed. He seemed to be analyzing her with almost as much scrutiny as she had been assessing herself internally. "I take it you're no closer to figuring things out with Matt than the last time we talked?"

"He's gone." She replied with the only fact she was sure of.

"I don't think so, Kate. It sounds like he's still around, judging from our meeting today." Whose side was Tate on? She felt resentment towards both men. She was tired of all the presumptions being made on her behalf. She was going to spend the rest of her life loving a man she couldn't trust and never finding that sense of happiness again.

"I'm too hurt to feel gratitude towards him right now, Tate, so don't ask me to."

"I wouldn't dream of it. What I am going to ask you to do is to go home. You have barely slept or been outside this building since Chloe got sick."

"Is this your way of telling me I look like hell?" Kate replied, a small smile at the corner of her lips.

"No. But I think if you tried to stay with Chloe again tonight, you would worry her more than you would help her."

It was odd, this new relationship with Tate. In almost every way it was new, except that it felt old and comfortable. It was true friendship and instead of their past intimacy making things awkward, it allowed for more honesty between them.

"You're right. She said the same thing last night. I give in. I'm lucky to have you both in my life, and in case you didn't realize it, you are both officially stuck with me."

She walked along the cement sidewalks towards home. The sun was out and the birch trees that lined the street were starting to show signs of spring. She smiled, feeling some peace at knowing this was not going to be her last spring in Boston, just one of many to come. It was going to be hard to go back to New York for her fellowship, but it was going to be worth it. Devoting her career to helping women with breast cancer would at least lay one of her demons to rest.

She had no idea where Matt was going to be or even where he was now. Was he going to stay in Boston, go back to New York, or was there somewhere else in the world where he spent his time? It was going to haunt her, not knowing where he was. She didn't want to have to worry about any more accidental encounters that would cause a resurfacing of feelings she wanted to move past. Still, she refused to call him, not again. She had finally said her goodbye.

She was lost in thought as she approached her apartment building. She looked up just as she reached the base of the stairs and stopped dead. Matt was sitting on her steps. He was still dressed in a business suit and hunched over with his forearms resting on his legs, hands clasped together. He looked as disconcerted as she felt surprised to see him again.

She decided not to make the experience any more painful than it needed to be and instead of challenging him took the spot next to him on the concrete, avoiding looking at him as she stared vaguely in the same direction he was looking across the street. In contrast to the cool concrete against her bottom she felt Matt's natural warmth radiating from him along her side. It reminded her of making love with him and it took every ounce of willpower not to cry at the memory.

"I don't deserve you." Matt's painfully confessed words broke into her internal battle.

Of all the things she had expected to hear, that was not it. Matt had always felt right in all his actions. Even when he'd confessed to lying to her about not loving her, he still had tried to justify his actions as being for her own good. When he had told Tate about them, it had been the right and honorable thing to do. After spending a decade not feeling like she was enough for Matt, it was surreal to hear him confess that he was the one who wasn't good enough for her. She couldn't respond, didn't know how to respond.

"I didn't know you were in New York. I wanted so badly to be with you that I erased all your messages and emails before I listened to or read them so as to do everything in my power to keep myself away from you. I thought I was doing the right thing for you." He sounded so honest, but she didn't believe what he was saying.

"Matt, you saw me in the coffee shop that spring. You took one look at me, turned your back and walked away from me. No looking back, no second glance." No more lies, no more misunderstandings, she was going to let everything out this time. It was the only way she was ever going to heal.

He reached out and took her hand, her small one completely engulfed in his. She didn't say anything and still couldn't bring herself to look him in the eye, so instead she concentrated on the sight of their hands together.

"I honestly thought I was hallucinating. I had already thought I had imagined your voice, and seen you on campus, so when I walked into the coffee shop and saw you that day, I thought it was my mind imagining what I so desperately wanted to see."

Her mind whirled with his last confession. She tried to put together the facts of the past, with her perceptions and now Matt's. She started talking and wasn't sure for whose benefit she was speaking.

"I need to understand this, Matt, because I can't tell what's true anymore. You're saying you were in love with me the night we first made love and you lied because you thought it was the right thing for me? You're also saying that you didn't know that I was in New York with you, and that you wanted to be with me so badly that you thought you imagined me the day you walked away from me in the coffee shop? And now you're saying that you know all this and you don't deserve me?"

"I'm saying that I loved you then and I still love you, but I know now I don't deserve you."

She let go of his hand abruptly and their eyes met for the first time in the conversation.

"When do I get to decide what I deserve, Matt? When do I get to decide what's best for me? Because I decided nine years ago that you were worth changing my life for and it's about time you let me make my own decisions because I love you, still, and always will."

As her last words echoed around them, Matt reached over and pulled Kate towards him. He held her close as his arms drew around her and his lips found hers. For the first time in their relationship there was nothing left unsaid. There were no thoughts about what the kiss meant or what the ramifications would be; instead, there was just love and honesty between them.

When they finally broke apart, he kissed her forehead and rested his against hers. Kate smiled. "Marry me?" he asked quietly. "I never want to be away from you ever again."

Kate's smile widened and she worked her hands between his shirt and jacket, feeling his shoulder blades beneath her fingers and holding him closer to her. It wasn't just happiness she felt, it was a sense of contentment and peace.

"Yes, I'll marry you, Matt. And you never have to be away from me again. You just have to agree to move to New York for two years and then back to Boston permanently because I've accepted a position at Boston General after my fellowship, and this time it's your turn to move."

He lifted away from her and smiled the same Matt grin she had fallen in love with so many years ago. "Anything for you, Katie. Always."

* * * * *

A sneaky peek at next month...

THE ULTIMATE IN ROMANTIC MEDICAL DRAMA

My wish list for next month's titles...

In stores from 7th March 2014:

❑ Waves of Temptation – Marion Lennox

☒ Risk of a Lifetime – Caroline Anderson

❑ To Play with Fire & The Dangers of
  Dating Dr Carvalho – Tina Beckett

❑ Uncovering Her Secrets – Amalie Berlin

☒ Unlocking the Doctor's Heart – Susanne Hampton

Available at WHSmith, Tesco, Asda, Eason, Amazon and Apple

Just can't wait?

Visit us Online

You can buy our books online a month before they hit the shops! **www.millsandboon.co.uk**

0214/03

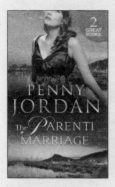

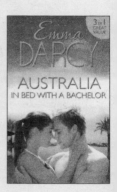

Work hard, play harder...

Welcome to the Gold Coast, where hearts are broken as quickly as they are healed. Featuring some of the rising stars of the medical world, this new four-book series dives headfirst into Surfer's Paradise.

Available as a bundle at
www.millsandboon.co.uk/medical

Join the Mills & Boon Book Club

Want to read more **Medical** books?
We're offering you **2 more** absolutely **FREE!**

We'll also treat you to these fabulous extras:

- **Exclusive offers and much more!**
- **FREE home delivery**
- **FREE books and gifts with our special rewards scheme**

Get your free books now!

visit www.millsandboon.co.uk/bookclub
or call Customer Relations on 020 8288 2888

The World of Mills & Boon®

There's a Mills & Boon® series that's perfect for you. We publish ten series and, with new titles every month, you never have to wait long for your favourite to come along.

By Request

Relive the romance with the best of the best
12 stories every month

Cherish™

Experience the ultimate rush of falling in love
12 new stories every month

Desire™

Passionate and dramatic love stories
6 new stories every month

nocturne™

An exhilarating underworld of dark desires
Up to 3 new stories every mont

M&B/WORLD4a

Discover more romance at

www.millsandboon.co.uk